THEY WERE
THE HORRIBLE

Charles got himself unt[...]
drew his sword. He had resheathed it while [...]
that might have been fortunate.

The sword looked like a toy. It *was* a toy, Merlain thought. Not even her father's sword would be a defense against the spider, and what Charles had was much smaller and more delicate. Magic? It had better be magic, if they were to have any chance at all!

The huge spider crept down the slope they had just rolled down. Merlain saw now that the ground was coated with webbing, making it smooth, so that anything falling here would not be able to stop. It would be hard to climb out. The spider's strategy was to drive its prey into this place, where it could not escape.

The spider had no difficulty, however. Its gnarled feet were sure on the webbed slope. It had perfect balance. It was a thing of beauty, in its appalling way. Its hairy front legs reached out toward them.

Charles swallowed. Merlain caught his thoughts. *I'm afraid, oh I'm so afraid!* But he clutched the hilt of his sword, and the sword seemed to give him courage. There was something about it, but no obvious magic.

Charles stepped forward, screwing up what little courage he had. *I'll stop it! I have to stop it! I'll kill it! I have to!*

She watched her brother brandish his sword, and she knew that whatever magic it had was not going to help him, and that he was about to die. She knew that once that happened, there would be no help for the rest of them. . . .

Tor books by Piers Anthony

With Robert E. Margroff:

With Frances Hall:

PIERS ANTHONY
AND ROBERT E. MARGROFF

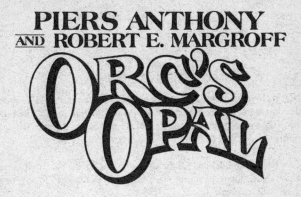

ORC'S OPAL

TOR
fantasy

A TOM DOHERTY ASSOCIATES BOOK
NEW YORK

This is a work of fiction. All the characters and events portrayed in this book are fictitious, and any resemblance to real people or events is purely coincidental.

ORC'S OPAL

A Tor Book
Published by Tom Doherty Associates, Inc.
175 Fifth Ave.
New York, N.Y. 10010

Cover art by Darrell K. Sweet

ISBN: 0-812-51177-8

Library of Congress Catalog Card Number: 90-39230

First edition: October 1990

First mass market printing: December 1991

Printed in the United States of America

0 9 8 7 6 5 4 3 2

INTRODUCTION

This is the fourth novel in a fantasy series in which the inhabitants of alternate worlds are distinguished by the shape of their ears. In the first novel, *Dragon's Gold*, young round-eared Kelvin and his point-eared little tomboy sister Jon managed to kill a golden-scaled dragon and later save the kingdom of Rud and their father John Knight from the clutches of evil, seductive queen Zoanna. In the process, Kelvin found love with round-eared Heln, and Jon with Lester Crumb.

In the sequel, *Serpent's Silver*, Kelvin's half-brother Kian discovered an alternate world where most folk were round-eared, but it wasn't John Knight's world of origin, Earth. Some folk had flop ears, and many folk were similar to those of the point-eared world, except that their characters were reversed. Here good king Rufurt was evil king Rowforth, and evil queen Zoanna was good queen Zanaan. Instead of golden-scaled dragons there were silver-skinned serpents. Again the forces of evil were finally thwarted—

but the mysterious Prophecy of Mouvar had not yet run its full course.

In the third novel, *Chimaera's Copper*, evil queen Zoanna teamed with evil king Rowforth to cross frames and take over Kelvin's home frame while Kelvin was away. Heln's developing baby was enchanted to become a chimaera, but the adult chimaera Mervania provided magic to fission the monster into three just before birth: a boy and a girl and a dragon. Zoanna was defeated and killed, and things settled more or less down again.

This fourth novel opens about six years later. Because the large number of characters carrying over from the prior novels may be confusing, this introduction is followed by a listing of the characters, approximately in the order of their first appearance or mention. They will be identified in the text, and some background provided, but that may not be enough. When you encounter one you don't recognize, flip to this list. Meanwhile, if you have ever wondered exactly what a fantasy convention is like, this novel will show you.

There will be one more novel to complete the prophecy: *Mouvar's Magic*. So don't throw away the prior volumes, unless you happen to like fumbling through a summary like this to get your bearings. One of the interesting things about those prior volumes is that through a fluke of magic the cover intended for this book, *Orc's Opal*, appeared instead on the hardcover edition of *Serpent's Silver*, two novels ago. So those who experience a mysterious déjà vu when reading the scene in Chapter 8 about Charles and Merlain and the great flying dragon-bird need by mystified no more; it simply means they made the mistake of reading these novels in order, in hardcover. Those who read *Dragon's Gold* in hardcover were in a different frame, because in this frame it was an original paperback.

CHARACTERS

Mouvar—fabled Roundear who made the Prophecy and set up a chain of scientific transporters linking the frames

Zady—ugly, evil old witch, Zoanna's aunt

Queen Zoanna—beautiful, evil former queen of Rud, now dead

Professor Devale—demon sorcerer and educator with a taste for beauty and mischief

Chimaera—monster with three heads: Mervania, Mertin, Grumpus

Kelvin Knight Hackleberry—the unlikely hero of the Prophecy, and thus of all the novels of this series. Son of John Knight, but his surname was changed when his mother married Hal Hackleberry, and not changed back when she remarried John Knight.

Heln Hackleberry—Kelvin's round-eared wife

Charles—Kelvin and Heln's son, age six

Dragon Horace—Charles and Merlain's sibling

Helbah—old sorceress of Klingland and Kance: a good witch

Katbah—Helbah's houcat (or "cat") familiar

Lester "Les" Crumb—Jon's husband, son of Mor Crumb

John—Kelvin's younger sister, whose ears are pointed

Charley Lomax—neighbor, formerly one of the king's guards

Cutie Lomax—Charley's cute kid sister

Charlain Knight—Kelvin and Jon's mother, wife of John Knight

John Knight—round-eared traveler from Earth, stranded in the magic realm, father of Kelvin, and of Kian, by Zoanna

King Kildom—boy-king of Klingland

King Kildee—boy-king of Kance

Zatanas—evil magician, Zoanna's father, now dead

Old Man Zed Yokes—river man who ferries others across water

Whitestone—convention wizard

Zudini—master illusionist and escape artist

Zally—Zudini's daughter, majoring in pedimagic

Fredrich—handsome young warlock, Zally's friend

Brudalous—king of the orcs

Glow—Charles' dream girl

St. Helens—familiar name for Sean Reilly, Heln's father from Earth, once a soldier in John Knight's Earth platoon.

Man—messed up Jon's loaf of bread

Policeman—picks up Jon

Desk Sergeant—recognizes the problem

Toastmaster—of banquet where Helbah is feted

Loopey—a drunk man in the form of a stargen

Phenoblee—Brudalous's orc wife

Phillip Blastmore—former boy-king of the kingdom of Aratex

Morton "Mor" Crumb—former leader of a band that helped Kelvin

Miss Pringle—attendant at children's suite

Ebbernog—little fat boy

King Rufurt—figurehead king of Kelvinia, a gentle and somewhat ineffective man

Mosday—orc officer, a general under Brudalous

Krassnose—resident orc wizard

Dawn—the sunwitch, Glow's mother

PROLOGUE

Night

The ugly old witch with beautiful warts on her face had an air about her. A bad air. It wasn't merely physical; it extended well into the supernatural realm and was almost artistic in its awfulness. Leaning there in the study on her artfully crooked stick, she could have stepped right from an ancient woodcut which had soaked in the foulest of sewers for a few centuries.

Professor Devale rubbed his polished horns, wondering who she was and why she had come. She was obviously competent in sorcery, or she would not have found him here.

"You *do* remember me, Professor?" Her voice grated like bone against gravestone. Her breath as she spoke staggered him. Her rheumy eyes cleared for a moment and glowed with the intensity of coals from a funeral pyre.

He thought rapidly, searching his memory, annoyed that his precognitive ability was weaker than it should be. Let's see—several centuries ago a witch such as this had brought a really beautiful girl to him. A girl named Zoanna, and it hadn't been entirely her fault that she hadn't wanted to study, then. With beauty like that, she had been able to have her way without magic. Later Zoanna had learned the limits of beauty and had come to him for help, as they all came sooner or later. What a joy she had been, when she wanted his favor! He had known exactly what she was up to, and that she cared not a pennycent curse about him personally, and she had known he knew. That was the way he liked it: proper understanding. There could be much pleasure in a business romance. But Zoanna was gone now, destroyed in the frame of dragons by another type of witch and that witch's amateur helpers. Helpers such as Kelvin Knight Hackleberry, the claimed Roundear of Prophecy, and his mother and sister. The frames were in a sorry state when louts like these could interfere with the projects of legitimate practitioners of magic. Vengeance was in order for somebody. Yes, yes, and so this had to be Zoanna's old aunt, who was as vengeful a creature as he could remember.

"Why of course I remember you, Zady," he said in his familiar manner. It wouldn't do to have anyone think he was other than completely sharp, and verging on omniscience. Especially a stinking crone like this! If she was so powerful, why didn't she make herself beautiful?

"Oh, very well!" the aged mouth snapped. An apparently feeble hand lifted, and fingers that resembled a bird's claws made a gesture.

Pink smoke puffed up from the carpet, spread out, thickened, and enveloped her, obscuring her form. In a moment a smooth white hand emerged from it and made a pass. The smoke dissipated.

There stood a voluptuous young-bodied redhead. It was the witch, of course; but her talons had been replaced by firm slender fingers, and her sour puss by a radiantly lovely face, and her scarecrow body by one that would shame an ardent hourglass. Her awful stench was now the sweet breath of roses. She smiled, showing even white teeth instead of gappy nobs on decaying gums. Only the knowingness of her eyes gave her away, and that was already fading to the perfect semblance of innocence.

Professor Devale drew an appreciative breath. This was better, much better! There was nothing wrong with the old hag's shape-changing or telepathic abilities. As a matter of fact, just looking at that luscious form . . .

But he was not so readily trapped by his appetites. "You want something, Zady. Out with it first."

The beautiful creature made a gesture the reverse of the prior one. Dark smoke puffed and dissipated, and her body metamorphosed back into the ugly witch. Professor Devale watched with regret. He knew exactly what she was, but her lovely form did not make his eyes smart.

"If you want business, it will be *all* business," the hag grated, making a grimace which was supposed to pass for a smile.

Confound it! She had really tempted him with her lush format. He was too smart to allow that to make him act foolishly, but he had really hoped they could work something out in the course of sensible negotiations.

Devale hated to be put at a disadvantage, but his mind did tend to be swayed by his desire. The crone was besting him at the game of manipulation. But it was a nice challenge, and perhaps he could recover some ground.

"I think I know what you've come about. Your niece's destruction at the hands of near amateurs. But surely you don't need my help for that. Just go to the dragon frame, work a few nasty spells, and—"

"Professor Devale, please have the courtesy to listen to me. First, it is not merely my niece who concerns me, great loss though she certainly is. Before that, my dear brother, the wizard Zatanas, was devastated by this brash, uneducated roundear. I must destroy that oaf above all, and do it in my own peculiar fashion." He had a notion of what her fashion would be: first she would use her luscious form to seduce the man away from his wife; then she would break his heart and spirit and finally his body. "But I must also deal with every righteous being who assisted in my kin's destruction. This is my unholy mission."

"Including the chimaera, I suppose?" Just how impractical was this old crone? She had some fine talents, but her overall perspective was deficient. The best magic was insufficient if used unwisely. Many an excellent witch and wizard had suffered because of a deficiency of larger vision.

"Not including the chimaera, dear Professor. As you know, that three-faced monster has the protection of certain others that even you dare not challenge. However, there is something of the chimaera's in the dragon frame."

"You refer to the twin children and the young dragon."

"Of course. They are of the roundears, but also of the chimaera, thanks to the complication of their undeserved luck. If they are allowed to live and grow to adulthood, they will present a real danger."

"Yes, I am aware of that." His precog had failed, frustratingly, when he attempted to see what would happen in those future years, as it tended to do when the purported Roundear of Prophecy was involved. He hated operating blind. Danger there was in these unnatural beings, but he could not foresee to what extent, or how it would manifest.

"That is why I may need your help in destroying them," Zady said, answering his thoughts as readily as his words.

"I see. That certainly makes sense. But why wait six years? Why didn't you come to me sooner?"

"Because, dear Professor, now is the proper time. With your help, I can arrange to use the youngsters against their elders before their final destruction. A cause of mine can be greatly benefited, and there is an incidental but hardly inconsequential prize."

She was beginning to interest him even in her present form. "Prize?"

"A certain stone. An opal endowed with certain magical properties."

"Zady, I know of that opal. The risk, even to me, would be considerable."

"Ah, but the exquisite irony if my plan succeeds!" she cackled. "My enemies' own children serving my purpose while bringing destruction to those they love!"

"True." He focused on the three dark hairs growing from

her jutting chin, repelled and fascinated. This crone had an intriguing mind. "All will suffer greatly in the process."

"Obviously. All the 'nice' folk. All the goody-goodies. When my family plots revenge, we plot *complete* revenge."

"The children too? They will certainly suffer when they discover what they have done, but what of them thereafter? Will they expire horribly?"

"Of course. Always the worse for the innocent."

He nodded. "A denobling philosophy, worthy of your ilk. But I would like to have them here at the university."

She was surprised. "To train them in evil magic? Do you dare, Professor?"

He shrugged with regret. "Probably not. The chimaera may not have forgotten them completely, and we can't rule out a possible reappearance by Mouvar."

"Mouvar will not be back to the dragon frame. Not after his defeat at the hands of my late brother, Zatanas."

"That was long ago, Zady, and your brother succeeded only with my help."

"I too may need your help."

"As," he said, making a motion so indecent that it would have appalled an ordinary woman and caused an innocent one to faint, "do I, in a more immediate manner."

The hag vanished in pink smoke. From the haze came her voice, at first scratchy but turning dulcet as the sentence progressed. "You do have a way with the inviting gesture, Professor!"

The smoke dissipated and the arousing redhead stood before him. Her breasts were heaving and her eyes were half-lidded. Some of the smoke clung to her body, forming a kind of cloak that blurred the rest. "Do that again, you rogue," she breathed.

Instead he reached for the gossamer covering. It became illusion as his fingers sought its texture, and he found himself touching her flesh instead. An electric thrill went through him: she had given herself a tactile aura. But he retained a sliver of caution. "Zady, promise me one thing."

"What's that, naughty Professor?" An aspect of her rondure slid into his hand, possessing a will of its own.

"Promise me you won't change your appearance in the middle of it."

She laughed in a way that suggested she had had exactly this in mind. "Why Professor! Doesn't my most basic form appeal to you?"

"Please. Indulge my little foible. At least while we're—"

He made a gesture with his smallest finger, the only part of him that was not engaged at the moment. Behind him his desk spread out to become a low and comfortable bed. Just in time; they were already descending. They fell on it together, locked, and bounced.

She twined around him, squeezing him here and there with this and that. Any reservations he might have had about helping her vanished along with the roaring flames of his not easily satisfied lust. "Zoanna!" he cried out climactically, unable to help himself.

"Hush, Professor," the voice of the old hag said from the mouth of the gorgeous creature embracing him. "After this is all over I'll be Zoanna any time you wish. Just remember that only I can be her, and that you are binding yourself to give all the help that is necessary."

"I'll give, I'll give!" he promised. He was uncertain whether the greatest part of his desire was for her body or for the satisfaction of aiding a suitably cruel and imaginative plan. Lust and cruelty: where did one leave off and the other begin? Or were they merely facets of the same devious pleasure?

Morning

Kelvin Knight Hackleberry lay in bed looking at Heln, his black-haired, still-beautiful wife. The flimsy nightdress showed off her form to best advantage where she stood in the ray of golden sunlight. It was hard to believe that she was the mother of ensorcelled triplets and had barely escaped with her health at the time of their horrendous birthing. She looked virginal at this moment. Well, not exactly that, but certainly young and desirable. If only she had been content to remain in bed awhile longer . . .

Outside their window the birds were singing, but he doubted that this was what had roused her. Instead of, sigh, *arousing* her. The only thing that caused her to react so alertly, so early, was the children.

"I'm certain they can't have gone far this time," he said reassuringly. He loved his children, but every so often he wished that they could go for a long visit with relatives so that Heln could give him her full attention. "I heard them when they left."

"You *heard* them!" Heln turned an angry face on him. "Then why didn't you *do* something?"

Of course he could not give his real reason. "Because, sweet love, the twins are very, very capable, for their years. It's natural that they want to explore. I did, at their age—or at least my sister Jon did—when we were young. Besides—"

"But they're only six years old! That's not old enough to realize the danger!"

"Believe me, they'll know if there *is* danger," he said with what he knew was a futile effort to reassure her. "I suspect they just went out to meet their brother."

"Don't call it that!"

"Well, he is. Or if you prefer, it is. You have to accept

that, Heln, even if we don't always like it." Actually Kelvin had adjusted to the notion fairly soon after the initial shock. It had certainly been better than the threatened alternative.

"Never! I will never accept that I gave birth to a dragon!"

He sighed. It was an old argument that never seemed to end. He hated having any source of dissension between them, but there was no getting around this one. Heln's attitude was understandable, but wrong, for she had indeed given birth to a dragon. As well as the twins.

Through magical evil their children had been distorted in her womb. Through good magic in the nick of time she and the children had been spared, and the monster within her had been fragmented into three. Kelvin felt, and knew that Heln did too, that the children were really theirs and not their benefactor's. Yet their son and daughter did bear a strong resemblance to the chimaera's woman-face.

"They are telepathic, you know," he continued, trying to satisfy her that the children really were safe. That ability bothered him during intimate moments with Heln, but at other times he saw it as a considerable advantage. "They do communicate in their heads. And Dragon Horace, whether or not he's their brother, is better protection than an armed guard. It would take an evil witch or wizard to slip up on them, and with Helbah as a friend I don't think that will happen."

"You just want them out of the house!" she charged with some justice.

"Well, sometimes that's nice. Their range is limited, and I admit I don't like to think of them peeking in at us when we're—"

"Kelvin!"

"Well, it's so," he said, nettled. He had never quite dared bring up this aspect before. He had sort of assumed that she had thought it out for herself, as far as she wanted to.

"You mean—when we . . . ?" He could hear the three dots of her ellipsis, each dot loaded with appalling significance. Evidently she *hadn't* thought it through this far before.

"Why not? Children are curious creatures, and it isn't as

if there's anything wrong with it. They probably are bored by it, because they're too young to have the, er—''

''I know what you're trying to say! Don't say it! Of course they're too young to have such urges! That's why they shouldn't peek!''

''But we can hardly stop them. However, now that they are out of peeking range, why don't we—''

''Kelvin, you are so exasperating at times! How could you think of a thing like that at a time like this? We have no idea where they are or whether they're safe!''

''Heln, I'm sure they're safe! They can read the mind of anyone or anything that might threaten them. They'll be with Horace, and he is extremely protective of them. We need to let them get some experience on their own. Meanwhile, if we want some real privacy, now is the time.'' He knew it wouldn't work, but what was there to lose at this stage?

She stared at him. Then she laughed, surprising him. ''Maybe you're right. Maybe they do peek, and certainly they need to have some freedom, lest we stifle them. So we can do what is good for us and for them simultaneously.'' She turned toward the bed.

He saw it at the same time she did. The small white square that materialized out of sunlight about the table and floated down. Magic—it had to be magic, but of what kind?

Heln picked up the paper. ''Why it's an invitation!'' she exclaimed, pleased. ''Look!'' She brought it to him.

He looked. In shimmery golden letters the message read:

Kelvin Knight Hackleberry
the Roundear of Prophecy:
Greetings from the Order of Benign
Wizards and Witches. You and your
spouse and your two human offspring are
cordially invited to attend this
century's Benign Wizards and Witches
Convention as guests along with our
Guest of Honor, Witch Helbah. Only

> under very special circumstances are
> nonmembers of our Order invited to our
> conventions. Time and place and
> traveling plans will be relayed to you
> through our guest of honor.
> The Committee

Kelvin swallowed. He had hoped that he and Heln were finished with the witching business. Yet Helbah had saved all their lives as much as he and his mother and sister had saved hers. All of them, working together, had defeated Zoanna and Rowforth, the wicked king from another frame. Through cooperation and magic and a bit of assistance from a chimaera they had saved the existing kingdoms in the federation. His mother and sister had in fact been recruited as apprentices. Much as he would have preferred to say no to this invitation, he knew that there was no way. Not only would it be a chore to attend, and not only would it interfere with the fishing trip he had planned to take with Lester Crumb, it had ruined his one chance to make love to Heln completely free of the children. If only the message could have arrived half an hour later!

Heln got a strange expression on her face. She seemed about to burst. Then she clapped her hands and shrieked with joy. She threw her arms around him, bearing him back down on the bed, almost smothering him.

"Oh, Kelvin, isn't it grand! They're honoring our Helbah at last! And we get to go with her and see her be honored! Oh my love, I'm so happy!"

Well, it was nice to have her happy, even if *he* wasn't. He held her, savoring the moment of closeness before she remembered all the womanish things she would have to do to get ready.

"Now I'm *really* in the mood!" she said, kissing him as she pressed close. "What are you waiting for, lover?"

Suddenly Kelvin was happy too.

* * *

Lester Crumb opened and closed his mouth. It had just come down, floating gently from the sky. Right into Jon's waiting, eager hands.

Jon caught the paper with its golden letters and perused it as if it were a letter. "It's come! It's come! Just as Mother said the cards predicted! We're going to the Benevolent Wizards and Witches Convention! All of us are going—she, you and I, Kelvin and Heln, and all the children!"

"Not I!" Lester said stoutly, as befitted a man. "I'm going fishing with Kelvin."

"You are not! You won't insult Helbah that way! I'm going, and you're going too."

"I am not! Kelvin and I have had this fishing trip planned for weeks!"

"Les, you're going to the convention. Or else."

Fighting was part of their relationship; they enjoyed it. "Or else what?" he demanded.

She pulled up her brownberry shirt, showing her breasts. "Or else you can forget about this." She dropped her shirt back and reached for her skirt. "Or this."

Lester sighed. This was getting serious! "Looks as if I'll have to get used to it," he said morosely. "Unless I can persuade that nice little Lomax girl to—"

He ducked as the clod of dirt Jon hurled narrowly missed. He had had that persuasive argument worked out for days. Of course Charley Lomax's kid sister was just a child to him, but she was awfully cute and could serve wonderfully to generate jealously.

"You big hunk of dragon bait, I won't have it!" Jon stormed. "You'll come with me or you'll regret the consequences!"

"I'll come with you over a dead witch's body!" Lester retorted. "And speaking of bodies, I'll bet your replacement's as ripe as they come!"

This time the clod struck him on his right pointed ear. It stung. He grabbed hold of that appendage and swore, carefully putting in some references to bruised witches' tits and suckling apprentices.

"You take that back, Lester!" Jon said. The fire in her eyes equaled that of a full-fledged witch and warned him that she meant it. Would she clunk him with a rock if he ignored it? That might be one way to get her to stay, but common male wisdom suggested another.

"All right, if you go, you go alone," he said. "You know how things will be here."

"But you don't know how things will be *there,*" she countered. "If two can misbehave here, two can misbehave there."

Of course she was bluffing, as was he. They were absolutely true to each other, though their constancy had not been rewarded with any babies, to their regret. But that aspect of their marriage was off bounds for argument.

"Take along your sling and plenty of rocks," Lester suggested. It was as mean and contemptuous a comeback as he could manage within the rules.

Jon didn't even hurl another clod. She simply walked straight-backed and nose-elevated to the barn and her waiting horse. It would be, he knew, almost nightfall before she finally came riding back.

Win, lose, or draw, he had bought himself one miserable day. If only he had had the wit to see this quarrel coming, so as to head it off. But that damned invitation had caught him by surprise. "Witches!" he muttered, disgusted.

Charlain held out the just-arrived invitation to John Knight. Its golden lettering, she knew, would be like a taunt to his face. "See. I told you. You said it was nonsense," she said teasingly. She was well past her youth, but remained an elegant woman, and certainly a good one.

"I always say the cards are nonsense," the big roundear said gruffly. But his disbelief in magic had long since become token; there was far too much evidence to the contrary, in this frame.

"And the prophecy too. The prophecy about our Kelvin." Without giving him a chance to squeeze in another grumble, she launched into the familiar words:

> A Roundear there Shall Surely be
> Born to be Strong, Raised to be Free

Fighting Dragons in his Youth
Leading Armies, Nothing Loth
Ridding his Country of a Sore
Joining Two, then uniting Four
Until from Seven there be One
Only then will his Task be Done
Honored by Many, cursed by Few
All will know what Roundear can Do.

"Spare me," he said, grimacing. "Spare me that doggerel. I wonder if it sounds better in its original language?"

"But you recognize that it's true. That Kelvin *did* kill dragons in his youth, *did* free our Rud of its sore of tyrannous government, *did* join Rud with the former kingdom of Aratex, *did* unite the newly united lands with those of Klingland, Kance, and Hermandy."

"Yes, yes, yes, I know, I know, I know."

"And the invitation came just as I foretold it would, from reading the cards."

"You're a whiz of a fortune-teller," her obstreperous old man said. "The prophecy's a *true* prophecy because if you use your imagination, it's partially worked out. That's what you want me to say, my coppery-haired, violet-eyed, pointy-eared witch?"

She elevated an eyebrow at him. "Sometimes I wonder what you ever saw in this coppery point-eared witch."

"Apart from the frame's most beautiful face and figure, I'm not sure."

"Oh? I thought those belonged to Zoanna."

He scratched his head. "That's right! There must have been something else. Maybe you were a better cook, or something."

"Or something," she agreed wryly. The truth was that Zoanna had used magic to enchant him, with imperfect success; his true love had been for Charlain. She had read of their love and marriage in her cards, and it had come to pass, though not without some fairly formidable complications along the way.

"Actually, I will say that you are good at explaining how

your cards say what we already know to be true. So after
we fell in love, your cards agreed. Will that do?''

"No. I want you to say that we're going with Helbah and
our son and our grandchildren to see her honored.''

"Do I have any choice?''

"Not a predictable bit, John Knight.''

"In that case I'll be delighted to attend. I understand that some
of the beautiful young witches can be quite attentive to a man.''

"In that case," she said smugly, "I predict that nothing at
all of what you're thinking is ever remotely going to happen.''

"But I don't believe in your predictions!''

"Then your disappointment will be that much greater.''

He sighed. Actually it required no magic to know that
nothing short of magic would separate him from her.

Kildom gave Kildee a sly wink and pointed with a grubby
finger at their guardian's back. Helbah had three of her
magic viewing crystals lighted and each showed someone
they knew well: Kelvin Knight Hackleberry, his sister Jon,
and his mother Charlain.

"She's planning something," Kildom said. "A trip, I think.''

"Are we going?" Kildee asked.

"I hope so," said Kildom to his mirror-image look-alike.
"Only I hope those *other* twins aren't coming. If they are,
I'd rather stay at home.''

"Who wouldn't! Think of all we could do with Helbah
away! We could eat our fill of sweets, watch women un-
dressing, and declare a war if we liked.''

Kildom considered the matter with his twenty-six-year-
old mind in his seven-and-a-half-year-old body. He and his
brother only aged one year in four, thanks to having been
born on Leap Year Day and dosed with magic. In theory
they had a long time to grow up and acquire the wisdom
for the practice of kingly duties. In practice childhood was
at times not really an enormous lot of fun.

"No, I don't think we dare," Kildom said seriously, after
completing his consideration. "Helbah would know, and if
she didn't, you-know-who would tell her.''

"Yeah, those brats."

Kildom thought of the pretty coppery-haired girl who had tormented them so. Peeking into their minds on one occasion, she had seen all and blabbed all. Instead of being outraged at her tattling, Helbah had been delighted. There had gone their adventuring plans, and also a curtailment of what Helbah called privileges. That was injury added to insult. For the past two years he had held the tattling against the little girl. She had then been four, by ordinary reckoning; now she was six, and no better.

"Saaay," Kildee said, catching him unaware. "Maybe we can—"

"What?"

"Get them to cooperate. They're six years old now and they should be smart. If we plan something and offer them a chance to be part of it . . . ?"

For a moment Kildom had feared that his brother was going soft on little Merlain. She was cute, but cute was as cute did, and she had tattled. He was relieved to see that Kildee had not lost his sense. It was almost impossible to nullify someone who could read your mind, but this just might do it. "Yeah! Yeah, let's!"

They set to work immediately, making plans for possibly impossible adventures.

Afternoon

Merlain was massaging Dragon Horace with butterin, rubbing the half-melted shortening and bread spread over his coppery scales. The scales gleamed brighter and brighter the harder she rubbed, particularly those on his snout.

"And so, Dragon Horace," she was saying, "our brother Charles didn't know what he was talking about! He's not going to get you any squirbet at all, I'll bet! Auntie Jon would knock one down from a tree with a rock from her sling. But Charles thought he'd do without! Just think at the little animal until it sees danger wherever you want, then have it run into a rock or a tree. Brain itself by itself. I knew it wouldn't work."

PLOP! The small gray body with its long ears and bushy tail lit right before Horace's nose, causing him to jump up a little and spill greasy butterin all over her dress. He sniffed once at the quivering small body, then shot out his forked tongue and tasted it. His mouth opened, revealing the rows of sharp teeth, each longer than the blade of Grandpa John's pocketknife. The tongue picked up the morsel and pulled it into the moist cave. Crunch, crunch, crunch, swallow, and then a satisfied dragon expression.

"So I was wrong," Merlain said, disgruntled. "You did get a squirbet."

"Yeah. Took me all morning just to find the right squirbet and the right braining rock."

"I'm getting hungry myself," Merlain said, patting Horace. "We ate all the cooakes and drank all our lemangeaid. We should have brought some of Mom's appleberry pie and some peajel butter and smackers."

"We should have but we didn't." Charles strode out of the brush and over to his brother and sister. He sat down by the young dragon's other side. His hand reached across and playfully teased the open nostrils just where the scales stopped growing. Horace was a handsome creature; they all agreed on that. In fact, maybe copper was better than gold, for scales.

"Well, don't you think we should go on back?" Merlain inquired tartly.

"Yeah. Just saying good-bye to Horace. Good-bye, Horace."

"**GROOMPTH!**" the young dragon replied. Smarter than others of its kind, it still refused to learn to talk. Horace did, however, respond to their mind commands when and as it suited his purpose. In that Horace was very much like an intelligent dog that Grandpa John had talked about.

The children watched together as Horace rose to his clawed feet and slithered and wriggled as he walked away from them. He would grow bigger than his present pony size in the years and centuries he probably had to live, if he didn't get into an ill-advised fight with a bigger dragon. Of course Mama talked madly of having him killed, but even their father argued against that. According to Auntie Jon, their father had actually killed dragons as a boy. When she had heard that, Merlain was so distressed and heartbroken that she had immediately peed on Jon's lap. That had been embarrassing, but she and Charles had been too young then to hear such stories. To Merlain, to this very day, it seemed that Auntie Jon had gotten exactly what she deserved.

"Someone's followed us," Charles said, squinting his weak eyes.

Merlain, who saw somewhat better than her brother, was able immediately to put him right. "It's our witchmother," she said.

Dragon Horace moved off a short distance. The witch made her nervous, so he tended to avoid her when he could. In a moment he disappeared into a nearby ravine.

A small, aged woman floated above the grass in their direction. One of Helbah's projections, without a doubt. They knew because they could not fathom its mind. "Hello, children," Helbah said.

"Hello," they replied together. In time Helbah would say what she wanted, and then the projection would vanish just as it had come. "Your mother's worrying about you."

"Mama's always worrying," Charles said. "But Daddy doesn't like us peeking into their minds when they want to get mushy."

"Yes, that's strange," Merlain said. "Why are they so interested in doing that, and why shouldn't we peek if we can stand the dullness?"

The projection's withered old lips quirked. "I am sure I have forgotten the answer, if I ever knew it. At any rate, they finished that business some time ago, so you won't have to be bored anymore. You had better scamper home.''

''We're going,'' Merlain said. Then, fearing to sound overly dutiful, she added ''We're hungry and we know she made a pie.''

The image of Helbah wavered in the air. Its feet lowered to the grass and the blades went into the feet and legs rather than bending. Still an image, but now appearing to be more substantial, the Helbah said, ''I wonder. I need to ask a favor.''

''Really?'' This was big stuff. If images had minds, Merlain would have been into Helbah's now! But of course the witch was way out of range, and she could close off her mind even when she was close, when she chose. She had never asked a favor before; indeed, it had always been the other way around.

''We're going on a trip, all of us,'' Helbah said. ''You, your mother and father, your grandparents on your father's side, your aunt Jon, and—''

''Not the kings!'' Charles said. He was, as always, undiplomatic, but accurate enough. The kings were royal pains.

Helbah's image smiled. ''They are kings, and kings must not be trusted far because they are so powerful. They have to come. You will have to see that they stay out of trouble. You will, won't you?''

Merlain saw Charles looking at her in despair. In his mind was a picture of two plump naked posteriors: a pair of asses. The thought of having to watch over those was almost too much for him. Horace, out of sight but remaining in mental range, picked up the sentiment and growled. But to the dragon, the vision of the posteriors was tasty rather than repulsive. Oh, for one good bite! That almost made Merlain laugh, but she managed to keep her face angelically straight. She was getting better at that. She hoped to be perfect at concealing her emotions by the time she was a woman and really needed the ability.

''Yes, I know that you both dislike them. I can't blame you. It was so mean of them, that trick they pulled. They knew better. But what did they do but feed you laxaberries and then lock you in their old abandoned dungeon. If you hadn't used your minds, you'd have made a mess for them to clean up.''

Merlain wished that she had had that piece of information a year ago when it would have done her some good. But this *was* interesting. ''You want us to tattle?'' she suggested with a trace more eagerness than was seemly.

''That is what you'll be along for. To tattle on them for their own good.''

Wonderful! Merlain loved tattling, and Charles didn't mind where the royal pains were concerned. This could be fun! They could put a lot of ideas in the pains' heads and then tattle on them.

''You are such *good* children,'' their unsuspecting witch-mother said. ''Go home now, for your mother will be anxious.''

Merlain waved, and Charles saw what she was doing and waved too. The image couldn't receive their ''good-bye'' thoughts. Helbah waved back, then vanished.

''WHOOF!'' Dragon Horace growled, emerging from the ravine with part of the body of a long-dead meer. He was thinking at them that he would share the intriguing scent.

''Oh, Dragon Horace, you're the bestest dragon brother in the whole wide world!'' Merlain ran to him, grabbed hold of his tiny wings, and pulled herself up on his back. Here the scent was overpowering, making her head swim. That meer must have died of a pus explosion!

''Wait! I want some too!'' Charles complained. ''Leave some for me!'' He ran up and threw his arms around Horace's neck, rubbing his cheek in the melted and now incredibly smelly ointment that had given the scales a shine. Horace must have rolled in the meer mess, as dragons tended to do when they found something truly rotten. ''Won't Mama be surprised!''

''I'll bet she'll know we're coming home,'' Merlain said, and laughed happily at the expression she knew would be on their mother's face.

By and large the human beings they knew just didn't appreciate a nose-wrinkling good scent.

CHAPTER 1

To Another World

"Now, you realize this is going to be a little different," Helbah began. Gathered together at the twin palaces, the Knights and Jon and Kelvin's family could simply look at each other and shrug. "I mean it isn't just an *ordinary* frame we're about to enter. No, no indeed. Oh, the geography is similar, the climate equivalent, but the living will seem quite, quite strange."

"Will there be look-alikes?" Jon asked. "I always wanted to meet look-alikes! Ever since Kel told us of his adventures in the silver serpent world and the chimaera's copper world I wanted—"

"Oh, shut up, girl!" Helbah snapped, addressing her minor apprentice severely. "I'll explain everything to you. You will each have a guide book, and then we'll go."

Jon was annoyed. Helbah's sometimes sharp ways contrasted badly with her mother's. Charlain had always listened carefully to her, then disregarded everything she said. Consequently Jon had grown up as a tomboy. That was the way to do it.

"As I was saying," Helbah continued, directing her speech more to Kelvin than to the rest of them, "there are real differences. You've never been to a city, though you may think that you have. Megapolis, our host city, is like nothing you've experienced. Even you, John, growing up in that barbaric frame with its horseless carriages, flying machines, atomic bombs, and absolutely no magic. Can you deny that, John Knight? I see you smiling."

"I've been in cities," Jon and Kelvin's father said. "True, there wasn't magic, but—"

"Then there wasn't anything! Magic is entirely different than your science. It can do things science can't."

"I have to admit the truth of that," John said. Jon knew that he could have given examples of experiences with Zatanas and his daughter Zoanna in this frame. In the silver serpent frame and later the chimaera's frame he must certainly have lost all doubt. So his antimagic attitude was mostly pretense.

"You'll find out most by doing, but for now just let me describe the Magi Towers where the convention is held," Helbah continued. "It's truly a magical hotel that sparkles and shines and has neither windows nor doors from outside. On the inside—"

"I don't believe that," Jon said, surprising herself. "If there aren't windows and doors on the outside, no one can get inside."

"How little you know about magic! Of course guests and hotel people go in and out. We'll show our invitations"—she held hers up—"and the doorman will sign for us and we'll walk through a wall that can stop people."

"Sort of like an electric eye," John suggested. Then, noting as Jon had that Helbah was displeased by interruptions: "Sorry."

Helbah looked from face to face most seriously. Her sharp eyes had a way of making Jon squirm. In this Helbah was not unlike a village schoolteacher who had taught both of Charlain's children. When no one interrupted or volunteered, she resumed: "Inside, all service is by magic.

Lighted signs will direct you. Travel to different floors will
be by your command. There are no locks. All practitioners
of benign magic trust each other—besides, one can always
lay on a curse. Luggage is transported magically, as are we.
There is running water in all rooms—something I'm certain
none of you will have experienced. The water is good for
drinking and bathing and there are fish swimming in it to
show that it is pure. There's a large banquet room and an
assembly room where some will give talks and others, I
hope, will keep their mouths shut. Everywhere in the hotel
there will appear to be no outside walls, but the walls are
there and will prevent unwary guests from falling. The convention program will consist of talks and panels on the craft.
There will be a room where books on the craft and various
bits of paraphernalia are displayed. There may be an auction
of rare works. There will be a furnished party suite, a
lounging suite, and most important of all, a children's suite.
In the children's suite the children will receive deportment
and other lessons and be kept out of the way of busy guests.
Now the—''

Jon had quit listening, but was pretending otherwise. Her
thoughts were on the children. Either pair of twins could be
trouble, but Kelvin's had to be the worst. They'd learned
early to keep out of heads, but at a large gathering of
strangers, who knew what might tempt them? She'd have to
speak to the royal twins and try to persuade them to tattle
on Kelvin's. The twin kings were after all men in all but
body. Kildom and Kildee must be around thirty years old,
their appearance to the contrary. if the two kings couldn't
control Kelvin's brats, maybe Helbah could cast a spell on
them.

''—and so that is why we will travel separately and meet
in the transporter in Megapolis. We with pointed ears—we
three ladies and our kings—will go by the water transporter.
You roundears—Kelvin, Heln, John, Charles, and Merlain—must take the other. I, of course, will provide you
with the correct transporter settings, and—''

How weary it all was! Jon hoped things would pick up a

bit once they were traveling. Poor Lester; he was going to miss it all! But what was this about a water transporter? How were she and Charlain expected to go underwater? Perhaps she'd better listen to what Helbah said.

Zed Yokes and assorted friends of the old river man carried the boat through the ruins of the old palace and down the ancient stairs. They launched it with the other boat and then they loaded. The roundears had the old boat and the pointed ears the newer one.

Helbah sat perched in the bow of the point-eared boat holding Katbah, her black houcat familiar, on her lap. Charlain took the stern seat, and Jon the middle seat, where she grasped the oars. Kildom and Kildee crowded as close to Helbah as possible, being both eager to see ahead and nervous about this particular business. They loved exploration and mischief, but anything relating to the Flaw was something else.

John had the stern seat in the roundear craft, Heln the bow seat, and Kelvin the oars. Like the other set of twins, Charles and Merlain preferred crowding near the bow.

The eerily glowing lichen-covered walls slipped by as Jon pulled the oars. Behind them, at no great distance, came the boat rowed by her brother. Jon was glad she had gotten Lester to teach her to row a boat, the summer before. She now wished she could race Kelvin. Turning her head to glance forward as well as she could, watching the clumsy splash of his blades, she knew she could win. Poor dear Kelvin, he had no real skill at anything, and yet he was acknowledged as a hero. With magic gauntlets, laser, the Mouvar antimagic weapon, the levitation belt and the electric-bolt-hurling chimaera's copper sting, there wasn't anything he couldn't defeat. But with all those things, there wouldn't be anything Jon herself couldn't defeat! Kelvin was on his own when rowing, the supreme, lovable klutz.

Now Kelvin, as if reading her mind, was drawing on his gauntlets. That would end that. With those on he was supreme; no one rowed a boat, aimed a weapon, or swung a sword better than her brother. Not for the first time, she wished that she had been born first, and with round ears, and male, so that the prophecy could have applied to her. But then of course she and Lester wouldn't be married, and though Lester could be a pain in the bottom and often was, no woman born had a better husband overall. Win some and lose some, as their father said.

The swirl in the water was right where it should be, just as Kelvin had said. She stopped rowing and waited. There were certain things that had just better not be pushed.

Helbah said some incomprehensible magical words and tossed a greenish powder. The powder settled on those in the boat, Katbah included. For a moment Jon felt annoyed. But only a moment. Then, WHOOSH, and they had become three long-necked, sharp-beaked birds, and two barely feathered out swooshlings straining to look over the boat's sides. There was no discomfort or disorientation; Helbah's transformations were of high quality.

Helbah swoosh waited patiently while something resembling a small rodent with very pointed ears crawled onto her back. That would be Katbah in batbah form. The rodent burrowed into the feathers, taking a firm grip on the heaviest ones at the base of the swoosh's neck. Then Helbah swoosh gave a quick come-on nod of her head and dived, neck extended, off the side of the bow.

Charlain swoosh and the two swooshlings were quick to follow. That left Jon, and she turned her swoosh head and vibrated her fowl tongue directly at Kelvin, just to keep him in his place. Then she dived.

Water was all around her, and her wings and her feet kicked, and it was as if she had been a water bird all her life. Ahead was the dome Helbah had explained about, and she ducked her head when it was time and followed on Helbah's tail feathers.

She came up inside the dome, where there was a pool for fish or swooshes or other diving birds. Here was air, magically supplied. Over there, past the pool, was the transporter, looking just as it had been described.

The water in the pool quivered. The swooshes and swooshlings became their human selves. The rodent grew in size, and as it grew it filled out into the beautiful black houcat with deep yellow, shockingly piercing eyes.

Katbah leaped to the platform and immediately began licking water drops from his fur. The rest of them climbed out more slowly, being only human. Kildom dipped his hand in the water before he emerged, then shook the hand just above Katbah. Kildee, not to be outdone, scooped out a handful and poured it over the creature's head.

If they had expected Katbah to screech and make a scene, they were disappointed. The familiar gave the kinglets a stare, then blinked at Helbah.

The witch got the message. She smacked both kings on both ears. They looked at her with expressions of shock. Jon suspected that this ear boxing was not the first time, and that this was why the kinglets, unlike Kelvin's twins, were normally well behaved. Their shock was not because of the punishment, but because it had been administered publicly. Certainly Jon had behaved after her foster father boxed *her* ears. Kelvin, goody-goody that he was, had never once had that happen to him. Now that she remembered, and her memory for that sort of thing was pretty good.

"That hurt!" Kildee cried.

"A lot!" his brother added. But their protests seemed more show than substance. The boxing hadn't been that hard. It had been more of a warning.

"Children, children, if you don't behave, you're not going on this trip," Helbah said sharply. "I can turn you back into swooshlings and leave you here. You can stay right here until the convention's over and I come for you. Do you want that?"

The kinglets looked down at their feet. It was the humility posture appropriate to penitents. At one time Jon had mastered it, and so avoided punishments quite as frequent as she had deserved. Kelvin, of course, had never needed to learn the art. That had always irritated her. It was a good thing she loved her brother, or she never would have been able to put up with him. She thought of it as disgust love.

"Oh, come on!" Helbah said in exasperation. She picked up Katbah and clutched him to her withered bosom as she walked around positioning knobs on the transporter.

Jon watched, not perfectly at ease. This looked just like the kind of transporter Kelvin had described, that accepted only roundears. She had always scoffed at the claim that pointears would be destroyed if they tried to use one, but her disbelief had never been total. Suppose it was true, and it was instant death to use one of those odd machines, and this was one of the wrong kind?

"Now you know how it works," the witch said. "You step inside and then you're there. I'll go last. Charlain—"

Without hesitation Charlain stepped into the small closet. Jon wanted to cry *No! No!* but stifled it, knowing she was being foolish, womanishly foolish, which was the worst kind of foolishness. Men like Kelvin were expected to be somewhat foolish; it came with the territory of maleness. But a woman—

There was a purple flash in the closet, forcing Jon to blink. When her vision cleared, her mother was gone, and there was the scent of ozone.

Jon swallowed. Few things scared her, but this was one of them. Magic was fundamentally understandable; a person just had to have a talent for it and learn the ways of it. But this was science, and was unsettling. It just wasn't *natural*.

"I'm next!" Kildom cried eagerly.

"No, me!" Kildee countered. They jostled against each other, trying to crowd into the closet.

What else could be expected of them? They were kings, Jon thought, and fools, and juveniles. They had no caution at all, except about getting boxed on the ears, and not enough of that. Whereas Jon herself, in contrast—

"Neither of you," the witch said. "Jon, you're next."

Jon jumped. She had to admit to herself that she was scared. But it would be worse to *appear* scared. Taking a firm grip on her sling, just as if the silly thing could help against the horrors of science, she stepped into the closet.

"Breathe, girl," Helbah murmured as she passed.

Oh. Jon forced herself to unhold her breath as she came all the way into the dread closet.

There might have been a purple flash, but she wasn't conscious of it. There was a twisting sensation all through her, a whirl of stars and lights, and—

The closet was almost the same, but now it stood in a row of closets. A long, low room stretched outward all around. There were people, here, too. People walking, people moving, people going about their business, people ignoring people. There were great lights on the ceilings and walls. Stacks of luggage were being floated through the air. All of this was so big, so confusing, so strange, that it threatened to overload her sharp eye and mind.

Jon shivered. She had been worried about the transporter, but this was *really* scary. All these strange people. Some of them were dressed oddly, and some weren't dressed at all. In fact they appeared quite naked. She could handle that, of course, but for the first time she was glad Lester hadn't decided to come with her. His empty threats might have lost some of their emptiness, if he had been here to see this array. But the unclothed weren't all women.

Where were Helbah and Katbah and the twins? Where was Kelvin and John Knight? And, come to think of it, where was Charlain?

Jon stepped out of the closet and had an immediate impulse to step back again. It was all so big and weird! She clutched at the side of the cabinet and shook.

"First time, miss?"

"Mrs.," she said automatically. The black-cloaked woman definitely had to be a witch. So old, so ugly—she was glad Helbah didn't look like that. And she smelled—bad. Like a herd of rotten animals soaked in spoiled brine. But at least she had inquired. "Yes, it's my first time to a convention."

"I'm not surprised," the figure said. "You don't appear to have lived much past a century. First transporter trip?"

Jon nodded. She had never felt so gauche in her life! Much past a *century*? This old bag of bones imagined she had lived more than a hundred years! She was badly out of sorts, here, but she didn't think it made her look quite *that* old!

The witch fumbled in a bag. She brought out a small blue phial, unstoppered it, and stepped in much too close for comfort. She thrust the vial almost in Jon's face. "Here! Take a whiff!" she urged breathily. "This will make the weakness go."

The weakness? It would be enough if it just made the smell go! "What—what is it?" Jon gasped.

"We call it displacement sickness. That's what you're suffering from. You can't reorient immediately. But this will cure it." The hag squeezed in even closer.

Before she knew what she was doing, Jon drew a breath. The odor of the potion was pungent. It bit her nostrils, prickling and sparkling through her air passages and her head. She closed her eyes. This potion wasn't curing her, it was making her overwhelmingly dizzy! She closed her eyes involuntarily, reeling. But in a moment she forced them open again as the dizziness cleared.

The witch was gone. Instead there was an absolutely beautiful and naked young woman, who, it seemed, was just leaving. Jon turned. Behind her a royal twin was stepping from the transporter. "That was fun," the kinglet said as he emerged, to be replaced by his look-alike redheaded brother.

"I want to go again," the second twin said. He exited the transporter and was replaced by Helbah.

Helbah stepped out. Charlain appeared around the side of the transporter on the arm of a red-caped young man with a pointed black beard.

"Here you are. I told you it would be all right," the man said to Jon's mother.

"Thank you," Carlain said to the stranger. "Thank you for helping me."

"Glad to have been of assistance. Don't feel bad. Many people panic when they think they're lost." The man walked away, smiling as if at a joke he had just told himself.

"That leaves those from the other boat," Helbah said. "I hope Kelvin and his father don't mess up." She looked around. "Oh, there you are, Jon; for a moment I didn't see you." She returned her attention to the others.

Jon opened and closed her mouth. She had wanted to say something—something she had felt was important. About smelly old women, or lovely young women. But it faded as she concentrated. Somehow, try as she might, she couldn't remember what it had been.

Kelvin rowed the boat to the ledge. He and Heln got out, followed by his father. With the help of the gauntlets he secured the boat with a line to an old iron ring that had gone unused during the other trips here. He walked to the great metal door, twisted the lever with the gauntlets, and turned back.

By this time John Knight had lifted the kids out. Wide-eyed, impressed by the trip past the great roaring Flaw just before their turn, Charles and Merlain had become temporarily obedient and unnaturally silent. They had actually obeyed the warning that they stay put.

The installation was just as Kelvin remembered it, with its curved walls and eerie lights and waiting transporter closet. Six years it had been, and it hadn't changed a bit. That was reassuring.

They entered the chamber and crossed to the parchment on its stand. The Mouvar Parchment, he remembered: perhaps the most significant document he knew of. Again he took the time to read the words that had been placed there, waiting for centuries, until a young man with round ears and a prophecy should appear. However unlikely or unwilling that man might be. He focused on the .ornate script, finding it even bigger and bolder than he remembered it.

> To whom it may concern: if you have found this cell, you are a roundear, because only a roundear could penetrate to it without setting off the self-destruct mechanism. I am Mouvar—and I am a round-ear.
>
> But because the natives look with disfavor on aliens, I masked my ears so that I could work among them

without hindrance. I used the technology of my home frame to set things straight, then retired, for it was lonely. I set up the prophecy of my return, or the appearance of any roundear, to facilitate better acceptance in future centuries. The tools of my frame are here, and you may use them as you find necessary. If you wish to contact me directly, seek me in my home frame, where I will be in suspended animation. Directions for using the Flaw to travel to the frame of your choice are in the book of instructions beside this letter. Please return any artifacts you borrow. Justice be with you.

"Hey!" His father stood with both grandchildren, one under each arm. "Time to go! I set the transporter. If we make Helbah wait, she will either lay an egg or have kittens. One of each, maybe."

"Will she, Grandpa?" Merlain asked, interested, her eyes bright.

" 'Course not!" practical Charles said, pricking her cuteness act. "He just says that."

"Yes, yes, let's go." Heln had been reading the document by his side and was only now finishing it. "Go ahead."

Heln looked him full in the face. "Kelvin, I never realized until I read this just how incredibly important you are! For Mouvar, that alien precog from another world in another frame, to have left this message here—here, for you, and long before you were born!"

There was a flash of purple in the transporter. Heln screamed and grabbed him with all her strength. Her nails bit in, and he wished he were wearing armor. "Oh, Kelvin—they've disappeared!"

"Of course," he said, glad for the chance to reassure her. It made him feel more competent. "Now *we* disappear. From here."

"But—"

Now was his chance to seem to be decisive. He scooped her up, holding her in his arms as he had done last time at a swimming hole. Only then both of them had been less dressed—in fact they had been naked—and definitely all wet. It was a fond memory. It had been some time ago, because once the children got big enough to get around—well, anyway, it had been fun. Maybe someday the children would visit relatives far enough away and he could swim with Heln again.

He walked across the chamber and toward the transporter. Heln was smiling, perhaps also remembering the swimming hole. But then she saw where he was going. "KEL—" she started as he stepped in, alarmed.

Everything twisted. Stars and comets flashed.

"VIN!" she finished, and reality changed for them.

They were suddenly in a very strange place. It was no swimming hole, unfortunately. There were floating platforms and floating luggage and all sorts of strange whatevers. There were also people all over, some of them less clothed than he and Heln had been when swimming. Well, that wasn't quite possible, but somehow it seemed true, because this was a public place. An unclothed body that was pleasantly nude in the water could be starkly naked in a marketplace. For that was what this most seemed like, at first startled glance.

He stepped out and put Heln down as he saw his father and his children meeting with Helbah and his mother and the rest. Jon, foolishly holding her sling, seemed to be trying to say something, but then women generally were.

He stood there and gaped, taking in the surrounding sights. Particularly absorbing was the sight of a young woman of statuesque proportions without a stitch of clothing on, who seemed completely unconscious of his staring.

Heln nudged him, not quite as unconscious of his guilty interest. She was not partial to that kind of company in his mental swimming hole.

Kelvin wrenched his gaze away. This just might, he realized, turn out to more fun than all except the most sensational fishing trip. Only mermaid fishing could be more intriguing than this. Lester Crumb had made a bad mistake, refusing to come.

CHAPTER 2

Megapolis

"Now we've plenty of time before the con starts," Helbah assured them, leading them through the gigantic terminal. People, most of them looking like witches, warlocks, and associated types, were headed purposefully in all directions, ignoring all else. Yet somehow Helbah threaded their way through, avoiding collisions without seeming to go out of her way. They walked past platforms, booths, and counters without seeming end. She motioned all of them to stay put and wait for her, then walked up to a Heravis Rent-a-Drive counter and started talking.

Kelvin recognized the man at the counter as an employee type he'd encountered at home. The fellow was not trying very hard; in fact he wasn't being helpful. He wondered if Helbah would unleash a spell. She was trying to be patient, but Kelvin was able to recognize the little signs of her annoyance. He saw the two kinglets nudging each other knowingly and knew that they had picked up on this too; they were looking forward to the explosion.

He held Heln's hand and she held Charles' hand and

Charles held Merlain's hand. Jon for some reason had a kinglet's hand in each of her own. This kept the young ones mostly under control; it was when they got out loose that trouble built up like a turbulent storm, one thing feeding on another. Charlain was quite by herself, evidently dizzied and bewildered by all the sights.

"It's all right, Mom," he said. "Really it is. By the way, where's Dad?"

"Right here," his father said, coming up behind him. "I was just out looking at the cars. This place is New York City, minus pollution and plus magic."

Kelvin hadn't the slightest idea what he meant. He was watching Helbah's irritation increase toward the warning flicker of anger. He would not care to be in the counterman's uncooperative shoes!

The kinglets watched raptly. "Now!" one murmured. Oh yes, they knew the dire signs! Their boxed ears had enabled them to calibrate Helbah's ire precisely.

In that moment there was a poof of whitish smoke behind the counter. The counterman disappeared in it. In a moment it cleared to reveal a large frog with a larger mouth and great bulging eyes.

Startled, the creature opened its mouth and said "**CROAK**!" in a loud, pained voice. He got no sympathy. People around them pointed and laughed.

A passerby paused, nodding. "Serves the idiot right, not to recognize a grandmistress witch," he said to his companion. "He tried to treat her the way the functionaries treat the rest of us." Chuckling, he moved on.

Helbah was too genteel to smirk. She simply made a gesture. The smoke returned. It dissipated in a moment and the man was there again. Possibly his transformation had been mere illusion. It didn't matter; it had made the point. He was shaking.

Hastily the counterman thrust papers before Helbah while she dug in her bag and brought out papers of a similar kind, only smaller. Helbah signed one of the man's papers, thrust it and some of her small papers at him, and turned away from the rental counter.

The kinglets lost interest. The show was over. It really hadn't been as much as they had hoped for.

"Let's go," Helbah said briskly. She led them across the terminal, past rows of platforms suspended in midair, seeming to know exactly where she was going. Each platform was equipped with a hunk of crystal in front of a couch and a back couch: two wide comfortable seats.

Helbah stopped at a platform whose number matched the number on a card. Despite her years she hopped in agile fashion onto the platform and seated herself behind the crystal.

"Well, all aboard!" she said, as if this were routine.

Oh. The rest of them had somehow not caught on that this was a conveyance, not just a place to sit. Kelvin let go of Heln's hand and helped bustle the four children into the front seat beside the witch. Then the five other adults climbed up into the rear seat. It was crowded, but sufficed. Jon was on his lap. He would have preferred to have Heln there; Jon was mostly all woman now, but she was his sister. Kelvin wasn't quite sure he trusted this wheelless, horseless carriage; he presumed there was some way to make it go, but could it be controlled? However, Helbah was Helbah; she knew how to do it if anyone did.

The witch ran her aged hands over the crystal. Her fingers remained just touching the faceted surface. The platform seemed to come to life, vibrating. Charlain looked worriedly about and Kelvin was tempted to. This felt a bit like riding the back of a dragon: one never could be sure what the monster was about to do.

Helbah's fingers remained just touching the faceted surface. The platform drifted out into a stream of other platforms, as if it were a boat entering a river and floating along with other boats. That analogy helped; Kelvin imagined invisible water, and determined its flow by the motions of the other boats.

Silently they glided down a tunnel, keeping perfectly spaced between the other craft, and in line. Katbah yawned on Helbah's lap, finding this dull. Jon shifted on Kelvin's lap, causing him momentary pain. She was looking around, as was her nature, but she was oddly subdued. The others seemed mainly to be holding on, still not quite trusting this craft.

They drifted out of the tunnel, and out of the terminal. The light of day brightened around them. Kelvin gasped; he couldn't help it. So many more wheelless carriages than he had imagined! Moving in both directions, two wide, never-touching lines. A street wider than any he had ever seen, bordered not by recognizable shops but by variously sized and shaped crystals of shop and building size.

Crystals? The only crystals he had seen before were of the size to be mounted in finger rings!

"I don't know whether to go to Hacey's or J.Z. Henny's," Helbah said musingly. "I suppose Hacey's. They should have what we want. They keep a good magical lookout for the needs of their future customers."

Kelvin slipped off a gauntlet and pushed his hand past Jon's rigid back to the far side of their couch. He tried to push his hand past the edge of the platform. He felt a slight tingle in his fingers and wrists. Something magical here, protecting passengers from falling, as he had suspected. There was no sensation of speed, but other platforms and the crystal chunks sped past. Now he noticed that the crystals had glowing letters on them, identifying them as shops or businesses. They went by a Sorcerer's Shack, a Zurgler Kling, and a Witch's Implement. Then they were headed for a really large emerald of many facets, and the central facet read "Hacey's."

The platform slowed. How Helbah managed it he did not see, but a green facet vanished before them and they slid into another tunnel. In a moment they emerged in a parking area, with many stationary platforms aligned in rows. Their own platform slowed further, swerved, and came to a gentle stop in what had been a space between two others.

Helbah, evidently impatient to get the dull details attended to, hustled them so rapidly off their platform and through one of the open doorways that Kelvin's head was spinning. He would have preferred to take time—maybe a day or two—to explore this area and get a better notion of its nature.

A glowing sign loomed ahead: OUTFITTERS, JUVENILE it read. Other doorways were labeled OUTFITTERS, MALE and OUTFITTERS, FEMALE. Well, at least that much made sense.

They were now in a very large store with a great crowd of adults and children. As in the terminal, there was every style and color and degree of dress and undress imaginable. Now Kelvin noticed that some of the unclothed women were not actually naked; they had some kind of translucent or outright transparent material on, which clung magically to their contours. That perhaps accounted for the lack of natural sag in certain portions, making them look impossibly healthy. Now if he could just get one of those outfits for Heln—

"We'll outfit the children first," Helbah said. "Next we'll go to the men's department for you lads, and finally the women's for us girls. Possibly you other girls can shop by yourselves while I accompany the men."

"Girls!" This barely applied to Heln and Jon, and it was inappropriate for his mother, and as for Helbah herself it was ridiculous. The old ladies' department would be more appropriate. But of course he kept his mouth shut. Life and marriage had taught him that much.

A large white bird flew down from a high perch and landed in front of them. Pinkish smoke poofed and there stood a smiling dark-haired girl in a light, gauzy dress. She turned to Helbah, instinctively recognizing her as the one with whom to do business. "May I help you?"

Helbah pointed to the children. "Them. Appropriately for the convention. These two boys are kings. The two others have powers they aren't allowed to use yet. Beware."

"You're Helbah!" the girl exclaimed. "The convention guest of honor! I have admired your magic for decades!"

Decades? To Kelvin the girl looked sixteen. But with witches it could be difficult to tell.

"You will be there?" Helbah inquired, seeming faintly interested.

"I'm flying over right after work. Oh, yes, Helbah, I'll fit them out for the con. It's an honor to serve you."

"In that case," Helbah said, taking the salesgirl's respect as her due, "the rest of us will go get attired while you're dressing them. Be alert; they can be quite troublesome."

"Oh, we have ways of dealing with youngsters," the salesgirl said, smiling. "Besides, when they see what we have here, I know they'll behave."

Lots of luck, Kelvin thought.

"I want to look like a hero," Charles said.

"Me too!" said a kinglet.

"Oh, you will, you will. When we're done, you'll look just the way you always wanted."

"Just be certain you keep them here until we're back," Helbah urged. "If you don't, they'll wreck the store."

Indeed, they were working on it. "There's girls on a high one!" Kildee exclaimed, pointing up and to the side, where a group of four women were gliding down on a platform. At least it seemed like a platform, because their feet were all fixed at the same level, but nothing was visible. They were standing, evidently holding on to a similarly invisible rail around its edge. "Quick! We can peek up their skirts!"

"Dumbbell!" Kildum retorted. "They don't *have* skirts!"

Sure enough: the two older women wore trousers, and the two younger ones were nude, or in invisible wrappings. Kildee turned away, disgusted.

Kelvin managed to refrain from smiling. Then he turned his eyes away, before Heln caught him looking at those body stockings again.

"Transparent elevator," John Knight remarked thoughtfully.

The salesgirl promised Helbah she would keep the children occupied, and shooed them ahead of her, up an aisle. Helbah sighed and led the rest of them to a squared area under an open shaft. Various colored blocks were underfoot, with numbers identifying the floor to which they related. Kelvin looked at the floor; surely just one number could identify it, if any such thing needed to be done.

Helbah pressed a number with her foot. Suddenly they levitated.

Oh. Kelvin couldn't have said he was surprised. He should have caught on that that was what the references to floors meant. His father had described the elevators of his home world, and this didn't seem to be that much different. It was magic, which made sense, but it did seem precarious; they weren't on anything, they were simply rising. Suppose the spell failed before they reached their solid floor?

"Like a glassed-in elevator, but I'd prefer a more visible one," John Knight remarked, almost echoing Kelvin's thought as he looked underfoot.

The first floor came to their level. They passed it and stopped at the second. They got off, and Helbah gave the "girls" instructions. Then she pushed Kelvin and his father back onto a lifting section. She hit the number for the third floor and up they went.

"Where's a salesman?" Helbah demanded, stepping onto the landing. Immediately a large dovgen with puffed breast lit at their feet, vanished in smoke, and became a man. Tall, blond, wearing blue trousers that had no sag, a shirt which was white and spotless, and a strange piece of cloth around his neck that Kelvin decided was a nose wiper. "Yes, madam, may I help?"

"These men." Helbah motioned at them. "Get them dressed appropriately for the big convention."

"Certainly, madam. This way, please, men."

The salesman led them to a large flat crystal set in an upright frame. The crystal reflected nothing. It was simply clear and polished and the color of water without depth.

"You first, Kelvin," Helbah said. "Just stand in front of it."

Kelvin did as she asked, not knowing what to expect.

The salesman made a pass with his hand across the surface and the crystal became a mirror. It reflected Kelvin and only Kelvin; none of the background.

The salesman eyed Kelvin's greenbriar pantaloons, brownberry shirt, and good heavy walking boots. His expression was blank; evidently he was suppressing his *country rube* assessment. He made a hand pass and the Kelvin in the mirror was newly attired almost as nattily as was the salesman. Kelvin had to touch his own throat to make certain he wasn't wearing the nose wiper.

"That's not quite him," Helbah said from the invisible area the mirror did not reflect.

"It would have been, on Earth," John Knight said. "The style is almost exactly what it was when I left."

If the salesman found the reference to Earth odd or confusing, he gave no sign. Kelvin wondered whether anything would shake the man's poise. Suppose one of the kinglets slipped a wet froog down the back of his shirt? But of course the kinglets weren't here. Too bad.

"What do you prefer, madam?" the salesman inquired politely, unaware of the fate he had escaped in Kelvin's imagination.

"Kelvin, what would you prefer?" she asked him in turn.

"A wet froog," he replied without thinking.

"What?"

Oops! He would have to watch that. Kelvin had a mind to say he was satisfied with what he'd been wearing; at least it was well broken in and comfortable. But Helbah was so serious, and his father had complained from time to time that the customary clothes they wore lacked imagination and were unflattering. Kelvin didn't believe that nonsense at all, but he did want to please Helbah. So he exercised his imagination, trying to come up with something suitable.

"Father, you said when you left your original home frame and arrived in mother's frame that you were wearing a uniform. Light green, of some shade called olive, I believe."

"The color wasn't that great, and I don't think you want a uniform."

"No, Dad, no uniform. I've had enough of war. But the color you said—I'd like to try it."

"It was more of a diarrhea brown than a green. Khaki. Unless you mean fatigues."

"No, I don't want to be fatigued," Kelvin said quickly.

"Khaki," the salesman said. "A favorite for uniforms everywhere."

"Oh for goodness' sake!" Helbah snapped. "You get fitted first, John. Show him what good dress is all about."

They changed places. John had his image dressed in khaki—just to show Kelvin, he said—and wearing a nose wiper which he explained was a tie. He frowned, touching his collar. "No tie."

The khaki tie disappeared, leaving khaki shirt and pants. "I like brown better," John said. "A little darker than the brown-berry. And the shirt—yes, match it to the pants. Maybe a leather tunic so I can look a little soldierly, and—"

Eventually it was done. John's image was still clad in what was essentially a uniform. No bags, no sags, everything fitting. It looked good enough to Kelvin too.

Helbah sighed. "Is that what you want? How about . . . ?" She moved a hand in front of the crystal and the image was clothed in blazingly bright colors that changed and shifted as light did in a magic prism.

"Nothing that showy," John said.

"How about—" Another wave of Helbah's hand and he was shown wearing blue tights and a red cape. The cape flowed out behind him as if he really could fly.

"No! No! Definitely not! What I had!"

"Oh, very well!" Helbah made a gesture and the image was back to wearing unpretentious brown with the only accessory a leather tunic. The boots were the same as when he had come in, but newer and brightly shined.

"Now that," John said, "Is right. You, Kelvin?"

"Me too." His father's stamp of approval was his best guide.

"But you will wear something different, won't you?" Helbah prompted, her tone warning him that she would not brook the same nonsense from him that she did from his father. "After all, this is the big con, and you are a hero."

That did put a different perspective on it. He didn't feel like a hero, and never had, but it might be awkward if someone thought he was and his clothing made him look like a dunce. "Whatever Dad settles on, that's the way I want to dress."

"I want this," John said. "What I'm in now."

"No further accessories? A plumed helmet, perhaps?"

"Plumes are for sissies," John said. "No, if I needed headgear, it'd be a hat. Not that stockelcap, but what fishermen and golfers wore on Earth. Something flexible with a brim and maybe a tiny feather."

"Something like—" and the salesman adjusted a series of hats on the image's head.

"That one!" John said. "The soft, crumpled hat with the smear of grease across it and the fishing lures stuck in the hatband."

The salesman groaned, echoing Helbah. It seemed that only those two had any taste. But father and son were firm in their tastelessness. They entered a booth where the outfits they had decided on had been magically conjured, and quickly changed. They were now dressed in what John called "American knockabout." Ready now to surprise the women.

"Oh, do come along!" Helbah ordered in her mother-hen way. She had evidently given up on taste.

Kelvin took one more look at himself in the magic mirror, now honestly reflecting. He looked, his father assured him, like a young college bum. Hardly flattering, but then possibly colleges on Earth taught other than the dark subjects of the necromancy schools. Maybe there it took real effort to master the status of bum.

Helbah was glaring at him, hands on naturally padded hips. He had better get a move on or he might feel her ire. She could change him into something, as she had that counterman, but he didn't think she would.

His father gave a curt nod and there was now no putting off going. He followed them to the descending squares and watched as Helbah pressed the number two for the women's floor. They floated down as effortlessly as they had floated up.

"Here we are," Helbah said, stepping onto the landing. The women were, as Kelvin had guessed they'd be, nowhere in sight. It was a known fact that no matter how long a man ever took to change his clothing, a woman took three times as long. It was magically programmed into them at birth.

"Oh, they'll be along," Helbah said cheerily. Naturally she could not criticize her own gender on this score. "They will surprise us with the new outfits they'll be wearing."

Kelvin, glancing randomly around as he mused fleetingly on what the women of his family might be wearing, encountered the bouncing breasts of another nude-body-stockinged young woman hurrying by. His eyes continued tracking of their own accord as her backside showed, the full buttocks flexing alternately. He certainly appreciated the view, but the idea of his wife, mother, and sister dressing like that—well, he hoped they did not choose this manner of surprising him!

Jon rubbed the smooth material of the diaphanous gown she had settled on as she crossed the store to the dressing room. Why did they even have dressing rooms? There were so many nudes around, the whole place was like one big dressing room! But she was glad they did, even though she had seen no men on this floor. She was a backwoods girl, with primitive ideas about privacy: she wanted certain parts of her body to be seen only by her husband, and not always even by him. She wanted to show exactly what she wanted to show, and not one bit more. Half a bit more, maybe, when she leaned forward, but that was the limit. This gown was set exactly at the limit.

What would Kelvin and their father think? But Heln had merely pursed her lips at the sight of the revealing gown on Jon's magical reflection. Her own mother hadn't said a word. *Do in witchland as do the witches,* she thought. But she could just imagine Lester's shocked face when she got home and showed him what she had worn! Poor Les, he didn't believe women should be equal to men, even after Heln's natural father had filled her in on it. Earth couldn't be such a terrible place if women were the equal of their men! Just the same, she was thankful that she had been born with properly pointed ears in a world where science was just a strange word.

That thought started another eddy-current of thought. She was glad for her ears, yes—yet sometimes she still wished she'd had Kelvin's round ears so that the prophecy would have applied to her. Certainly she had the makings of a hero, and with the help of her trusty sling she had proven it at times. If she had been a round-eared male—

She reached the dressing room and was waved inside by the most stunning salesgirl she had seen yet. That girl shouldn't be here; she was bound to make the customers feel inferior. That would not be good for business. Surely the store would know that!

Jon went in, hung her sling on a clothes hook, and draped the gown over a convenient chair. She unbuttoned her plain brownberry shirt and greenbrier pantaloons and pulled them off. No help for it, she thought ruefully: her underwear would have to go if she was to wear the gown, because it covered a good deal more of her tender flesh than the gown did. How would it feel, slinking around in that skintight garment, knowing that under it she was all the way bare-nude-naked? But then some warlocks and witches were reputed to have what John Knight called X-ray vision. Maybe in truth her shaggies concealed nothing.

She took hold of her underblouse and started to pull it up over her head. At that moment the door opened and the stunning salesgirl stepped in, red hair swirling.

Jon opened and closed her mouth. This shouldn't be happening! She was supposed to be alone in here. "I don't need any help, thank you," she said curtly.

The salesgirl's face changed like melting wax. So did her form. Her magnificent bosom sank into a shape more like a sack of produce, and her tiny waist fattened in the manner of thirty years of undisciplined eating. Her lovely flowing hair turned into limp string. In a triple heartbeat she became the squat and ugly witch Jon had met in the terminal, but somehow had not been able to tell the others about. Only now, seeing the crone again, did she remember the episode.

This surely meant trouble! Jon started to reach for her sling, then froze. Those evil yellow eyes were holding her. "Relax, dearie," the old witch said. "Transfer spells don't hurt. In fact you won't even know it happened."

Until too late, Jon thought despairingly. She knew that something was terribly wrong. Then she ceased to think of anything.

CHAPTER 3
MegaCon

Kelvin had to admit that his mother and wife both looked spectacular. Heln had chosen a modest form-clinging blue gown that appeared to be a piece of summer sky and had fluffy white clouds drifting magically over it. Charlain wore a green gown covered all over with magically growing flowers. His mother's gown reminded him of verdant woodlands, and there was even an accompanying scent of grass and flowers. But Jon's! His sister's gown was formfitting and revealing at one and the same time. Off the shoulders, off the bosom, transparent everywhere yet somehow concealing the vital areas. There was only one word for Jon's gown, and her father said it: "Wow!"

"Jon, you're not really going to wear that!" Kelvin said. "It looks as if you're ready for bed, and not alone, and not for sleep!"

"It's supposed to, stupid!" Jon retorted.

John Knight laughed. "I've seen them as sexy on Earth."

"But Dad," Kelvin persisted. "This isn't a sexy woman, this is my sister! To have her dress like this in public—"

"I'm not *what?*" Jon demanded. "I'm your *what?*"

John headed off a sibling spat by turning to their good witch. "Is it appropriate, Helbah?" he asked.

Helbah looked admiringly at Jon's firm contours. "If she was as short and dumpy as I am, it would be obscene. But Jon has the form for it. Let's proceed—the con awaits!"

Kelvin looked despairingly at his father, then tried to stifle it. He just had to get used to the way other people were. Other frames, other manners. Jon had always been an uncomfortably independent creature; it just hadn't shown in this way before. In fact, he had not realized how much she had developed, or just how eager she had been to flaunt it. Apparently she was now not trying to compete in manly things, but in womanly things. That made him distinctly uneasy, but at least it would only be for the convention. He hoped.

He was thankful for one thing, and that was that Heln had picked the blue sky and clouds, with the clouds covering the right portions of the landscape, instead of the shockingly transparent gown. At least she retained some decorum.

They left the store carrying their traveling clothes and gear in packages. The children were beautifully dressed. Charles was in a near replica of his father's and grandfather's near uniforms, but with an undersized weapon harness. Charles also wore a helmet complete with side extensions of what looked to Kelvin to be ass's ears. Merlain had on a royal purple shirt and short, pleated skirt; in addition she had gotten boots with laced-up leggings extending to her knobby knees. Still more alarming to Kelvin's notions was what he hoped was a purely ornamental dagger she wore across her skirted butt.

The two kinglets had also copied him and his dad to an extent, though they had chosen a blue color for their non-uniforms and added waist-length leather jerkins and wide leather belts. At least they did not sport swords. Kelvin had no idea what had possessed Helbah to dress them that way;

if she wanted them to look like little adventurers, she had done right.

The streets were glowing with a comfortable amber light. Kelvin though how beautiful it was as Helbah glided them to their destination. Jon, as if taunting him for what he had said about her revealing gown, contrived to rub its slickness against his face.

Helbah pulled the platform into a great emerald needle that opened before them, just as the store had done. Here, in the hotel terminal, was an assortment of odd-looking people, some of them hardly qualifying as human. There were men with horns on their heads and girls with what seemed to be angel wings of the type his father had once described. There were many who were actually birds. Here and there a large mother hen with chicks became a dowdy matron with young ladies as they approached and somehow were swallowed by a blank wall.

"Now we'll need to have our invitations," Helbah said. "All out."

She had told them of the importance of the invitations days previously, Kelvin thought distastefully. He fumbled out his own and watched his father fumble out his and Charlain's, and then Jon somehow produced hers from the midst of her nearly invisible costume. As Jon handed the invitation to Helbah he wondered where she had her sling. Surely Jon wouldn't be without it, but it certainly wasn't in evidence.

"SPAT!"

"Katbah!" Helbah exclaimed, shocked. As Jon was handing her the invitation, the witch's familiar arched his back and struck out with a clawed paw.

Jon jerked her hand back, just in time. "Filthy animal!" she snapped.

Now it was Kelvin's turn to be shocked. Jon and Katbah had always gotten along well together and had been the best of friends. In fact it had been Katbah, acting as an extension of Helbah, who had brought out Jon's latent talent and enabled her to rescue all of them from evil Zoanna and the impostor king. How could such a quarrel occur so suddenly, without cause?

Helbah was staring at Jon as if she didn't believe it. Jon melted gradually under the stare. "I'm sorry, Helbah. It's the excitement. I didn't mean—"

The witch set it aside. "Quite all right, my dear. Katbah must be a little excited himself. He's been to conventions before, but they are after all a century apart."

The cat gradually settled down on Helbah's shoulder. The children stared at him and then at Jon and then at Helbah with widened eyes. The adults were evidently forgetting the matter, but the children knew how strange it was.

"Oh, I'm certain everything will go well once we're inside," Helbah said. "Won't it, Jon?"

Jon nodded, acting, Kelvin thought, definitely strange. But than a tall, dark wizard in a purple cloak was taking their crested invitations. After he scanned each invitation, it puffed instantly into smoke. Apparently they did not need to keep them beyond this point.

They walked through the apparently solid wall. The convention materialized all about them. They weren't at the edge of it, they weren't standing just beyond the wall, they were right in the center of everything.

People were everywhere, most of them exceedingly strange. They were of all possible shapes and sizes: roly-poly men, flat-chested women, children who could have been and possibly were little dwarves. Everyone moving. Everyone talking. Men and women wearing glasses, which were something Kelvin had only heard about: sets of glass lenses perched on faces. People with armloads of books. People with paintings. People with suitcases and luggage of all imaginable sorts.

Helbah led then straight to the registration desk. A tall, dark wizard type noted their arrival in a large book.

"Welcome, Helbah!" the wizard said. "These are your honored guests?"

"You know it, Whitestone." Helbah glanced around. "Good turnout."

"The best! And tonight it's only the registration. Tomorrow when the program and the meetings get under way—"

"Yes, I know. Then it will really sway!"

Helbah turned to them. "We'll keep together, mostly. But there will be times when we may have to separate."

Kelvin was finding it hard to keep his eyes off passing displays of flesh. He had thought he would have become acclimated to the sexy women by this time, but apparently it was not to be. He tried to fasten his eyes on Heln, but his wife seemed to be more interested in seeing whether he was noticing than in noticing herself. Jon, uncharacteristically, was all big-eyed and smiling at the approach of any dressed or undressed male, and eyeing their codpieces.

"Well, maybe we can just peek into the hawkers' room," Helbah said. "I haven't looked at the literature in several centuries. There just might be a new book."

They followed her into a crowded room where thick, leather-bound volumes were displayed in piles and inspected and talked about. Helbah picked up a volume entitled *Necromancy Updated*. She glanced through the thin, almost translucent pages. "Disgusting!" she said, tossing it back on a pile. "As soon as this sort of thing is stopped, the better! The old spells are best; we don't need any recent modifications."

In a short time they had traversed the entire room, seen most of the displays, and met the sellers and buyers. Kelvin was for his part relieved when they were back out.

"I think we could each use a cup of brew," Helbah said, and Kelvin realized that the hawkers' room, however novel an experience for the rest of them, was old, tattered hat to her. She had made her required appearance. Now that chore was done, and she could relax a bit. "The coffee shop is this way. You can get coffee or tefee, and there's pepacola or whatever for the children. I'll get a witch's herbal for myself, and a saucer of dognip cream for my intuitive half."

Kelvin knew she meant her familiar. He watched Katbah on Helbah's shoulder as they entered the shop and seated themselves. Their table had a view of the doorway and the strange types coming and going. Katbah seemed not in the least disturbed by any of them. Why, then, had he taken that swipe at Jon? Kelvin had seen it happen: the cat had definitely started it. Could it be her dress? For all he knew it could be a magical dress that affected the wearer more than the viewer. Look at the way Jon was eyeing that man out there! She should not be doing that. It was mostly all right for married men to look at pretty women, but not for even unmarried women to look at men, and Jon was married. Lester wouldn't like his wife doing that. Kelvin didn't even like his sister doing that.

The white-uniformed waitress had nipples that pressed the fabric on her blouse to the verge of tearing. Kelvin had to look at what was almost in his face while she took the order. Somehow he knew that Heln had a reversed notion of just which partner in a marriage should be looking at what, but surely even she could appreciate the fact that it would be impolite for him to turn his face away. Assuming his neck muscles would work. He was more or less paralyzed at the moment, staring dazedly at the amazing view.

True to her word, Helbah ordered a witch's herbal for herself and dognip cream for Katbah, John Knight ordered coftee, as did, after a reminding nudge, Kelvin. Heln and Charlain both ordered tefee. The kids got their heads together and came up with orders for chokabola, an unmagical potion. The waitress assured them that there was little or no magic in the stuff, nodding emphatically so that her bosom quivered, almost rubbing Kelvin's nose in her points of interest.

Meanwhile Jon was hesitating, her eyes luridly tracking a nude man's passing crotch. Actually he seemed to have a flesh-colored codpiece there; still, Kelvin was annoyed at the man for seeming to show all and at his sister for staring at it. Finally she said: "I'll have what you're having, Helbah."

Helbah stroked her chin. "Are you sure, Jon? It may not be to your taste."

"As long as it doesn't kill me," Jon said.

"It won't. But it may waken your dormant witch senses. That's what it's for."

"I want all my senses open," Jon said. She spoke with the hint of a smirk, totally unlike her usual self. She was normally rebellious, not smirky.

The waitress smiled and finally heaved her tight blouseful of breasts out of Kelvin's face. He blinked, as if recovering from a trance.

"You could have closed your eyes," Heln muttered in his ear. She was mistaken; his eyelids had been locked in place. He had picked up everything else by peripheral vision. But he merely nodded amenably, knowing when to cut his losses.

They waited only a minute or so before their orders arrived by magical materialization. Each appeared before the appropriate person. His own steaming mug of coffee sent its aroma up to warm his face. He savored the aroma for a moment, then picked up the mug.

There was a pattern in the swirls of vapor: twin full breasts. He stared. The waitress had known! Then, quickly, he sipped it, and the image disintegrated. It was good coffee, though not exactly like the type he had at home. This mix had a flavor of tight blouse.

Kelvin watched the others sip their potions, and tried very hard to relax. He hoped Heln never caught on to the extent of the visions he had been seeing. There was a faint smile on his father's face that suggested that his coffee, too, had shown something interesting.

Jon was doing it again: ogling. Should he tell her? Didn't she know how obvious it was? She looked just as if she was pondering the betrayal of her vows to Lester. Of course his sister would never really do such a thing. Just the same—

"Goodness, Jon," Helbah said. "You drank your brew as if you're accustomed to it."

Jon looked as if she might give a sharp retort, then simply drained the last of her cup and went back to ogling.

Kelvin wondered more strenuously whether he should say something to her. But suppose he did? Jon never had been very respectful of him, and to tell her not to do anything was worse than useless. She would merely tell him to get his own eyes out of the waitress' cleavage. It wouldn't matter that the waitress was long since gone; the damage would be done.

How about their mother? Surely she could see what Jon was doing! But Charlain, he saw with dismay, was enraptured with everything all about them, and was paying little attention to those at the table. No help there.

Help came from the least likely source. "Looket Auntie!" Charles piped, putting down his chokabola with its ice still intact and a big brown mustache of chok on his face. "She's a-lusting!"

"Charles!" Heln said. "That isn't nice!"

"I'll bet what she's thinking isn't nice!" Merlain said, eagerly joining in on the mischief. "I'd like to know, but you said don't peek on other's thoughts."

"Quite right, Merlain, and that will do!" chided Kelvin. Certainly he didn't want his own thoughts monitored right now! He looked at his wife somewhat helplessly even while he strived to be the authority figure. Ordinary children could be a handful, but when they had the ability to look into minds, they were a mindful too!

"Oh, do quit fussing," Jon said. "I'm just quietly enjoying myself, the way you are."

Kildee dug Kildom in the ribs. Both smirked. How much had they observed?

Kelvin was stuck in it now. His sister was striking back exactly as he had feared she would, but he couldn't simply let it drop. "Now see what you're causing!" he said. "Sister Wart, I don't want to criticize, but—"

"What d'ya mean, 'Sister Wart'!" Jon bridled. She really seemed angry with him, yet he had called her that since before she was the age of the twins. She had liked to go out exploring with him, dressing like a boy, and he had called her Brother Wart. When she grew up and manifested as a girl, he had changed it to Sister Wart. "And if you don't want to criticize, don't!"

Kelvin swallowed. There was a fire in Jon's eyes that he had never seen before, and a frost in her voice that he had never heard before. What was going on with her?

Could Helbah and his mother be oblivious to this strangeness? He studied them now as carefully as he could. If anything, they were both a little too casual. Witches could not read others' thoughts, but witches were by nature—it was necessary to face it now—prone to deceit. Helbah had been as tricky in her ways as evil Melbah and Zoanna had been in theirs. It was a witch's nature to suspect things and intuit without giving away what she felt. Thus Charlain had always been one step ahead of her children, or several steps, even when they really were children and making plans to run away.

"People behave differently at cons," Helbah said. "We all do at first. Particularly those who aren't professional."

"Who's not professional!" Jon snapped, the fire rising again in her eyes. Then, seeing the looks exchanged by Helbah and Charlain, she backed off. The fire died and a flush suffused her cheeks. Clearly there was no reason why Jon should resent what Helbah had said.

"I mean," Jon countered lamely, "it's just that I'm not used to this. All these naked men and no one saying I shouldn't look."

"*I* say you shouldn't look," Kelvin said, stepping back into it. He knew that he had made another clumsy mistake the moment she turned her eyes on him. "I mean, you wouldn't stare like that at home."

"We're not at home," Jon reminded him. "That's the point."

Irrefutable logic! That of course was what Helbah had suggested. So somehow, as usual, he had succeeded in turning Jon's misbehavior into his own embarrassment.

"Helbah! What an honor to meet you!" the gray-haired wizard with spade beard and green cloak swirled over to meet them. The elderly witch locked eyes with the elderly wizard and clasped hands. Then the wizard was drawing up a chair from a neighboring table.

Helbah introduced their entire party, brat kings and all. She started with Charlain, who had been her apprentice during the war with Zoanna and the false king. She concluded by introducing the wizard to the rest of them. "This is Zudini, a master illusionist and escape artist. In his youth he actually studied for a while with Mouvar."

"Mouvar the alien! Mouvar the creator of the transporter!" Kelvin exclaimed. He was so excited that he couldn't contain himself. Whatever had been bothering him a moment ago had been swept from his mind. He hadn't known that any person alive had known Mouvar!

"The same," the wizard said. He was tall and maturely handsome, yet probably a contemporary of Helbah's. Witches and wizards lived, like dragons and other magical creatures, for a long, long time.

Kelvin tried to control his excitement enough to be coherent. "You were around when he built—"

"Oh, no!" the wizard protested. "Don't put that on me! I'm old but not that old! Mouvar dates back from before there were people in *any* of the frames."

What? "But—"

"He came here, probably with others like himself. I'm not saying he created people or worlds, but certainly he built the transporters."

"You—you learned . . . ?"

"Only what he wanted me to. He sees ahead. He knows, he plans."

"Precognitive," John Knight said. "I'd guessed that because of the prophecy."

"Precognitive, yes," Zudini agreed, evidently comfortable with the strange term. "But don't expect me or anyone here to have Mouvar's degree of expertness. There was something about his originating on another world, possibly a world revolving around another star. I don't know how he foresees or what he plans. But Kelvin, yours is an exceptional legacy."

"You mean the prophecy? Yes, I guess so." Kelvin did not feel it necessary to add that like his father, he had once thought it was all nonsense. He still had formidable doubts, as much about himself as about the prophecy. In time he might even come to fully accept it, if things continued to fall into place to fulfill it. Maybe.

Zudini reached across the table and took his right hand. There was a slight tingle similar to what Kelvin often felt while wearing the magical gauntlets. The old wizard held his hand between his own two and seemed to concentrate.

"No, no, I can't do it," Zudini said, gazing into his eyes. "I can't read what is to be, except within narrowly prescribed limits. But there has never been another to whom the prophecy has or could have applied."

"It originated after Mouvar fought Zatanas and was defeated by him."

Zudini shook his head. "I don't believe Mouvar was ever defeated. But it was probably within his planning that he seemed to be defeated. To his kind a few centuries may not seem as long as to the rest of us. I believe he left certain enemies as challenges to prove out his prophecy."

"Challenges!"

"Consider it this way, Kelvin. If the prophecy meant notoriety and power for an otherwise undistinguished person, who would try to claim to be the one?"

"Why, anyone! Everyone!"

"Precisely. So the position could not simply be there for anyone to claim. There had to be some challenge to it. Something to make it possible for only the genuine person to assume the mantle. So it was limited to a roundear, and to one who fulfilled certain tasks. Such as destroying the evil Zatanas."

Kelvin was amazed. It made so much sense! An ordinary person who challenged Zatanas would have been destroyed. Only someone extremely brave or skilled or just plain lucky could have any chance. Also, maybe, stupid, because it was a bad business to go up against big magic.

Zudini had known Mouvar, and lived far longer than most mortal human beings, Kelvin thought. Undoubtedly the wizard was correct. But what a revelation! It was still hard for his backwoods mind to grasp.

The wizard unclasped Kelvin's hand. He did not seem disappointed. Yet how could he fail to be, since surely each of them, with the possible exceptions of Helbah and Katbah, looked and felt so ordinary? None of them were heroes; all were simple country folk. Kelvin himself was mostly bumpkin, a hero in name only.

"Helbah, I need to see you about some of the programming," the wizard said. "That's why I searched you out before you got properly into the convention."

"Of course, Zudini. I believe we're all finished."

One of the royal twins sucked loudly through a straw. His brother, never to be outdone, gave a rude and probably totally unnecessary belch.

Helbah sighed and almost absently reached down to cuff one twin on the right ear and the other on the left. Both boys let out appropriate "Oh's" of faked innocence. Charles and Merlain both smiled. It was a ritual: crime, punishment, and cover-up.

"Perhaps," Zudini observed thoughtfully, "the children would like to visit the children's suite?"

Charles, Merlain, Kildum, and Kildee looked at one another. They knew, as did all children their age, when they were being shunted aside. Yet it had been suggested that the suite could be fun, and whatever children were there would have to be out of the ordinary. They had enjoyed their refreshments, but were bored with this dull dialogue. They needed to get out from under the watchful gazes of their parents and/or guardians.

"Let's go!" Charles said, sliding out of his chair. He grasped the edge of the table and tipped the chair until his feet touched the floor. Merlain and the two royal pains were quick to follow.

CHAPTER 4

Children's Suite

The enormous room, a combination of playroom and gymnasium, was a humming hive of potential pests. Kids of every age and description and size were there, up to an apparent age of twelve. There were instructors and nursemaids and teachers, all of whom had to be witches or the representatives of witches, conducting numerous and varied activities. There were footraces and other athletic contests conducted with the help of magic. There were games designed to teach and exercise magical skills as well as physical and mental abilities. There were kids talking among themselves. Kids fighting. Kids screaming. Kids everywhere. In short, it was routine.

Kelvin breathed a great sigh. He had expected something like a large cage. This, though noisy, was better than anything he had visualized.

The children looked around, wild-eyed. In an instant they were off, getting closer looks at unfamiliar objects, intruding in conversations, being typically rude and bothersome and satisfied. The adults just stood and watched, each undoubtedly thankful that these little demons would be here and not enlivening the convention proper.

A light-colored bird flew down from above and lit by Helbah's feet. There was a puff of white smoke and a most attractive blonde wearing horn-rim glasses replaced the bird. The blonde smiled at Kelvin.

Kelvin gulped. She wasn't nude, but to his mind glasses and a body stocking hardly counted as clothed. It seemed impossible to get used to this style of (un)dress, assuming he wanted to. Naturally he had to be standing next to Helbah, who would not miss a thing.

Zudini made quick introductions. "Zally, my daughter, majoring in pedimagic at Magicon U."

Kelvin stammered something appropriate. Her nearness and bareness unsettled him in somewhat the manner the waitress had, squared. He had to focus his mind on Heln and leave it there.

"I wonder, Witch Zally—" Jon began.

"It's *neophyte* witch Zally," the beautiful creature corrected her. "I can't be just Witch Zally for at least another hundred years."

Jon frowned, though only briefly. "I was wondering about adult visitors—"

"Any of you may come and go as you wish: Our only restriction is for the safety of the children and the peace of adult conventioneers. No child is allowed to leave here unaccompanied."

"That means any of you," Zudini said to Merlain, who had come back to listen, trailed by the kinglets. "There are no bad people here, and we intend to see that none enter."

"Do practitioners of malignant magic ever show up?" Charlain asked.

"Infiltrate, you mean?" Zudini said with a grim smile. "They've tried it a few times in the past. That's why we take all possible precautions, especially with the children. We've never lost a child or had one harmed. Shall we get to that meeting, Helbah?"

Helbah made a pass. One of the kinglets jumped as if an

ear stung, and put his hand back down without smacking Zally's pretty bare bottom.

"Yes, better get it over," Helbah said, seeming not even to notice her own background activity in the disciplinary arena. "Charlain, Heln, John, Kelvin—why don't you go to the rooms and wait? I know you'll be comfortable. Or you can just browse around the con. We'll all meet here when it's time to go for lunch."

Kelvin watched as Helbah and the handsome old wizard walked away toward what he'd heard called the "liftivators." He felt, irrationally, that she was abandoning them.

The children disappeared into the melee of the chamber. Those remaining, of the intermediate generations, exchanged glances. "I know we can get to our suite," John said. "The elevators here are just like those in the store. They call them liftivators, but I call them elevators. Anyone want to do anything else?"

"I think I'd rather stay here," Jon said, surprising Kelvin as well as their father. "I'm interested in what the children are doing."

Kelvin wondered whether the failure of Jon and Lester to have children of their own was affecting her. He knew Jon wanted a child, but she had refused to invoke any magical remedies. For that, at least, he could not fault her. After what had happened to Heln's pregnancy, because of magic— she had given birth to twins and a dragon—Jon had reason to be well wary of it. But she did want a child. Maybe she thought it was Lester's fault, so she was looking at other men's anatomy, wondering whether there was more fertility there. That just might explain her weird attitude here.

"The children are mainly making noise," Heln said, clapping her hands to her ears.

"They'll quiet down," Zally said. Her form was as pretty from the rear as it had been from the front, as she walked out into the battlefield to try to arrange a truce. These witches must be using magic to make their bodies so good! Kelvin realized he was staring again when he felt Heln's warning touch on his arm.

"You can do whatever you want, but I want to stay and watch the children and their instructors," Jon said.

"Anyone else?" John Knight asked.

Kelvin wondered whether his sister could be planning something involving one of the handsome wizards. No, that thought was simply unworthy of him. But try to rationalize it as he might, she *was* acting strange.

No one mentioned Jon's decision as they left the suite, but seeing all the nudity and near nudity forced Kelvin to wonder. Just how different was Jon in her revealing dress from Jon in greenbriar shirt and brownberry pantaloons? She was an adult, and she was married, but just the same, the way she was acting bothered him. In addition to showing an uncharacteristic interest in men other than her husband, there was something else: Jon, impudent, saucy Jon, his irrepressible little sister, had taken lately to being entirely too polite.

Merlain was rapidly tiring of the games. Children's games were, after all, of only limited interest to real children; they were mostly the adults' idea of what children should enjoy. She had beaten Kildom and Kildee and even Charles without difficulty. The teacher had beamed at her and called her a "little natural," but she didn't care. It was all so easy to know what cards were coming up, and in fact she didn't hardly have to cheat. She wondered whether Charles had known she mind-peeked. Had he mind-peeked himself? The teacher didn't know; in fact she had made sure of this. Kildom and Kildee were just too dumb to know.

"That concludes our precog series," neophyte witch Zally said. Her smile was nice, but Merlain had peeked a little too deeply and knew that at times she thought naughty. That young-man warlock who went around without clothes and some pretty good male contours really flamed an instinct Merlain would not encounter in herself for years. She was in no hurry to grow up, seeing what mush it made of the mind of an adult, though some of the bodily contortions it seemed to want to lead to were interesting. Why should anyone want to do *that* with *that?* But since that was the way it was, why didn't Zally just *tell* the big-muscled hunk? Maybe if she whispered to him herself . . . ?

"Oh, Zally," the young warlock said, coming close to their teacher with all his male equipment. "I was wondering if we could have lunch together."

Zally's pulse leaped so high it almost made Merlain wince. But she affected indifference. "Oh, of course, Fredrich," she said. She wanted more, much more, but Fredrich wasn't supposed to know. What a curious business it was, being adult!

"And a talk in the bar," Merlain suggested. "And then maybe during your off time, a visit to her room, and—"

"Merlain!" Zally's cheeks flamed. Then, to Fredrich: "I'm sorry, but she's a natural."

"You're not sorry at all!" Charles piped, proving that he too had peeked. That was just as well; Merlain had begun to worry about him.

"Chimaera," Fredrich whispered. "They have to be the ones."

"You think?" she asked, seeming awed.

"I know. Helbah brought them, didn't she?"

"Oh. Oh, dear!"

"So they can read minds. We're both practitioners of the art, and adult."

"Yes, yes, that is true."

"You can go at it now and we won't tell anyone," Merlain suggested. "Will we?" She looked around at her brother and the nominal kings. Kildom and Kildee were clearly puzzled, but Charles had his head bobbing, and an expression to go with the way Zally felt: guilty desire.

"I know you both want to," Merlain persisted.

Fredrich squatted down, not without a certain difficulty, until his face was at Merlain's level. "Young lady, didn't they teach you *anything?*"

"I was told not to peek. I don't, usually. But—"

"But you did."

"Uh-huh. Because it's interesting." She knew he wanted her to feel uncomfortable. Adults were so predictable.

"Merlain, what happens or doesn't happen between grown-ups is none of your concern."

"That's what Mama says."

"You won't do it again? Not ever again, at least during your stay here?"

"N-no." She made some tears come to dress it up a little. Why did adults always want her to lie?

He stood up, more readily than he had squatted. He looked the blonde straight in her blue eyes. "Well?"

"They have things to do and it's not as if they're unsupervised," she said, her flush not quite fading out. "Here comes that girl who was here."

"Auntie Jon!" Charles exclaimed.

Jon stood alone where she had been earlier. She had some packages: possibly presents.

Merlain didn't try to stop herself; she just had to peek. Auntie Jon was thinking something about two pearl drops put into a chokabola shared by Zally and Fredrich. Then Aunt Jon's thoughts got dark and ugly and then blank.

Merlain gasped aloud. Never before had she experienced this mental shutout. Auntie Jon was smiling a smile that was not a smile at all under the surface, and that suggested she was going to punish her for peeking. But Auntie said nothing of the kind; her thoughts, Merlain realized, were now hidden.

"Oh come, Zally!" Such urgency in the hunk's voice. At first Zally had been the interested one, but once Fredrich caught on to her interest, his interest had leaped way up.

"Oh yes, Fredrich!"

The two of them walked away, as if guided by some unheard instruction, arms circling each other's waists.

Their passion tempted Merlain not at all, now, though a moment before it had been weaker and she had been far more interested. That was odd! Even if she had wanted to break her promise, there was now Auntie. There was fire in the eyes that were usually mischievous. It held Merlain, preventing her from diverting or dividing her attention.

"This is for you," Auntie Jon said, placing a package in her hands. The wrapping felt smooth, almost like skin. "And for you," she said, placing a similar package into the hands of a red-haired king.

"Can we open them now?" Charles asked eagerly. It was a natural law: anything in a surprise package was exciting.

"That would be unwise. You must not let adults or even children see you try these on."

Oh, then it was clothes. That was the glaring exception to the law: clothing was almost never interesting, especially if an adult picked it out. Merlain tried to stifle her disappointment. She was quite satisfied with the outfits that Helbah had bought, if only because Merlain had really chosen hers herself.

"You are going to have fun with these," Auntie Jon promised. She made a sweeping gesture with her hand that completely circled them. "There! Now no one will hear or see and you may try."

Merlain hadn't realized that Auntie Jon could do that kind of magic. But if she could now shield her thoughts, it made sense that she could do other witchy things. She must have been practicing in secret. It didn't matter; it just might mean that the packages really were interesting.

Hurriedly they ripped open their packages. The strings, so much like dried guts, came untied without Merlain doing any picking. Magic indeed! The skin—yes, it definitely felt more like skin than paper, and looked it too!—peeled back from her fingers. She held in her two outstretched arms—nothing.

The twin who was either Kildom or Kildee—she couldn't tell without peeking into his mind, because she had forgotten which mirror image was which—was standing exactly as she was, as if Auntie Jon had commanded it. He was similarly baffled, and about to make a loud and probably indecent protest.

"There are two cloaks in each package," Auntie Jon said. "One for each of you. Put them on."

Merlain felt gingerly in the nothingness. She found substance after all. Almost without willing herself to, she took hold of what her fingers touched and lifted it. It was very, very light, with no texture feel at all. Only the slight resistance of it against her fingers satisfied her that it was even there.

"Be careful not to drop them," Auntie Jon warned. "They can be difficult to find."

Ignoring Auntie and the rest, Merlain felt out the lines of a cloak. When she put her hands and arms under it, they vanished. Oho! This was a magic cloak! She whipped it up and drew it around her shoulders. She felt the same, but now she couldn't see herself. Could anyone else?

"You are now invisible, Merlain," Auntie said. "You can go anywhere and not be seen. Even witches and warlocks won't see you. But you will have to be quiet, lest they hear you."

"Oh, Auntie! Auntie!" Merlain was overwhelmed. It was the best present she'd ever had!

"You can go right into people's rooms. You can take their things without their knowing."

The kinglets and Charles were now donning their cloaks. Charles left his head uncovered so that it appeared to float in the air. Then he drew the cloak all the way up so that his face seemed to disappear into some invisible hole, from the bottom to the top. Kildom and Kildee put theirs on from the top of the head down; their bodies seemed first decapitated, then cut off at the chests, waists, and legs, until only their four feet were standing, and then nothing. No one now seemed to be present except Auntie.

"Take things?" Merlain whispered. This disturbed her. She had always been taught that stealing was wrong.

"Of course," Auntie Jon replied. "Taking is fun. At this convention there are many, many magical things that you can enjoy without anyone catching you. Books that tell secrets. Elixirs that make people do things and behave in many different ways. Love potions can really be fun, and hate potions even more fun—especially when you slip one to one member of a couple and the other to the other. Toys that you'd never, never get to play with without your cloaks. You can play tricks on people and never get caught. Not as long as you are careful and quiet. You can see things children are forbidden to see.''

"Like what Zally and Fredrich are doing?" Merlain asked, her interest in that subject returning. It wasn't that the subject fascinated her; it was the idea of spying on something the participants didn't want spied on.

"Exactly like that," Auntie Jon agreed, smiling.

"Tricks?" a kinglet asked. "You mean like kicking butts? Pinching? Fun things like that?"

"Oh yes, yes. I see you do have a quick imagination. Only you must not allow people to know you're there. If they realize, they will use magic on you and then you will be caught and punished."

"Helbah would box our ears," said one royal.

"Or spank our butts," the other pain continued.

"Maybe take our cloaks away," the first added.

"Possibly worse," Auntie said. "Remember, this is not your home. If you are caught in mischief here, there is no telling what your punishment may be. Any people you hurt here will enjoy hurting you more than you enjoyed hurting them."

"But," Charles whispered, confused, "hurting people is *wrong*."

"Pooh," said Auntie, and made a naughty gesture. Merlain had not realized that adults were capable of such gestures. Then Auntie made motions of throwing a cloak over her own head and pulling it snug. Her body vanished as the rest of them had. Merlain could see clearly, but there was nothing but empty floor where she knew they all stood.

"What should we do first?" asked a kinglet.

"Go back where we had lunch and get chokabolas," the other kinglet replied.

"Yes," said Charles. "Let's."

Merlain felt a little disappointed. She wanted first to see what Zally and the hunk were doing. She thought she knew, having mind-peeked her mother and father. But seeing it, actually being there in the room to see with her real eyes instead of her mind's eye—what fun!

"Maybe we'd better join hands," Charles suggested practically. "We don't want to get separated or lost. We can't talk where anyone might hear us."

"That's an excellent suggestion, Charles," Auntie Jon said. "I can see you have an aptitude for this. You children run along. Have fun, be naughty. Auntie Jon is going to be doing some naughty things herself."

"Like with that hunk?" Merlain asked, interested.

"Perhaps. We shall see. 'Bye." There was a *poof* as that same dirty gray, really ugly bird appeared on the floor. It hopped into the air, its wings beating, and took off. It passed over their heads, then over the heads of others in the room, dropping a large squishy dropping in some unlucky wizard's upturned eye. Then through the doorway, out of the suite, and it was gone.

Merlain was truly amazed. Auntie Jon had really learned a lot of magic in a short time!

"Let's go!" Charles said. She felt a tug on her hand, and started walking. It was strange, not being able to see her own feet; it made her a bit dizzy. But it was worth it. First they'd drink all the chokabola they could hold, and then—

It was later in the day after they had seen many things that children weren't supposed to that they decided to revisit the hawkers' room. "We haven't stolen anything yet," one of the kings explained. "The stuff we ate and drank wasn't important. We need to steal something valuable that will be missed."

"Yes, watching that old woman in the bathroom wasn't much fun," the other king said. "And Fredrich and Zally were just lying there, hardly moving at all. What's the fun in that? We have to *do* something."

Merlain felt less than enthusiastic. She had managed to

dissuade the kings from pinching women's bottoms, because that would have led to an instant clamor that could have resulted in them all getting caught. But watching things without interfering wasn't much fun either. Also, she had guzzled one big chokabola too many and gobbled one too-rich desert more than her tummy wanted to handle. Now she wanted more than anything to go back to the lavatory, lest she do something truly spectacular right where she stood. Of course she knew the boys would wait for her as they had before. At least she hoped they'd waited; there might have been a suspicious sound that wasn't hers. Maybe she could wait a little longer.

"Now everyone's quiet," the kinglet's voice persisted. "Lot of people in here. Don't stumble against anyone. Don't get caught."

"I've an idea," said the farthest kinglet. "Let's let go of each other's hands. We'll each take something, hide it under our cloaks, and then get together in that room we were in."

"Great idea, Kildom!" said the closet kinglet. "I know because I thought of it first. Once we're together in the room, we'll see what each of us got."

"I think I'd rather take something from one of the other rooms," Merlain said, thinking of the lavatory.

"Me too," Charles said.

"But," Merlain said, thinking of her need for privacy, "we'll each go to a different room. Kildom, Kildee, you can start your stealing here, if you like. Or if you want, you can go steal somewhere else."

"I'm going back to the kitchen," Charles whispered. "I'm hungry!"

Hungry! The very notion made her yearn for the lavatory!

She felt her brother's hand loosen and she knew that now they each were entirely on their own. It was scary, but scary could be fun. She decided to go straight to the lavatory, knowing that none of the others could see to follow. Once she'd done what had to be done, she could get down to some serious thieving. Strange, Auntie Jon suggesting that. But then Daddy had always

said Auntie was strange *and* adventuresome. She was beginning
to think she knew what he meant.

She followed a pretty, dark-haired witch into the lavatory,
and did what was proper. It was a great relief. No one saw
her, she felt. But when the witch closed off the running
water before Merlain had her hands washed, she was annoyed; that stickiness, after all, had bothered her ever since
she spilled the chokabola. So as the witch walked away
Merlain stuck out a foot and tripped her. The witch fell,
inelegantly, and Merlain choked on a laugh.

"Sooo, Krissie, you *are* jealous!" the witch said to the
empty air. "Two can play at that! Just you wait until I get
my spellbook! You'll be sorry you did that!"

Merlain shuddered delightfully at the young witch's anger. Some witch who might have done what Merlain had
done would get her punishment. What fun! What a way to
get even with someone!

For the moment the lavatory was empty. She went to the
sink and turned on the water herself and washed her hands.
It was all right, as long as no one could see. Now at least
she was clean; the smell wouldn't give her away.

She waited patiently by the door until another witch entered, then went out, catching the swing of the door at just
the right place. Down the hotel corridor was the one who
had left. The dark-haired witch was quite recognizable because of her shoulder-length glassy hair and alabaster bottom. Why did Mama and Daddy concern themselves that
some people were undressed? It was warm and comfortable
here, and inside there could be no rain. In fact, rain would
hurt those who were clothed more than those who weren't.
Maybe, just maybe, she'd try going bare herself—someday.

The witch's back was very straight and there was no question
that she was angry. Merlain decided to follow her. She did. Up
one corridor, down another, and to a room with a number on
it. The witch made a short, angry clearing pass with her hand
before going inside. Merlain followed right after her.

The witch went straight for the wooden dresser on which
was cluttered a lot of stuff. There were unguents, powders,

creams, jells, and potions. The witch hesitated over these,
picked up a large stoppered bottle, then set it back down. She
opened a drawer, took out a large, leather-bound book, and
flipped through its pages. Muttering to herself, she left the
hotel room, book in hand. Krissie, whoever she was, was
in for trouble.

Merlain sighed. Here she was alone with an array of stuff
used by witches. She should take something; it was only
right that she fulfill Auntie Jon's faith in her. But what? She
picked up the bottle the dark-haired witch had hesitated
over. It had a label: "Alice Water."

Alice Water? Alice Water? Where had she heard of that?
Surely it did not mean water *from* Alice; no one would want
to save that! It was probably something magical, but what?
There had been a girl named Alice in a book. What was it
called? *Alice in the Appleberry Patch? Alice and the Squir-
bets?* Close. Close. But not quite.

Then she remembered it. It hadn't been Alice anything,
though it had been about Alice. *Down the Squirbet Hole!* It
had been about an ordinary girl with pointed ears who
couldn't mind-peek. There had been a bottle in it labeled
"Drink Me." Take a drink from the bottle and it made you
big or it made you tiny. Nice story, and now here was something that reminded her of it. Just possibly a drink from the
bottle would make her big or small. But which? Maybe she
could get the royal pains to drink from it, and then if they
got small, she and Charles could get even with them for
those laxaberries!

The door started opening again. Oh-oh, the witch was
back! Hurriedly, hardly thinking what she did, Merlain
opened her cloak and pulled the bottle out of sight. She'd
just barely gotten the bottle under her cloak and the cloak
closed when the witch was at the dresser.

"That'll fix her!" the woman muttered. "See how she likes
having all her hair fall out! Steal my warlock, will she!"

Steal her warlock? All Merlain had done was trip her!
There must be an ongoing feud, and the tripping was taken
as a reminder of it. Merlain had been lucky—maybe.

The witch put the book back in the drawer and slammed the drawer back. She looked at the contents of the dresser and saw that the Alice Water bottle was gone. Oh-oh!

"So you got in here, did you, Krissie? You're going to regret that! Last time I borrow anything from you! I hope you drink the entire bottle! I hope it changes you so much you'll never get back to your normal size! Assuming anything about you is normal, ha-ha!"

So it *would* shrink a person, or make her big! She'd been right, and she hadn't mind-peeked. But now maybe she should. Just in case she was misunderstanding about the bottle. Suppose the size change was in the head instead of the whole body? Or the belly? That would be horrible!

She tried to read the dark-haired witch's mind, but it was as closed as Auntie Jon's had been. She should have expected that. She had not encountered many witches before, and wasn't used to their abilities, but she was learning quickly!

The witch started circling the room, feeling with her hands as though for someone invisible. Merlain moved back and aside, keeping the witch's hands from touching her, holding her breath when she had to keep quiet. How glad she was that she had washed off the chok smell; that would have given her away for sure! Once, the witch reached right over her, almost touching her head.

It really wasn't hard remaining clear, but Merlain was afraid her beating heart would give her away with its thumping. All she had to do was keep her nerve, but she wasn't sure of her supply of nerve right now.

Abruptly the witch gave up in disgust and went out. Merlain followed in her steps. The witch turned left; Merlain turned right. In a moment she was clear. Phew! It had been easy, yet also nervously difficult, and she would be much more careful next time she blithely followed anybody into a private room.

She paused for her heart to settle back to its normal place in her body. Then she resumed motion down the hall. It was time to go to the vacant room and meet the others. Now that she had done the right thing and stolen something.

She wondered what Charles and the royal pains would

have gotten that could offer quite so much fun—maybe—as a bottle of size-changing potion.

Charles felt as if he were being led. He couldn't have explained it, but his invisible feet had carried him right to this door. Something just made him want to come this way.

No one was in the hallway with him, so he opened the door and went on in. For a moment he was disappointed; it was just a room, not much different than their own. There wasn't a lot of baggage scattered about, let alone magical paraphernalia. It was more like a storage chamber for the convention, with boxes of props and things. He was wasting his time here. What stupid whim had led him to this washout?

Then his eyes fell on the bed, and on the small weapon lying across it. A toy? No, surely not!

Charles gasped. It was a short dragon-leather scabbard with jewels on it, and protruding from its widest end was the jeweled pommel of a sword. On the pommel, worked into the precious metal, was a design of a shining sun wearing a smiling face. It was beautiful to look at, and right away he wanted it.

A sob sounded. Was his sister in this room? If so, what would she be crying about? No, she couldn't be here. No matter, he had to have this sword.

He picked it up in both hands, as gently as if it were alive. He grasped the handle and drew out the blade. The blade shone as if held in bright sunlight. It was beautiful, this sword, and just his size. It was probably part of someone's costume for a play, a child's role; everything had to look authentic. A hero prince!

As he bent over the blade, studying it, testing its sharp edge with a careful touch of his thumb, the sob came again. It seemed close, and sounded heartbroken.

He glanced at the dresser mirror. There, looking cutely forlorn, was a little girl in a nightdress. It seemed as if she were getting ready for bed. She had long, light hair that glowed as he looked at it. Blue eyes, soft, with tears. She was astonishingly pretty.

For a moment the ghost, or whatever she was, looked at him from the glass. Then, in the manner a spent candle guttered, dimmed, and went out, she faded. The mirror was just a glass. It reflected the room with the sword and the scabbard apparently floating in midair.

Charles mentally shook himself. That girl had seemed to see him—but she wasn't really there. A magical something was here, but maybe only an illusion. Something set up to make an intruder think someone was watching. But it seemed to be no threat. Had it been an unfriendly dragon in the mirror, it might have been more effective. The girl wasn't scary at all. Still, it was a warning of sorts; he had best take the weapon and go.

He put the sheathed sword under his invisibility cloak and made certain he could not see it in the mirror, and that his hands and feet did not show. Weren't Merlain and the pains going to be surprised when he showed them what he had found!

Happy that he had done the right wrong thing, Charles left the hotel room, closing the door gently in his unseen wake.

In the room the redhead who said he was Kildee—he was lying, Merlain thought, as both pains often did—had a book. Its title was *Spells* and it had a cover that felt like the wrappings on their cloaks: peeled human skin. On the first page was a warning: "Adepts Only."

"With this," the kinglet said, "we can do magic. That's what it's for. Helbah had a book of spells but it doesn't have these pictures."

Merlain and Charles looked at the pictures. They were gross. Did witches really do things like that? She had never suspected! Butchering babies. Pulling out people's guts. Chewing on people's parts. Some pictures were confusing, but she suspected that if she were old enough to understand exactly what they meant, she would be utterly appalled. One section labeled "Ectoplasm" showed funny taffylike, cloudlike stuff coming out of several different orifices of witches. Didn't that *hurt*?

"I've got another," the twin pretending to be Kildom said.

He took it out from the cloak now lying invisibly on a chair with no apparent bottom. It was a book, but it didn't have the same cover as his brother's. This one was titled *Opal*.

"Opal's a girl's name," Merlain said. She was proud that she knew that, and could read, a little. What had the royal brat imagined he was taking? Another volume of magic?

"Wrong!" the pain said stoutly. "It's a gem. A very magical stone with very special powers. With it anyone—you don't have to be a witch or a warlock—can go anywhere in an instant, even into another frame! We could go home if we wanted to, kick some butts, and then disappear back to here."

"Just by wanting to?" Charles was skeptical. "Without a transporter?"

"Yeah, and look here—this is who has it."

Charles squinted at the picture. The pictures were prettier than those in the other book, Merlain decided, but not by much. This one showed a creature resembling both man and fish: it showed a fish's scales, fins, and eyes, and a man's arms, legs, nose, and forehead. It was a giant, judging from the trees that came to its scaly elbows. Maybe they were small trees; still it was scary. There were gills on its throat and broad greenish nostrils. It was crying out something and brandishing a club that dangled tree roots from the giant's greenish hand.

"Ugh," Charles said. "What do you call that thing? It sure isn't human!"

"It's an orc," the kinglet said smugly. "You babies are really dumb, aren't you! Nobody teaches you anything!"

Merlain grabbed Charles' arm before he could do more than make his customary fist. There might come a time for him to fight the little king, but that was hardly now.

"What did *you* get, Charles?" she asked him, hoping to distract him, and also hoping it would be something more impressive than the efforts of the kinglets. She had figured them for something better than mere books. Maybe they had done it just to spite her expectations.

She was too successful on both counts. "This!" Charles said, and whipped up his folded cloak to reveal a shining sword. He brandished it before the twin faces, still in its scabbard.

Charles, don't kill him! she thought desperately.

Why not? He insulted us!

He's a king. They're both kings. Pains and brats, but also kings. Helbah wouldn't give us presents if we hurt the kinglets.

Yeh. You're right. I wasn't going to anyway.

She had picked that up as she mind-talked to him, but it hadn't seemed expedient to remark on it. Charles, like all males, liked to make a bold, dramatic play, even if it was a bluff, and the kings certainly deserved to be scared.

Carefully, almost reverently, Charles drew a polished blade from the heavily jeweled sheath. The blade gleamed, and though it could have been used by a grown man, it was as if it had been made for a person of Charles' size. It was a small weapon, but definitely a real one.

"That's a *sword!*" the kinglet of the insults said, admiring the thin edge. "Is it magic?"

"I don't know. I just took it from the room I was in. There seemed to be magic there, like someone watching, but it didn't stop me."

The kinglet reached out and grabbed his brother by a lock of red hair. He pulled out one of the hairs as the other yowled a protest. Those two didn't treat each other any better than they treated others!

"Have to test the edge," the hair puller said. He held the hair between thumb and forefinger at either end. Slowly, respectfully, he brought the middle of the hair against the edge.

With no apparent pressure the hair parted. It hardly seemed to touch the blade; it fell in two parts.

"Sharp!" the kinglet exclaimed appreciatively. "What are you going to do with it?"

Don't say it, Charles! Merlain warned her brother. *Don't tell him you're going to ram it up his—*

I wasn't going to. You think I'm as dumb as they? Actually, she read on the next level down, he had been mollified by the kinglet's appreciation of the weapon. "I'm going to

wear it when I can. Take it home if I can. Slay a bandit
with it, maybe."

"*You* slay a bandit?" The kinglet was skeptical.

"Or assist Dragon Horace with his lunch."

"Now that I want to see! Your dragon Horace."

"You will when we're back. I'll show you." *Maybe feed
you to him, too!*

You wouldn't! Merlain thought, alarmed.

*Naw. You know what a delicate gizzard Dragon Horace
has. Raw meat is one thing, but rotten meat is another.*

Actually their brother dragon could get quite intrigued by
rotten meat too, as the episode of the stinky smell had
shown. Still, she feared what might happen if Charles got
mad while holding the sword. *Don't even think that way!
We have to get along with the kinglets. It's been a long time
since they fed us those laxaberries. Besides, I told Helbah
every naughty thing they did until Mama and Daddy made
me stop. We got our revenge.*

I still don't like them.

*So what? They know better than to play king with us.
After Helbah made them eat all those naughty words they'd
written, they were sicker'n us.*

Charles smiled. *I made them feel even sicker when they
vomited.*

*You did! That was brilliant, Charles! Why I never even
thought of that!* A little flattery never hurt.

*Copper-haired girls can't think as well as copperhead
boys,* he thought smugly.

This was getting out of hand. She used her flattery judiciously, but he was believing it. *You start calling me Sister
Wart the way Daddy does Auntie Jon and you'll get the point!*

Truce. Charles was not wholly stupid about interpersonal
relations. *I won't think that again. Not to you, anyway.*

Truce, she agreed. They had to get along as a brother and
sister should. They might not agree on everything, but they
had to be united against the pains.

"Why are you two looking at each other like that?" the
kinglet demanded suspiciously.

Charles shrugged. Merlain smiled in the manner she knew adults loved. The brat might not love her smile, but now he'd worry about what they might have been thinking to each other inside their heads. That would make him cautious. Any caution they could encourage in the kings was a good thing.

"That orc," Charles said, buckling on the sword. "What's it doing with the opal?"

"The orc is king of Ophal, the water country right next to the Kingdom of Rotternik. There are other orcs but mostly in different frames. Ophal's king is Brudalous."

"What a silly name!" Then she thought of what Brudalous looked like and changed her mind. Certainly it shouldn't have a name like a person.

"What'd you get?" Charles asked her.

She showed him the bottle of Alice Water. The other two were immediately unimpressed.

"Perfume!" a kinglet pronounced.

"Toilet water!" said his brother, sniggering. When the kinglets spoke of toilet water, they had something other in mind than women did.

Merlain didn't feel like arguing the matter. Just then Charles, showing unusual compassion, helped her out. "It's obviously a potion. They can be anything from love to poison."

"Yeah," the kinglets agreed together, learning respect. Potions could indeed be fun, in the wrong hands.

"Let's get back to the children's suite, before we're missed," Charles said.

It was such an obvious suggestion that each of them put on a cloak. Merlain, though she now felt embarrassed about it, carefully retained the bottle of Alice Water and held on to it on the way back.

CHAPTER 5

Changing Time

"I tell you," the stout magician was saying, rubbing his rear where a royal pain had recently kicked it, "there's Malignants at this con!"

"Maybe not," squeaked the tall witch with lavender hair. "Malignants don't play jokes. They go for serious mischief."

"I don't call this a joke!"

"Kids do."

"Kids? Children? Little monsters?"

"Right."

"But the children's suite is supposed to take care of that! No children are allowed loose in the main convention."

"Maybe some escaped. Maybe some who stumbled on an invisibility cloak."

"Just what the con needs: invisible brats underfoot and interfering!"

Merlain couldn't help it: she stuck out her tongue and blew air over its tip. Just the way her grandpa Reilly on her mother's side of the family had taught her.

"BRAAACCCKKKK!" It took real skill to get out that fourth *K* at the end, but it was worth it.

"There! You hear that? You hear it?" The short warlock standing between them and the open doorway was as excited as the other.

"Yes," Lavender Hair said, and tossed a powder.

Merlain sneezed, and as she did her face appeared. Hastily she shook and brushed the luminescent powder grains from her head as she ducked behind a couch. What an obvious trick to fall for! Maybe she shouldn't have relented and let the kinglets have their fun, because they were getting more children than kinglets into trouble.

"There, convinced now? We'll have to complain to the management and the con committee. They'll get these kids and find out who's responsible for them. Someone may get expelled from the con for this. Someone besides those kids!"

Merlain felt a tug on the hand gripped by Charles, and followed. As she had done before she slipped by the short warlock and into the hallway. She was glad to get away from that group. Enlivening adult room parties was getting boring and she was almost glad she'd almost gotten caught. The first few piercing female screams had been hilarious, but the kinglets had tended to overdo it, and some of those women had not seemed like very good sports. Goosing had its natural limits, it seemed. Now would Mama and Daddy and Grandpa and Grandma Knight and maybe even Helbah get in trouble because of them? Maybe Auntie Jon would confess and take all the blame. But somehow Merlain doubted that last.

Back in the children's suite they found their old corner and removed their cloaks. No one seemed to have missed them. They had led a charmed life, perhaps literally, for the past hour.

"What do you think, Kildum?" a kinglet asked.

"I dunno, Kildee. I think these two are in trouble."

"Us!" Merlain bristled. How like a royal pain to be saying that!

"She's your aunt," Kildum said reasonably. "She's the one who gave us the cloaks."

"You're the one who kicked butts and pinched bottoms!"

"I pinched people. Kildee kicked them. We're not in trouble. We're kings."

"In an evil eye!" Charles glared at them. Just as if he had become a warrior grown, he drew his sword.

Charles!

I just want to remind them. They don't get by with that king stuff with us!

Merlain sighed. What a trial they all were at times! Mama had said that just about her and Charles, but with the kinglets it was true. This could be very serious. They could all end up with their ends up, getting spanked.

"Why children," Auntie Jon said, materializing right in front of them with a sudden sweep of cloak. "Whatever is the matter?"

They all told her at once, each accusing all the others and protesting his or her own innocence. Of course Merlain knew that she of all of them really *was* innocent, but she knew better than to try to get an adult to believe that!

"Oh pish and tosh," Auntie Jon said, making it sound dirty. The meaning of pish was obvious, and the other word could be figured out by elimination, as the adults put it. Only they didn't laugh. "All you sweet, dear little children have to do is do something for the others that is particularly nice. Then they'll forgive you your transgressions. Otherwise the least they'll do is send you home, probably with your little posteriors steaming."

This didn't sound like Auntie Jon. But then nothing Auntie did or said had seemed quite right since they'd reached the convention. Was this what her father Kelvin meant when he said his sister acted crazy?

"But what can we do?" Charles asked. "We're really in trouble, and maybe you are too."

"Oh my dear," Auntie Jon said, her hand reaching down and stroking Charles' forehead. "Your auntie is much more durable than you."

Whatever did she mean?

"Here, Kildom, let me have your spelling book."

Reluctantly, it seemed to Merlain, the king who had lied about who he was when showing the book handed it over. How had she known which twin he was and that he even had it? Had Auntie been along when they did those things, watching? Had she been there invisibly when they stole and again when they were back together showing each other what they'd taken and, amazingly, gotten away with? That seemed hard to believe, but it was not all that easy to disbelieve, either.

Jon's fingers opened the book to a picture and showed it to them. The picture was of a little girl clothed in flames. Mean-looking wizards and warlocks and witches were dancing around the girl, laughing cruelly.

"See what can happen when you steal and get caught?"

"B-but they wouldn't burn us!" Charles protested. But he looked as if he thought they might.

"Don't be too certain. Naughty children have to be dealt with. That's why there's the children's suite."

"But how can we—"

Auntie ignored him and stretched out a hand to Kildee. "Now let me have *your* book, Kildee. The orc text."

The kinglet handed her the book. She returned the spellbook to his brother. There had not been a bit of hesitancy as to who was who when she asked.

"Now here," she said, displaying another picture, "is the opal, the magical jewel that makes travel between frames as easy as thought." She glanced quickly at each of them in turn, her eyes disturbingly knowing. "Don't you think Helbah would be pleased if you could get it for her?"

"The orc has it," Charles said, looking somewhat nervous. Merlain could appreciate why.

"Oh, piddle on the orc!" There was another naughty word! "It's nothing but a big, clumsy old fish shaped like a man. Hit it with a few spells and it won't be a bother. Besides, all you have to do is get the opal without getting caught."

"But—"

"You are most unusual children, all of you. Merlain, Charles, you have special powers. You can use them against the orc while you steal his opal. Nobody will know until afterward, and then they'll call you clever."

Clever? Somehow this did not seem clever so much as crazy. But Auntie Jon was an adult, and should know.

"Isn't Ophal a long way off? Even at home?" Merlain asked. She was scared of what Auntie Jon was suggesting. What was even more scary was that it was seeming more and more possible. They *were* unusual children, and they *did* have the special power of telepathy. And they had stolen things that might have other powers. Still—

"Oh, not with spells, dear child!" Auntie exclaimed with a gesture of pooh-pooh that made the very notion of distance seemed ridiculous. "Once at home, you can fly."

"But we can't fly! We can't even become swooshes the way you and Kildom and Kildee and Helbah did."

"A detail, I assure you," Auntie Jon said. "Imagine how pleased Helbah is going to be on your return."

Merlain wavered. She felt as if she were teetering at the brink of an impossible cliff, but also as if it was the way to launch into glorious flight. Maybe. "But I—I'm just a girl!" Normally that was a token of superiority.

"And your companions are just boys, an obvious liability, I agree. But you do have your loving auntie."

"You'll come with us?" It seemed just too much to believe, but the notion was reassuring. Auntie would know what to do; she was very certain of herself.

"Partway. Until you're home and started on your way for Ophal."

Oh. Not all the way. Merlain didn't like that. She would rather have Auntie's company at the other end, where the danger was. "But—"

Auntie Jon sprinkled some powder. Merlain sneezed once. She heard the others sneezing too. Her head seemed to swell and she knew that they'd get the opal. When they returned and gave it to her, Helbah was going to be very, very pleased. She couldn't see why she had ever doubted this.

* * *

Wearing their invisibility cloaks, they followed a group of conventioneers out of the hotel. There, unknown to the young witches, the children joined them on a platform for the ride, and exited with them at the terminal. With a few whispered words from Jon they wormed their way through the crowd to a vacant transporter. They waited until a neighboring transporter booth was empty as well; then Auntie Jon set the controls on both. Kildom and Kildee went into the first transporter and disappeared. Their destination was the underwater installation of the pointears.

Merlain and Charles entered the second. There was a confusion of lights and stars, a twisting in the tummy that spread through their entire beings, and an awful moment when uncertainty became absolute doubt. Then they were there, in the installation chamber they had used with their parents. Here, alone except for the Mouvar book and parchment, they were to await Auntie Jon's help.

"D-do you think she'll do it?" Charles asked, his worry only made more evident by his attempt to mask it.

"She said she would." Merlain had been worrying about that herself. Auntie Jon was so different these days!

They waited, and they waited, and then they waited some more. Just as Merlain was getting sniffly and ready to cry, and Charles was trying to find some manly way to avoid doing something similar, the three water birds flew squaking down the river.

Suddenly Merlain herself was flopping her wings and flying away from the chamber, to her surprise, and with her was a young swooshling who had to be her brother. The three approaching birds did not have to reach the ledge; they turned, and the party flew up the river, up the stairs, and across the ruins of an old palace where their grandpa Knight had once fought the evil Queen Zoanna. Now she, with the others, was climbing into the sky. The blue, blue sky, more glorious and exciting than it ever was when she was in human form.

Ahead, she knew, there would be adventure. But still Merlain's little swoosh head harbored a stupid little worry, even as the scenery changed so prettily. Could she really trust Auntie? Did she really *want* to trust Auntie? Auntie Jon, who hadn't known such magic as this before leaving home, and who ever since their shopping trip had been acting more and more strange?

The old woman stared with incomprehension at the somehow familiar clothes hanging on the wall of the store's dressing room. Greenbriar pantaloons and brownberry shirt—where had she heard of these? Her own clothes were dark and none too clean. Her face in the mirror was unbelievably ugly, all nose and warts and sunken eyes. She was an old, old hag, the utmost crone, and she smelled bad even to herself. Worse, she had no memory of who she was or how she had come to be here.

The clothes on the hanger were almost certainly those of a young person. Had she come in here to try them on? Was that what she was doing—shopping? But then why wasn't she clean? Certainly any woman bathed before shopping for clothes. Had she any money? Could she buy any of these things?

Carefully, slowly, because her joints and bones caused her pain, she stripped off the black, sacklike dress. It was such a dress as was often worn by witches, and more often evil witches than good ones. Did that mean that she was a witch? That she was evil? Her body really stank; she wished she had something to clean it with. There were rough bare spots of scaly skin and mats of kinky, curly hair. She had never seen such a body in her life, she felt certain, yet somehow it was, either temporarily or permanently, her own.

There was something hanging beside the clothing: a pouch of stones and a leather sling. She took these items down, fondled them, sniffed at them, and knew somehow that these were hers and hers alone. Then she put them back and tackled the clothes.

She put on the underclothes first; they were clean and modest and a reasonable fit. Now, feeling a little better about it, she stuck her skinny arms into the sleeves of the brownberry shirt and pulled it on. The shirt hung loosely on her. Where were her breasts? She should have magnificent young, firm breasts. Why had she thought that? She was an old woman; old women didn't have breasts, they had bags.

She reached for the sling and pouch of stones. She hung them under her left arm. She looked in the mirror at herself: a crone with ugly facial hair and warts now dressed as a rustic visitor from a faraway land.

What thoughts! What thoughts! What thoughts! She had to get out of here. Once she was out in the store, someone would recognize her. There would be help for her, from the salespeople if from no one else.

Taking a firm resolve, she left the dressing room and emerged into a busy togging shop for females. There were young and old folk feeling dresses and underthings. Birds swooped overhead, now and then landing and changing instantly into salesclerks. There was a big window, magically concealed from those outside who might try to peer in, she was sure. Looking out, she saw building without stain or glass, beautifully lighted and displaying names: Charters, Rowward, BuckSears, Aberrommie and Fish. A familiar scene, certainly, though somehow she knew she had never seen it before.

Down below, a street. Platforms, some with bubble covers, some without, moving in fast or slow lines. People on sidewalks, often getting off stopped platforms, sometimes with packages. So conventional, so normal, so strange. She stood contemplating what she saw, wondering and feeling and knowing nothing, nothing at all that was in any way clear.

Wings whispered behind her. She turned, and there was the clerk she had been hoping for. Broad of shoulders, handsome as anything, he would have been a dream of what a young girl traditionally longed for. Why she should think of him that way wasn't clear.

His face now bore a frown, and his mouth was pursed. "What, madam, are you doing here?"

"Shopping." The response was spontaneous and took no thought.

"Shopping." He looked dubious. "May I ask for what?"

"Clothes." Why else would she be in a clothes department?

The clerk looked at her pantaloons and shirt. "Frankly, I can see why. Do you have anything in mind?"

How odd that he should ask that. "No, I have nothing in my mind." That might be more literal than he knew.

"Hmmm. Do you have credit?"

"Credit for what?"

"An account with the store. To pay for your clothes."

"I have to pay for these?" She touched her pantaloons and shirt. Would he make her put on that horrible black rag she had been wearing?

"*Those* are not ours. *Those* must be what you were wearing when you came into our store. What money do you have?"

"Money?" She tried to think. She felt the pantaloon pockets and found them empty. She might have had a purse. Why couldn't she remember?

"I probably had a purse," she said, answering the salesclerk.

"Probably." He seemed unconvinced. Perhaps that wasn't surprising; she was unconvinced herself. This whole situation rang false—yet she was stuck in it.

The clerk whistled, and a white dove landed and became a lady salesclerk. The young lady looked at her, eyes widening.

"She's dressed like that other. The young woman who was here."

"The young woman was with this one?"

"No. The young one was with two others. I've never seen this one before."

"Could she have a purse?"

"I'll check." The girl made a pass, said some words, snapped a small capsule under her own nose. She took a breath. "No purse belonging to this woman."

"People?"

The salesgirl blinked. "No people of hers here. I don't know how she can be in the store, frankly."

"She's not going to be for long. Back entrance, not the front."

"Right."

The salesgirl made a pass with her hand and left behind a cloud of flower scent. The old woman savored it, reminded of an unremembered home. Then she was standing in a grimy alley that did not smell nearly as nice.

Magician laborers were unloading platforms at an unloading dock and floating their cargoes inside the store. She watched them for a while, as they directed shipments with waves of their wands and spoke the proper spells carefully. No one paid any attention to her.

Then one of the laborers took a break from levitating racks of clothing up a shaft. He turned and spoke. "They throw you out, Mother?"

How perceptive of him! "Yes." But she did not feel as old as he took her for.

"Store's all heart. No money, no business your being here."

"That's what the clerk said." And he had been such a handsome one, as if that related.

"It's their business," the laborer said. "Can't fault it. Do you know where you are?"

"Outside. Not in the store."

"Right. Privileged Street's that way. Underprivileged Street the other way. If you have any friends in the city, don't go on Underprivileged. Mainly failures and bad people live there."

"I haven't money and I haven't friends. That means I'm a failure. Maybe on Underprivileged I can find out why."

"Luck to you, Mother." Another platform slid into place, piloted by a rough-looking man who could logically have come from where she was going. "Well, back to work."

She watched for a little while longer. Then she walked past him on her way to Underprivileged. There, if anywhere, might be the answers she needed but did not know how to seek.

CHAPTER 6
Adventuring

Sean Reilly, familiarly known as St. Helens because of his volcanic nature, was playing chess with Lester Crumb. They had set up their game well within sight of the ruins of Rud's onetime capital palace. Only one day had gone by and already Lester was missing his feisty wife.

"You know, Les," St. Helens said, scratching his shiny black beard, "you could have gone with her."

Lester moved a pawn. As big a man as either St. Helens or his own father, but without the stomach of either (physically or emotionally), Lester was just as stubborn. That was why he and Jon, the sister of the Roundear of Prophecy, made such a perfect match.

"I could have," Lester agreed. "She told me over and over. I said no, I don't want nothing to do with witches."

"But she was an apprentice—sort of. Helbah and the Roundear couldn't have done without her. She conked Zoanna with a rock so that it was possible for them to nab her."

"I still don't like witches. Oh, Helbah's nice enough, I guess, but she looks exactly the way Melbah looked."

"Don't mean she's evil. There's probably an evil man who looks like you in another frame."

"I'd prefer a world without magic."

St. Helens scowled. "You wouldn't. I've lived in such a place."

"Earth. But from the stories you've told, there was magic. Horseless carriages, talking boxes with the images of living people in them, flying machines, at 'em bombs—"

"That's atom bombs. Nuclear fission."

"New clear fishing?"

The man laughed. "Not exactly."

"Magic," Lester said.

"All science. Where your wife is now, they probably have the same things, only they work by magic. I don't pretend to understand the difference. The commander, John Knight, and I used to discuss it, but even we couldn't come to decisions. Now me, I'd have liked to have gone along into that other frame. Unfortunately no one invited me."

"You aren't married to a Helbah helper."

"No, but my little girl's married to the Roundear. Has children by him."

"With the help of a chimaera," Lester said. "Jon was there, remember?"

"Yes, yes, I know. But they're still his and Heln's. The magic of the chimaera saved the kids' lives and allowed them to be born. The fact that they've got coppery hair is just coincidence."

"And the dragon?" Lester inquired dryly.

"Heln says it never happened."

"Jon says it did. I believe my wife."

St. Helens had an impulse to reach across the board, grab Lester by his reddish throat, and strangle him. It was only an impulse. Both knew that the children were and weren't Kelvin's. Starting from the lad's seed, warped by prenatal influences, then magically unwarped right at the moment of their birth. It wasn't strange that Charles and Merlain resembled their unhuman savior, but only that they were two of the nicest six-year-olds in existence. But unnaturally smart and, he suspected, possessed of a talent. On Earth he had heard of telepaths but never believed they existed; he had also seen the products of some most unusual births.

"It's your move, St. Helens."

"Oh. Oh, yes." He moved a knight. He'd beat Lester in about two moves, he thought. The lad had some ability but he just wasn't concentrating.

"Look there! Swooshes!"

St. Helens looked where Lester was pointing, his own concentration pulled from the board. There were the swooshes, flying up and out of the ruins. Four young ones scarcely old enough to fly, and one adult swoosh of an unusual dark color and a buzvald's ugliness.

"Do you think . . . ?" Lester asked.

"Could be. But so soon! Of course there is the river, though even swooshes generally don't go underground."

The birds saw them, came close, and circled above their heads. The little swooshes dived down. The big swoosh blocked them, trying to indicate with a toss of its head that they should fly on. Some hesitated, but one of the little ones landed, and promptly, magically, transformed. It was Kelvin and Heln's strange and beautiful chick, Merlain.

"Merlain!" St. Helens exclaimed. "What are you doing here?"

"Oh, St. Helens, Uncle Lester, we're on our way to get the magical opal the orc has! We're going to steal it and take it back to Helbah as a gift."

"You're *what?* You can't do that!" St. Helens had seen a lot of action and a lot of trouble in his day, but this was twice as much of both as he would have cared for. For this child to try . . . ! "Ophal's a long way off! The orc is dangerous, and stealing's not even nice!" He knew he sounded like a prissy old maid, but it was true.

"Oh, Grandpa, you're funny!" Merlain said. "That's Auntie Jon squawking up there. She got us some magic cloaks so the orc won't see us, and she learned from Helbah how to change us into birds. We can fly there, steal the opal, and—''

"No, no, no you can't!" he insisted, hating himself for sounding prissy again. "It's crazy! Your mother and father would never allow—"

"They don't know about it," she said brightly. "Just as you always said, what they don't know won't hurt them. It's a surprise."

A surprise! St. Helens opened his mouth to protest.

The big bird flew low. Lester reached his arms out, as if expecting his wife to fly into them and receive his embrace. The bird rose slightly and just skimmed his head. A dropping fell and splattered on his upturned face.

Lester scrubbed at his eye, disgruntled. "Jon, I knew you were mad at me when you left, but not *this* mad! Come down and we'll talk."

"Mad at you! Mad at you! Go home!" the big bird screamed. "Come, Merlain! Come! Follow us!"

Merlain was again a bird. St. Helens made one desperate grab at her but she eluded him and flew off, following the three smaller swooshes. The big swoosh flopped on ahead. St. Helens watched them, as he saw Lester was doing. The birds got rapidly farther away, and soon, too soon, they were out of sight.

Lester finished wiping bird excrement onto a rag. He wore an expression of bewilderment, not completely unmixed with shame. St. Helens sympathized. He had never thought the girl was so hard to handle. Evidently he had underestimated her.

"What do you think, St. Helens?"

"I think Jon's one helluva girl!"

Lester looked further pained. "I mean, about this business of—"

Oh. St. Helens had never been known for diplomacy, and every so often he regretted it. "I think if they get to Ophal, there'll be another stage of the prophecy," he said grimly.

"War with Ophal?"

"If they get the gem. Gods, how could there fail to be

war?'' It would be, he realized, as if a foreign power sent gem thieves to steal the crown jewels of England.

"But they can't get the opal! Regardless of what she said!"

"If they don't, but they do get close, there still could be trouble. Those orcs aren't exactly pupkits! I just don't understand Jon aiding them in this. It must be her idea; she's the adult and she found the magic."

"Yeh," Lester said thoughtfully. "If that big bird is really her."

"Who else could it be?" St. Helens asked reasonably. "It can't be Helbah. She'd never have shat on you, even if you made her mad."

"I don't think my wife would have either," Lester said. He finished cleaning his face and threw the rag away with an expression of distaste. "St. Helens, I think that was an imposter, and I think it's leading astray my niece and nephew, your grandkids."

St. Helens sighed, knowing that Lester had to be right. He focused his eyes on the empty sky and tried to think what they might do about this situation. It was too big for them alone, but just where in or out of the Confederation were they to find help?

Dragon Horace lifted his fine coppery snout from the mess of maggots festooning the carcass of a meer he was feeding on. There was a strange thought in his head: that head that seldom thought of anything but eating and eliminating.

Horace! Horace! It's me, Horace! I'm your sister Merlain!

There was a pesty, snoopy bird flying just below the carcass. Did it plan on eating some of the maggots? He'd stop that! He would roll out his tongue and snap that bird into his mouth before it could land. The feathers would tickle his throat, but that was his price for dining undisturbed.

No, no, Dragon Horace! It's me! I'm the bird!

Merlain? His sister? A bird? This was an odd thought, even for an unusual dragon.

The bird lit on the tip of one of the meer's antlers. Its

long beak and beady eyes were directed at him. If it wasn't
Merlain, it was a really careless bird.

*Dragon Horace, Charles and I are going on a trip with
those terrible twins I told you about. You know, the royal
nothings with the crowns on their heads.*

Dragon Horace snorted, almost blowing the bird off its
perch. He hadn't liked what Merlain had told him about the
twins. Once, long ago, she had even told him he could eat
them. Now she and Charles were going someplace with
them.

*Auntie Jon is along too. It's an adventure! There's this
big monster in a place called Ophal who has this wonderful,
magical gem! We're to steal it and take it back to Helbah!
That will make Helbah happy and she won't punish us for
all the naughty things we let the royal brats get away with!
It's going to be such fun! I wish you could come, Horace,
but I don't know how to make you fly. Besides, I don't have
an invisibility cloak for you.*

"Merlain! Come!" a large ugly bird called, flopping over.
Horace stifled an impulse to jerk his head high and snap his
jaws at it.

That's Auntie Jon, Horace. She's impatient. Good-bye.

Horace watched the bird fly. It followed the big bird and
was joined there by three the same size as herself. Strange!
The doings of humans were incomprehensible, even if two
of them were his siblings.

Dragon Horace licked up a tongueful of squirming maggots that had crawled away from the carcass. He sucked
them down, then lowered his snout into the meer's rib cage
for another mouthful of fragrant, well-ripened flesh. Fresh
blood was great, but mature meat was better. Munching
away, he thought mostly thoughts appropriate to a young
and hungry dragon. Few dragons or humans would suspect
that he was strikingly different in two ways; he was telepathic, and he had been born of a human woman.

They flew all day, buoyed by magic, until Merlain's wings
were tired. She knew she should be enjoying the view, as

she seldom had such a chance to see the mountains, valleys, plains, and rivers from such vantage, and they were beautiful and ugly and shades of in between, but mainly she just had to concentrate on pumping her wings and keeping the pace. As night threatened they landed on a cleared area at the extreme edge of the twin kingdoms of Klingland and Kance. Here was glowing moss and a large gray stone bearing a pointing arrow and the dark warning: ROTTERNIK.

As they touched ground, they reverted to their natural states. Merlain remained tired, but mainly in her arms; her legs had not been used for flying, so standing and walking were easy enough. Still, the notion of her nice warm bed at home was tempting.

"You will cross the border tomorrow in the morning," Auntie Jon said. "You will travel on across Rotternik to the Kingdom of Ophal. It will be a long journey, and dangerous. You will have to use your magic and your wits."

Merlain experienced sudden alarm, which cut through her fatigue. "But *your* magic and wits should protect us, Auntie!"

The woman shook her head. "Auntie Jon will not be going with you."

"But," Charles protested, catching on. "You said—"

"I said *you* would get the opal. You children, not Auntie Jon. What good would it do if I got the stone for you? Then the credit would be mine, and you would have nothing to redeem yourselves. You must do all of this entirely by yourselves."

That did make a certain sense to Merlain, though she was not completely at ease with it. Why couldn't Auntie Jon come along with them, and let them get the opal, and only help protect them from the orcs? The credit would be theirs, and they would be more likely to return with their skins on.

"But—" said Kildom or Kildee.

Auntie Jon looked at them. Her eyes blazed. It was as if flames flickered within them. They shut up. Merlain was glad the kings had taken the rap for the protest she had not quite had the courage to make. It wasn't courage for them, of course, it was stupidity, but the result was the same.

Auntie Jon made a pass with her hand, said some strange words, and a cloud of smoke puffed into existence. In a moment it dissipated, and there was a banquet prepared for them: bottles of icy cold chokabola and peajelnutly butter sandwiches. That made the three boys forget about any questions they might have had, and Merlain almost forgot. They ate, and it was delicious.

Then Auntie Jon reminded them: "Tomorrow. Tomorrow you children are on your own."

Merlain knew she meant it. She tried to salvage what she could from what she feared might be a disaster. "But we can't become birds," she said. "You do that for us. We don't know how. We have a long way to go, and we won't get there if we can't fly."

Auntie Jon was unfazed. "Kildom, you have your book of spells. Merlain, you have your Alice Water. Charles, you have your magic sword."

Merlain was startled. She didn't think she had told Auntie Jon about that bottle, though it seemed the woman knew anyway, just as she knew about what the kinglets had stolen. Charles looked surprised too, and Merlain knew why: magic sword? They had assumed that it was merely a nice ordinary weapon.

"Y-yes," Merlain said. She tried again to penetrate Auntie Jon's mind, and found none of her thoughts accessible. The woman had become like another person, no longer the fun-loving aunt who had been really more like another child than the sister of a parent. This showed how treacherous it was to trust the nature of adults.

Kildom or Kildee—whichever one was stupider at the moment—started another protest. "But—"

"You children," Auntie Jon's voice said with a steely edge to it, "haven't experienced anything." She clapped her hands, and at the smack of the palms Kildom and Kildee fell over as if dead. Then Charles rolled his eyes upward, yawned, and fell beside them.

"Auntie Jon, you shouldn't have—" Merlain started,

knowing she was being as foolish as the kinglets, but unable to help herself. But she couldn't finish her sentence. She was very, very tired, and—

He was standing knee-deep in a pool of crimson. It was blood. No, no, it wasn't blood. It was tall red grass, and it was this color simply because of the light of the rising sun. There were feathery pink stocks to these grasses, and they waved in a cooling breeze coming across an open grassland. In the distance were many animals with horns and antlers. The scents of strange, wonderful flowers came to him with every breath. Charles was alone in this landscape, and he did not for a moment question its reality.

There was a horse under him, though a moment before this he had been standing. It was a big, firm war-horse of magnificent chestnut brown. Charles now filled the big saddle. A man grown, he held a sword, and it was *his* sword, grown large enough to fit a warrior's hand.

The horse carried him for days, possibly for years. He realized that this was not exactly reality as he knew it, though it did not seem exactly like a dream either. It was interesting, so he had no objection. He saw many sights, and fought many a fight, using his sword, which did indeed seem to be enchanted. It wasn't that it moved for him, but that it was so compatible that he knew how to guide it to the proper spot; he was highly competent with it, because it seemed like a close friend. So he slew many orcs and many bad men, knowing that they were like fantasy figures in a game, there only to challenge him. When they died, they did not suffer; they were merely pieces being removed.

Back on the plain, he found the sun still shining, and it even seemed to have a human face. His sword was no longer in his hand, not because he had been disarmed but because he had no need for it now. Before him was a little girl in a flimsy nightdress. She had light hair and blue eyes, and she glowed just when he looked at her. She looked familiar, and in a moment he recognized her: it was the girl he had seen in the mirror of the room at the big convention, who had been crying. He had heard her sob and seen her tears. Then he had been caught up in his mission and forgotten the matter.

Now that memory came back with force, and he realized that he was more interested in this little ghost-girl then he had realized before. She was pretty, and about his own age, and her sorrow made him hurt; he wanted to comfort her, if he could only figure out how. Maybe she was a princess being held captive somewhere by an orc, and he could be the prince who came to rescue her. Then she would cry "O my hero!" and kiss him, and he would really be a hero. That notion appealed.

Did you enjoy it? the girl thought-projected.

Charles did not think her question odd, though he realized in the background that maybe he should. Only his sister, and his dragon brother in a more limited way, had ever thought-talked to him this way.

Enjoy what? The riding? The fights?.

All.

Yes. Very much. It was a good adventure, and I was a hero, I think.

She nodded, as if this were only to be expected. She was easy to get along with. *Would you like to play?*

Who are you? He knew from the nuances of her thought that her idea of fun would be very similar to his, only modified for girl nature. No mushy stuff, no argument, just games and things they both enjoyed and could contest against each other without really meaning it.

I am Glow.

Glow, as in light? That's not a name.

She shrugged. *It's a witch's name. It can mean goodness.*

You're a witch? Now he had a little alarm, for witches could be anything.

My mama was.

A good witch?

Of course.

That was a relief! *Are you dead?*

Does it matter to you?

Noooo. Here he knew it didn't, since this whole thing was a dream or a vision or whatever.

She set her little fists on her narrow hips. *You want to play or not?*

Yes. He couldn't have said no to her anyway. *What game, Glow?*

Hide-and-seek, then.

There was a forest around them, instead of the sunny plain with the red grass. That was all right. She ran away from him, her fair hair flying back behind her, her nightdress flapping in the breeze of her motion. He ran after her. She stayed just ahead, going down a long path. She ducked in and out behind great trees and many bushes. He would gain on her, and almost touch her, and then she'd be far ahead, laughing, telling him to hurry up and catch her. She must know the magic of this place, so she could jump ahead without seeming to. That was all right; it made the game more challenging.

A cottage was ahead. Now Glow was at his side, holding his hand. Either he had caught her, or she had changed the game. It didn't matter; it was fun to be with her. Flowers bordered their path, smelling sweet, looking pretty, sissy but nice. The door of the cottage was open, and together they walked through it and inside the cottage.

I love you, Glow, he thought. He was unsurprised even at this sudden declaration. What he meant was that he loved being with her, playing games with her, and even holding her hand. She was just so perfectly right for him that it could not be otherwise. Even if she was dead. She hadn't quite said about that, but either she was dead or alive, and he could accept it either way. Just so long as he could be with her in his dreams.

I love you too, Charles.

I want to marry you when I grow up. But how could he do that, if she was dead? What did he know of marriage, if she was alive? Maybe he was lucky this was only a dream!

She laughed, her thoughts running right along with his. *You can't, if I'm not alive.*

Then it matters?

Not if you forget me.

Now he felt alarm. *Will I forget?*

Do you want to?

No!

It's only a dream. You'll forget.

Never! But he was afraid he would, because that was the nature of dreams. His happiness was being replaced by grief: grief for what he feared he would do, and what he would lose. He *did* love her; and though his dream emotion might diminish when he woke, he did not want to lose her entirely.

Charles, if you do remember, remember to be good.

I am good!

Not always. Lately you've been bad.

That had an uncomfortable ring of truth. *How bad?*

Stealing is bad. You know that.

Then I won't steal again.

Even the opal?

The opal? Oops! He was already committed to that. *Yes, the opal. I have to steal that. But after that I'll do what is right. I promise.*

You must not steal the opal, Charles.

The opal's magic. Magic should belong to everyone. At least that's what my aunt says.

That isn't your aunt, Charles. Your aunt isn't evil. The person telling you to steal is bad—witch bad. I am in a position to know! Do not obey her, Charles. Please!

As she thought to him, the little girl named Glow grew shimmery and hazy. As before, like a light from a candle that has guttered out, she was there, and then she was gone.

Glow! he thought, knowing it was useless. But at least he could remember her, and be guided by her, and maybe he would meet her again sometime.

Charles' back hurt, and he realized that he was waking up. He clung to his memory, but it slipped away like vapor between his grasping fingers. Whatever the little girl in the dream had thought to him was in the process of being gone. *No! No!* he thought, and then lost even that.

* * *

The old woman was hungry. She had walked a long way and her bones ached and her head hurt. She still did not know who she was or how she had come to be in this city. She felt as if her body were not really hers, and that this was not a city she had lived in. She felt these things, but could not actually form them as coherent thoughts. It was as if she were under some kind of enchantment, but she couldn't focus on that either.

Was she human? That seemed likely. What sort of human? She couldn't know or think. She was here, and that was an end of it, except for a faint cloud of doubt and confusion that impinged on the dubious clarity of her thoughts.

Sniff! Sniff! Her nose, almost without her decision, picked out the tantalizing aroma of cooking meats from all the scents around. The smell was coming from a diner. She peered at and into it. Dirty windows, ragged customers seated at a counter. The word on the window was "Jake's."

It wasn't appetizing, on the whole. But neither was she. Here was food. She hesitated not a moment. She went inside. A stool was vacant between a fat man and a woman almost as ugly as herself. She moved forward, grasped the counter with her clawlike hands, and pushed her rump onto the stool.

The unkempt man frying patties of meat ignored her. A hatchet-faced woman pushed a plate of what she knew were fries before the big man. The man looked at her, wrinkled his large red nose, and turned his back. The woman on her other side said, "Whew! Stinks in here!"

"You want something?" the counterwoman asked. Her expression indicated that this old intruder should leave.

"Food," the old woman said. "I'm hungry."

"Tough, crone." There was no sympathy in the woman's voice. "You got any money?"

"Money?" She knew she hadn't any and she knew instinctively that it mattered. Perhaps if she just didn't say . . .

"Jake! This un's for outin'!"

"No money, huh." The fry man moved away from the grill and around the stools. "Off your butt, Granny!"

Disrespectful, the old woman thought. Possibly a knot on

his head would help. She looked for something to hit him with but, seeing no sympathy in surrounding eyes, desisted. She would only get herself thrown out, probably bruised, possibly badly hurt when she landed. She couldn't even blame them; they weren't in business for her health. With difficulty, she unstooled herself.

"Whew! This one's ripe!" Jake said. "You ever take a bath, old woman?"

"Go—" She caught herself, not quite certain what she had been about to say, except that it related to something obscene that would make him angry. There was no point in making things even worse.

Meanwhile, Jake had taken her scrawny arm. As she tried to make up her mind whether to struggle to even a token extent, the customers gawked and Jake led her firmly out the back way.

"You going to have your will with her, Jake?" The speaker was rodent-faced as he leered out of a rear booth.

"Funny," Jake said, and propelled her out into a worse alley than the last. Here there were garbage cans and scrawny, flea-infested cats. He pointed to an open can where a large tom was chewing at something burned or spoiled.

"Your dinner, Grandma. *Bon appétit.*"

She watched him go back in, feeling the urge to do violence. But if he were to strike her, as she knew he would if she gave him any pretext, she could guess the damage she would suffer. How had she come by such a fighting spirit, in such a frail old body? She didn't make sense, even to herself!

She took the lid off a can and sniffed. She put the lid back on, firmly. She was hungry, but there were limits.

But her hunger was gnawing at her stomach. Eventually she would have to eat what was available. She hated the idea of garbage, but she knew that if that was all that offered, she would return to it. Eventually.

CHAPTER 7

Growing Magic

They woke in the morning, stiff and sore from sleeping on the ground. Merlain could see at a glance that both the royal pains and her brother were suffering in much the manner she was. But where was Auntie Jon?

"Where's Auntie Jon?" Charles asked, perhaps picking up her thought. He stretched his arms, seeming uncomfortable about something more than the woman's absence, but his thought was fading even as she tried to tune in to it. Just a picture of a cute little girl, and a warning of something bad.

"I want my breakfast!" said one of the royal pains. It was obvious that *he* had no concern with either a girl or a warning. What had Charles dreamed about? Almost, she could remember it; she was always connected to his mind somewhat, even in sleep, and sort of knew what he was dreaming. That little girl—it certainly wasn't Merlain herself! But who *was* it? As far as she knew, neither of them had ever met her. But she didn't seem like a pure dream, either. There was something disturbingly real about her.

"Me too," said the other pain, interrupting her chain of thought. Whatever conclusion Merlain had been about to come to was shattered. That hurt, because she had the notion that it was important.

They looked around, but Auntie was not to be seen. "Maybe she's hiding from us?" Merlain suggested. "Wearing an invisibility cloak."

Though they cried out again and again, Auntie Jon did not appear. The woman really had left them here to fend for themselves, after putting them forcefully to sleep. That reminded Merlain of Charles' dream again. Something about Auntie Jon—

"Appleberries!" a pain exclaimed, spying a bush.

Merlain gave up. She simply could not concentrate on anything elusive with the royal pains around. Anyway, she was hungry, and those appleberries did look good.

They breakfasted on the fruits and spring water. Then, as bravely as possible, they set about making plans. Rotternik lay before them, great trees, incredibly voracious wildlife, and people who had the reputation of not liking visitors. Auntie Jon had said that they would have to cross the border by themselves, but Merlain did not want to believe it. Now she had to.

Resolutely they shouldered their packs, straightened their clothing, and took the never-to-be-taken-back step across the luminous green border. Past the great ugly gray stone with its pointing arrow, into the scary territory that was hidden by a deep ugly blackness, as if it lay in perpetual night. Into the fabled forbidden kingdom of Rotternik.

"I do wish," Merlain said plaintively, "that we could be birds again."

"Me too!" Charles said. "Kildom, look in that book of spells."

Kildom promptly sat down at the side of the trail and opened the volume. He had in fact had it ready, taken from his pack the moment he woke up and not replaced. Merlain felt a little envious of his reading ability, but then she knew why he had it. Kildom and Kildee might look and act like age seven and a half, but both had been born during the same year as her father. Of that too she could fell envious—a childhood that would be lasting many more years. When she and Charles were boring adults like Mama and Dad, Kildom and Kildee would still be doing kid things and being brats. They had all the luck!

As they had stepped across the border the blackness that lay beyond the stone had changed to trees and streams. It was really rather pretty, once it became visible. It wasn't dark at all, merely somewhat gloomy.

The trees were way, way high—higher than anything she had imagined. The river in the distance was wide, wide, wide. Strange animals gamboled in the very high grass. In the distance—too far for her eyes to see clearly—mountains rose with green and brown and a few snowcapped peaks. The luminous border behind them was replaced with a simple end to sight. Blackness on this side, blackness on Klingland's side. With a border that kept out light, and, she understood, sounds and signals, Rotternik hardly needed to fear invasion by foreign armies. No army would be able to communicate with its home base, to organize an effective campaign. At least that was what the adults said. Rotternik was forbidden territory, the place everyone talked about but nobody ever went. Not by choice.

Kildee, not to be outdone by his brother, got out his own stolen book and opened it. While Kildom read spell after spell to himself, Kildee was busily tracing lines on a map.

"We have to go through or over the Dreadful Forrest; that has to be it straight ahead," Kildee announced. "Then we have to climb Heartbreak Mountain; that's in the distance. Then it's down the other side of the mountain and through or over Dismal Swamp. That bring us to Ophal. The border here looks like just an ordinary border on the map."

"Where do we come out in Ophal?" Kildom asked.

Kildee frowned more deeply and turned to another map. He studied the two, making comparisons by moving his hands back and forth between them. "We can come out on an island or we can come out where there's water. That's all Ophal is: water, islands, and land below water."

Merlain did not like the look of this at all. The forest, mountain, and swamp were bad enough, but land below water was worse. How would they breathe?

Charles caught her thought. "Auntie Jon," he said. "Are you here?"

No answer. Merlain wondered whether he had thought there would be. The woman could be watching them invisibly, waiting to take a hand, but Merlain doubted it. The Auntie Jon they had now wasn't like the Auntie Jon of yore. What was it that Charles had dreamed about her? Something that—

"How far across this kingdom?" Kildom demanded of his brother.

Kildee measured with his fingers and a scale at the bottom of a map. "Can't really tell. Mountain's at the bottom of this picture. Mountain's high. Dreadful Forrest may be magical. Road through forest goes to capital, Beraccck."

"Beraccck? Like when you stick your tongue out?"

"See for yourself."

Kildom did, then stuck his tongue out at Charles and went "Beraccck!"

Charles bristled. He looked as if he wanted to fight. His hand went for his sword.

Don't be stupid, Charles, Merlain told him in his head. *We need them to read the spells and the maps. Also, you know someone may have to take some blame when we get back. Everything bad that happens will be their fault. Besides, you know how old they actually are. If you tried fighting them, you'd get hurt.*

Not with this sword! It's magic! Auntie Jon said so!

But there was something about Auntie Jon. Merlain no longer quite trusted what she said. But until she was able to remember what it was she had heard in Charles' dream, there was no point in saying that. *Then you save your sword for the orc or something equally dangerous.*

Awwwwww.

You know I'm right.

The kinglets, quite oblivious to the conversation she was having with her brother or to Charles' menacing gesture, had their faces cheek to cheek so that they resembled one red-haired boy and one mirrored reflection. Unless Merlain looked into their minds, she was never sure which was which, and then sometimes she was doubtful, because their minds were as alike as their bodies.

"I dunno, Kildom. If we fly straight across and nothing happens—"

"Maybe half a day, Kildee. But if we walk, and if we climb the mountain . . ."

As if cued by the royal brats' discussion, a flock of small birds—very dark and very long of beak—flew over. Merlain was trying to decide whether they were starrows or sparklings or some more sinister creatures, when the sky darkened above the flock. A horrendously great bird dropped through them, snatching little birds in either set of talons and snapping up two or three others with its sawed beak. The flock dispersed in terror, while the big preybird halted its dive, flopped its gross wings, and flew away over the forest. Both its mouth and its claws were full, and dripping blood.

Merlain looked at Charles and Kildom and Kildee. They had all seen what she had. So much for the suggestion that they turn themselves into tender young swooshes and fly the rest of the way. They would have to walk, at least to such a place where flying might be less dangerous. Maybe some broad plain, where an enemy bird could be seen as far away as the horizon.

Actually, Merlain felt relief. She just knew that the royal pain would never get the spell right. There was no telling what forms they might have assumed if a kinglet tried transformation. She felt safer as she was.

Dreadful Forrest appeared even more dreadful close up. The trees were sooo high, and the stretch of prairie with

head-high grasses was wider than Merlain had expected.
Kildom and Kildee both sneezed all the way through the
grass, to Charles' ill-concealed delight. They couldn't see
ahead in the grass, and then the meer path they were following came out abruptly into trees. Now they could see
ahead a short distance, and behind a short distance, but not
overhead. There were twisted branches and vines and flocks
of birds and assorted animals in the trees that they hoped
were harmless; now and then something odorous was falling on their heads. Light that reached them on the path was
filtered green by large spade-shaped leaves. On either side
of their path the tree trunks were as big around as houses
if not actually palaces. Looking up, Merlain wished mightily that she could see all the way up to the trees' distant
tops.

They had been walking for half a day. Merlain's feet hurt
and she was becoming bored. She wasn't sure which was
worse. She was beginning to wish that something interesting would happen, even if it was a little threatening.

Suddenly Charles stopped walking and drew his sword.
What is it, Charles? For her part, she saw nothing dangerous.

Straight ahead! In those bushes!

She strained her eyes. Lights danced in them. She could
make out some peculiarly bent branches in the bushes, and
an assortment of red eyes. *What?*

*I can see better than you and I don't know what. I just
know we don't want to get eaten by it.*

Eaten? She shivered. This was *too* interesting for her
taste. She wondered how Charles had been alerted to it.
What had tipped him off?

Charles raised his voice. "Kildom, Kildee! In the
bushes—"

The kinglets responded like truly grown-up men: they left
off whispering to each other, turned a significantly paler
green, and ran for the trees. Their young, royal legs moved
remarkably fast. As they ran, a hairy branchlike thing
reached out for Charles. Also at that very moment, a loud

hoot sounded from overhead and a hairy creature dropped from a higher to a lower branch. Other hoots sounded, and soon the branches above were filled.

Merlain looked up at a face she would have preferred not to believe. A babkey, she thought, and a large one. But the forest dwellers were interested not in the children, but in the creature in the bush. One of them threw a chunk of tree bark and then another threw a rotted tree branch. Soon the air was filled with missiles raining down on and around the bush. It was a fight between hairy babkeys and a thing in the bush, and each side seemed worse than the other.

Charles! Merlain thought to her brother. *Let's go!*

But stupid Charles was liking his sword and his stance. He switched the blade as if he knew how to use it, ignoring the primates overhead. What had gotten into him? Auntie Jon had said the sword was magic; was it working some kind of spell on him, making him think he was bigger and bolder than he was? Yet he did seem to swing it with a certain competence, despite not having had any practice with it. Only magic could account for that.

But magic could not change the fact that he was only six years old. He had no business tackling any unknown monster.

"Charles!" A big bumpy thing rose from the bush as she resorted to voice. It *was* the bush, with legs that resembled brown and hairy branches. Many, many hairy legs, reaching feelers, and red eyes. It was what Merlain had always feared most: a spider. Unable to control herself, she turned and fled.

"Charles! Oh, Charles!"

Who was that calling? It wasn't herself, Merlain realized, for she was running as fleetly as she could, away from the threat, in a manner that would have been cowardly had she been a boy.

She looked back to see the spider begin a scuttling charge. Missiles rained down on it. Could it be that the babkeys were trying to help the human children? No, she realized;

it was more likely because the babkeys didn't want the spider to eat the children before the babkeys could.

The spider's feelers batted away the missiles. Now and then a leg helped, when a missile was large. The spider evidently did not fear the babkeys; maybe it liked to feed on them when there wasn't something juicier to catch, like a child.

The spider was fast, but Charles was faster. He was running now, finally convinced of the necessity. Maybe the spider would have been faster, but not when it had to keep knocking away the missiles. They might be no more than a distraction, but they did slow it down.

"HELP! HELP! HELP!" Now she placed it: the voice of royalty, calling so shrilly that the words could be heard above the din of the chase and battle. Running as hard as she could in their direction, Merlain found she was getting a dusting from huge flower stems. Tree roots that must have been the size of the great silver serpents her father talked about were treacherous as they continually blocked her and forced her to change direction. Everything was happening at once!

She looked back again, and saw Charles coming hard. He looked breathless. She *felt* breathless! Her breathing hurt her lungs. Not for the first time she wished that she had big air bags in front. A grown woman would be able to run much faster without running out of breath!

"MERLAIN! HELP US!"

She abruptly stopped running. Right in front of her was a long, damp slope. At its bottom, quite some distance ahead, the two royal pains were lying on their backs. Around them, heaped there, were the greenish skeletons and loose bones of animals. The royal pains were surrounded by skulls and arm bones and leg bones and—

BUMP!

"HELPPP!" Charles' voice came. He had run into her, trying to look back. Now they were both tumbling, sliding, falling. . . .

Greenish blur and muddy slide changed places and

changed places again as she somersaulted. Her bottom finally plopped down, and there she was on the bone pile, with the royal pains cushioning her.

THUMP!

Charles landed against her, heels uppermost. Now they were all stuck in this boneyard. Ugh!

The royal pains began howling to them. The azies and chimpees and babkeys howled and screamed overhead. They were shouting insults at the huge spider, which was crouched now at the mouth of this trap which had taken so many of their kind. As well as four terrified children.

"Oh, Charles! Oh, Kildom! Oh, Kildee!" Merlain said. She had never before been this scared, even when stealing. There was nothing she could imagine that could save them. The babkeys, monboons, azies, and chimpees had to be as frightened as she felt. They were all trapped in the horrible spider's den.

Charles got himself untangled, climbed to his feet, and drew his sword. He had resheathed it while running, and that might have been fortunate.

The sword looked like a toy. It *was* a toy, she thought. Not even her father's sword would be a defense against the spider, and what Charles had was much smaller and more delicate. Magic? It had *better* be magic, if they were to have any chance at all!

The huge spider crept down the slope they had just rolled down. Merlain saw now that the ground was coated with webbing, making it smooth, so that anything falling here would not be able to stop. It would also be hard to climb out. The spider's strategy was to drive its prey into this place, where it could not escape.

The spider had no difficulty, however. Its gnarled feet were sure on the webbed slope. It had perfect balance. It was a thing of beauty, in its appalling way. Its hairy front legs reached out toward them.

Charles swallowed. Merlain caught his thoughts. *I'm afraid, oh, I'm so afraid!* But he clutched the hilt of his sword, and the sword seemed to give him courage. There was something about it, but no obvious magic.

Charles stepped forward, screwing up what little courage he had. *I'll stop it! I have to stop it! I'll kill it! I have to!*

She watched her brother brandish his sword, and she knew that whatever magic it had was not going to help him, and that he was about to die. She knew that once that happened, there would be no help for the rest of them.

"Auntie Jon! Auntie Jon!" the two kinglets began calling. But Auntie did not come, and Merlain thought the kinglings stupid for thinking she might. Auntie Jon had brought them to the edge of Rotternik and dumped them; she was responsible for this. She must want them dead, crazy as that seemed. No, there would be no help there! They would have to help themselves. Charles was trying, and the royal pains were useless, which meant it was up to Merlain. If only there was something she could do!

A long, hairy foreleg darted at Charles. His sword shot out to meet it. The foreleg jerked back minus its tip; a drop of greenish substance dripped from it. The spider clicked huge mandibles and emitted a foul stench.

Maybe Charles actually *could* fight the monster! Maybe the sword enhanced him so that he was fast enough and strong enough and skilled enough. Maybe—

The foreleg darted a second time. Again foreleg met blade, but this time not directly on. With one fast sweep the spider whipped the sword expertly from Charles' hand. He was defenseless.

She had to do something! She had to!

A second leg grasped her brother. It yanked him off his feet. Charles screamed as he was slowly pulled toward the waiting mandibles of the monster.

"Help him!" Merlain cried.

How they found the courage she did not know, but Kildom and Kildee actually responded. Each boy grabbed one of Charles' legs. The spider pulled as they pulled. A tug-of-war was on, Charles was screaming, the furred audience in the trees producing a cacophony. But all that was only noise; something more was needed.

Merlain tried to help the boys, but their combined weight and strength was not enough. If only she weighed more! If only she had magic. If only she knew one of the spells in the kinglets' speller, or—

Maybe she could do it with her mind! She concentrated her thoughts at the spider: *STOP! LET GO! GO AWAY!*

The spider merely pulled harder. Evidently it was not receptive to such messages. But maybe if she changed it a little:

These creatures probably taste bad. I don't want to eat them.

The spider's mouth orifice dripped drool. It was even hungrier than before!

It just wasn't working. Obviously the spider, like most creatures, was not receptive to mind talk. Merlain and her brother could snoop on the thoughts of other people, and could send their thoughts to them when they made a special effort, sometimes. It helped to be close to the person they were sending to, physically and emotionally. She couldn't even read the thoughts of this monster; it was too alien. But its slaver spoke for it clearly enough.

Meanwhile branches and bark, nuts, fruit, and excrement came down from above in a blinding shower. Merlain winced as a particularly large chunk of bark bounced harmlessly off her head. The tree dwellers were trying to help them, not do harm, but it was clear that they were not magic.

Something *had* to be magic! That book—that *had* to be the answer! But she didn't have time to read it even if she could understand what was in it, and the screaming kinglets were no good for that at this stage. There had to be something else.

Charles' feet were moving higher, and the kinglets' bodies were now being drawn up off the ground. Merlain clung to one kinglet, feeling the hideous strength of the spider through the linked bodies. *What was there she could do?*

The Alice Water! Maybe that was it! But she didn't know which way it worked. If it made her as small as the girl in the storybook, that would be no good. Well, she could hide among the bones. Maybe all of them could. But then the spider would just move the bones and keep moving them until it found them. Still, if they were small enough, say the size of ants, they might hide in the skulls for a while and maybe find a hole in the ground. If they were small enough, the spider might lose interest in them, because they wouldn't be enough to feed it. And there might be other predators, no danger to them now, that would pounce on them when they were small enough. So that was no answer.

Unless she could take a small sip, and if it made her smaller, then she could dump the bottle on the spider and make *it* small, and then it would be no threat to them.

The kinglets screamed in unison as the straining spider's limb pulled all three closer to the opening and closing mandibles with their dripping drops of digestive liquid. Merlain would be the last one to be eaten, but that was small comfort.

She had to try. It was the only thing. Quickly she took out the small bottle from her pack, scattering the extra underwear and stockings. It was impossible to be neat when she had to keep hanging on to the kinglet's leg with her other hand so that the others would not be hauled into the maw even faster. She brought the bottle to her face and unstoppered it with her teeth. Not giving herself a chance to think, she turned it up and took more of a sip than she had intended, because of the motion of the bodies she was touching.

Nothing happened, except that something seemed to slip away from one hand. Disappointed, she replaced the stopper, though it seemed pointless to save unmagical water.

Then she realized that the noise had diminished. She looked around, and saw that the spider and children were gone. So were the trees. There was shoulder-high shrubbery all around. Tiny bugs scuttled in it.

She looked down at her feet, and—

She was standing in a shallow hole. Two little chimps, or were they azies, pulled at a third. But all were dressed as humans! Right at the edge of the hole, holding on to the brown-suited azie with the winged helmet was—a spider.

Suddenly she understood the situation.

Merlain hardly thought at all. A spider was a spider, and one this size she could handle as she would at home. Careful so as not to step on her brother or the kinglings, Merlain raised her right foot out of the ankle-deep hole. She moved it over the group, then over the spider, centering the heel of her boot above its body. She lowered her foot.

The spider, no dummy, scrambled back out of the way. The three boys tumbled heels over heads in the other direction. The little fleas swarmed through the brush—actually the trees—to pursue the spider in its retreat. Charles and Kildom and Kildee stared up, shouting at her. But it was the mental voice she received best.

Merlain! You're big.

Oh, I know that! The water hadn't made her small; it had made her a giant! That had certainly solved their problem with the spider.

She looked around again. That rough rise a short distance away was the mountain they had been traveling to. She could carry them all in a few steps. That would be better than being a bird! But she'd have to hurry. Magic had a way of wearing off.

She leaned down and put her hand out in front of them. Charles ran and got his sword, and in a moment he and the two kinglets climbed on.

Well, Charles, she thought, straightening, *now I know what it is to have three boys on my hands.*

She had to smile, though Charles, hanging tightly to her little finger, probably wasn't smiling.

The old woman *was* that hungry. Her stomach growled in the manner of a subdued dragon, and she knew it hadn't had nourishment since she'd awakened in the store's dressing room. She had spent the night in an alley, crouched between garbage cans. Now it was morning, and she was awake and cold and stiff and sore and dispirited. In fact, it would not have been too much of an exaggeration to say she felt bad.

Holding on to a can she pulled herself to her feet and took off its lid. Nauseating odors came at her. She banged down the lid and closed it tight. Possibly the other one.

Cautiously, so as not to choke on its fumes, she lifted the lid on the second can. Inside were the remains of meals, together with bottles and cans. But there, right near the top, was a partially eaten, partially clean loaf of bread. Obviously someone had dropped the loaf, so that it got soiled on the ground, and tossed it into the garbage. It had been there all night, right next to her, just waiting to be discovered. If she was careful, she could eat from the clean side. If she was careless, she would eat some of the dirt, but even that side of it would feed her, and that was much better than nothing. She lifted the bread to her mouth and prepared to bite.

"What you got there, sister?"

Startled, she looked. He was big and he was ugly and he probably needed the food as much as she did. He reached out a ragged sleeve with a deformed hand protruding from it.

Alarmed, she pulled back her prize. "It's mine," she explained, fearing his intent.

"Give it here, hag!"

"We can share. If you're really hun—"

He made a sudden grab, got the bread, and pushed her away with his free hand. She fell back against a rough wall, the collision making her gasp. He turned his back, walking away with her food, not even interested enough to rape her. Insult added to injury.

Anger filled the old woman's cloudy mind, invigorating her for the moment. Hardly knowing what she did, she got to her feet and slipped the sling she carried out from under her arm. She took out the pouch, shook out a stone, placed her rock in the sling pocket, and twirled the sling like an expert. There was a whistling sound as the sling built up velocity, and she sensed the precise moment to release. The rock flew, straight and true.

The ragged man dropped the bread in the alley and put a hand to his neatly wounded backside.

He turned back to face her. "OHHHH! You filthy crone, you—"

She fitted the sling with another stone. "Next one's for your head," she warned.

He was lurching into a clumsy charge. Then he saw the sling, saw her starting to whirl it, and the significance of her words sank in. He changed his mind. He reversed directions and lumbered away.

The old woman held her fire. There was no point in wasting a good stone on a bad target. Momentarily the man was outlined in the mouth of the alley by the morning light; then he was gone.

She waited until she was certain he was not coming back, possibly with a club or some other weapon. Then she hobbled over to the bread, picked it up, and examined it. Grease and filth clung now to every crusty side and soaked into the interior. The thing might as well have been a sponge, and it had landed in a foul puddle. No part of it was remotely edible anymore. She sighed, dropping it back.

She made her way to the stone she had hit him with and picked it up. Good hurling stones were valuable. She had learned something about herself: she was not defenseless. But that was all; her memory remained too confused to enable her to make sense of any more.

Somewhere, somehow, there had to be a bit of nourishment in this city for one poor and hungry old woman who didn't know whether she was coming or going.

CHAPTER 8
Flight

Merlain had been invigorated by the Alice Water, but now she was tired again. The mountain had proven to be farther away and higher than she had expected, and even shoulder-high trees were an impediment to swift travel. Especially when she had to carry three boys in her hands. She had gotten scratched, and had put her foot carelessly in a soggy stream, and tripped over a foothill—now she knew why they were named that!—but had made progress. She was approaching the top of the mountain. The trees had gotten shorter and the grass more normal on the slope.

Now she was almost at the crest, and her cupped hands felt more crowded than when she started. She realized that possibly when she shrank back to her normal size, it would not be all at once, but gradually; it might be happening already.

She forced her feet to carry her giant self and passengers the last few steps. It had been like a steep hill, and had she tried running, she knew she would be even more tired. She wanted desperately to see what lay beyond the mountain crest. She hoped it was not another great long distance to travel by their regular small feet, with giant spiders and who knew what else lurking along the way.

She peered over. There were rolling mountains and fog. Her heart sank. It seemed that the distance was much farther than she had thought. Kildee had said nothing at all about all the mountains between Dreadful Forrest and Heartbreak Mountain. Obvious *this* wasn't Heartbreak, though it almost broke her heart to realize it. Feeling dizzy, she bent and put the others down on normal grass. She knew that they all had a long way to travel.

What do we do now? Charles asked in her head. *Why did you stop?*

I think I'm shrinking. Do you want me to drop you? Think where we are and where you might land.

Charles looked from her hand down off the mountain for what was even for her an impressive depth. *You sure you're shrinking?*

I have to be. I'm dizzy.

I'm dizzy too. It's the height.

Trust Charles to argue! But if she was very careful, maybe she could get them off this mountain range and over another. Only how many bumps and hunks of ground and rock were there? The map showed somewhat more mountain ranges than forest. Could she cover that distance, even as she was now? It was starting again to look like a hopeless task.

One of the little kings was muttering something. With her head up here she couldn't quite hear.

Kildum says let's change into birds. Why don't we?

You saw why not!

That was down there. Here the sky is empty.

Yes, empty for now.

Kildom's got the book out. He's reading the spells.

She hesitated. She was really tired of walking. She wished she had the book but the book was now small. When she had enlarged herself, her clothing and her pack and the bottle had all enlarged as well. Magic did things like that;

it wasn't like what Grandfather Knight called science. Had she been holding the book, it would have grown with her. But she hadn't been holding it, and it hadn't grown. However, a kinglet could read it.

So did it make sense to invoke a bird spell now? It should certainly help them get where they were going, but the risk— suppose a big predator bird came swooping in, and they didn't have time to get out of the way or change back to children? But maybe they could change into big birds themselves, so that they could fight in that form if they had to. If the spell was right.

She decided to mind-snoop. No one would know and it couldn't be worse than stealing. She looked down at little Kildom reading, and—

He was reading the index. Birds: Bird Ordure, Bird Feathers, Bird Flight. *Bird Materialization! That it?*

Before she thought for herself, Merlain replied: *It is! It has to be!*

Merlain! That you? Kildom was looking at her.

Who else? I want to help.

You can't even read!

I can so! A little at least. You read for me.

Kildom read. It took time, but gradually the spell for bird materialization was in both their heads. There had to be a symbol marked on the ground with fresh blood. She hadn't known Helbah did that sort of magic, as blood was a characteristic mostly of evil spells. But if that was what it took to fly, they'd have to do it. The odd thing was that Auntie Jon hadn't needed any blood when she changed them to swooshes. So this was evidently something else. But it was what they had to work with.

You do it! Kildom ordered.

What?

Make the symbol. You are shrinking, I can tell. One drop of your blood will be as much as a cupful when you're shrunk. You can draw the symbol now, and then when you're the proper size, you can dance in it.

She didn't like doing it but what he suggested made sense.

She drew her dagger. She hated pricking herself because it hurt, but she knew she had to.

Taking the dagger, she placed its point against a thumb and pressed. The blade cut in, and blood oozed, and pain came. She suspected it didn't hurt as much as she thought it did; it was just that a deliberate injury was worse than a surprise one.

She used the blood to make the symbol, stood within its points, and dabbled blood on her forehead. She was now three times the height of Charles, which was pretty small compared to what she had been. She had to hurry.

The symbol she had drawn was now roomier. Carefully, hoping she was doing it correctly, she twirled as the book had directed and pronounced the magical words. She had never tried this sort of magic before, and it made her nervous. She feared that any little error she might make could have dire consequences.

POOF! Thunder?

Flop, flop, flop! From the sky.

"Bird!" Charles called, pointing.

"You expected a fish?" a kinglet asked sarcastically.

Merlain strained her eyes. It was a bird, a huge bird. As it flopped closer she saw that it wasn't really a bird but something closer to a dragon. It had feathered wings, a great scaly neck, and a head far more reptilian than any bird.

"No, she expected a monster," Charles said, not willing to let the royal pain get away with it. But he too was daunted by this apparition.

The thing opened its mouth and there were needlelike teeth that weren't at all birdlike. Great talons hung below the creature.

Now the naughty king had done it, Merlain thought. He had brought destruction to all of them. Or was it her fault? She had thought the spell was right, after all. Or could it be just accidental that this thing came flying overhead? Maybe the spell had failed, and this was just another predator coming to gobble them up. In that case, they were lucky the spell hadn't worked, because if they had been flying as birds, the dragon-bird would have caught them all.

But what about that clap of thunder she had heard? She just knew she had done the spell right! Yet none of them had turned into birds. Instead *this* had come. She was in a dither of confusion about what had really happened, and whose fault it might be.

Meanwhile, the monster was coming rapidly closer. It swerved and turned, cocking its head in their direction. Definitely it saw them.

The kinglets seemed ready to flee, but weren't sure where they could hide up here on the top of the mountain. So they stood petrified.

The monster descended. It circled them twice, thrice. Its great talons opened and closed as if uncomfortable being empty. It seemed about to pick up one of them on its next pass.

The two kinglets shouted something, then started down the too-steep mountain. One of them stumbled, of course, and tumbled. The other twin tumbled after. Merlain couldn't watch them; they would be bruised if not badly hurt, depending on how far they fell and where they landed.

Charles drew his sword. So far it hadn't helped any, but it did seem to give him confidence. He waved it and took a stance. Merlain winced. The teeth in the mouth of the monster were longer than his sword.

Stop! Stop, Bird! Don't hurt him! Merlain was startled by the desperation of the projected thought, before realizing that it was her own. It hadn't worked on the spider; why should it work on this new monster? Yet she was getting a notion, and if she were right—

The bird pulled back its wings, put its feet down, and came in on the narrow mountaintop in a rough landing. It flopped over, its head almost at Charles' feet.

Charles aimed the sword high, aiming for the eye of the creature. Their father had killed dragons that way, terrible man that he had been in the bad old days before Dragon Horace came on the scene.

No, Charles! No! Now it was to protect the dragon-bird she was projecting. *It's magic! I brought it! Think at it!*

Charles' blade wavered. He screwed up his face. She knew he was thinking. As if responding to his thought, the huge creature blinked an eye, once, twice, thrice. It was responding! She had been right!

Charles put away his sword. He walked over to the bird and scrambled upon its huge, scaly neck. The bird lifted its head, easily lifting Charles as well. It sat upright, its big, feathered wings folded at its sides.

"My brother—" One of the royal pains had suddenly shown his face. The sturdy clothing Helbah had gotten him had survived well, and the leather jerkin must have been especially effective in taking up much of the abrasion of his slides. He looked at Merlain with a pleading expression. Then he looked at the bird monster, and his jaw dropped.

"Not now, whoever you are," Merlain said. She was not at all sure the situation with the bird was under control yet.

"I'm Kildom, and my brother—"

The huge dragon-bird flopped its wings, raising a breeze that she felt and that almost blew Kildom off the mountain. It lifted up, Charles hanging on to the rough scales near the back of its head. It was carrying Charles—but was it under his control?

The bird flew, and circled. It flew overhead and to the side. Charles waved to them. Merlain waved back, relieved. Hesitantly Kildom waved as well, realizing that all was just maybe well.

"That's our steed," Merlain explained, as if she had always known. "It's magic. I brought it here for us to ride. No other predator birds will attack us when we're with this one!"

But Kildom had something else on his mind. "My brother—"

"What about your dumb old brother?" she snapped impatiently.

Kildom swallowed. "He needs help."

Disgusted, Merlain went to the very edge of the cliff with

him and looked where he was pointing. Kildee, very white-faced, was hanging with both hands to a small, insecurely rooted tree. Below Kildee's boots was a long drop to the start of Dreadful Forrest and the river she had crossed. If Kildee were to let go now, he would drop and roll almost back where she had grown big and started carrying them. Or so it seemed at the moment.

"Kildee, can't you pull yourself back?"

"No!" the kinglet gasped. "The roots are giving! HELP!"

What a bother! But Helbah would be angry if Merlain didn't save his royal butt. Merlain was still the size of a tall adult, and strong, even if she was tired.

She reached down to Kildom and grabbed him. "Hey!" he protested. "It's my brother who's falling, not me!"

"I know. Shut up." He struggled, but she lifted him over the cliff's edge, then changed her hands until she had him by the ankles. He screamed as she held him over his brother, thinking she was going to dump him.

"STOP! LET ME GO!" That was nonsensical at this stage, but no one had ever accused the kinglets of having much sense in any crisis.

"Oh, shut up! I'll swing you down and you grab his hands." She had see that she could not reach the stranded kinglet while retaining her balance; this was better.

."HURRY!" Kildee shouted. The roots had just pulled out more and bits of dirt were raining down on his face. Small clods fell all the way down, maybe to fall into the distant river. But if there were any splashes, they were too faint and far away to hear.

She swung Kildom down so that he could reach his brother. The brothers locked hands just as the tree let go. The tree fell, turning end over end. She felt sorry for it; it really hadn't deserved that fate.

Merlain felt herself reduced in size as the tree dwindled with distance. Oh no, no, no! She was just a little girl! She strained to hold on to Kildom's ankles, but her hands were now too small and too weak. She was slipping over the edge herself! She opened her mouth to scream.

THUMP!

That wasn't exactly the scream she had had in mind. Something was holding her. Something like a big, rough hand, crossing her shoulders and back and curling around the rest of her, terribly strong. She shut her eyes, hanging on to the kinglet.

Then Kildee was grasping her arms, having climbed up over his brother. A moment later both Kildee and Charles were prying her fingers from Kildom's ankles. With her watching, gasping for breath, they pulled the clumsy young king back onto the mountain and away from the drop.

Merlain let out a long sigh, flexing her cramped fingers. By turning her head slightly she saw the talon holding her. Charles must really have control of this thing!

Kildee screamed. He had evidently just realized that the pleated belly and the hanging feathers were parts of the flying creature he had sought to escape.

"Oh, shut up!" Merlain told him in as kind a manner as Auntie Jon's. "It's only a little bird!"

But Kildee had fainted at the end of his scream. Not to be outdone, Kildom rolled up his eyes and joined his brother in a heap.

Merlain dug her fingers into the grass and discovered that she was really pinned. That was lucky, for she might have slid over the edge, the combined weight of the two boys giving her no choice.

Charles, if you'll get this bird's foot off from me, we'll wake up the pains and continue our journey.

Charles tweaked the creature's strange scaled ear—something that certainly belonged on neither bird nor dragon!—and the great talon lifted. She slid out, got to her feet, straightened her dress, and found herself whole and uninjured.

A moment later she and Charles were doing something they had both dreamed of doing for years: slapping the kinglings' sleeping faces to get them awake.

* * *

"What are you doing, Grandma?"

The old woman blinked. The policeman—she knew he had to be one, because he was uniformed and had that manner about him—had flown up behind her so quietly that she had not seen him until he spoke. She had been trying to find something edible in a pail of garbage, hoping for another nice soiled loaf of bread but knowing that the one she had lost had been the only one in all the world.

"Hungry," she said. What use to explain that not only was she starving, she still had little or no memory of her life before yesterday, but thought she wasn't who she thought she was, so was almost as hungry for memory as for food? He would deem her crazy, and she wasn't sure he would be wrong.

"Hmmm, let me see your identification." He did not look like a *mean* policeman, but then one couldn't always tell. He might just be making sure she was helpless and of no consequence, before he satisfied his sadism. So she wouldn't tell him about the sling and stones, just in case.

"Identification?" she asked, perplexed. "You mean like a mole on my cheek, or—"

"Papers. Levitation license, unsocial insecurity number, credence card, pas-sport."

"I'm long past sport," she agreed ruefully. "I don't have any papers or cards or numbers."

The man nodded as if unsurprised. "No identification. You'll have to come with me to the station house. We can't have you wandering all over the city. There's a big convention with a lot of important tourists in town. We don't want to give a bad impression."

"But—" What *was* it she was almost trying to think of? That convention—

"We'll feed you there. We'll let you clean up and we'll get you some different clothes. We are not barbarians. You'll be all right, unless you have a criminal record."

"I don't have any record of anything!" she exclaimed.

"Oh, you have a record," he said grimly. *"Everyone* has

a record. We'll find it. The only question is whether it's a good record or a bad record.''

"You'll find it?" she asked, bemused and almost hopeful. "You can find out who I am, when I don't even remember?"

"We have ways."

She decided to shut up. Maybe going with the policeman wouldn't be such a bad idea. To get fed and clean again—how wonderful! Even if her record turned out to be bad. Yes, she would be satisfied to go with him to the station.

She started to tell the policeman this. But he had his baton unclipped from his belt, and was pointing it at her, and—

POOF! She was a bird. A pretty white dovgen whose feathers shone as if just washed. This was certainly an improvement on her prior form!

The policeman gazed down at her. "Well, Granny, I didn't expect you to look like this! Maybe you're an enchanted princess of the type the romances describe! Follow me, please." He didn't seem to be mocking her; he really seemed impressed. That almost jogged part of a memory. She wasn't a princess, but enchanted—could she be . . . ?

POOF! Now the policeman was a big, strong preybird resembling an eagawk. He took off, brown wings flapping. She followed: up over the roofs and the streets, so that she saw all the buildings and floating platforms and parks and the pattern of roads extending through the city like spiderwebs. At any other time she would have been fascinated. As it was, she was making a reasonable try for it. All those big squares of buildings, like blocks of blocks, and some round puddles she knew were lakes or reservoirs, laid out like the artifacts of a doll city. Then down to a large, boxlike building all by itself.

The policeman flew through an open window and lit before a large desk manned by a large policeman wearing sergeant's stripes. She flew in after him and landed on the floor at his side.

"Sarge," her rescuer said (at least she hoped he was that,

and not her captor), materializing from the preybird shape, "you aren't going to believe what I've got here."

The sarge lifted himself far enough off his chair to look down at her. "The centerfold from next month's *Police Enquirer,*" he said with irony.

"That's right! Feast your eyes!"

Another pointing of the baton, and—

POOF! Jon waved at the smoke, which quickly dissipated. She was standing before a desk manned by a man in an unfamiliar uniform. A younger, similarly uniformed man was staring at her with open mouth. Oh, joy—her memory and body were back! Only where had she been, if she had lost them? The last few hours were fogging out.

"My gods, Sarge, this *is* a centerfold!"

"So I see. Not dressed like one, though, is she?"

"Sarge, she was an old woman when I found her. An *ugly* old woman. Looked like one of those malignant witches we're always hearing about. She was going through garbage. Sarge, something isn't right!"

Jon felt she had to agree with him. She stank! Partially it was these filthy rags she had on. They were her own, but smelled like what that old woman had been wearing in the transporter terminal and later at the store. Jon realized that they had also taken a beating, and now her brownberry shirt had tears in it that were showing parts of her torso. The biggest tear was along the side, and the young policeman was staring at it, or into it, where her left breast was exposed. Now she understood his remark about a centerfold: those were reputed to be pictures showing similar flesh.

She tried to shift her posture to make the tears close up, without being obvious about it. She didn't know exactly how she had come to be in this state, but she didn't want to annoy these men if she didn't have to.

"She does look a bit bewildered," the sarge remarked.

What had happened to her? Where was Kelvin and their father and mother and Helbah and the children? And how could she get out of these stinking, tattered, exposive clothes without making a scene? No matter how she squirmed, those tears just seemed to gape wider.

"Sarge, do you think this is what it looks like?" the policeman asked, his eyes firmly focused on that rebellious rent in her shirt. Jon felt a flash of annoyance. Did he think it was artificial?

"We'll soon know, won't we?" Jon was alarmed, then realized that the sergeant did not have the same view of her shirt. It was only business on his mind. "Who are you, Miss?"

She swallowed. "I'm _Mrs_. Lester Crumb." She felt it important to make her married status quite clear. "I was on my way to a convention. We left the transporter station and went to a store and—" She paused, trying to piece together the significance of events which at the time had seemed inconsequential. That was anything but the case, she now knew.

"Yes?"

"There was this old woman—a real hag. She was dressed in dark clothes"

"That's it, Sarge!"

"Sounds like it." The desk sergeant gave the policeman a warning glance. "Miss, you claim to be here from another world. Are you registered at the hotel? Are there people there who know you?"

"I never got to the hotel," Jon said musingly, just discovering the sling and pouch of stones under her arm. That was reassuring! "I was going to try on a dress. I took it into the changing chamber, and that woman was there."

"That tears it, Sarge!" the policeman exclaimed. Jon wished he had not used that particular expression. She shifted her arm, trying to cover the tear. "She has to be—"

"Shaddup. Mrs. Crumb, is your husband at the hotel?"

"I doubt it." How she wished that he were! What had their stupid quarrel been about, anyway? She should have sweet-talked him into joining her, instead of getting mad so that he got his stubborn back up. "He didn't come with me.

He said he didn't want to be around witches, even good ones.''

"But you're here; how is that?"

"Guest of the guest of honor. I helped Helbah and my mother and brother when—"

"Helbah? You're with Helbah?"

"I—was." Obviously something awful had happened, and that old crone had been connected. But her mind was blank from the time she was in the changing chamber until now, except for some wisps of memories about being old and feeble, and garbage cans. How could such things relate to her?

"Sarge, this could be big!" The policeman's eyes were bugging again; she had forgotten to keep her arm tight against her side.

"I'm thinking that myself."

"Could be what we've always feared—Malignants infiltrating the convention."

"Could be."

"Now wait!" Jon protested. "I'm not malignant!"

"Of course not, Mrs. Crumb," the sergeant said quickly. "We are referring to witches. We suspect that the old woman you encountered, and who seems to have given you her form for a while, is such a person."

Oh. That certainly made sense.

"We'll have to send a Slap Team, and—" the policeman started excitedly.

"No. We'll just have to alert the Wizard Patrol that's already there."

"But Sarge, if there are Malignants, shouldn't we go in with everything we have?"

"And mop up innocent old women who have been enchanted to look like witches?" the sergeant responded with irritation. It was obvious that he had a better handle on this than the policeman did. "Mrs. Crumb, here, must have been enchanted, and her memory fogged so she couldn't protest. You want to smash folk like her?"

"No!" the policeman exclaimed. This time Jon had

moved her arm out of the way deliberately, to make sure he answered correctly. "I guess I wasn't thinking."

The sergeant nodded, having made his point. "Wouldn't want to disrupt the convention prematurely. Don't want any birds slipping through the net."

Jon listened, but hardly understood. Just so long as the sergeant knew what he was doing, as he seemed to. One thing she did understand was that she was hungry and needed a bath and clean clothing. But if there was a big mess at the convention, could it be her fault? Shouldn't she warn Helbah about the old woman, and try to help Helbah identify her? She touched her sling, and a memory came to her of using it to stone an evil old witch to unconsciousness; her brother and her mother and Helbah had taken it from there.

"Officer," Jon said, "may I see your baton?"

He seemed about to refuse. Then she moved her arm clear of her torn shirt again, and he changed his mind. Smiling, the young policeman handed it to her.

Jon studied it. Now, how had he done the changing? He had just pointed it, and—

POOF!

She had pointed it at herself. She flopped her wings and took off even before the smoke had cleared. Behind her she heard the sergeant's exclamation. "Grab her! Don't let her out! She's a material witness!"

"Some material," she heard the policeman mutter as he tried to grab the bird.

Then she was outside, climbing above the streets, into the pretty blue sky.

CHAPTER 9

Disruption

Kelvin walked briskly, almost naturally, by Heln's side. They had just left the children's suite, he realized. They must have seen Merlain and Charles, but oddly he couldn't remember. Things had been awhirl ever since they arrived, and sometimes he wondered whether it was all really happening. It was a good thing that nothing had gone wrong; he wouldn't have known how to cope!

"I suppose we'd best be getting ready," Heln said, sounding very much the wife. "Helbah says we'll have to go up on the stage with her after the banquet."

"Yes," Kelvin said, wondering what was happening to his mind. "When we're all to share in her award."

The chicuck was what John Knight called rubbery, and the salad was hardly garden fresh, but no one was there for the food. Nervously Kelvin sipped his wine and looked over at Jon. She had a triumphant, even smug expression. Was it just that she would be sharing Helbah's glory? His sister always had been strange, but since the purchase of her dress, she had seemed like another person.

John shoved his plate aside, having eaten everything. He must have an iron stomach! Everyone was finished, clean plate or not.

Plates and silverware and empty cups began rising from the table and drifting unaided back into the kitchen for washings. Waiters merely pointed fingers and their magic did the rest. Kelvin had found the frequency of magic a bit unsettling at first, but now he was getting used to its comforts. If things could be like this at home . . .

A speaker stood at the great clear table-sized crystal in the center of the stage and rested his palms on it. His voice was heard clearly throughout the immense auditorium. Crystals had many properties, the magical conveyance of sound being one.

The speaker told how Helbah had been a good and proper witch who had applied her craft judiciously in the service of benign mortals and humans. It was starting to make some sort of muddled sense to Kelvin when a convention wizard motioned them to the stage.

Kelvin soon found himself seated between his wife and his mother; on his mother's right sat his father, and on his wife's left was the stranger he tried to think was Jon. He felt guilty for doubting his sister, yet he did doubt.

The paean to Helbah was long, flowery, and nice. Then Helbah was at the crystal, her aged fingers on its surface. She cleared her throat, and somehow the crystal converted the sound into a loud, uncouth burp. People laughed, some of them nervously.

"I must apologize for that," Helbah said. She frowned, seeming as bewildered as Kelvin. People waited, and there was a feeling of tension before she began her formal address.

"Besotted witches and warlocks," Helbah said. She paused, clearly considering what she had said. "I mean, of course, reputed witches and warlocks. Eh, no, that's not right. I—" Her face flamed red.

Kelvin looked at his relatives. Jon was doing something with her fingers. Her expression had become fiendish. Her eyes spoke of anything but gentle fun. What was the matter with the girl?

"I'm sorry," Helbah said to the audience. "It must be the wine. Either that or a blather spell. Now I want all of you to know I deserve this great dishonor." No one laughed; people fidgeted with embarrassment. "I mean—you know. Zoanna, the rightful queen of Rud learned witchcraft late, but she learned from a master. She and her chosen consort, Rowforth, a strong king from another frame to replace the weakling Rufurt—"

What was she doing? How could she be saying these things?

"—were bringing stability to my home frame when I interfered. Together with my sniveling accomplices, the pitiful bunch sharing this stage with me, I—"

"Helbah," the toastmaster's words went clearly to the audience. "Something is wrong! You are not giving the speech you rehearsed."

That was hardly news at this point! But Helbah kept doggedly on, as if unable to stop.

"And we destroyed them. By luck and treachery, assuredly, rather than ability. Destroyed the magnificent beings who could have made our worthless frame a magical center of power! Destroyed them through trickery and deceit and the improper application of a chimaera's sting! We—"

"Helbah, *please!*" The toastmaster pulled at her arm. Helbah glared at him and threw him back with a magical shove that sent him all the way to the rear of the stage. There was a general gasp of shock.

"You are honoring the worst witch who ever lived," Helbah told the audience. "Instead of feting this ignorant bag of bones, you should be honoring sweet, gentle, beautiful Zoanna whom she has so treasonably slain." She gazed around the audience, her face grim. "And you should not be honoring roundears! Roundears are never magical in any frame! Roundears should be exterminated, especially *these* roundears. As for her helper and apprentice Charlain, that ludicrous excuse for a woman, she should be executed also. Anyone who helped Helbah should be destroyed, and—"

There was a great cracking sound, and Helbah fell sense-less onto the crystal top. The toastmaster at the far side of the stage was struggling to his feet as security wizards burst onto the stage from the wings. It was one of these, evi-dently, who had hit Helbah with some counterspell.

The audience was now on its collective feet. Many people were shouting. "Infiltrators!" someone called. "Abomi-nable Milignants wrecking our convention!"

Well, they had gotten that straight, Kelvin realized. Now the little oddities made sense. Except for the way his sister was acting. Jon seemed pleased rather than upset.

The toastmaster reached the crystal and lifted Helbah's face. Helbah's eyes opened. She looked, Kelvin thought, surprisingly angry.

"The spell has been dispersed now," the toastmaster said. "Now you can give your rightful speech."

"Who wants to," Helbah snapped, "with an infiltrator around?"

Kelvin wondered again about Jon and about the way all of them had been acting, and the peculiar way he still felt. He turned his head to look for his sister—and saw a vacant chair.

"I think," Helbah said clearly, "that we all know what has happened. I appreciate the honor that brought us here, but—"

SPLAT!

A large darkish something that smelled like what it was had dropped from above to land with unerring accuracy on Helbah's head. The dung splattered, spotting those on the stage and in the nearest rows. Immediately the security wiz-ards had their faces turned, staring up into the rafters above the stage. Something had to be up there!

At that moment there was a flutter of wings, and a great cloud of bats swooped down from the rafters and then out over the audience. Witches screamed and grabbed for their hairdos. Wizards and warlocks made passes with their hands. Someone finally made the right spell and the bats vanished.

"Just an illusion, folks," the head security wizard said. He made another pass of his hand, and the dung and stench were also gone.

Kelvin breathed a sigh. It was over, then. At least until they caught the one who was causing this disruption. Obviously Helbah still had a strong and talented enemy. But where was . . . ?

Jon came strolling out of the right-hand wing. She smiled sweetly and resumed her chair. "I had to go to the bathroom," she announced. "Did I miss anything?"

Kelvin wondered, and then as he started to realize that he wondered, he saw Jon's eyes. They seemed to light up yellow, and to blaze at him. This wasn't like Jon at all! What could be possessing her?

But then he lost track of whatever he had been thinking, and merely knew that his dear sister was with them and was safe. For a moment he had feared . . . but he wasn't even certain what he had feared and when.

"It's all right, miss," one of the security wizards said. He was smiling at Jon, seeing her revealing gown, bewitched by her beauty and "available" signs. Strange; Jon had never been a flirtatious girl or a woman who forgot she was a wife; she had shown her flesh only when she had some most specific reason to, and not much then. Now she seemed eager to show and promise. "A little disturbance that you're lucky to have missed."

"Only a little disturbance?" she inquired sweetly. "Back in the bathroom it sounded as if a war was starting."

"That won't happen, miss." The wizard remained fascinated by her heaving décolletage, as she evidently intended. "You're better protected here than anywhere."

"Oh, Officer, I hope so!" Jon batted her eyelashes and quivered her flesh in a way that was almost indecent and not at all like her. It was as if a stranger had usurped her skin, and—

"Yow!" Kelvin grabbed his head. The pain had been so quick and so lancing that he thought of nothing else. He had been thinking something, but that was something vaporous that dissipated as the agony abated.

"What's the matter?" the officer asked him, wrenching his eyes from Jon's body. Jon seemed to be going elsewhere, so that was possible for him to do now.

Kelvin shook his head, freeing it of the last vestiges of ache. "It was as if an ax was buried in—"

But now his skull did not hurt, and there was no blood where he touched. What had the officer been saying to him?

The wizard was gazing into his eyes. "You got hit with something just now, didn't you?"

Kelvin continued to feel his head. "I—"

"Don't worry. We have fine psychihealers here. They'll check you and the others."

Dazedly, Kelvin looked around. He saw Helbah standing as if to resume her speech.

Hit? Me? Maybe he had been. There had seemed to be an alien presence in his mind. But his headache threatened to return, and he found it easier not to think about the matter.

Helbah sighed and her eyes rolled up. She fell over onto the crystal, as she had before.

Then, as quickly as she had collapsed, she straightened up again. She stared at the audience with burning eyes, much like those of Jon a moment before. "You fools! You're dead! All of you are dead!"

"Quickly!" one of the security wizards said. Suddenly there were wizard batons extending from their arms, pointing, sizzling at the ends and glowing hot. They were making an obvious sweep, searching for the hurler of the malignant vibes. The batons pointed up into the rafters, into either wing, above and around the audience.

Meanwhile Helbah was pulling off her clothes. She ripped off her gown and her modest underclothes and stood there naked and gross. Her hands reached out, grabbed the arm-length golden broomstick trophy on its crystal pedestal, and aimed its rounded end at her own groin. Her arm muscles bunched.

"THIS IS FOR YOU, HELBAH!" Helbah cried in a voice totally unlike her own. "FOR YOU AND YOUR SILLY AWARD!"

A burst of magic energy from a baton froze the trophy and held the aged witch in her obscene posture. She stood there, a statue, award trophy held suspended at arm's length. Gently a security wizard took the award from her and put it back on the pedestal. Witches came up on stage and wrapped Helbah in a cloak designed for outer wear by a wizard. When Helbah was properly covered, the security wizard touched her on the forehead. There was a flash of blue light and Helbah was again Helbah.

"Oh, I'm so embarrassed!" Helbah said, and her voice was carried by the crystal so that everyone heard. "How could I have done this? How could I have let it happen?"

"You didn't let it happen, Helbah," the wizard told her. "You were magicked."

"Outmagicked." Helbah sighed. "But to say those things and know I was saying then, but not to be able to help myself! To stand here naked and—"

"Don't worry. We'll get the guilty party. We have to. The dignity of benign witches and warlocks everywhere has been insulted this night. We won't any of us dare to rest until all of us have been properly avenged."

Looking at the young wizard's grim face, Kelvin not only saw and heard the determination of the words, he felt them as if he were Helbah's son or brother.

They were waiting for her on the roof. When she had landed and did not immediately change, one of them walked over and changed her from her bird form. She was immediately Jon again and had the feeling as she looked at the stern wizard faces that she was in more trouble than she had been in at the police station.

"Ma'am, are you a guest here?"

"I'm with the convention. With Helbah."

The tall wizard seemed suspicious. "Then why is it you are not with her now?"

"It's a long story. I need to see someone in authority. There may be trouble."

"You wish to see someone in security?"

"Yes." What was security? she wondered.

The tall wizard said, "I'm security. He showed her a star that suddenly gleamed bright and golden in his hand. "We had a report you were coming."

"Who—"

"From headquarters. You left abruptly and were traced."

She might have known! But maybe it was just as well. These people were, after all, authority. They should help her destroy the evil witch, or at least see that she did no further·harm.

"I'll cooperate with the police," Jon said. "But—"

"Then you can appreciate that we need to keep you out of sight. There may be another who looks like you but isn't. There may be a malevolent infiltrator in the convention."

Oho! "That old woman—"

"Is whom we suspect." The wizard made a gesture.

POOF! Jon was a bird again. She raised her wings, determined to take off and find the witch on her own and deal with her, or at least to find Helbah. But the wizard was pointing at her, and she couldn't move; she was as frozen as she had been by the witch's gesture in the store. An ordinary person just couldn't compete with magic!

The tall wizard motioned to the short wizard. The short wizard picked her up in his hands, carried her a short distance, and placed her in a cage. He shut the cage door. She still could not move. She wanted to protest, but couldn't even squawk. So she waited.

He levitated her onto a platform identical to the one Helbah had driven but marked with a large glowing star. He got onto the platform at the front, seated himself, and activated the platform. The platform lifted vertically above the roof, then lowered until it was in a stream of traffic moving just above the street. After a few twists and turns they were at the station.

The wizard levitated her and the cage through the window and onto the sergeant's desk. Face fixed firmly ahead, she yet saw him as he drove off. The young policeman and the desk sergeant looked down into her cage.

Mercifully, the young policeman pointed his baton. She expected to become Jon again inside the cage, but she remained a dovgen. The only thing that was different was that now she could move. She opened and closed her beak.

"Sorry, Mrs. Crumb," the desk sergeant said. "For your own safety and the safety of others you are going to remain in our custody. As soon as you can be released, you will be."

The sergeant motioned to the young policeman, who looked disappointed that she hadn't been returned to her natural form, in the shirt with the tear under the arm. She was disappointed too; she had used that tear to escape once, and might have used it again.

The policeman picked up the cage. She watched his hands come around it; then the walls and desks flashed by. He was carrying her swiftly through the office and into an outer room. Here were bird cages like the one she occupied. Some had residents; most did not. He hung hers on a wire beside a cage containing a droopy, rough-feathered stargen. The stargen hiccuped at her.

"Mrs. Crumb, this is Loopey. He drank too much Happy Potion, as he does at every convention, every century. You can keep each other company until it's safe for you both to return."

He went out, leaving her with a sick-looking Loopey and her own scattered thoughts.

"Kelvin! Oh, Kelvin!" It was Jon, hurrying along the hotel corridor. Obviously something had gotten her excited, and he couldn't imagine what. It couldn't be the panels; all of these were dull enough to put a tree to sleep.

He wasn't actually anxious to meet with Jon. Every time

he thought about her too closely, he got a sudden splitting headache. It was safest not to think about her at all. But it seemed he couldn't avoid it now.

Come to think of it, he hadn't seen his sister at all since yesterday. Had he visited the children, even? He tried to think, but his thoughts were fuzzy. Hadn't he done *anything* but attend endless panels and move around from room to room looking for the others? Where were Helbah and his mother and father? They had eaten lunch together, and then somehow separated, each going a different way. As far as he knew.

"You look as if you've got connesia," Jon remarked.

Kelvin wiped his brow. "If you mean I'm losing track, right. What have you been up to?" He had to be polite, but he wanted to save his head from another mental ax chopping too. Would just talking to her set it off?

"Well, Kelvin, I met this simply adorable warlock with the biggest, reddest—"

"JON!" She had shocked him before, but this . . . !

"Cloak," she continued, unperturbed. "And we went to his room and—"

No, no, no! It couldn't be. Not his sister.

"Watched what was happening around the convention on his crystals. You don't need to run your legs off or attend things, you can just stay put."

Kelvin released half a sigh. No mischief, no headache. So far. But she remained in her too-revealing outfit, and she still seemed excited. That boded ill.

"So nice, just lying on the bed all day with someone pleasant and—"

He shuddered. He knew she wasn't talking with him just to pass the time.

"And watching things. Well, Kelvin, I hate to tell you this, but I think the children skipped out."

"What do you mean, skipped out?" Had Jon ever in her life chattered at him like this before? Face it, she just hadn't been herself since they'd arrived here.

The headache loomed. *But it didn't matter!* he thought desperately. The headache backed off.

"I mean they left the children's suite. Left the hotel."

Alarm of another nature surged. "How could that be? There are young witches and warlocks watching them all the time."

"Well, dearie, if you ask me, some of these young witches and warlocks get to watching each other. If you'd used a viewing crystal the way I did—"

"You mean you spied on them? Invaded their privacy?"

"They must subsist entirely on aphrodisiacs. When they're not birds mounting each other in the corners, they're planning on which room they'll visit. I tell you I haven't witnessed such passionate fumblings since—"

"Oh, shut up," he said, fed up. Jon had spoken crudely sometimes trying to sound grownup and equal when they were both young, but never like this.

"Why what's the matter, dearie? Don't you like hearing about it? Maybe if I tell you what the warlock and I were doing while we watched—"

"The children! The children!" he said.

"Oh, yes, they're gone. Not here in the hotel anymore. They've been gone since yesterday."

"WHAT? Why didn't you tell us?"

"I'm telling you now. Besides, you could have been watching them yourself, you know."

"But they'll get in trouble!"

"Probably. You know your brats."

He shook and trembled. Never had she called them that before. It was as if she were perfectly indifferent about what had happened. "Where can they be? What can they be doing?"

"Anything their little depraved minds can think of, dearie. They had invisibility cloaks. All four of them were using them, but then the warlock and I got a bit distracted."

"Invisibility?" he said stupidly. "Cloaks?"

"Oh, yes, they probably stole them from one of the guests. They were stealing everything in sight once they had the cloaks. The boys were pinching and touching women right and left, and the girl—''

Kelvin both did and did not want to hear about it. If this was what came of coming to conventions, he never wanted to attend another. Thank Mouvar they had only one a century! Why couldn't this—this person who looked like his sister—get to the point? Was she *trying* to torture him with worse and worse news?

The headache be damned! He had to think this through. Could it be that she *wasn't* his sister? Could it be . . . ?

He stiffened, anticipating the headache, and it did come, but its severity was only half what it had been the day before. The magic was wearing off.

Which meant that he had been enchanted, and that was a sure sign of other mischief. His head hurt, and he had to ease off on that line of thought, but at least he was starting to face the truth. His sister was somehow mixed up in this— or something had happened to her too, to make her act this way. That would explain a lot!

''Well, you know brats will be brats, and yours, dearie, are the brattiest. Except perhaps for the kinglets. They stole a book of spells and a book on the orc's opal and a sword. They went all around the dining room tasting desserts. They tripped people and started fights. Those little kings have a real talent for goosing pretty women! You should have heard the screams! Oh, they had just a wonderful time, and the best part of it was that they were clever enough to stay invisible and never get caught.''

Kelvin was sickened. ''I just can't—can't believe it.'' But he was starting to.

''Oh, now don't look so stricken. You would have done the same things when you were their age if you had been fortunate enough to steal a cloak.''

''My children do not steal,'' he said grimly. She was making him wish he had on his gauntlets; he almost thought they'd choke the life out of her as they had once choked an enemy who had been slowly killing her. But was this the same person? Was this Jon? His headache was diminishing, and as it did, his suspicion of her increased.

"Well, Kelvin, old witch's poop, they might not steal, but they certainly get sticky fingers. Not only that but they are oh so interested in life! They not only went into people's rooms, they watched while they bathed, eliminated, and copulated. Really, Kelvin, if you knew how precocious those brats are, you'd want to lose them fast!"

His hand flew out. It was almost as if it wore a magical gauntlet, though it did not. His right palm smacked her left cheek. Her head rocked to the side, then straightened to pierce him with blazing, hate-filled eyes. What had he done? What had he done? His sister!

"You'll pay for that, warlock's crap!" the Jon facing him hissed. Then there was a loud poof of air rushing inward, and where she had been there was now a bird.

This was a larger, uglier bird than he remembered her being before; certainly not the dovgen or the gawky swoosh. It took off, veering around conventioneers and skimming over their heads. It sailed down the hallway, around the bend, and out of his sight.

"What have I done?" he asked himself, horrified on several levels. "Oh, what have I done?"

Conventioneers looked at him oddly, some a bit pityingly; none of them spoke.

CHAPTER 10

Ophal

Kildom and Kildee were scared. All of them, including Charles, who would never admit he was scared, hung on tightly to tufts of great feathers where the scaly neck began. Down below, dizzyingly far, were spread out valleys, and in the distance were purple peaks. How long would it have taken them if they had had to walk this distance? Merlain wondered. She didn't think that they could have done it, even if she had remained a giant.

Now there was a town, actually more like a village. People were looking up. There was hair on the faces of these Rotterniks—much hair, almost like the creatures in the forest. They were curious, and could hardly be blamed for that.

Then a man wearing a helmet drew a bow.

Merlain screamed. She couldn't help it. But the arrow merely bounced off the scaled area under the great bird's ear. The bird tossed its head and hissed like a great annoyed snake. Merlain feared it would dive down at the man and eat him. She held on all the tighter to the feathers, anticipating that dizzying descent. But their carrier merely flapped on. Apparently a miss did not warrant retaliation, and they were already out of range.

Mountains, valleys, and mountains again. It was all quite scenic, for those who might actually enjoy that sort of thing. Merlain just wanted to get where they were going and get out of the sky so she could stop hanging on for dear life and rest. If there turned out to be any safe place to do that.

Then, quite suddenly, there were great patches of water, a swamp, with creatures great and small moving among big trees. The swamp thinned, the water patches broadened, vegetation became less dense, and trees seemed far behind. The great bird slowed, circled, and came in for a landing.

Oh no, Merlain thought. *I don't want us to land here. I don't!*

We have to! Charles responded. *We need to get the opal.*

Charles, I want to go home!

Tough titty, he responded. using one of the neat new expressions he had snooped from an irate conventioneer. *We go back without it and they'll skin us and eat us. Remember what Auntie Jon said.*

She shivered. Auntie Jon had changed so very much! She remembered those horrible pictures she had shown them: witches, some of whom resembled Helbah and others of whom were beautiful, dancing around a fire, skinning a child, feasting.

I didn't know they did it either, Charles thought to her. *But it's as our grandpa St. Helens said, seeing's believing.*

But we only saw the pictures! Auntie Jon might have been lying to us.

You know what our uncle Lester says, a witch is a witch is a witch is a witch.

He only says that to tease Auntie, she reminded him.

That's what our daddy says. You know how wrong Daddy can be.

Yes, but so can Granddaddy be. They don't call him St. Helens because he's never wrong.

No, because he has a temper. BOOM! Like a big, fire-

puking mountain in a land called the state of Washington.
He seemed to enjoy the description of the mythical mountain. Everyone knew that only dragons puked fire.

*There's no such place. Our other granddaddy made it
up.*

You sure?

*Nooooo. But Daddy always said that neither of our
granddaddies should be believed when they tell stories about
that place named Earth. No magic there at all! You just
can't believe that!*

No, but then Daddy tells some whoppers too, he thought
with a certain envy. *Like about how the chimaera aided our
birth. He says you look just like one of the chimaera's heads
and that you're named after it. I look a little like the other
human head. And there's Dragon Horace.*

*Whom Mommy doesn't admit exists. Yes, yes, I know all
that. But still—*

*Did you ever look into Daddy's mind when he told that
story?*

No, not after he told us he could tell, she admitted. *Besides, both he and Mommy said not to.*

*I went in when he told us that story, Merlain. It's true.
We are different.*

Different because we can go into people's heads?

*Yes, and maybe in other ways too. We're smarter than
others. Smarter than the royal pains, at least.*

She knew it was true, but this wasn't the time to discuss
it. They were coming in to land on what seemed a very
large lily pad. The great bird dropped gently, folding its
wings, and they were there.

The wide green surface, like a carpet, bounced a bit, and
water lapped its far edges, though once down she discovered that the edge was farther away than she could see. An
insect the size of an ordinary bird took off. She hoped it
wasn't a weltquito; they were bad enough in tiny size.

First Merlain, then Charles, and then the two pains together slid down the feathery slope, coming to rest on the
pad. They stepped away from the bird, and the bird took

off again. Merlain was not quite at ease about that; how would they get away from here once they had the opal? But it was a bit late to do anything about the bird. Maybe they could summon it again later, with another spell from the book.

They watched it climb into the sky, its wings beating heavily and creating a breeze that threatened to blow them down. Merlain was glad that she didn't have a hat; she would have lost it. Charles clung to his helmet with both hands. The pains, most fortunately, had left their royal crowns back at the convention so they would not get lost. Of course now the kinglets might get lost instead!

"What do we do now, Merlain?" one of the royal pains asked her. Though nominally kings, both now looked to her for guidance. That was the consequence of her having a little magic, while all they had was the power of life and death over people. Of course Charles had magic too, but Merlain was more assertive.

"Orc's castle is supposed to be on a small island in deep water surrounded by rocks and waves," she said, "It's south, I think, and not too far from here."

"Turn us into swooshes, then," the brat king demanded.

She glared at him. "You know I can't. I'd have to be Helbah. Or Auntie Jon. We'll have to walk."

"On water?" the pain asked nastily.

He had a point, unfortunately. Well, there was the Alice Water, but she feared to take more of that except in a dire emergency. The witch who owned it would be angry with her for taking it. Even if they got Helbah the opal, there were others they would have to face. Why had they stolen things just because Auntie Jon told them it was fun? How could they ever have thought anything like that was fun?

"She can make herself into a giant and carry us," the other pain suggested.

"Good thinking, Kildee," his brother said. Then, to Merlain: "As royal sovereigns of Klingland and Kance and effective rulers of the Confederation we command you!"

She would like to command *them!* But there was probably

no help for it. Maybe when they got back, Helbah could help them get more Alice Water to replace what she used. Or maybe they'd find some in the orc's castle.

She held the bottle up and shook it. When she had seen Charles in the clutches of the spider, she had been distracted, being scared, and might have gulped too much. She might have spilled a few drops too, though she hoped she hadn't. The level of the liquid was significantly down.

There was no use putting it off. She opened her mouth, tilted the bottle up, and let a tiny bit trickle down onto her tongue. Phew, that tasted bad! Worse than before.

Without warning, her feet broke through the green surface. Water, wet and cold, gripped her ankles. Her legs and hips were wet and her new purple skirt—

"HELP! Merlain, help us!"

Bothersome kids! But there they were, clinging to the green platter that had folded up around the edges. The kings rolled their eyes up at her and even Charles looked scared.

She stoppered the bottle and put it carefully away in her pack. Then she reached down to them.

"Me first!" cried one of the kings.

"No, me, I command it!" cried the other.

Annoyed, she was tempted to duck them both with a flick of her finger. But at that moment Charles disappeared, leaving a trail of bubbles.

Help, Merlain! It's got me!

She reached down into the water, quickly, without thinking about it. Charles grabbed her fingers. Each of her fingers was now at least the length of their arms. She lifted him up and out, and there, dangling from him, holding on to a foot, was a creature like a kittyfish. Only this fish didn't have whiskers around its big mouth, but tentacles, three of which were wrapped around Charles' ankle.

Carefully she unwound the tentacles with her left hand. Then, shaking an enormous finger at the creature, she said, "Bad fishie!"

Merlain, get rid of it!

Oh, very well! She flicked a finger and sent the tadwog

flying tail over head. It lit with a splash that raised a small wave and promptly swam off. The wave in the meantime was threatening the edge of the pad where the two kings were. She grabbed again, and then she had all three of her companions right in her palm.

Take us out of here, Merlain, before that drink wears off!

You sound like Grandpa St. Helens!

I don't sound like anything! I'm thinking at you! GO!

She knew he was right. She tended to get overconfident when she was big. Maybe that accounted for the way adults were. She hadn't taken nearly as much Alice Water this time, and knew how quickly it wore off. It was funny, though, to have Charles sounding in her mind like St. Helens. It had been at their parents' anniversary party that she had last heard the man say, "Now before we drink our toast I have to tell you that you have to find an excuse to invade Ophal, Rotternik, or even Throod. You've got the prophecy to consider, Kelvin, and none of us are getting younger."

Merlain! What are you doing? Don't just stand here! Move!

Charles, you want me to throw you back to that fish?

Carefully she raised her left foot and found vines holding it. She'd have to be careful or she'd trip up and go down holding her companions. She wouldn't get hurt in this shallow water, but she could get her dress dirty and they could get drowned. She smiled to herself; of course it was more important to save them from drowning than to keep her dress clean! But it was easy to lose track when they were so small and her dress was so big.

She bent down and reached underwater with her free hand to feel along her leg. Her right foot was snagged on something. She grasped a vine that was anchored fast to the bottom. She pulled it out without difficulty and tossed it away.

MERLAIN!

I have to walk, don't I? Charles thought she was just playing, but she wasn't. If she tripped and fell, it would be one awful crash!

Walk she did, splashing step-by-step. She picked the shallow places to step, and though her feet wanted to sink into the mud, she pulled them free and went on. The water didn't seem so cold, now that she was used to it. In some ways it reminded her of the time when she and Charles had gone wading in the creek. Dragon Horace had splashed after them and herded them some fish. That had been fun, and even Mama's getting mad at them hadn't spoiled the day. Dragon Horace had eaten most of the fish himself, but they did have some. Charles had pretended they had caught the fish on hooks and lines, and Auntie Jon—so different then— had pretended to believe him.

Merlain! Watch where you're going!

Without thinking, she had veered off her course into water that was for her waist-deep. Her passengers were clutching her fingers, looking down into the water at fish that were longer than the children were. From up here, her head almost scraping the sky, she could see farther than they could, and she spied boats with sails on them in the distance. Should she splash over to those boats and ask the boatmen directions? She was going in the right direction, she believed, but where was that castle?

You know we'll have to get our cloaks of invisibility when we enter the castle, Charles thought. *We won't dare risk being seen.*

So Auntie told us.

Don't you believe her, Merlain?

Of course I do. But did she? Did she really? She wasn't certain she believed anything Auntie Jon had said to them. Auntie had told them that taking things from the rooms would be fun, and that everyone stole. Merlain knew she wasn't right about that. Her father had never stolen anything, and she knew their mother hadn't. Just why had Auntie Jon told them that everything they had been told before was wrong was right? And if she was wrong about stealing—and Merlain was pretty sure about that—maybe then stealing the opal would be wrong.

And if that were wrong, what were they doing here?

Maybe they should just turn back now, and admit what they had done, and take their medicine. The could return the things they had stolen and—

But how could she return the missing Alice Water? She knew she couldn't. So she would have to go on, and hope she found a way to replace it.

Merlain, there's a sign!

Where? She didn't see any.

On that tree.

Tree? She didn't see any trees. Oh—those knee-high shrubs sticking their tops up out of the water.

She bent low and somehow dunked her burdened hand. Charles and the royal pains were sputtering as she raised them above the surface. Now and then being of great size had its problems. Now she saw the sign, but it was too small to be intelligible, though it didn't seem to have many regular words on it. *You read me the sign, Charles.*

You keep me dry! he retorted. Apparently he didn't like having his clothing soaked much better than she did. *It's just an arrow sign. Points toward the sunset and says—* There was a pause while he consulted with a kinglet, who could read the actual text. *"Orc's Castle, Thirty Milli-miles."*

What's a millimile?

I don't know. I'll ask the pains.

Charles asked. They answered. She tried but couldn't hear their faint piping voices. Charles' mind talk came in as strong as usual; apparently that wasn't affected by size.

They say it's a day's march for an army, Merlain. I don't know if they know or not. But you'd better get us there before the magic wears off.

Don't fuss. If it wears off, I'll just take some more. But should she? There was not a lot of Alice Water in the bottle, and she had already taken about half of it. She might need all there was left to get them away from here after they got the opal.

But if she didn't take any more, she could shrink and

they would be caught in deep water. That wasn't any good—not with these mean fish and other monsters around.

Then there was the sun: it was heading down toward dusk. When it went all the way down, it would take away their daylight. How could she hope to find a dark old castle then?

The more she considered their situation, the less she liked it. But what was there to do, except plow on?

Ahead, she couldn't see too well, but she thought it might be the island. She strained her eyes, and then she thought of how the royal pains claimed to have good eyesight. She held up her hand with her brother and the pains on it and commanded that they look ahead and tell her what they saw.

"That's it!" one of the kinglets piped in his shrill little voice. "That's the island with the castle!"

"He's right!" his brother echoed. "I see it too!"

I don't see anything, Charles grumbled in her mind. *But maybe they do.*

She brought her hand down to a more comfortable level and cupped it up against the bodice of her dress. She didn't want to drop anyone. She didn't like it that the royal pains could see better than she could, even in giant form, but then they couldn't read others' thoughts or mind-communicate. That was a comfort.

She forged ahead, going as fast as she could without stumbling, swinging her free hand wildly to keep her balance. The motion might make her passengers seasick, but she wanted to get where she was going before darkness or shrinkage stopped her.

After she had splashed a fair way, she began to see a hazy lump in the distance. Then she saw something moving on the water—something almost the same size as herself.

She lifted her hand again, carefully holding her other hand ready in case someone fell. She was about to ask, but the pains were ahead of her.

"ORCS! Swimming! Get down, Merlain, before they see you!"

She squatted uncomfortably, further wetting and dirtying her dress. At home this wouldn't have bothered her, but here there was no one to clean it for her. She wondered what she should do. Then she chided herself again for her foolishness: a soiled dress wasn't as important as their lives!

Now is the time, Merlain! Charles thought urgently. *Use your cloak!*

Hastily she did as he suggested. She brought out her cloak of invisibility and covered all her head and body and her handful of boys. But he could still see her legs. The bottom of the enlarged cloak wasn't sinking under the water. Well, this way she could at least see her feet and where they were going. Unless those orcs got really close, they wouldn't be able to see her at all. Her task was to keep away from them. And to keep herself and the boys from drowning.

Let's go right to the castle. While you're still big.

Very sensible of Charles, though she thought she might have thought of it herself. She was really getting worried about the Alice Water running out before they were done with all this. She splashed determinedly ahead. Then she thought about the orcs and the pictures of them she had seen, and that made her think she really shouldn't splash.

Hold us up. The pains can watch out for orcs better.

She lifted them up under her cloak and held her hand cupped. She had now to make certain nothing came uncovered, that she didn't drop anyone, and that she didn't splash. Life was becoming more and more difficult. She realized that size wasn't everything.

"Keep going, Merlain," a kinglet said. "There's no orcs close, now."

"None of them see you, Merlain," the other added.

The pains had their uses, she guessed. She slid one foot ahead of the other—and stepped right off an underwater ledge.

She struggled to keep her balance and almost went down. She could feel the pains and her brother holding on to her fingers. She made only a little splash and got them only a little wet.

"They see us!"

"No, Kildom, they saw the splash!"

"Move carefully, Merlain. Better yet, don't move. Wait until they turn away."

She waited, worrying again about the state of the Alice Water and how much longer her present dose of it would last. She was getting what her mother would call a fixation on that bottle! But with good reason. If she became small now, they'd drown here or be caught and probably eaten by those terrible orcs.

"Now, Merlain, but don't splash."

She moved one foot and then another. The bottom seemed slippery here, not at all the way it had been. She did not trust it at all. She was almost as afraid of falling down as she was of the orcs.

The water got deeper suddenly, and the boys bigger. It was up to her waist. Was she shrinking, or was the water deeper here? Each possibility seemed worse than the other! Either way, they were going to get dunked.

"Hurry, Merlain, hurry! You're shrinking!"

She knew that she was. She should have had no confusion: with the boys getting bigger, it had to be shrinkage, not the water. She moved faster, and the water continued to rise as she shrank down into it. It came up around her neck.

She held the others high in her two hands, though they were now overlapping them and getting heavy. She took three more steps; then all four of them were in the water together.

She could see the castle on the island. It seemed far away. Very far. She was too tired to swim well; she could never get there.

She took a breath, swallowed water, and sank beneath the heaving surface.

CHAPTER 11
Zady

"And she couldn't have known where they went if they were invisible," he finished the story for Helbah some time later. "Magical crystal or not, she couldn't have followed them."

"Oh, I quite agree," Helbah said thoughtfully. "That definitely isn't Jon. It couldn't be her, even with a spell on."

"What is it, then? A look-alike from another frame?"

"Hardly, though barely possibly. I'd say more like an impostor achieved through an identity exchange. Of course these things are never perfect, but—"

"Can *you* save her, Helbah?" Charlain demanded.

"Oh yes, yes, of course if she's not—" Helbah hesitated, then finished it. "Destroyed."

There was a pause of silence in their hotel room which Kelvin found painful. After he had found Helbah and Heln and his father, they had come straight here at Helbah's suggestion. She suspected something, he thought, but he wasn't certain what.

"Helbah, could this be an enemy of yours?" Charlain asked her. She was holding on to her husband's hand, her expression and voice earnest; it was, after all, her child and grandchildren.

"Undoubtedly," Helbah said. "If not an enemy of mine, an enemy of goodness."

"Can't you do anything?" John asked. "I mean now. So that we don't have to wait for the next attack."

"Of course. Just give Helbah time. We have the best practitioners of magic here at the convention. Certainly there are enough of us to deal with one of the evil kind. We are no longer ignorant of what is happening."

"One?" Kelvin asked.

"Possibly. Almost certainly. But one of the evil kind can be quite a challenge."

"Aren't there authorities?" John asked. Then, explaining what he meant for Helbah's benefit: "Police. Those trained to deal with bad witches and the like?"

Helbah didn't answer. She positioned one of the three crystals on a stand, passed her hand over and around it, and started it swirling inside. A man wearing a light blue uniform sat at a desk.

"Sergeant," Helbah said to the image. "This is Helbah at the convention. What news of Mrs. Crumb?"

"Safe. In custody as you urged."

In custody? Kelvin jumped. They must have acted immediately, for it wasn't that long since he had been talking with her. No, wait—that had been the fake Jon.

"May we see her?"

"You may."

Helbah directed the crystal vision with motions of her fingers. Seemingly they drifted down a corridor to a large room filled with bird cages. Many of the birds were very ugly, but there was one that wasn't: a white dovgen.

"Jon!" Kelvin breathed, for even in bird form he recognized her. She was sulking in her cage, her back turned on the tipsy spargen in the next cage. Just looking at them, he could tell that the two birds had little in common.

"May I speak to her?" Kelvin asked.

"You may." Helbah made some motions and nodded her head.

"Jon, this is Kelvin," Kelvin said.

The white dovgen straighted up, hearing and recognizing his voice. Several of the other prisoners fluttered; evidently the sound carried to them too.

"We know you're there, Jon, and we'll come to rescue you," Kelvin continued. "But first we have to find whoever has been impersonating you. It shouldn't take much doing. There're witches and warlocks and sorcerers all through the hotel. No one wants an evil person here. No good person does, I mean."

The bird opened and closed its beak as if it wanted to speak. But Jon had not yet learned how to speak while in this form. The bird looked frustrated.

"Please be patient, Jon," Heln said at his side. "We know you've been through much and it's not your fault or ours. Whoever the malignant agent is, she's used a variety of spells."

The bird agitated its wings and made a head motion of violent pecking.

"Yes, I know you'd like to get out and deal with her yourself," Kelvin said, understanding his sister's mannerisms despite the form change. "But that's no good, Jon. First, she's a really powerful evil witch; she would use magic on you and destroy you before you managed to pull out the first hank of hair. Second, we would not be able to tell the two of you apart, and our good witches would be as likely to bash you as her. So you're safer right where you are, Sister Wart, until they are through bashing your likeness."

The bird relaxed. It was evidently beginning to make sense to her, despite her extreme annoyance.

"We'll singe her feathers proper," Mother Charlain promised. "We'll get you back again, and the grandchildren."

The bird froze in place. Kelvin could almost hear his sister's thought: *The children are missing?*

"Not to mention the two kings," John Knight added. "Your impostor did something with all four children."

The white dovgen squawked.

"Oh, no, we don't think she's hurt them," Charlain said quickly. "But they're missing. Tell her, Helbah."

Helbah explained in soothing tones exactly what had happened and how they had gradually learned how things were amiss. She omitted certain embarrassing details, understandably. "It's certainly a Malignant doing this, Jon, and one who has strength. We want to do more than just expel her from the convention. We want to punish her."

The dovgen clicked its beak as if it were a preybird.

"Yes, yes, I know you'd like to tear into her," Helbah said. "Possibly we'll need your help before we're done, but for now you can help most by staying where you are. You'll be safe here in custody, and as Kelvin said, it would otherwise be too easy to confuse you with your impostor. She won't keep us confused with her spells forever. You'll be released soon, I promise you."

The bird did not look fully satisfied. That was Jon, certainly! Helbah waved a hand, and the crystal went blank and was again simply a many-faceted piece of quartz.

"What do you think she's up to, Helbah?" Kelvin wanted to know. He was tiring rapidly of sitting in the hotel room watching undercover police wizards move about the convention. There was no pattern to anything that he could define. The authorities were simply searching, now and then questioning someone and showing them, with a careful wave of a baton, Jon's image. They were, as near as he could see, getting nowhere.

"I think she's here, hiding, laughing at us," Helbah said. "She doesn't have to remain in Jon's form, or in any form at all; she could be invisible."

"How very astute of you, Helbah," a whispery voice said in the room. Katbah, perched on Helbah's chair arm, instantly raised his back fur and spat.

"Yes, Katbah, yes, it's the wicked witch Zady," Helbah said. "You tried to warn us when she impersonated Jon." She spoke with seeming satisfaction, as if she had long sensed the enemy's presence.

"And you know me too, don't you, Helbah?" the voice answered. "How very, very perceptive of you, dear."

Even Kelvin bridled at the enemy witch's irony. But he was sensible enough to keep his mouth shut, as were the others. Nobody with any sense messed in with a witch's quarrel.

"I knew you'd be after revenge sooner or later," Helbah said evenly. "I expected you to wait six years for the convention so as to make a bigger splash. You have not disappointed me."

"Then you prepared for me?" Zady asked, her tone suggesting her derision.

"Of course." With one quick motion Helbah threw the handful of powder she had kept concealed. It flew to the spot at which Katbah was staring.

An ugly old hag materialized, chilling the blood and terrifying the soul with her warty countenance and malignant expression. They all stared.

"Hello, Zady," Helbah said calmly.

"You—you cheated!" the apparition screeched. "You had that powder ready! You threw it where the familiar was looking!"

"Where else? I told you I was prepared."

"That was supposed to be a bluff!" the hag screeched, outraged. Then she straightened. "Well, counter this!" One hand moved.

Kelvin knew that witches had fast reflexes, no matter how haggard they might look. But a cat's were faster, especially when it was a witch's familiar. Katbah leaped with outstretched claws, and sank them into Zady's bony hand before she could complete her gesture.

The old witch shrieked more with indignation than pain, and clubbed at Katbah with her free hand.

Now Helbah glanced at the men. "Muscle," she murmured.

Propelled by her word, Kelvin and his father each grabbed one of Zady's arms. She was astonishingly strong, and for a moment Kelvin thought he'd need his gauntlets. Then Helbah tripped Zady with a stabbing kick to an ankle. The evil witch went over and down on the floor, with Kelvin and his father on top of her.

Whew, but did she stink! Kelvin fought as hard to hold his breath as to hold her pinned. Katbah was on her face, menacing her eyes. Even so, it was no sure thing.

"I'll get you for this, Helbah, you sneak!"

"Sticks and stones—"

Kelvin heard them enter the room. He couldn't look, being preoccupied with the witch. He heard the door open and the thump of their feet. He hoped they were on the right side and not the wrong side.

"Get the net over her!" ordered one of the undercover sorcerer police. "Careful now, she's got a million tricks and we don't want her to get away."

The police deployed the net. "You'll have to tell us about the children," Helbah said as Katbah got out of the way.

"I do, do I?" The hag cackled despite her exertions. "They're with Devale. He's going to do things to them that will make them Malignants."

Kelvin experienced a shock of horror. His wonderful twin children—evil creatures?

But Helbah wasn't fooled. "I know better than that. You always lie, Zady."

"Sticks and stones will break your bones—"

The woman became a great serpent as Kelvin and his father helped the police to cover her with a net. He strained to keep her pinned. To keep *it* pinned. The net slid over, worked by other hands, but it seemed that the serpent would simply writhe out from under it.

"The snake's an illusion, son," one of the cops said.

Kelvin was relieved. He had had quite enough of big serpents in past adventures, though witches were bad enough.

Now the snake was gone and in its place was a big, ugly bird with saw teeth. He new a buzvald when he saw one, but he knew this one for illusion. So when it made a peck for his arm, he ignored it, confident that it couldn't actually hurt him. Why block a phantom beak?

Instant agony ballooned and exploded with the snap of

the beak. The terrible bird, all too real, had taken a good-sized bite from his heroic young arm. The witch wasn't limited to illusion!

Katbah grabbed the bird by its warty neck and held on. His orange eyes lifted in his dark feline face, looking to Helbah. "Not yet, Katbah," Helbah said. "First we must make her talk."

The bird emitted a hilarious cackling. How could they make her talk?

Then she changed again. Now she was a voluptuous red-haired young woman. Kelvin was holding on to one sleek slender arm, his nose nudging one extraordinary breast. She was naked, and her beauty was spoiled only by the ugly cat whose teeth were digging cruelly into the white column of her neck. On the other side John Knight was grabbing her other arm, as if such a delicate limb could ever cause harm to even one man.

The eyes came to rest on Kelvin. "What is it that you do to me?" the red lips inquired softly, chiding him.

Suddenly Kelvin felt guilty. It was virtual rape—that was what they were doing to this lovely creature!

"Let me go, O handsome man, and I will be most grateful," the beautiful woman said. She moved her legs, which remained free. They were bare and perfect, from their dainty tinted toenails to the dark shadow of their juncture. Abruptly he wanted to tear off his own clothes and—

"Suffer yourself not to be deceived," Helbah said. "Whatever form she may assume, either physically or in illusion, her nature is unchanged. She is old and evil inside, and without scruples. Whether she caresses you or bites you is a matter of indifference to her, just so long as it is effective in accomplishing her purpose."

Kelvin thought of embracing that inviting body, and trusting part of his body to that tempting crevice—and getting it bitten in the manner his arm had been. His foolish interest dissipated.

With that change of his interest, the woman's attitude changed too. "Fool!" her beautiful face said—and became the ugly beak of the bird. The torso and legs returned to the buzvald form. "You could have had it all, and your children safe too," the beak squawked.

It was hard not to believe that, despite his knowledge of her real body and personality. He was a married man, and he loved his wife, but had he been faced with this temptation when alone—he just wasn't sure what he would have done.

Somehow the five of them—Kelvin, his father, and three undercover officers—got the net over, under, and around the ugly bird. The other officers materialized with a large cage. They maneuvered the witch/buzvald into the cage and locked it. The lock made a satisfyingly loud snap.

The luscious young woman reappeared, staring straight at Kelvin. "If you should change your mind, handsome man, you will know where to find me," she said.

No one else paid attention. Apparently this was an illusion for him alone. He knew it wasn't real, in substance or essence. Yet the sight of those perfect legs, and those perfect breasts, and that perfect face, and the luxuriant red hair flowing out and down and around like a voluminous cloak—made his knees feel weak and his heart flutter. She had had centuries of experience; she knew better than any other how to please a man. And she would; he believed it now. She did not depend entirely on magic; she captivated men by giving them what they most desired, in full measure. He *knew*.

He tried to close his eyes, but her gaze held him locked. His very soul seemed in thrall.

Then someone threw an opaque cover over the cage, and it stopped. The witch could no longer ensorcel him with her eyes. The spell was broken. He was free—yet somehow he was grieving.

Kelvin struggled to his feet. He felt dizzy and his arm hurt. He had felt no pain while the witch's gaze held him, but it returned with a vengeance now. Blood dripped from his wound to the carpeting.

The police were already levitating the covered cage with the witch prisoner in it out of the room. One of them turned and spoke to Kelvin. "We'll send her right back to you."

"We don't want her!" he protested. Yet on another level he did, guilty as he felt for realizing it.

"He means your sister," Helbah explained.

Oh. Of course. "Thanks."

"I'll have to fix that arm," Helbah continued. "She may have poisoned you. Witch's saliva can send an ordinary person into hallucinations or worse. Katbah too; he's sick from biting her. Officers, be quick and careful!"

Hallucinations . . .

"We will, Helbah," an officer was saying.

"And be certain the bird you release is really Kelvin's sister!" Then, to Kelvin: "Don't worry about it. They really know their business. Now, about that wound—"

Kelvin was all too ready for a magical healing. He probably needed more than physical repair. Soon the policemen were gone, and Katbah was licking a great saucer of charmed cream with a bit of magical dognip seasoning. Kelvin wondered whether the houcat had suffered any similar visions, perhaps of the softest and prettiest female cat, who purred to him invitingly and suggested tempting things.

Katbah raised his eyes and met Kelvin's gaze for just a moment. Then Kelvin knew that they were indeed brothers in hallucination. But the cat had known better than to yield to it.

"We have to find out, Helbah," Kelvin pleaded. He stared at his family's witch benefactress with all the earnestness of his being. He tried to suppress the notion that he was being even more concerned than usual because of guilt about almost being seduced by Zady's vision. Now that his sister was really back—and now that he knew it had been Zady instead of her, he understood much better about the way she had been exposing her flesh—he was wondering despite himself if any of them should trust Helbah. True, the grand old witch loved them and they loved her, but she had brought them here knowing there was danger.

"Of course we do, Kelvin," Helbah smiled, confident again now that her arch enemy was in custody. "But remember it's not so easy. Zady is a trickster and at least as powerful as a Malignant as I am as a Benign. She put up counter- and recounter-spells to make it impossible to follow their tracks.''

Kelvin now knew from personal experience just how tricky Zady could be! Of course she had fixed things so that even her own captivity would not undo all her mischief.

"Try again, Helbah," Heln urged. "They're our children!"

"Please," Charlain echoed.

"Oh, very well, since you're all insisting. I'll try just a little more nullity powder this time."

Helbah shook some purple powder over the square crystal. She made some passes and said some words. The crystal flashed, flushed, and held a scene.

"Merlain, Charles, Kildom, and Kildee," she announced. It was the children's suite. Zady in Jon's image was giving them the cloaks of invisibility.

Kelvin glanced sidelong at his sister. He would not have been surprised to see Jon appalled or furious. Instead she seemed mostly curious and intrigued. Apparently the outfit Zady had put on her was giving the real Jon some ideas. Perhaps she was seeing herself as she could be, if she chose to be, and was not entirely turned off.

Now they followed the invisible adventures of the children. They saw them take food from people's plates. Saw them take drinks that were intended for adult witches and warlocks. Saw the Jon likeness whispering, making passes, spilling more of a powder. Now they were tripping people, pinching, kicking, and slapping exposed adult rears. The two kinglets seemed to take great pleasure in seeing which of them could evoke the shrillest screech from a firmly goosed woman.

"Inhibition release," Helbah murmured, watching. "A component of the powder. Certain mischief for children."

Now the children, still invisible, were entering rooms, tittering and giggling. They were alarming people, scaring them, starting fights. At room after room the Jon fakery remained just outside the door. Zady was making sure that the children misbehaved!

Kelvin trembled. All that he had discovered was that his

children—his and Heln's—were monsters. So maybe Zady had put something in the powder to help them along; it still wouldn't have worked if that mischief hadn't been inside them, waiting to be released. He couldn't even blame the kings, for he had seen Merlain and Charles' hands emerge from invisibility as often as theirs. He had watched helplessly while he knew they were watching people bathe and eliminate and perform very private actions. He had heard Merlain titter while adults in the crystal were engaged in lovemaking. How could he and Heln have produced them? How could he even think of wanting them back?

Yet what were they doing, other than satisfying their curiosity about the very kind of thing Zady had just used her young illusion to tempt him with? Heln had been right with him, yet that fascination had taken him. If his children were to blame, what about himself, for passing on his fickle nature to them? So he was answering his own question: he knew how he had produced such children.

"We're getting to the place," his sister whispered. She seemed quite subdued for Jon, possibly because she had been an old hag and then a bird and finally a prisoner. She had had a rough night and day! At any rate, she was right: it was the spot.

The young kings' hands reached out of nothingness in the hawker's room and took books: first a big leather-bound volume and then another. Charles' hand took a sword from a storeroom of some guest exhibit. Merlain's hand emerged again to take a bottle from some lady witch's dresser.

Kelvin shook all over. He couldn't stand dishonesty. It made him sick to see his children practicing thievery.

"How can they do such things?" Heln demanded.

"All of us have mischievous desires," Helbah replied. "The process of growing up is to learn to curb those desires, and to behave in civilized fashion. The twin kings are more of a handful than most, and at times I despair of ever straightening them out. In this case, Zady saw to it that they would have very little restraint, because of her magic. So they are being normal, given the situation. It doesn't mean that they're bad children, just that they have temporarily lost their guidelines. They will straighten out again when returned to a proper environment.''

Heln looked relieved. Kelvin knew he was.

Now they were back at the children's suite and Zady in her guise of Jon was explaining something to them, meanwhile making passes and sprinkling powders behind their backs and over their heads. Now it was obvious how much control Zady had had. It was here that the spying had ended, before; the scene had simply stuck.

Zady as Jon was looking fiendishly right at them from the crystal. It was as if she had anticipated their replaying of this scene, and catching her here. Her hand sprinkled a sparkling powder over the children's heads, and as the powder settled, all movement ceased.

Jon/Zady grinned at the crystal, resuming her natural appearance. She must have wanted them to get this far so she could laugh at them!

Helbah dropped some powders on the crystal. She mumbled words and made passes. The scene remained the same. Zady's gap-toothed grin was neatly framed: a portrait.

"What will we do!" Heln cried. "Helbah, you have to—"

"It won't work," Helbah said. "Even a linkup of power won't help. It isn't a matter of energy—it's magic of a different kind. She prepared for this investigation of ours, just as I prepared for my meeting with her.''

"And you're helpless before it, Helbah?" Heln was incredulous. "You can't do anything to counter it?''

"Not this particular spell," Helbah said. "Had I known it was coming, I might have interfered with it as it was invoked. I'm afraid, friends, that there's nothing at all I can do to make the crystal follow the children beyond this point.''

"Then you can't do anything?" Kelvin demanded, still feeling guilty, as if it were his fault for being bemused by the vision of the luscious redhead. "Nothing at all to locate the children?''

"Nothing that I know of," Helbah confessed.

CHAPTER 12

Castle

Merlain was going down for the third time, which she knew as the final one (all the storybooks agreed on that) when she felt something grab her hair. She held on to the invisibility cloak, fearful that it would be swept away. Then she gulped water and choked and—

She was lying on stones almost under a great rock which towered above her. She was on her stomach and someone was pressing hard on her back. She choked and spat out water, and then she vomited.

"You all right, Merlain?" one of the royal pains asked. He was sitting astride her backside, and his weight was squashing her bottom uncomfortably when he wasn't putting weight on his hands. That made him a royal pain in the rear: she finally understood what that saying meant.

"Get off me, pain!" she gasped.

"What?" he asked, sitting heavier.

"Thank you so much for helping me," she gritted. "Now will you please let me get up?"

"Oh." He got off her, evidently understanding her second statement better than her first.

She turned over, sat up, and gasped. Her new dress was ruined. Her pack lay be her side, and—where was the invisibility cloak? She must have lost it! The thought made her want to cry. She started to raise a hand to her eyes and realized there was something she couldn't see wrapped around her fingers and arm.

"I still have the cloak," she said, relieved.

"Of course you do," said the pain. "I wouldn't have rescued you without it. I could see most of you but not your hand and arm."

"Oh. My broth—"

The pain pointed. The other kinglet was astride her brother's back, pushing down on his shoulders. For a moment she thought he was hurting Charles, but then Charles opened his eyes, choked, and vomited water and the food he had eaten way back in Rotternik. Goodness but he was sick!

Then she tasted the bile in her own mouth, and knew exactly how he felt.

She got to her feet, feeling very weak and wobbly herself. She took one step toward Charles, wondering how it was that the orcs had not spotted them. It was cool on this side of the island, and the sun was going down and making large shadows of the rocks. The kinglets had done well to haul them here, much as she hated to admit it. The pains were good for very little, but they could see well and they were, it had turned out, better swimmers than Charles and Merlain. They had known what to do, and had done it. She and her brother probably owed their lives to the kinglets. What disgrace!

Charles, are you all right?

No, I'm drowned! he thought, sick and disgusted. *They saved us, the pains! Now I can't get back at them! I can't feed them to an orc as I intended!*

Don't worry about it, she soothed, gratified that he felt

exactly the same about it as she did. *They did save us. Now maybe you can save all of us.*

How? He had picked up her underlying sympathy for/and irritation with the kinglets, and was mollified.

How do I know? Men are the heroes, aren't they? That's what you always tried to tell me.

The castle. The orcs. The opal.

Right. We have to hurry before they catch us.

The cloaks.

I've got mine. Proudly she swished it over her shoulders and saw herself disappear. Now they would enter the castle unnoticed.

In a moment they were all four invisible. Hand in hand, using the technique they had practiced at the convention, they moved around the rocks on their way to the castle.

At first they saw no orcs. Then they saw several. They were big, all right, almost as big as she had been. One of them carried a basket of flopping fish through a giant doorway while two younger orcs scampered among the rocks, chasing each other. One of the orcs ran so close to her that Merlain feared he'd run into her. Seeing that it was a boy who probably deserved it, she stuck out her foot and tripped him. He fell with a crash, then got up, unharmed, and said words which sounded so villainous that they had to be an orc curse. She did not understand the language, but the tone was a guaranteed wash-your-mouth-with-soap-naughty-child.

"Which doorway?" one of the pains whispered.

She was about to reply when the pain's brother whispered, "This one. Has to be the servants' entrance."

Kings would know about such things, she thought, annoyed that the pains now seemed in charge. She followed her invisible hand and the pain's invisible grip on it. Slowly, very slowly so as not to alert the big, gilled creatures doing kitchen work, they crept through the kitchen and into a large room with tables and chairs. A dining room, she thought, and look at the size of everything! There were stairs going upward, and each step was so high that they would need to boost each other up each step. She did hope they weren't going to have to climb the stairs.

"The opal is supposed to be in the throne room," Charles whispered. "I read that in the book."

With a kinglet's help, she knew. But what did that matter, so long as the information was correct?

"It has to be the big room ahead," whispered one of the royal rescuers. "This room should adjoin it. Kings like to eat a lot."

"You should know," whispered back his brother.

"SHHH." Merlain shushed them louder than she had intended. If an orc did not hear them, it might hear her.

A servant was walking their way, carrying a mop and a bucket of soapy water. It was a female, though with orcs it was hard to tell. This one had on a skintight garment that was more swimming suit than dress. Merlain wondered whether it was considered a sexy outfit by orc standards. It certainly wasn't by human standards.

The female set down the bucket, scratched herself, and wrung out the mop. She looked down, looked hard, then bent until her face was just above the floor. She went "HISSS," and her finny crest erected on her bobbin-shaped head.

Oh-oh, she sees our tracks! What'll we do, Charles?

Keep calm. She doesn't know what she's looking at. Charles' foot shot out as hers had a short time before. It kicked the top of the bucket, and with a full leg stroke tipped it over on the floor. Water and suds splashed and flowed everywhere.

Charles, that was stupid!

As if proving her right, the orc woman was calling out something in a great hissing voice. It was no language Merlain had heard, except possibly the one the child had cursed in. In response to the servant's calls other servants came from the kitchen and down the stairs. The woman was waving her mop, gesturing at the overturned pail and the spreading water and suds. Merlain had some sympathy; it really wasn't the female's fault.

Let's get the opal fast! Charles thought. *That distraction won't hold them long.* Fortunately neither of the pains emitted a whisper; there was no telling how sharp an orc's hearing was.

They moved at a fast shuffle across the parquet floor with its interlaid blocks of stone, and into the throne room. There was the throne, even bigger than Merlain had anticipated. There was the opal, as beautiful as she had imagined, sitting all by itself in a velvet-lined case to the right of the throne.

The opal was the size of a small viewing crystal back at the convention. Remarkable colors were dancing in the huge gem, pulling at her attention: blue, green, bluish green, greenish blue, sky, water, watersky, skywater, sunrise, noon, and sunset. Sparkle, sparkle, sparkle, sparkle. Depths, depths, depths.

"And now that you've seen it, perhaps you will explain how you happen to be here?" The voice, so loud, so unexpected, so harsh, in a room otherwise much like a shrine, made all four of them jump.

Merlain looked up to see a great gilled throat and flaring green nostrils. As she did, she realized that neither she nor the boys were now invisible. This great orc, whatever it was, had done something that had changed their cloaks to transparent coverings.

Auntie Jon hadn't told them this would happen, Merlain realized with a certain developing bitterness. Auntie Jon hadn't really told them anything.

The large, brutal-seeming face was that of the orc in the stolen book: Brudalous, king of Ophal.

Charles drove his small sword hard into the stomach of an orc who was just his size, made a hard slicing motion, and watched the guts coming out. The warrior's fish eyes rolled up. "You win, Charles!" he gasped, and vanished.

In the orc's place was a large crimson flower. In Charles' hand there was now not a sword but another hand—a girl's.

As he looked on the small hand where the handle of his sword had been, Charles saw the outline of a young girl in a nightdress. Gradually she took shape and form, glowing in the manner of a fragrant candle.

"Glow!" Charles said, thrilled. "It's been so long! I thought I'd never see you again."

She smiled at him. She spoke, using her voice now. "You were wrong. It has been only two days."

"Can we play in the fields and woods as we did before?" How could he have forgotten her? He loved her! Now she was back, and everything was returning, all the wonderful memories.

"Yes, Charles." Abruptly she was running and hiding in tall grass, and he was eagerly running after her. As before—when had that been, anyway; she said two days, but they had been on this quest for the orc's opal all that time—she kept just out of reach. Now and then his fingers would touch her long, soft hair, and then she'd be on farther without him. She was teasing him, and he loved it!

Finally, a long, happy day having passed in what seemed also like a moment, they lay side by side on a pinkish bed of moss. He held her hand, and sissy or not, he felt happy.

"Charles, you've been doing great wrong."

"Playing with you?" How could that be? She was the rightest thing he had ever encountered.

"No, my love. In your waking life."

He was surprised, but not completely. "This is a dream?"

"You know it is, and always has been."

"You mean you're my dream girl?"

She laughed. "In my way, yes. But the evil you are doing is no dream, Charles."

He thought that over. It seemed to him that maybe she was right and that he had known it for a long time. Yet he didn't see that he could help himself.

"Why, Glow?"

"Don't you know why you do wrong? An evil person has misled you in your waking life. You must not let her. Don't do her bidding, Charles. If you do, you will never dream of me again."

Even in his dream, that hurt. He wanted to see Glow

again and again and again. In fact, he never wanted to leave her. He had never understood why adults made such a big thing of love, but now he was getting a solid idea. To be with her forever, like this: love.

Why was she saying this? He had to know, had to understand, so that he wouldn't lose her.

"Don't you want to play with me, Glow? Ever again?"

"I can't, Charles. Not if you do evil. I cannot abide evil."

He thought of the orcs and Merlain and the pains in their prison with him. He knew he'd have to wake. He didn't want to do that. He wanted to be with Glow and dream of her always. The thought of anything else was too painful to bear.

"What must I do?" he asked. "How can I make it right?"

"I'll try to tell you, Charles. You and your sister and the two kings. But you must not do evil, you must not, ever again."

"I won't," he whispered. But even as he whispered, he was waking up. There around him were the orcs' castle walls, and there was Merlain crying, and one of the kinglets comforting her.

He sat up, breathing deeply of salt-scented air. That had been so real, so magical. He could love that little girl, love her even when the two of them grew up. He *did* love her!

But already he was forgetting. He was able to cling to only one thing, the only thing that would ever bring her back:

DO NO EVIL.

CHAPTER 13

Castle Break

Merlain was crying. She just couldn't help herself. It was partly Charles' beautiful sad dream, that she was forgetting almost as fast as he was, leaving her with a sense of appalling loss. But it was mostly their present situation.

Here they were, the four of them, shut in this ugly, dank cell that smelled of the sea. Three boys, no privacy at all, and no real excuse for a bathroom. At least the dream girl had privacy!

"Don't cry, Merlain," one of the kinglets said. He was reaching out one of his royal, very dirty hands to her, reminding her of how she herself looked, how they all looked.

"I—I can't help it." She choked, almost as upset at being comforted by a pain as by the rest of it. The sob she tried to swallow hurt.

"They didn't take our things," the kinglet said reassuringly. "Brudalous only took our cloaks and then called those fish faces to take us to this tower. They didn't ask for our packs. Charles still has his sword. You have the Alice Water. My brother has the spelling book."

"Yes, but I'm still afraid." What, after all, could they hope to do? The orcs were almost as big as she had been as a giant. The cell they were in stretched for a long distance in both directions, being scaled for orc prisoners, and it was in a tower. The ceiling was far, far overhead. Suppose she did make herself big, could she fight Brudalous and all the fish faces?

He's got a point about that spelling book, Charles thought to her, recovering from his grief because he had forgotten it. *Why didn't they take our magic things?*

Because they don't realize that we have other magic, she responded.

So we can use another spell! It's a great book.

Yes, but I'm afraid of it.

What for? It got us out of the mountains in Rotternik and into Ophal.

Yes, and now we're locked up! It's just like the dungeon the royal pains put us in, only bigger and aboveground.

At least no one here fed us laxaberries.

She sniffed, wiping her nose. Charles was trying to make her feel good, and maybe it was working. He had forgotten his dream, while she hadn't quite, maybe because the enchantment made him forget itself, while her memory was of him experiencing his dream, and the forgetting didn't apply to her so well because she wasn't the one being enchanted. That thought confused her so much that she lost it.

She had actually been afraid of the gruel that had been brought, but she had been so hungry that she'd eaten it. Now it was much later, after each of them had excused himself or herself—actually she had excused herself twice—and gone to the dark corners for relief. She didn't know what Brudalous intended, but she knew they had to leave. If they could get out, she didn't even want the old opal! All she wanted was home.

"Take a look in the book," Charles suggested to Kildom. "I don't think the orcs realize we can do magic. Maybe they don't know that magic can come from books." That was her realization he was taking credit for, but she let it pass.

She watched them, not liking it. It wasn't that it was evil—*do no evil!*—for the books were really neutral, not evil. But they were dangerous. Under Kildom's directions she'd done a spell to turn her and them into swooshes, the way Helbah and then Auntie Jon had done. She'd done just what Kildom and the book had told her, and what had happened? Somehow they had called up a big and powerful bird! If Charles hadn't done things to its mind, she thought it might have eaten them. The magic in that book could turn either way, and they might not be quick enough to make it work for them, next time. Maybe adult witches with centuries of experience had nothing to fear from such powerful spells, but they were children.

"Well?" Charles prompted her.

But what else was there? Certainly they did not want to be left to the horrible mercies of the orcs!

She hated even touching the book, with its feel like baby skin and the ugly pictures of monsters in it. But as Charles had just reminded her, it had saved them once. She took the book from Kildom, opened it, and wondered what to look for.

"See if there's a spell to break out of cells," the second pain suggested, coming back from the corner.

No, Charles urged in her head. *Make me into a powerful swordsman, the way Daddy is supposed to be.*

That's with his gauntlets, Merlain reminded him. *His Mouvar gauntlets. Without them, he's just a klutz.* A lovable one, of course, but a klutz.

So find a spell for my sword. Or have that bird bring me gauntlets as magical as Dad's.

I can't do everything, Merlain complained. *I can't even read very well.*

So get the pains to read for you. You did before.

Yes, but I don't want that bird.

Then get something else. Get anything else. We have to get out of here!

Again, he had a point, though she was annoyed by his impatience. Merlain clenched her jaw and handled the book. She flipped pages, looking for something not too bad. If the orcs discovered them with the book, and caught on why, they would surely take it. If she was going to perform magic, she'd have to do it now.

Ugly picture followed ugly picture. Her stomach turned. She just couldn't believe witches would do such things. Not good witches. That was, of course, the key: this book was not intended for good witches.

"Use the index, Merlain," one of the kinglets suggested.

Index? Oh, yes, that listing in the back. She'd tried looking up a spell for bird and look what she'd gotten! She flipped to the index, and both pains helped her. They were as eager to get out of this cell as she was.

In the index they read: "Break: body, control, desire, home, imprisonment." Merlain winced at the early listings, having a faint ugly notion of their significance.

"That's it! It has to be!" Kildom said. "Turn to that page and we'll read that spell."

"To break someone's body?" Charles asked, frowning.

"To break our imprisonment, dummy!"

Merlain turned the pages, distracting them before they could work up a boyish quarrel. Somehow it seemed that no matter what the subject, the page number was always 666. That's where they'd found the bird spell. Now, book again in hand, she was on that same page, but the spell number and subject were entirely different. What good the index was, when the page numbers were all the same, she wasn't sure, but it did seem to have helped her find her place. Maybe the index made the page of whatever was looked up in it change to page 666.

She read. "Symbol drawn in blood." Well, she could make herself big and prick her finger, as before, but then it would take a while for her to get small. She had to be inside the symbol's lines to work the spell. She wasn't sure how much time they would have before the orcs came to eat them.

"Can we help, Merlain?" Kildee asked in her ear.

Could they? Yes, she supposed they could. If Charles were to cut one of them with his sword . . .

Forget it, Merlain. We owe them our lives.

But—

Make one of them big. Let him cut himself and bleed big drops of blood.

An excellent idea, if an orc didn't catch them at it. She explained what she wanted. At first the kings were appalled at the notion of shedding royal blood, but then they started daring each other and calling each other chickling, and in a moment they were matching fingers to see who would have the privilege of making the donation.

Kildom won. Soon he was taking a precious sip of Alice Water, while Merlain worried yet again because of the diminishing supply. Now it was over half gone; they had less big time remaining than they had used before. "Give me back the bottle!" Merlain cried. "I have to stopper it again!" But she was too late.

Almost instantly the little pain was a big pain, very big, his head almost touching the ceiling. As with Merlain, all his clothes and the Alice Water bottle he held had also grown. That was the way of magic: it made sense only on its own terms. At least he had heard her plea about the bottle, and was putting the huge stopper back in it.

"I'm big!" Kildom boomed down. "I'm not afraid of orcs now. Let 'em come! I'll—"

"Your blood, Kildom!" his brother called up. "Hurry, before you learn just how strong you'll have to be!"

Charles held up his sword by its handle, and two big fingers took it from his hand. It was hardly more than a pin to the giant, but maybe it would cut him as well as her own dagger had cut Merlain.

"Why do I have to do this? I can just break us out! I can knock down some walls and—"

"And the orcs will be all over you," Kildee said. It was amazing how reasonable he seemed to have become by *not* getting large. "You know they've got giant weapons and how strong they are reputed to be. Besides, if they can change frames with the opal and nullify invisibility cloaks—"

"Oh all right." Kildom stuck his pinky with the—to him—needle-sized sword. Drops of blood rained down, big drops. One drop fell on Kildee and soaked his filthy clothes right through. Another drop almost hit Merlain, but she had had sense enough to be alert for this, and stepped out of the way just in time.

"Ouch!" Kildom boomed in a voice that surely roused the entire orc castle. Then, sounding surprised even in his deep voice, "That hurt!"

"You expected it maybe to feel like Helbah's kiss?" Kildee called up sarcastically.

Kildom started to laugh. "Yes, that's exactly what it felt like!" In a moment they were both laughing, with huge ho-ho-ho's and shrill hee-hee-hee's.

"Quickly now," Charles said impatiently. "We have to get through this spell before the orcs get their cooking pot hot!" That sobered both kinglets rather suddenly.

With Kildom's big help they drew the lines around Merlain's feet. Quickly she dipped her fingers in the fresh blood and transferred some of it to her face. A half-moon drawn on either cheek, and horn-type marks on her forehead.

She spoke the words. She didn't have to look at the open book. Somehow they just came to her. Witchcraft got easier to do, not harder. She had a deep-rooted queasy feeling about that, but there was no time to think about it now. Just so long as she used magic only for a good cause.

Something happened. There was a trembling that shook the entire room. It was as if the island itself were shaking. Merlain wondered if it were, or if that was only part of an illusion.

CRRRRRRAAAAAACCCCCKK!

Merlain looked up to see a band of daylight widening above their heads. The band ran all the way down a wall and was becoming wider.

CRRRRRRAAAAAAK!

Now the floor widened at her very feet. There was a gap there, a terrible gap that went down through the floors below. She could not see to the bottom of it; it seemed to have none. It reminded her of the fabulous Flaw, the crack between worlds. That made her feel a bit dizzy.

"Kildom!" she called up. "Get us out of here!"

Kildom walked the two big steps for him to the huge door. For him it was now an ordinary door in a playhouse, and he a tall adult. He reached down, placed his hand against the wood, and shoved. The hinges and lock snapped and the door exploded outward.

There was the hallway beyond, the stair landing, and the stairs. But a great tear was running through them all, sagging the carpet down into the crack. The fissure was getting worse!

Kildom hesitated. Well he might! Merlain knew that everything would soon collapse about them, and that they would never make it down those stairs. Throughout the castle orcs were running, screaming, calling to each other, and in general being properly disorganized. Many orcs were departing as fast as they could run.

Kildom turned from the doorway. If he was surprised by his great strength, he had no chance to exclaim about it. The castle tower was coming apart in two halves, precisely in the middle, with fracture lines radiating to either side. There was the major split that cut off the stair landing, and a minor crack that crossed their cell. The center of the whole business seemed to be right in their area. Merlain thought that might be just because they couldn't see the rest of the breakage, but more likely it was because it was their spell that was responsible. The magic in the spelling book was horrendously powerful!

Kildom looked out the small window. He could reach it now, far over Merlain's head. He reached out a hand and pushed, and the window exploded outward. With quick hands he broke away large sections of masonry. Now there was a hole big enough for him to go through, but below was that awful drop and the lapping dark waves of an angry sea. She'd be angry too, if the ground around her were cracking up and messing up her system!

"Kildom," Merlain started to tell him, "you can't—"

To her great horror Kildom unstoppered the now-grown bottle of Alice water, held it to his lips, and tilted it up.

"NOOOOOO!" Merlain screamed, fearing the loss of the last of that invaluable elixir. The absolute fool!

Then something grotesquely big, huge, and monstrous was coming down and picking her up. A drained-white Charles and a pallid Kildee were beside her on something far too big to be Kildom's palm. She closed her eyes and felt a lifting, and then a flying, and then a tummy-tickling drop. Water was splashing down below, far below, and then she felt a shock that went all through her.

She opened her eyes to see both boys flat on the bumpy, hilly surface they shared with her. Water was still below them, but not nearly so far below as it had been. Overhead white clouds floated, in a perfect blue sky.

CRRRRRAAAAAACK!

Kildom, impossibly huge, stood in water that was waist-deep for him. He stood uneasily, buffeted by the tiny waves. His head was between them and the clouds. The hand they were on was above the water at a height several times as great as Merlain had been able to carry them. Fingers the size of tree trunks were bent protectively over them. To Kildom, Merlain thought, they were now the size of flies.

"Look at that!" Charles said, pointing.

Merlain shook and rubbed seawater from her eyes. Above them, not nearly as far as she had imagined, was the cliff and the castle, and—

The split and fallen sides of its tower.

She cried out, and then she shook all over as she had never shaken before. What had they done? What had the magic done? What had she done? The orcs would be angry, with a certain justice. Brudalous would want a war!

They might have found a spell to make them all very small so that they could have crept out through the normal crevices of the castle and reverted to normal size once they had escaped undetected. They might have found a spell to make the walls porous to their bodies so they could walk through them and go home. There might have been plenty of ways for them to escape without making any fuss. But what had they done instead?

They had broken imprisonment. Through evil magic they had not just found a way out; they had broken the very walls that had held them confined. In the process they had practically guaranteed calamitous trouble between the orcs and the human folk.

Merlain shivered. How she wished they had never gotten into any of this hideous misadventure!

CHAPTER 14

Little Fish

Merlain hardly could see Kildom's head in the clouds. Only magic could do this. Her grandfather John Knight would have pronounced it scientifically impossible. And it was, she guessed. But in the meantime she lay on pores the size of her hands, in skin that now resembled some substance nearer to Dragon Horace's unscaled hide.

In back of them was the collapsed tower, burying with it all the hope they had of getting the opal and not creating a disaster. Orcs, big orcs, though now far below, were lining up with bows on the island. The orcs had drawn their bows full length. They were well within arrow range. Those arrows might seem small to the giant Kildom, but they would sting his hide something awful. Then he would roar and maybe drop his passengers. Merlain didn't want to watch, but was morbidly fascinated. Now the orcs were releasing their arrows.

Big tree-sized fingers curled protectively over her and the two boys on the outstretched hand. She felt a sense of motion and then lifting. After that she heard something like a strong wind. Was a storm coming up? She had not seen any clouds.

The platform of flesh lowered, the fingers unclenched, and there was the island and the ruined tower. The castle roof was now gone, and its broken windows were sad, open eye sockets. Orcs were scattered all over the island, and some were in the sea. Some orcs were unmoving, but a few were shaking fists in a rather humanlike gesture.

What had happened? There was still no sign of a storm, yet she had heard the terrible wind.

Kildom stuck down a finger. He poked it into a window, then withdrew it, cracking stone. The walls shivered and fell, stone upon stone. He inhaled hugely, pursed his monstrous lips, and blew down a terrible blast. His breath alone completed the castle's destruction.

The surviving orcs stood in the dust of the fallen castle, facing it. Where the castle had been there was now only a pile of rocks.

Oh, Kildom, what have you done! What have you done! Merlain thought in anguish.

He blew the orcs down! Charles thought gleefully. *Windy, ain't he!*

Oh, Charles, must you make jokes, even now?

It's true. He did blow on them!

Do you think you could reach his mind? Get in it, as you did with that big bird?

Huh, you know I can't. The bird was receptive; your magic had summoned it. It was waiting for traveling orders. But Kildom is just a dumb king. He's not waiting for anyone's orders.

You tried?

Yes. He doesn't block the way Auntie Jon did. I can get his thoughts but I can't influence them.

Merlain had to try herself. It was strange. Kildom's thoughts were Kildom's thoughts, recognizable as an individual's voice, but now larger. It hurt her head just receiving him.

MISSED EYES. WOULDN'T HAVE HURT ANYWAY. I'M

TOO BIG. NOTHING CAN HURT ME. BUT TINY LITTLE ARROWS MAKE ME ITCH. I DON'T LIKE THAT. MAYBE I CAN SLAP SOME MUD OVER THEM AND RUB THEM OUT?

"Kildom, watch what you're doing!" Merlain called out. But she knew there was no chance of his hearing. He was intoxicated with the power of hugeness.

Kildee grasped her hands, terrified. She held him. "It's all right. Your brother's going to get mud."

A hand the size of a ship's sail swept past her vision to the island. It dug into the solid ground as if it really were soft mud, then lifted a gigantic load of dirt and rock. The hand dipped into the ocean and squished there, raising huge bubbles. Kildom's great face flew down. The hand, dripping rivers of newly made mud, smudged carefully all around the neck and cheeks and ears. To Merlain's real horror, arrows of an unusual size dripped down from that mountainous face and those fingers, and fell the long distance into the waves far below. He really had gotten hit by those arrows!

Kildom straightened up. *I FEEL BETTER NOW,* he thought. *LET'S SEE, WHAT DO I WANT TO DO?*

Take us home! Merlain thought at him fiercely. *Take us home this instant!*

I WONDER IF I'M TALLER THAN THE DEEPEST PART OF THE OCEAN? I WONDER WHERE THE ORCS' UNDERWATER CITY IS? I'D LIKE TO SEE THEIR CITY WHILE I'M HERE. I WONDER IF I CAN BREATHE WATER?

"What's he thinking?" Kildee asked. His face was still white, and he hadn't stopped holding on to her, she noticed.

Merlain swallowed. "He thinks he wants to go wading in the ocean. He thinks he wants to see if he can breathe water."

Kildee's face became swiftly a very red shade, to match his newly dirtied hair. "Kildom, you dummy! Take us away from here!"

There was no indication that the giant heard. Instead there was a sucking noise as a gargantuan foot lifted and the sea rushed in to take its place. The giant lifted a second foot—splash!—and then the first again.

Merlain peered down. Below, it was like an incredible storm, as each foot disturbed the ocean. Kildom was walking, carrying them away from the island, away from any hope of rescue when he returned to normal size. And how soon would that be? She had no experience with Alice Water gulped on top of Alice Water!

Fog rolled in, soon surrounding them like a blanket. Still the giant splashed on, seeming happy and carefree in his explorations. Oh, the arrogance and carelessness of size!

Looking down now, Merlain could see nothing but gray. Then suddenly, very suddenly, there was a WHOOSH feeling, a dropping as if in the department store's magical raiser and lowerer. The waves lapped just beneath the hand. No, he wasn't getting smaller, yet, for the size of the hand hadn't changed; he was just wading into deeper water.

The hand raised just a bit. Now she could see Kildom's giant leather jerkin and just beneath the water his impossibly wide buckled belt. Kildom was wading now, in an ocean that for him was waist-deep. He seemed to be buffeted by the water more than she would have expected. Would he have to swim? Would he lose his footing? If he had to save himself, would he be able to save the rest of them as well? At their present normal size they could vanish under the water without him noticing. Merlain could imagine the difficulty she would have seeing little flies in the waves created in a dishpan.

WHOOSH again, and the hand elevated as the water rose. Water splashed them, wetting them, and then there was Kildom's enormous head and neck like an island in the sky. He was looking all around the water, searching.

"Kildom, take us home," Merlain pleaded. She knew it was useless. Those great ears, large enough to walk into, might hear well, but hardly the buzzing of small insects such as the three of them.

"KILDOM, YOU IDIOT! GET US HOME BEFORE YOU SHRINK!" Kildee was standing upright, grasping a huge thumb, shouting at the face the size of a building. It was a good, even heroic try.

Kildom stared well past his hand. It was as if his enormous eyes saw something the rest of them could not yet see. Suddenly a great triangular sail loomed, and below it a ship with a long, sharpened bow. The bow of the boat was for ramming other vessels, but at the moment its objective was to ram at full sailing speed into the face of one normally small but now giant boy.

Merlain screamed and threw up her hands. She knew this was a useless gesture, but she couldn't help it: she was a girl. The ship bearing down on them was loaded with orcs—armed orcs. It was toy size to Kildom, but a toy that was downright dangerous.

Fingers tightened over them, shutting out the light. She heard the blowing and knew that Kildom had expanded his cheeks and was now emptying them. But this was no fishing vessel. This was a warship, and even a giant windbag would be hard put to send it down. Merlain had blown against the sails of toy ships, but only the small ones made of lightest material had ever moved for her.

Now there was the sensation of quick motion and an enormous splash. The fingers opened slightly and there was the floundering ship with orcs in the water and clinging to its sides. Kildom's free hand was lifting up from the water, far, far in front of them.

Merlain shook. All Kildom—who was now an incredibly powerful king—had done was slap the water once and make a huge wave. It was sufficient to stop a warship. But suppose the orcs sent a navy? If there were a hundred ships, could he splash down the entire fleet?

He's going to get us in trouble, Charles thought.

I know. Can't you stop him?

How? What about you? Can't you use magic?

You know I'm not a witch! Merlain was indignant, though she had never in her life—before this adventure—thought that witches were anything other than good.

But you've got the book! Maybe something there.

I doubt it. Besides, you know I need blood and a place to make those lines. In his hand, here, it wouldn't be possible.
Look anyway.

She did, trembling while she turned the smooth pages. She didn't want to use the book ever again, but if there should be something here that would help, then she would do it. What should she look for this time?

She raised her eyes from its pages and saw that the orcs were abandoning their ships and diving underwater. They had no fear of drowning, of course. Once under, they stayed under. They had gills, she remembered, and could breathe the water as well as they breathed air.

Craning her neck upward, she could see Kildom looking down; he was studying the situation from his great height.

Kildee took the book from her and turned its pages. His face was pale but intense. He evidently did not trust his brother's judgment any better than she did, and he should know, because his mind was mirror-image similar. He could read much better than she could, and now she was glad of that. They needed to come up with something quickly.

"Here, Merlain, here," Kildee said, excited.

"What?"

"To breathe underwater. We may have to when Kildom the dummy giant shrinks."

She looked at the recipe. Words to be said. Dance to be danced within the lines of a star. It seemed feasible, and if that was all it did, it should be safe. She hoped.

"If he would straighten his hand out, and if we had the blood—"

"I know just the thing," Kildee said. "Charles, now's the time to use your sword!"

Charles' mouth fell. "You want *me* to . . . ?"

"We have to get his attention. I know my brother: he won't give this a thought unless we tell him. First we have to get up to his face, and I don't want to climb."

Merlain shivered. "It's so high! Do we really have to?"

Charles drew his sword. He looked at it and frowned.

"Right here," Kildee said. "Just a prick on the pinkie."

"Suppose he squeezes us or puts us underwater?"

"He won't. I know my brother, I tell you. He knows he needs us, and he doesn't want to lose us. Right here."

"The skin's tough. I'm not sure I can—"

"Put some weight on it."

Charles did, pushing hard. Blood welled up around the sword tip in one enormous drop. From far overhead came an "OUCH!" and the hand they were on lifted swiftly. Kildom's big nose was pointed down. It seemed as if he had an entire flaming forest for hair.

Kildee cupped his hands and shouted. Kildom turned his head and presented a huge ear with a dirty tunnel leading inward. He pointed to it with his other hand. Again Kildee shouted: "KILDOM, WE HAVE TO DO MAGIC ON YOUR HAND. HELP US!"

The hand moved away from the ear. The fingers straightened. On either side of his hand clouds drifted by.

"All right, Merlain," Kildee said.

"B-but the star!"

"Make it, Charles." Kildee was taking charge in annoyingly kingly fashion, but he seemed to be getting the job done.

"You want me to cut him?" Charles sounded unaccustomedly scared. "He won't like that, Kildee."

"Maybe you could use the blood from his pinky," Merlain suggested. But she saw that that drop of blood was far from the center of the hand where they had to make the diagram. It would be hard to carry the blood there, and it would take a long time. They needed a source of blood closer to the action.

"Oh, I'll do it myself!"

With that Kildee marched up the pinky and smeared a little hand with the drop of blood there. He went to the center of the big hand and began drawing lines. But he soon ran out of fluid.

"Charles?" he said, recognizing the problem.

"You do it. He's your brother. If he gets mad at any of us, it might as well be you."

Kildee took the sword. He raised it high and plunged it down.

Blood erupted at its point. Kildom's howl almost blew them off the hand. Each clung tight to an enormous finger.

In a moment Kildee was back to marking. Now he had a copious supply of blood. It seemed a terrible wound to Merlain, but actually she knew that the great gaping hole was for Kildom little more than a pinprick. The hole filled with blood, buckets of blood from their viewpoint. Kildee took off his shirt, soaked it in red ink, and rapidly finished the five-pointed star.

"Now, Merlain."

She got into it, and it was as before. A power, a force took over from her. She danced the steps, said the words that she did not know she had memorized, and felt a deeply buried qualm. *She was becoming a witch!* At another time, under different circumstances, she knew the words would have become twisted on her tongue and her toes would have stubbed and her ankles turned. But having looked in the book of spells, and having been influenced by it on more than just a reading level, she did the spells perfectly. That both exhilarated and frightened her.

Lightning flashed, blinding her. Thunder thundered, deafening her. It was no natural storm; it was the action of the spell.

She was falling. Air whipped through and over her. She had the sensation of growing lighter as she fell. She swished her tail in the air, wriggled her fins, and—

SPLASH!

Water came up around her. She fell through it for a distance, bubbles escaping her mouth. Her gills worked. She was breathing water. She was—

She was a fish. A fish! And what of the others?

She moved her fins and her tail and her body and found herself traveling through the water, smoothly and comfortably, feeling competent. She gazed out of her fish eyes.

Two other fish swam beside her. One had red fins and tail, and other more coppery shades. Both were about her size.

Charles?

Me, Merlain. That's Kildee.

What about . . . ?

He was gone when we were falling. Perhaps he shrank.

A fourth fish, identical in appearance to the one with red fins and tail, swam up from below to join them.

Kildom? Merlain wondered.

Has to be. You see, you were just in time. He did shrink!

But we're fish. We're all fish!

And we're breathing water. We're safe.

Until the enchantment wears off. If it does. She was worrying again.

That might be a long time. That big bird never vanished, did it?

No, it didn't. Of course that was a conjuration rather than a transformation, but it did suggest the continuing power of the spells in the spelling book. The Alice Water wore off after a while, but that was incidental magic. The book was deeper magic; she knew it in her being.

She wanted to cry, but here underwater that was difficult. Here she was a fish, and she hadn't been a little girl very long. Phooey on magic anyway!

A shadow loomed over them. A big one.

Oh-oh, that was one great fish! As big as those she had seen while a giant in the lily pads. This one, whatever it was, could swallow them if it had a mind to. Big fish did eat little fish, she remembered, and the thought was especially scary right now.

Almost without her willing it, she was diving. The others were swimming close at her sides. As she twisted and turned, her fish body doing what came naturally, the great shadow deepened and darkened. Then she was at the bottom of the sea among spears of long grass, chunks of rocks, long feathery weeds, and the remains of a sunken ship.

Almost instinctively, she swam for the best cover. She made for the derrick and swam down under its deck. Heart pounding (she hadn't quite realized before that fish had hearts or that they could pound) and senses whirling, she hid there and saw first one red-finned fish and then a coppery-scaled fish enter the hole in the planking.

Merlain?

Here. Kildom?

I don't know.

A second red-finned fish entered the hole just as the region darkened. A seemingly endless shadow slipped by. They were hidden. Just four little fishes hiding from a big fish intent on eating them. Routine. How she wished she were elsewhere!

A great claw reached out at her. A horrible body with waving eye stalks swam after it, and she knew there was a lobscrab or crabster holed here. This good place to hide was a bad place to hide!

She swam immediately out of the opening, not wishing to be dinner for a crustacean any more than for a vertebrate. The others schooled with her, evidently having similar sentiments. They swam outside the ship and down amidst grass and weeds and shells, many of those shells with reaching tentacles, and some with half a fish outside them. There were great hungry shadows darting all around.

She hid under a rock, and fortunately there wasn't anything hungry hiding there first. Was this what a fish's life was like? Just one escape after another, until one fail-to-escape? She wanted to go home. She wanted to be a little girl again. She definitely, most certainly, did not want to remain a fish for the rest of what was sure to be a short life.

Merlain?

I'm here, Charles. Under a rock.

We're all under rocks, or between rocks and hard places. Terrible way to live, isn't it?

I suppose you want me to do more magic?

That would be nice.

Charles, you know I can't Not while I'm a fish.

Yes. But it will wear off.

You hope.

Yes.

Charles, it's not fun, is it? I wish we were back at the con and in our true forms.

Who doesn't!

I wish we'd never let Auntie Jon talk us into coming here, she thought fervently. *I wish we'd never listened to Auntie Jon at all.*

Me too, though it was fun taking things. Just reaching out invisibly and taking someone's sandwich or drink or piece of cake.

But it was wrong! You know it was.

Why did we do it then? he asked, avoiding the charge.

I don't know. Maybe we're bad. Maybe Auntie Jon is bad.

You believe that?

No, not exactly. Maybe sometimes we're bad.

Yes, and maybe Auntie Jon too.

Right, she agreed, uncomfortably. *Only—*

What?

Sometimes I think she's not out auntie.

She had expected him to argue with her, but he didn't. *You thought that too?*

Yes, since the time she got that dress.

You think she shouldn't have? Did you feel something, just then when she got it?

I don't know. I don't know if it's the dress. It could be magic. Charles, maybe it's not really Auntie Jon in that dress. Maybe it's somebody who looks like her. Maybe somebody bad.

Maybe, he agreed. *There, I felt it again!*

This time she felt it as well. A sort of bumping sensation, as of something big moving about just above the rocks. Dare she peek out and see?

The rock above her vanished. In its place was a large orc's face, its gills moving rhythmically. She sought to flee—

A net was suddenly over her, keeping her from swimming anywhere, no matter how hard she flipped her tail. The top of the net closed, capturing her in a mesh bag.

Oh, Charles! she managed to mind-scream.

Too late, Charles thought.

Through the mesh she could see him dashing helplessly around in a similar bag.

The orcs had caught them again. This time, she knew, they would not escape in the way they had before.

CHAPTER 15

Brudalous

The orc ruler looked into the mesh fish cage that now held all of them: all four miserable little fishes. Here they were not about to be eaten by other fish, and here also they were not about to escape.

Bubbles came up from the great orc's wide mouth. It spoke to them, and the words, though they sounded strange, were transmitted by the water surrounding them.

"Little pests! Do you realize what you have done? You have brought down an ancient landhome! You have buried the precious opal! You have caused a state of war to be declared between the Federation and Ophal—a war the Feds surely cannot win. All of this, you immature little imbeciles, and even more!"

Merlain wanted to cry. But there was just no crying when she was a fish. She doubted she could even answer him. If she could, what would she say? She knew that he was right, and that they had indeed done these awful things.

"I should leave you in your fish forms forever, or feed

you to something without your sentience. I will not. I am far too kind."

Yes, Your Majesty, Merlain tried to think. But she knew there was little or no chance of his getting her thought. What did the monster mean? Was he really going to help them change? And if they did change, wouldn't they drown?

Brudalous moved a webbed hand above their fish cage and opened it. From his greenish fingers sparkling specks were propelled down into the water of their cage. At the same moment he pulled a braided grass rope, and the cage itself sprang apart.

Merlain felt something sparkling enter her gills and tickle. She choked. She felt herself without air. She breathed, and water bubbled through her mouth and was sucked painfully into her chest.

She was breathing. She was breathing water—and she had her right form!

Beside her, sprawled as she was on a green carpeting of intertwined grass, were Charles, Kildee, and Kildom. All of them were gasping and choking and finding that they could, after all, breathe.

Brudalous waited, so big above them. He was such a truly giant, ugly form!

When their breathing became halfway regular, the orc leaned down closer. "What have you troublesome polly-poles to say for yourselves?"

Charles managed to speak first. "It wasn't our fault. It was magic."

"Yes, magic, obviously," the orc leader said. "But whose?"

"Auntie Jon's," Merlain interrupted. Charles should know better than to speak up first; he'd just get them in trouble. If he blabbed about the Alice Water or the spelling book, they would be even further done for than they already were.

"Auntie Jon?" The huge orc grimaced. He certainly had the mouth for it. "Your father's sister with the pointed ears?"

How did he know that? "Uh, maybe. We're not really sure."

"Not sure? What nonsense is this?"

Merlain started to cry. She was surprised to find that she really could. She touched the drops coming out of her eyes underwater and had to marvel at it happening; in turn, she ceased to feel the need for shedding tears.

"She may not be our real aunt," Charles explained.

"No? Whose aunt is she, then?"

"We don't know. But Auntie Jon was different at the convention."

"Convention? The Human Century Convention of Benign Witches and Warlocks?"

"Yes. We were there. Helbah was to be honored. She and my father and grandfather and aunt. They worked together to destroy two evil beings the day that my sister and I and our dragon brother were born."

He was telling too much, but Merlain wasn't sure how to stop him. A mental warning at this time might just cause him to give away that ability of theirs, too.

The orc king was definitely interested. "Destroyed Zoanna, the former queen of Rud gone malignant witch, and the rightful king's evil look-alike from another frame?"

Then again, Brudalous already seemed to know so much that it might be foolish to try to deceive him on anything.

"That's what they told us, Your Majesty," Charles answered.

"They told you well. Now this aunt who aided Witch Helbah in defeating the former queen and her consort—she was replaced?"

"She was with us, but then she got a new dress—"

"With a wow neckline!" a kinglet put in.

"And a sexy attitude," the other kinglet added.

The orc nodded. "Ah. Identity switch. Probably an enemy of hers."

"She had no enemies," Merlain spoke up. "I mean Auntie Jon hasn't any. She's just our father's nice sister."

"But there are evil witches in many frames," the orc

said. "A relative of the former queen, perhaps." He had an amazing understanding of human events.

"Maybe. We just don't know." Merlain wished that she did.

"Yes, you are only children, after all."

"We're kings," one of the pains said. "Those two aren't. We rule not only Klingland and Kance but the entire Confederation."

"Yes, your Helbah was wise in arranging that," the orc said. "Nor are you two kings quite the children you appear. Ophal may be distant and different than your kingdoms, but we are informed."

That was what alarmed Merlain most. This orc was no ignorant savage, and that was more dangerous than if he had been a ravening beast. "W-what will you do with us?" she asked, not trying to hide her nervousness.

"Why, we shall send you back."

All four children were surprised by this. "Back?" the two kinglets asked together.

"Once the Confederation has been defeated," Brudalous said. "And it certainly will be."

"You declared war on the Confederation?" one of the pains asked.

"No," the orc said, making a ghastly smile. "The Confederation foolishly declared war on us. The acting ruler is now King Rufurt of Rud; Helbah arranged this before leaving for the convention. He is of course a gentle man and an ineffective leader."

He was disturbingly on target. "But—" Merlain began.

"His minion, Sean Reilly, the grandfather of these two nonroyals, whom you call St. Helens, delivered the message in the form of a declaration."

Merlain sighed. That was her grandfather all right. If only the kingdom wasn't run by men! Probably he had gotten mad, as she had seen him do one time, and blown his top. Back as far as she could remember, Grandpa St. Helens had talked about how the Confederation needed to declare war on somebody. There was something about her father being part of a prophecy that had to be fulfilled through warfare.

Brudalous made a motion. Other orcs came, picked them up, and lifted them into the air—rather, the water, which now seemed just about like air, so that they didn't even float—and held them there. The orcs were truly the size that she had been on the mountain, and later among the lily pads. And they had magic too. The Federation was surely doomed!

"Take them to Orc Castle," Brudalous ordered.

Orc Castle? Wasn't that on the island? Hadn't she seen its tower fall with her very own eyes?

But the orcs were carrying them to an enormous underwater pile of rubble. The rocks were very large and overgrown with grasses and weeds and attached shells. The orcs went between two boulders in the center of the pile and inside there was greenish light filtering from outside. In fact it was quite impressive.

There were rooms—rooms upon rooms—furnished as an underwater castle of orcs. Grasses were growing here, fish were swimming, crustaceans crawling, and yet there was also furniture, and decorations to suit orcs. How could this be, the sea and ground together?

They were taken through several rooms of similar furnishings, down under, deep, to where luminescent creatures of small size crawled and swam and emitted light. There were no outside windows here, and the only door led to a cell-like chamber at the bottom of the stairs. This was where they were set down.

The orcs withdrew. There was a sliding, grating sound, and a great slab of rock now blocked the doorway. They were locked in—really locked in!—in an underwater dungeon from which escape would seem to be impossible.

"Well, Brudalous, I hope you're satisfied!"

"Don't start with me, female!" the orc leader told his distraught wife. If she would just get this reproductive bit out of her mind and concentrate on magic the way he wanted! But Phenoblee, wonderfully good witch or not, was all orc female.

"They're only taddies after all!" she persisted. "Shutting them up in that ugly old jail without even a chance to swim! Don't you have feelings?"

"I have many feelings! But those tads have to be punished."

"How? Set upon by vicious bullfishes? Taken above surface, dried into kindling, then burned?"

"That might do for a start." Phenoblee, loving mate though she was and had always been, could be a source of irritation comparable to scaleworms.

"Oh, you think so, do you!" Her anger shook their seaweed bed, sending their pet bullfish streaking off with gills flapping. "Well, consider this, those taddies didn't act alone."

"They didn't?" He was playing dumb; he had already ascertained that there had been an identity switch that had affected the children. But he also knew that the tads weren't ready to come all the way clean about their involvement. That little girl was disturbingly cunning. Some isolation in the cell would help soften their attitude.

"No, someone filled their tiny heads with stories! Someone misused them and misled them, to the point where they felt they had to steal our stone."

Exactly. And he intended to discover exactly how that had been done, and exactly who was responsible. He knew it hadn't started with the children. Once he had the correct information, he would be able to formulate a truly devastating plan of action. But he wasn't going to explain all this to his wife. She was, after all, only a woman. "That's why the Confederation has to pay for the damages. It's only fair."

"Fair to you, maybe, but not to them."

"Female, I'm not going to feed them to a pack of bullfish! I'm not going to take them to the surface, dry them off, and have them burned, no matter what you imagine! All I'm going to do is feed and shelter the little monsters until I'm satisfied that they should be returned." Which would be after they told him all he needed to know, and after the defeat of the Confederation.

"You're lucky they didn't actually get the opal!"

That was for sure! The notion gave him the shivers, and he did not shiver readily. But the female did not need to know that, either. "How could they? With you and Wizard Krassnose to do magic, there's no chance."

"Oh, Husband Brudalous," Phenoblee said, mollified. As always, it pleased her to be complimented for her rare and precious art.

Brudalous sighed. Whatever his intent, he would now have to adjust his thoughts to lovemaking. Someday, he supposed, her eggs would even get fertilized.

Sean Reilly, familiarly known as St. Helens, also known as the father of the Roundear's round-eared wife Heln who was indirectly named after him, and grandfather of the two strange kids, swore. It was something that came naturally to him. The riding in this brush was just too much! How he wished he had the levitation belt or even an old fashioned jet-pak. Horse traveling never had suited him, and that son-in-law of his hadn't left him with the means of flying. Kelvin, typically, had taken all his magical paraphernalia—the belt, the gauntlets, the Mouvar weapon, and the chimaera's sting—with him. He wondered what they were getting done at the convention and what would be their reactions when they learned that the kids were prisoners of orcs and that the Confederation was declaring war.

The brush got denser and denser, and the soldiers sent ahead were clearing it at a less than magical speed. Wasn't that ever the way of it! Magic, that was what was needed. Well, he didn't have any. At a convention in another frame were old Helbah and her cat and all sorts of friendly witches and warlocks. Plenty of magic there! But for the old saint, trapped here in this minor frame, nothing.

"You know, St. Helens," Phillip Blastmore said, riding up to him, "we're not apt to get permission to cross Rotternik."

"I know. We'll go around."

"By ocean?"

"That's where Ophal is, isn't it?"

"Sort of. Partly, they say. But we haven't ships."

"We'll build ships."

"That will take time."

"Yes." Indeed it would, and he hoped that the convention foolishness would be over by then and he'd get the reinforcements he knew he was going to need.

"St. Helens," the maturing young man, formerly the nominal king of Aratex, said, "do you know what we're getting into?"

"War," St. Helens said with satisfaction. This was obvious, and always had been.

"I mean with the orcs. They aren't just people, you know."

"I know. They are bigger, uglier, and they have gills."

"Besides that. The power they have."

"A little magic. I've heard about it."

"More. With the opal they can switch frames."

"So?" What was the young whippersnapper getting at?

"They can disappear from in front of you and reappear in back of you. They can bring others like themselves in from other frames. There's no fighting that, St. Helens, even with any magic I've ever heard about. That one power makes them just about invulnerable to attack and, I'm afraid, undefeatable. Just how can we fight them when they have that?"

St. Helens had to wonder about that himself. He had not realized just how significant a tactical weapon that opal was. This was a bad situation. Since he had no clear plan, he gave up and used the all-purpose answer of a seasoned officer.

"Newly commissioned officer Blastmore," he said, "shut the hell up."

The youth had no fit rebuttal for that. In time he would learn the correct response: "Yes, *sir!*" expressed so sharply that it plainly showed what a fool the senior officer was. Until that time, St. Helens was safe with it.

They rode on through turgid silence.

Dragon Horace crouched in the tall grass. He squeezed his copper scales flat and tried to appear to be just a part of the sun-dappled landscape. In front of him, well within attacking distance, the soldiers on their horses rode on and on, trampling brush and making a noise disturbing to game. What a nuisance!

Who were they, these annoying men? He sensed that they were going to Merlain and Charles and that they meant no harm. The leader of the men was a man Merlain had said was their grandfather. That meant Dragon Horace's grandfather too. It probably would not be right to eat him.

Dragon Horace decided that he was going to follow them. At least, he thought, snapping up a brushy-tailed squirbet and crunching it in his jaws, they were scaring out game. So they did have some use after all.

Lester Crumb faced King Rufurt in the Royal Palace and frowned his ugliest. "Rufurt," he said, in exactly the tone his roughneck father would have used, "you made a mistake."

"Why do you say that, Les?" Rufurt inquired, studying the chessboard. "My white king's protected by the—"

"I mean letting windbag St. Helens take the troops. You know he'll gt in trouble."

"Now, I don't know that, Les, and you don't either. Commander Reilly, or St. Helens as we all like to call him, has proved his leadership qualities. Without his military sense we might never have won against Aratex, and Helbah's look-alike would be alive and directing our destinies."

"Yes, and just maybe the trouble with Aratex would never have happened in the first place!"

"He had to save his daughter after the witch had her

kidnapped. As for his wanting that war, well, you know what things were like there.''

"I don't deny that we needed to fight Aratex. But the war Zoanna and your look-alike started was something else!''

"Yes, but you were all a little bewitched, weren't you? Don't blame a man for what he does under the influence of magic. You and your father fought in that war as well.''

Lester pushed back his chair and stood up. He paced the carpet for a few steps and turned back. He hadn't suffered from nerves in the past, but he'd never before been in a situation that felt so frustrating.

"You're planning something, aren't you?'' Lester asked, catching on. Rufurt was not quite as soft a touch as most folk took him for, fortunately.

"Well, a little kingly strategy,'' the king said.

"What? Are you depending on Kelvin coming back and saving the day for us?''

"There is the prophecy,'' the king reminded him. "According to it, he's supposed to unite all seven kingdoms. I never really understood that myself. There are, after all, eight kingdoms in our frame counting Throod where everyone goes for mercenaries.''

"Suppose,'' Lester challenged, "the prophecy's not what we think? Suppose Mouvar intended it not for our frame but for another?''

"Another almost like ours? But with seven kingdoms instead of eight?''

"Could have happened. How much do we know about Mouvar anyway? All we know is that he's an alien and that according to that robot Kelvin met, he's from a science frame rather than a magic frame.''

"I never understood that either,'' confessed the king. "Major and Minor world frames, according to what the robot said. Yet predicting seems like magic.''

"Precognition, according to John Knight, Kelvin's father.''

"Yes, precognition. But what does it mean?''

"The ability to see what will happen some way into the future."

"Magic."

"John says there's a difference."

"Yes." King Rufurt toyed with his chess piece. "If it's true, as we've been told, that some frames only differ in very minor, sometimes almost undetectable ways . . ."

"There could well be a frame just like ours with people nearly the same, but without one kingdom."

"But how would Mouvar make such a mistake?"

"Who knows? Mouvar is said, by that same robot, to be an alien."

"If the prophecy applies to another Kelvin in another frame . . ."

"Then we're in trouble."

"What would you have me do, cancel my orders making St. Helens commander of the troops? That would make him very angry. Besides, knowing roundears, especially St. Helens, I doubt he'd obey."

"Then he's running things, not you!"

Rufurt turned a suspiciously vague glance past him. "Lester, it isn't good to get angry with a king."

Lester considered the words. King Rufurt had become a close friend, but kings were more than army officers and civilians. Kings were known to have whims, even such gentle, bumbling kings as Rufurt. St. Helens might have fired off his notorious temper at him once or twice or even more often, but St. Helens was after all a roundear. Being a roundear related to the Roundear of Prophecy through marriage gave St. Helens a special status. Superior, even, to that of friend and war hero.

"All right, I'm not angry with you. I shouldn't have said that about St. Helens. You're the ruler of the entire Confederation until the rulers of Klingland and Kance are back."

"At least the ruler of Rud."

"Yes. I didn't mean to imply differently. It was your wine. I'm not used to wine."

"You have something on your mind?"

"I was thinking"—Lester took a deep breath, wondering how to phrase it—"that someone should advise Helbah, the young rulers' guardian. And the Roundear of Prophecy, of course."

"In the frame where they are having their convention?"

"Yes."

"You would go there?"

"Yes."

"How? You know the warning Mouvar left. Only round-ears can use the transporter."

"The one above water, yes. But there's that other that possibly Mouvar had nothing to do with."

"The underwater one that was used by Zoanna and Rowforth, my enemy look-alike?"

"Right. My wife and mother-in-law were to have used it with Helbah. The young kings were to have used it too. My ears are no more rounded than theirs. If they can use it, so can I." Not very far to the rear of Lester's mind was the fact that Jon was there, and that he had been wrong to refuse to go. He couldn't actually apologize to her, in so many words, but if he came to her there, it might be enough, and their quarrel would be over. Jon could be very pleasant to be with, when a quarrel was resolved. Regardless, he just wanted to be with her again.

"You know nothing about setting it," Rufurt pointed out. "Remember what happened when Rowforth apparently changed the setting on the transporter used by roundears? Kelvin, his father, and his half-brother transported to that world with the chimaera. That was almost the end of them!"

"It shouldn't happen if the controls aren't changed. Helbah won't have changed them, and Zoanna and Rowforth are six years gone."

The king sighed. "You do want to try, then? To go underwater and use the transporter?"

"Yes."

"Very well, then. I'll even ride out to the ruins of the old palace with you and row you out to that little dimple that marks the installation. After that, you're on your own."

Lester swallowed. It occurred to him then that just maybe the big-nosed, corpulent king might be a more clever player than he had realized.

"Checkmate," the king said, moving his previously unnoticed knight.

Rufurt was as good as his kingly word. He did not tell anyone else, and did not order a servant to do the rowing. He had no pretensions. He just got the job done.

Lester marveled as the king himself rowed the two of them to the spot where the water dimpled. Here, according to Helbah, was the installation concealing a second transporter that had been used for centuries by pointy-eared witches and warlocks.

The king leaned on his oars. Lester had already stripped to his undershorts, not wanting to get all naked, and unable to turn himself into a bird. He had always been a good swimmer. His lungs would hold out, he hoped.

"I'll get them as fast as I can," he promised. With those words still ringing in his own ears, he took a deep breath and dived.

Water was all around him, and he was letting the last of his breath escape when the dome was there like an underwater hornee hive. He swam under it, as Helbah had said they would, and then up a little, and—

Air. Lights. An interior exactly as Helbah had described. So far so good; he was relieved. It was a strange place, a very strange place, but he wasn't here to see what it was like. He wiped his hair back, rubbed water from his eyes, blinked, and looked carefully around. The transporter—that must be what they had all talked about.

He climbed free of the pool of water, crossed the platform and the room, and stood before it. _Don't touch the clocks or anything else,_ he thought, _just step into that space._ It was what Jon would have had him do if he had agreed to accompany her.

He took as deep a breath as he had taken before diving. Then, controlling his thoughts as well as he could and ignoring a fear that Jon would not have believed he possessed, he did it: he stepped into the closet space.

Something happened. Star-whirl, and a pulling and apart and a repulling together and—

"Oh, look, Mama, look at the man who just arrived!"

It was a little girl with golden hair, and she was pointing at him. The mother was beautiful and point-eared. There were lights and people and floating platforms all around. It was like a big tunnel, but probably magically made.

He realized that he was standing in this booth in this very busy place in a condition of near nakedness. He swallowed again, wondering if he dared step out, wondering if he could hide himself. It hadn't occurred to him that he would find himself this suddenly in a crowded place with so little on. He just hadn't thought it through.

At that moment he looked beyond the pretty red-haired woman with the smiling face and saw a man with dark features who wasn't waring anything. There were people in robes, people in assorted trousers and shorts and every other description of dress. All of them were very busy; only the little girl, now being reprimanded by her mother, seemed to have noticed him. His state of undress didn't matter, here, after all.

He had arrived. But where oh where was he?

CHAPTER 16

Lester

The crystal flashed, and in its depths the face of the security officer appeared. He looked right at Helbah, but it was everyone in the room he addressed: Kelvin, Charlain, John Knight, and Jon as well as the good witch.

"We have taken someone into custody who may be from your frame. Here he is."

Another face filled the crystal. A not-unhandsome dark-haired man of Kelvin's age. The man's eyes were widened and his mouth was opening and closing as if with astonishment or shock that couldn't be contained.

"Lester!" Jon shrieked. She stepped forward, squatted by the table, and put her face near the crystal. "Is that you or are you a witch?"

"It's me, sweetie," Lester said, evidently relieved to see her. "What do you mean, am I a witch? If I were anything, I'd be a warlock, which I'm not."

"If you're really Lester, you know what you said to me just before I left."

"I didn't mean it, lovebit. I was angry and I was scared for you."

"Your very last words to me the morning I left. What did you say?"

"I said"—the image swallowed a still-prominent Adam's apple—"that I wouldn't go anywhere with a witch—even my own witch."

"And what is it you call my witch's mark?"

The image of Lester eyed the rest of them. "You want me to tell it? In front of all these—"

"Yes."

"Well, it's that purplish-blue spot on your left—"

"You're Lester!" Jon exclaimed. "How'd you get here? Did Zady get to you, or—"

"Zady? What's a Zady? I followed you, lovekins. Had to. It's really important."

"Oh, Lester! I knew you loved me, but—"

"That too," he said, looking gratified. "But there's something else. About the kids, and the war St. Helens is starting with Ophal." His eyes turned to Jon's brother. "Kelvin, you're needed back home! There may be a disaster if you don't act!"

Kelvin looked to Witch Helbah and saw that she was smiling. "I think, Kelvin," she said, "that the answer to what Zady did is about to come to light."

"And so," Lester explained in their room some time later, after Jon had thoroughly kissed him and found him some clothing to wear, "that's all I can tell you. Somehow they got to Ophal, obviously with the Zady's help. They caused trouble there and the orcs responded as orcs are bound to. The children are prisoners and St. Helens is getting the Confederation involved with King Rufurt's approval. I disapproved of St. Helens' actions because—"

"So do I!" Kelvin said.

"So do I!" Witch Helbah echoed. "Orcs are not to be casually warred against, and not just because they generally mind their own business and are no trouble to us. They are

formidable opponents. In fact, about the only reason they
didn't conquer the rest of the frame long ago is that they
don't have the interest to do so. They prefer the sea and
islands; vast expanses of solid land dismay them. But they
can handle it when they have to.''

''Well, we can fight them on dry land, then,'' Kelvin
said. ''We can set up barricades they can't pass—''

''Not so, Kelvin. Orcs can change frames rapidly, almost
instantaneously, with the help of a certain stone.''

''The opal,'' Charlain said.

''That's it, Charlain. The one and only, as far as any of
us know.''

''But—'' Kelvin said.

''In and out, Kelvin,'' Helbah explained to him. ''Behind
you with weapons, maybe with troops. Somehow with the
opal's magic, their orc leader, Brudalous, not only can cross
frames and be anywhere he wants to be in an instant, he
can move that way at home as well.''

''But there's antimagic with the Mouvar weapon,'' Kelvin
said. He was thinking that the powers of the opal resembled
those of a valuable chess piece. ''With that I can reverse
the magic of the stone and send him back.''

''No,'' Helbah said firmly.

''No?'' Why did he always feel slow when he got into
these dialogues?

''No. The frames aren't magic and that antimagic weapon
won't affect them or the opal. Your Mouvar weapon counters and reverses hostile aggressive magic that is in use,
nothing more.''

''The copper sting? That did for Zoanna and Rowforth
when witch's fire and the weapon weren't enough.''

''You're right. The sting utilizes electricity, which is science, not magic. But of what worth if your enemy can appear suddenly and take it from your hands?''

''The gauntlets—''

''Are no stronger than an orc. An orc's strength is said
to be that of ten strong human warriors, and for once the

legend is not exaggerated. Are your gauntlets stronger than that?'' It was a rhetorical question.

"With a sword—"

"Orcs are almost impervious to sword thrusts or slashes. Their scales are very tight and strong, and they overlap to leave no weakness. The orcs' reactions are swift. They are not mere human beings."

Kelvin thought rapidly. There had to be something. Then he remembered a bit of magical apparatus an orc could not have and would not be able to counter. "The levitation belt!" he said triumphantly.

"Helpful, perhaps," Helbah conceded. "But remember, Brudalous is no clumsy chimaera waiting to be confused. You can start to fly and then he disappears and then you're the one confused. Then when you land, he pops out of nothing and takes your belt."

"You sound as if orcs are undefeatable," Kelvin complained. She had never been that pessimistic when they went up against Zoanna and Rowforth.

"Kelvin," Helbah said, laying her hand gently on his arm. "I'm afraid that in that you may be more realistic than you now wish to believe."

That wasn't exactly the reassurance he had hoped for.

It was dark in the jail in back of the police station. None of the viewing crystals were lit, and there were only three jailbirds. The largest was dark and ugly and wide awake. The other two were sleeping well with a bit of help from magic.

The bird clucked to itself. It had been so easy to convince them! They thought her safely in confinement, and all the time she had this simple holdout spell, courtesy of her visit to Devale and a sweaty night. Men were so easy to manage, even the smartest ones, even when they knew better. Too bad she had not quite had time to make a proper impression on that nerd Kelvin. She could have taken him out right then! Well, this game was not yet over.

Carefully, wishing to make as little noise as possible, the ugly bird twisted her neck until she had hold of one of her own dark wing feathers. She strained at it, sucking, pulling it into her beak and far down her throat.

Her bird body responded, vomiting. Up and out came the feather in a nauseating mass; up and out came the pod planted by Devale. She pecked the pod with her beak, splitting its gelatinous surface. Something unholy leaked out, forming a little cloud. She breathed deeply, sucking in the greenish vapor before it dissipated.

Her head swam, as it always did when subjected to magic. Normally she was doing to others, not being done to herself, and so it was their heads that swam. But she did not hesitate to apply her spells to herself when she had reason, and she had excellent reason now. This was powerful pharmaceutical enchantment.

As the fumes cleared, she took hold of the bars of her cage with her beak and twisted and pulled them apart as if they were wet maccagettie. Devale might be a bore and a chore as a companion, insisting on repetitive delights of the flesh which had little point for one who was sterile, but his spells were first rate. She was now the frame's strongest bird.

Soon there was a hole in the side of the cage as big as its locked entrance. She stuck her head out, looked carefully around, then launched herself to the top of the next cage. She rattled the bars with her beak until the bird inside unwinged its tired head and took her reptilian gaze straight in the eye.

Zady's neighbor, she gleaned, was an apprentice wizard of tender centuries who had indulged in too much elixir and become objectionable to his fellow conventioneers. He could have been sobered and put right, but that was not the way to instill a lesson. Now missing the doings at the convention, now confined, now having to sleep off his excess without official aid, he was for her fowl purposes perfect.

Zady tore out the side of his cage as she had torn open her own. She directed him with pulsed stares to fly from this cage into hers. She then carefully bent the bars back on the empty cage, flew back to the first, and repeated the barbending.

When the cage was again intact, she delivered the triple-whammy stare and rendered him into another form. Then she shuddered as she changed into a young male bird with a terrible hangover. Inside the cage was now, to all appearances, the great ugly bird that was her natural bird form. It had been no harder than changing forms with that young hussy Jon had been. In fact it was easier, thanks to Devale's helpful preparation.

Chuckling in unbirdlike fashion, Zady flew out of the station and into the night's streets. There was no alarm sounding; she had taken pains to nullify their simple magic. The police had much to learn about trying to confine a witch of her caliber!

When it was discovered that a prisoner had escaped, it would seem to them to be the young wizard. She, the powerful Witch Zady, would still seem to be confined. They would not worry, since the wizard was due for release anyway. They would probably not even make a report on it, so as not to mar their record for efficiency. By the time the dullards realized that they had made a mistake, she'd be well gone, long beyond any hope of recovery. Then there would be a reckoning for the police, though it really wasn't their fault. It was the fault of their superiors, who had deluded themselves into thinking they were competent.

She flew over the convention hotel, carefully dropping a wad of excrement on a couple who were necking out on a balcony. He was just about to kiss the heaving hollow of her cleavage when the glob of dung went *splat!* in there first. A perfect score! Who said old witches had no sense of humor? Her scream and his cry of dismay were music to Zady's ears. With luck a beautiful romance had just been demeaned into disgust.

Chuckling again, she winged her way on to the transporter station, just one more cock out spying hens and blessing the human folk with presentations of fertilizer. There was a good deal more to life than this, of course, but such innocent fun was good for a witch.

It was time that she get serious, however. She had to return to Helbah's golden dragon world. Now she had to institute Phase Two of her revenge.

* * *

Zady arrived at the transporter station, flew low over heads to an isolated booth, landed, and resumed her natural form. This was a calculated risk; she assumed that no one would recognize her, because she was believed to be safely caged in the police station with the other jailbirds. She could have assumed her luscious young red-haired likeness, but that required special effort and tended to attract the gaze of too many men. It was best to reserve that for business: when she wanted to obtain a favor from a man who knew better. Such as that lout Kelvin, the alleged Roundear of Prophecy. She would see about that, in due course. She would play with him for a while before destroying him utterly. As it happened, her risk paid off: no one gave her any attention.

She set the destination coordinates, entered the booth, transported, and exited in the underwater installation. Here she turned herself into the particularly ugly swoosh she had been before, in imitation of Helbah. She dived into the pool in her bird shape, which was well suited to this activity. She flew through the water in swoosh fashion, bobbed to the surface, and took off again with strongly beating wings. She well knew the way, and wasted no time.

She flew along the underground river, by its luminescent walls, up the ancient staircase, barely pausing to admire the way it was crumbling with age, and across the ruins of the old palace. Zady felt a special affinity for decrepit artifacts. She was now in especially familiar and hated territory.

Oh Helbah, I'll get you! Zady mentally promised her arch enemy. *Your victory will be turned to dust and your triumph over Zoanna into mockery. The kingdoms ruled by your darling twin brats will be destroyed and that silly prophecy of the roundears nullified. Helbah, my pretty, your nemesis Zady is about to bring all of you defeat and shame everlasting. You will know Zady's revenge and Zady's torment before the extinction of your goodie, goodie, nicie, nicie lives.*

CHAPTER 17

Opal

"Mind you, keep an eye on them this time," Brudalous told his wife. "I have to depart to fight the Confederation, so I can't watch them."

"Certainly I shall," Phenoblee agreed. "It is obvious that they performed some kind of spells of great strength. We must discover how mere children can have such power."

"Precisely. They may be children, but it seems someone has given them potent magic. Watch them, and intercept it when they try to use it. Only then will we know exactly what we are dealing with. Perhaps then we shall be able to turn it to our own advantage." He headed out to round up his minions for the invasion.

Phenoblee had the best intentions, but she was tired from recent exertions. She tried to keep her attention on the peep-hole mirror which showed the interior of the chamber confining the children, but soon she relaxed and fell asleep. In plain view the children went about their nefarious business, undisturbed. That was unfortunate for the orcs.

When events jerked her back awake, it was too late to

stop the mischief, even with magic. Her husband was going
to be furious when he learned!

Merlain voiced the idea first. Since they were alone in
their underwater prison, it was inevitable that one of them
would.

"We're breathing water now, but if we could get up to
the ocean's surface, out in the air, and then do magic to let
us breathe air . . ."

They pondered that, and found it good. "You find the
spell," Kildom said, digging in his travelsack. The orcs had
been so confident of their power that they hadn't bothered
to investigate just how the children had performed magic
before, and still hadn't deprived them of their packs. Maybe
it was stupidity instead of confidence, though Brudalous
hardly seemed stupid.

The kinglet handed her the book, not even bothering to
open it. It was she who was the witch, his actions said. He
was as arrogant as the orc king, in his stupid young fashion.
The attitude must come with the territory.

Merlain felt very strange. She had promised herself that
the spell that had turned them into fish would be the last
one she would do. She distrusted this magic, partly because
it seemed to be of evil derivation, and partly because of the
hint of a memory of a dream her brother had had. Charles
had promised not to do evil, but he lacked the wit to know
exactly what evil was, so it was her business to follow
through. If *she* could just be sure what it was.

She had also thought that the book would be gone if they
ever resumed their proper forms. But once they had been
changed back by Brudalous, all the things they had on their
persons changed back too. Magic was quite illogical that
way. They did magic with clothes on and travelsacks on
their backs, and became fish; then they changed back and
had all their clothes and things back. Only now everything
was wet—or was it? Surprisingly, there seemed to be a layer
of air surrounding them and everything they had with them.
Thus their travelsacks and equipment were dry.

She turned to the index, shuddering. She didn't like doing this, but just didn't seem to have much choice.

Her fingers found it: Escape from Sea. She flipped to the page with the recipe: 666.

"Kildom, Kildee, Charles, we'll need blood," she announced.

"So what else is new?" Charles complained. "Kildom, any Alice Water left, or did you drain it?"

Kildom shook the bottle. "There's some in there yet. Who wants to grow big this time?"

"Don't you?" Charles demanded.

"I did last time. It's not my turn." The kinglet had showed every sign of enjoying it at the time, except for the blood donation, but now he was off his high of hugeness and had evidently reconsidered.

"I just thought of something," his brother said. "We're underwater, right? So blood will wash away, right? How are we going to draw anything with blood, Merlain?"

Merlain squinted at the book. The lettering entered her eyes and mind, not at all like the lettering in other books. "It doesn't say," she said. She had the feeling that she might figure out a way if she kept gazing at that print, but that frightened her more than the prospect of failure did. This was a powerful, evil book!

"I think I know," Charles said. He took off the shirt Helbah had bought for him. Then he took his brownberry shirt out of his sack. "Kildom, Kildee, if we take off all of our shirts and tie the arms together, then soak 'em in blood, then weigh them with rocks . . ."

"Wouldn't work," Kildee said.

"Why? You got any better ideas?"

The two kings whispered to each other. In a moment off came their shirts. Chests now covered only by their undergarments, they knotted their shirt arms together and arranged them on the floor. Charles drew his sword and slashed here and there, and finally they had a couple of sections of crude rope. They put these down in the shape of the magic star.

"Now all we need is the blood," Charles said.

"Maybe it will work without blood?" Kildee suggested.

"It won't," Merlain said. She didn't know why, but she was certain.

They looked at each other and nodded. "One of us will have to take the Alice Water," Charles said. "There's enough for one more dose in the bottle. Then a nick on the pinkie and enough blood to soak the shirts."

"You?" Kildee suggested.

"Yeh." Grimacing, Charles tipped the bottle and sipped the last of it. His face grew large and soon he was crowding the rest of them. In a moment he had become as big as an orc, but unlike the kinglet, he did not let his size go to his head. He knew that the last thing they wanted to do was call attention to themselves or their ability to do magic again. He kept his head low and did not speak.

Charles held the shirt rope—now hardly more than a string to him—in his right hand. Carefully he applied the edge of his now-huge sword to his giant thumb. His chest heaved and the blade cut deep—a mere nick to him—and blood flowed into the water.

Stifling his outcry of pain, Charles wrapped and re-wrapped the string around the wound. He moved it so that the whole length of it came into contact with the gore. Then he dropped the shirts and stuck his hurting thumb into his mouth.

There was blood smeared on the entire length of the rope of shirts. Quickly the pains rebuilt the star. Merlain stood in its center, nerved herself, and spoke the dread words.

SHURRRRRBLAK! With the mind-numbing sound there were prickles at their necks and in the roots of their hair and bases of their fingernails.

There was a trembling of the water and the rock walls. Then a great crack appeared in the rock ceiling. Was this to be another castle-destroyer?

Merlain looked up and felt herself being sucked upward as by a giant straw. Charles and the pains were right beside her. They left through the great crack in the rock pile, legs kicking wildly. They were pulled up through the water at a dizzying speed; up and up until air exploded around their faces and they bobbed like floats on the surface of a still sea. So it wasn't a castle-destroyer, just a castle-escaper. She was relieved; the less damage the better, because it meant less evil done. She saw the legs of the others, kicking vigorously below the water level.

Merlain breathed, and choked. One of the pains grabbed her hair and pulled her head up. "You can breathe air now but you can't breathe water," the kinglet reminded her.

She spat. She was finding that out. She had kept her face in the water when she inhaled, not realizing. This last spell had nullified the orcs' magic as soon as they hit air.

Charles remained orc-sized. His legs and arms thrashed, making waves. Now Merlain wished it had been one of the pains who had taken the last of the Alice Water. Charles couldn't swim, in his natural form, while the kinglets were swimming as if they were part orcs. Evidently the Royal Pool they had at their home was not merely for show.

Moving her own legs and arms, keeping herself afloat in the choppy sea as well as she could, Merlain saw the pains clinging to the coppery cables of Charles' hair. They were shouting in his ears: calming him, getting him to move and breathe right. Merlain choked on seawater, and then one of the kinglets had her and was swimming with her. She flailed, and caught hold of what had to be Charles' undershirt. Soon she was above the water on Charles' shoulders, and the pains were there in his hair, and Charles was actually swimming.

Merlain hung tightly to the fabric that had grown with her brother's increase in size. Now the weave was as coarse as a net. She held really tight and hoped that he would keep swimming and that he would not suddenly shrink.

There were no boats on the water, but ahead, far, far away, was something that could be the island. At first she didn't think it was the island, and then the water shook from her eyes and she definitely saw the pile of rocks that had been the castle. She heard one of the kinglets shouting, "Keep going! Keep going! You can make it!"

Water splashed, and her position changed as Charles found his footing on shallows and stood up. There were the rocks, and there the ruined castle. For the moment there were no orcs. Charles was wading ashore.

Suddenly he stopped, his hand reaching back to his enlarged travelsack. He bent down, plunged his hand into the sack, and emerged holding the giant Alice Water bottle. He bent, placing the huge bottle on the shore.

Merlain was wondering what her brother was doing when he roared out, "Maybe a little Alice Water inside. You try it."

At that moment one of the pains let loose Charles' hair and dropped onto the rim of the bottle. "Kildee! Kildee!" the other kinglet shouted.

Kildee looked up at them, made a futile grab, and slid down the neck of the bottle. Listening, Merlain imagined she heard a small splash. A tiny drop in the bottle would now be a pailful, and a small fraction of a drop should be enough to make one of them into a giant.

Nothing happened for a moment. Then the sides of the bottle simply flew apart. Kildee grew up mightily, passed Charles in size, and towered with his head in the sky. He must have gulped down all the Alice Water he could, before it started taking effect! The huge dose was making him truly huge.

"GRAB HOLD!" Charles called, and started climbing Kildee's pant leg.

Kildee reached down a hand fully as big as giant Kildom's had been. Charles climbed on it, rested on it, clung to it, and lay on it as the hand lifted higher and higher into the sky.

Charles, what are you doing? Merlain thought at her orc-sized brother as she and Kildom were carried up with him. The height was dizzying, and she felt twice as precarious as before.

Too busy, Merlain. Have to talk to Kildee while I can.

Merlain clung to the shirt weave and looked to either side where the clouds floated. She looked up and saw Kildee's chin, now a large cliff. She heard her giant brother shout to the giant giant: **"THE OPAL! DIG IT OUT IF IT'S STILL THERE!"**

Kildee's hand tilted, clouds vanished as her tummy tickled her, and then her brother and his passengers were put down on the shore. Two enormous Kildee fingers and a thumb lifted great rocks from the old castle and dropped them into the sea with fearful splashings. Far faster than an army of orcs could have done it, the giant uncovered the lower floors.

Suddenly Charles waved his arms and shouted: **"STOP!"**

Kildee either heard or remembered. His hand came down and Charles grabbed a finger. They rose up, Merlain and Kildom supported by Charles and Charles by the finger. Seemingly forgetting that they were even there, Charles swung out, making no effort to pull himself up onto the palm. The gleaming opal lay undamaged in the wreckage, down below Charles' feet. Hanging on to the weave, seeing it there, Merlain grasped her brother's unspoken intention. "Let me! Let me!" she cried.

He heard, though Kildee couldn't have. Charles dropped a fearful height for her, an easy step down for him. His finger poked to his undershirt. She grabbed the finger—so large, yet so much smaller than Kildee's. She held on tight and was lifted over and down into the jumble of broken rock and plaster and ruined furniture and art. She let go when her feet touched the top of a table.

The orc's magical opal lay like an overlarge egg in a rumpled nest of velvet. She reached out and touched. To her it was the size of a large ball, heavy and a bit slippery as she grasped and lifted it. She was about to shout up or think up to Charles, but there his fingers were, gently taking her waist with his big thumb. The ruins receded from beneath her feet and—

THUMP!

She lay on the ground, a little dizzy but otherwise unharmed. Charles, now normal size, was flat on the rocks above her. Kildom was there with her. She had fallen maybe twice her height as Charles shrank.

She gazed up at what seemed a great tower of smoke: Kildee, still unshrunk. He had taken a bigger dose, later; it would be a while yet, for him.

"Oh-oh, look there!" Kildom pointed out to sea.

Merlain strained her eyes, wishing they were stronger. Ships, she guessed.

Charles touched the side of Kildee's boot, now the size of a large ship. He seemed determined to climb it, but something white and enormous moved down to a spot above them. It was Kildee's face, now the height of a windmill. His ruddy cheeks expanded. There was a terrible blowing sound, and what little Merlain could see of the ships were quickly carried backward.

Kildee's hand appeared by his feet. They climbed on it, no more than the size of bugs to him.

Kildee lifted them high. His great right leg lifted and he stepped into the water. He splashed through the shallows where the rest of them could have drowned, and out to where it was for him waist-deep. The little waves seemed to tip him, and he struggled with them and every little breeze. Yet despite his difficulties he made swift progress from the perspective of the little flies. Merlain hoped that none of them fell off, because it would be unlikely that Kildee would notice or could rescue them if he did. It wasn't as if it were easy to gain his attention.

SPLASH, SPLASH, SPLASH. Step by big step, going back, back, Merlain hoped, in the direction of Rotternik. Oh, how much she hoped!

St. Helens gasped as the tall, ugly orcs appeared suddenly right in front of them. All were at least the size of the trees on both sides of their path. Yet they had not just materialized or dropped an invisibility cloak, but had come walking up from the distant sea.

Drops of water glistened in the sunlight on the greenish

scales of Brudalous and his long, incredibly sharp looking sword. At one glance St. Helens could see that it was really the leader he had spoken to with Helbah's crystal. In the magic communication quartz that was for him so highly reminiscent of television, the orc had appeared almost laughable in his ugliness. Of course there had been no clue to his size, and St. Helens naturally had not thought to inquire.

"ST. HELENS!" Brudalous shouted. "Do you surrender unconditionally? You may surrender or die here, as is your choice."

St. Helens swallowed. Just what had he gotten himself into? He had thought the stories of the size of orcs exaggerated. Stories were always exaggerated! He knew, because that was the only kind he told. Now he could see that one of them could easily lift a man *and* his horse, and hurl both at the sky, if the orc liked. Those muscles swelling beneath the overlapping scales were in every way gigantic. Scales over muscle? For orcs it must be natural. Anyway, this ended any thought of building ships to take them to where the orcs lived. St. Helens knew himself to be a fool at times—more often than he liked to admit—but he wasn't *that* big a fool!

"Well?" Morton Crumb demanded of him. "You going to reply to that?"

Crumb would like to make the reply himself, St. Helens thought. Not that Crumb begrudged him his leadership, but he had done his best to talk him out of this foolish mission. Crumb had been right at his side when he made that call, shaking his head negatively and indicating with his hands that he should use a milder, more polite tone of voice. Naturally St. Helens had ignored that. Now, seeing the orcs up close, St. Helens wished that he had heeded his second in command's advice.

"WE FIGHT!" St. Helens bellowed, frustratingly unable to match the sheer authority of the orc's voice. Wish that he might, there wasn't another thing that could come from his mouth in reply to that challenge.

The orcs came forward, step by unhurried step, swinging their sharp, long, deadly swords.

"How?" Mor demanded of him. "Those swords of theirs can cut through trees! They're so long they can slice through us before we're in arm's length. *Our* arm's length. How do we get within striking distance?"

St. Helens knew his old friend and irritating companion had to be right. Yet there was a way or two, and he had planned on these just in case the orcs should be more than he had bargained for. That was certainly the case!

"Catapults!" St. Helens ordered. They should have time to set these up, considering the speed with which the orcs were advancing. Barely time.

The brush was whacked down with swift sword blows, and the catapults wheeled up in a staggered, though imposing line. Heavy boulders brought all the way from home and chosen for their sphere shape and probably accuracy of flight were loaded. The catapults had been tied down for travel; the moment the ties were cut, they would hurl their burdens.

At his command, the long timbers flashed upward, and the great ammunition balls shot outward in sizzling hot flight. They arced toward the advancing enemy. It was wonderful!

St. Helens saw one of the orcs clutch his stomach where a boulder struck. He was going to whoop with joy, but at that moment Brudalous reached high to grasp with his own two webbed hands an identical projectile. The chief of the orcs staggered from the weight and speed of the boulder, but stopped it and held it up as if it were an overlarge beach ball. To the orc, St. Helens realized with shock, the boulder was playing size and catchably light. He just had to get his balance and be ready for it.

St. Helens winced. Then he gulped. The rock was coming back at them, hurled by the superb arm muscles of the enemy orc.

CRASH!

Bits of broken timber flew in all directions. More accurate than the catapult had been, the orc had dropped the boulder squarely on its extended arm. The timber had splintered into wood chips, sending broken cables off in all directions. The catapult crewmen crouched low and hid their heads.

"I don't think we can stop them with catapults," Mor remarked.

The pointed-eared Rudian had told him that before. St. Helens smoldered. Why hadn't he listened? Now he was in the extremely awkward position of having to back down from a stance, and his army wasn't doing well either.

Someone screamed "RUN!" and his troops were abruptly in fast retreat. Some discipline! An ordinary man could hardly blame them, after the business with the catapult. St. Helens did, though. He started in on a long, convoluted, and probably useless curse.

"Best idea," Mor said. "They'll let us escape, I think."

St. Helens had a different notion. "Charge!"

"You crazy?" Mor's demand was a whiplash to his burning rage.

You know it! he thought. *Cursed son-in-law left without leaving a decent weapon! Damn him! What I wouldn't give for a laser, or just that beautiful little old levitation belt!*

"Move it, Sean!" Mor was already wheeling his big warhorse.

St. Helens did the thing that he knew was least expected. He shouted "CHARGE!" just the way Teddy Roosevelt had at San Juan Hill. Just as loudly and senselessly, though certainly not as well backed. He dug his spurless heels into the sides of his war-horse, demanding the equine's attention. The animal shied, shivered, and then obeyed his master's incomprehensible command.

St. Helens charged all with leveled, sharp, and deadly dragon lance. That lance should account for anything living, he had felt. But as he drew closer to those tree-trunk legs, he was less certain.

At this speed the lance should go all the way through Brudalous' scaled middle. It should bring him down, spouting orc blood and dying. With the orc leader dead, slain at the outset, there should be some remote chance of a Confederation victory. *Think victory,* St. Helens told himself, concentrating on the target. No way at all dare he now think about himself. Or the fact that he had no support at all from his army.

Brudalous' great sword tip was suddenly in front of him. Just before the spear head reached it, the awful blade swung away. Then it swung back, fast, catching the shaft of St. Helens' ponderous weapon. The spear head of a size to do for the largest living creature coexisting on St. Helens' Earth flew up through tree branches and on its way in diagonal flight to an unknown destination.

Brudalous, giant leader, was unperturbed. With an almost casual motion of his sword he had rendered harmless St. Helens' single best weapon.

CHAPTER 18

Dragon's Tail

Merlain experienced a falling, rushing sensation as the clouds vanished and the water rushed up. She gasped, thought to scream, and then with a slight shock that produced wavy motions she was down. She found herself on a flat green surface surrounded by other green carpets, some with huge whitish flowers on them. Kildom and a normal-sized Charles were sprawled beside her. Swiftly, very swiftly, Kildee was shrinking down to their size too.

Water lapped up on the lily pad, wetting her, and then receded. They were back in Rotternik, having outdistanced the orcs and escaped from the kingdom of Ophal. She was still clutching the opal she had stolen, and hadn't the slightest notion what to do with it.

In fact, she was confused about what to do with herself. She had resolved not to steal anymore, yet here was the opal. How could she set that right? She didn't know, which meant she would have to follow the lead of the boys, which was no good thing.

Kildee pulled himself out of the hole in the great leaf just before he stopped shrinking. His weight as a giant had made the hole in it even while he was getting smaller. Now that he was a little boy again in size as well as brain, he was light enough for the leaf of the water plant to support, and it was leveling out. He lay on his back, panting.

He was also small enough to tempt a predator insect that appeared. The long-abdomened creature was the size of a preybird, its four wings raising a breeze. It hovered a moment, then lit on Kildee's chest. Its horrible mouth opened as it prepared to bite off the boy-king's foolish head.

Kildee lay there, petrified, evidently unable to twitch a muscle. Merlain was no better; her scream was stuck in her throat.

Charles!

SWISH!

The insect's head bounced on the great leaf and rebounded into the water. A fish leaped up and snatched the faceted-eyed horror, splashing them all on its way down. The decapitated body spurted green goop that missed Kildee's face as he squirmed out of the thing's embrace. The insect had been served as it had thought to serve him: it had lost its head.

"Thanks, Charles," Kildee gasped a moment later. Charles nonchalantly cleaned his sword. His smug expression said what he wanted them to think: that as his father's son he was naturally heroic, and slaying ravenous insects was all in a hero's day's work.

Merlain knew better, for she could read his mind. He had been as stunned as the rest of them, but the little girl Glow had called to him, jogging him into action. Glow had almost forced his arm to grasp the sword and swing it accurately.

Glow? There was no such girl here! Who was she?

Merlain strained to get her thought straight. There *was* someone they knew by that name, but—

"None of us will get big again," Kildom complained, and Merlain's thought slipped away like an elusive little fish. Trust the pains to ruin anything significant, even if it was only in her head! "Charles busted the bottle when you drank."

Kildee, former giant, shrugged. "It wasn't his fault. Besides, what would have saved us and gotten us the opal if I hadn't gone super giant?"

Charles nodded. He had not done the deed; he had merely jogged the stopper loose. Kildee had burst the bottle by his increasing size. But he evidently saw no point in debating technicalities. "There wasn't much time. I didn't want the bottle broken."

I know you didn't, Charles, Merlain thought at him. *The Alice Water was all gone anyway. But the pain is right: we can't any of us grow big again.*

We won't need to. We've got the spelling book. We can call up the big bird to carry us all back.

I hate it! I won't call up the bird again! I won't do any more witch magic! She was finally finding the place to put her foot down. Stealing and witch magic: they seemed to be linked.

Well, we can walk. Or the opal—we do have the opal.

Yes. They had been wrong to steal it, but at least the opal itself wasn't evil, as far as she knew. They could use it without further compromising themselves. Maybe it would even be possible to return it to the orcs, after the four of them were safely home.

But *could* they use it? Would it take all of them through the frames, or just some of them? They had no book of instructions for it; how could they possibly make it work?

Not really intending anything, Merlain stared hard at the opal. She was sitting cross-legged with it resting in her lap. The sun beat down hotly, and the lily pad had a definite smell to it, and it made her think about the children's suite they had left an aeon ago, it seemed. Her fingers stroked the smooth, cool sides of the opal. How nice it would be to be back there, safe, as if all this had never happened!

She heard the little fat boy shriek. He was staring at her, all big-eyed astonishment.

Fat boy?

"Look, Miss Pringle! Merlain just appeared right out of the air! She's sitting where I threw up my chokabola!"

"Hush, Ebbernog! That fibbing of yours has to stop!"

"But Miss Pringle, just look!"

"I haven't time. I have to read this numerology lesson."

Point-eared children and shapely young witches and handsome, muscular warlocks were all around, busy with their concerns and not interested in this corner. Merlain wished for the invisibility cloak. She was still cross-legged, still holding the opal between her fingers. Now that the brat had mentioned it, she could definitely feel and smell his vomit. *I will never,* she thought to herself, *drink chokabola again!*

Auntie Jon's face was suddenly near her own. Under her arm she could see Ebbernog with a big playball, still wide-eyed. Auntie Jon, or whoever this was, had popped out from an invisibility cloak.

"So you got it for me, Merlain! That's my bad girl! I knew you could do it! You have the makings of a truly malignant witch! It comes naturally to you. Give it here!"

Merlain's rebellion had been sputtering, overwhelmed by the onrushing circumstances. Now it solidified. "No! No, you can't have it! You said it was for Helbah! Besides, you're not really Auntie Jon!"

The smiling face turned ugly. "Now, what makes you think that? Give it to me, brat!"

Merlain shied away, but strong fingers pried at hers. The smell of Auntie Jon, or whoever this was, was worse than the vomit. Merlain felt nauseated, as if she might throw up herself. She didn't want to give up the opal, because then she'd have no way to return to the others, to rescue them. Yet how could she, a little girl, resist anyone so strong?

Her mind reached to Ebbernog just as the big clawed fingers started to nip through the skin on her hands. She thought of the fat boy throwing his ball, bouncing it against her tormenter's back. She was normally unable to influence any ordinary person this way, but this was exactly the kind

of mischief such a boy enjoyed, and she was desperate.
Maybe a strong nudge—

THUMP!

An ugly old witch was revealed, grasping the back of her
head where the ball had struck. This was what the imitation
Jon was really like! This wasn't Auntie Jon at all, just as
she had thought! This was someone whose image belonged
in that spelling book!

A blond witch screamed. A wizard with bulging muscles
ran across the suite, magic baton raised above his head, eyes
on this corner. Help was coming!

The witch who was not Auntie Jon threw an invisibility
cloak over Merlain. She disappeared herself, and a cloud of
smoke obscured the running wizard. She was going to do
something dreadful to get the opal from Merlain.

Merlain tightened her fingers even more on the opal, so
very hard they hurt. She must not give it up! She wished
she was home with her mother and father.

The air changed. Instead of sanitary suite with a background of brat vomit, it was now warm and pure backwoods
country with a background of animal manure and soap and
a foreground of delicious.

She was sitting cross-legged on the kitchen floor, holding
the opal on her lap. Her hands still smarted where the
witch's claws had stabbed her. She was still invisible: she
could see right through herself and the opal to the well-
scrubbed floor. Her mother was just cleaning out the scrubbing brush with the point of a knife, dropping dollops of
soapy dust back into the bucket. In a moment her mother
would take the bucket aside and empty it on a bare spot
away from the back door.

Merlain sniffed. Her mother had baked cooakes and
frosted them! Her favorite kind—peajel butter! Her father
wasn't in sight, and neither was Charles. This was wonderful, but there was something odd about it. If her parents
were here, how could they be . . . ?

Merlain got to her feet, quietly, keeping the cloak of invisibility in place. She looked out the window into her back-

yard. The flowers and the fence looked a bit different, but this was home. It looked like home, it smelled like home. Just why her mother was here scrubbing the floor she didn't know. Mother should be back at the convention. Father should be too. And Helbah, and of course Grandma and Granddad and Auntie Jon.

Merlain ran from around the side of the house shouting something. She was pursued by Charles, who caught up with her and grabbed her by a shoulder and pulled her around. Charles had mud in his hand and he was going to wipe it on her, maybe in her lovely coppery hair.

Merlain screamed loudly. Her mother looked through Merlain and the opal and out the window.

"Now, Charles, you stop that!" Mother said. "You stop teasing your sister."

"She started it," Charles said. He was looking back through Merlain and opal to Mother."

"I did not!" Merlain-outside said. "He called me old dragon poop!"

"No, I didn't!"

"Yes, you did!"

"I called you *fat* dragon poop."

"Children, what am I going to do with you!" Mother said rhetorically. Merlain wasn't sure what the word meant, but knew it was the right one.

It was about the only right thing about this situation. For this couldn't be right, invisible Merlain thought. This couldn't be her home at all. This had to be one of those almost-the-same worlds where a Merlain and Charles were almost like her and her brother, but misbehaved. But then she and her brother did often misbehave, so that wasn't certain.

Something else nagged at her, and after a moment she identified it. There had been no mental communication. It had all been verbal. Why hadn't they been thinking insults at each other, instead of yelling them?

Charles, you're serpent poop! she thought at the boy outside.

There was no reaction. She knew he hadn't received her thought. He wasn't telepathic.

Now she knew this wasn't right, and that she shouldn't be here. She didn't *want* to be here. She wanted her own frame, not an almost frame. She wanted to be back where she had left Charles and the royal pains. She knew they needed her, and she needed her own folk.

She closed her eyes just a moment, no more than a heavy blink. Then she found herself looking not at duplicates of Charles and herself, but at giant lily pads. The sun beat down hot and the headless body of the giant insect was being feasted on by reasonably sized gnats and ants. This seemed to be the place, and there was even the hole in the lily pad where Kildee's giant feet had been before he reduced to ordinary size. Everything was as it had been before she wished herself back at the children's suite. Only one thing was different.

Charles and the pains were nowhere in sight.

St. Helens pulled his horse up short and threw away the worthless half of his dragon lance. Now all he could do was wait for that huge, merciless sword. In a moment it would swish down and lop him and his war-horse into two halves. It was an abhorrent picture, but one all too likely to occur.

But Brudalous did not strike. Instead he stuck his sword in the ground so that it stood upright. He leaned down, his great hands grasping.

St. Helens saw the hands approaching and tried to avoid them. He was too late. Before he could move, he was caught.

He felt himself lifted free of the saddle as if he were a small pet. His sword, sheathed and unbloodied, went along. He had the feeling that if he had not left the saddle, his whole horse would have been lifted too.

"Now I've got you, St. Helens, you loudmouthed troublemaker!" Brudalous said. Up close, his face was a formidable sight: shark's teeth gleaming in a mouth reminiscent of a bigmouthed trass. Eyes that were less attractive.

St. Helens thought of drawing his sword then, useless

gesture though it might be. The neck gills might be out of reach, but there was that big nose. A blade rammed up a nostril would hurt. It was a small price the orc would pay for taking his life. He tensed his shoulder muscles, about to make a lightning sword draw.

But just then a finger as muscular as his own arm pinned his forearm to his side and scabbard. He couldn't even start his move.

"Coward!" St. Helens cried. It was hardly more than a hint of defiance, all that he could manage at the moment. Unfortunately his voice sounded less than heroic.

Brudalous put his head back and started a truly gargantuan laugh. His mouth sucked in breath and he started with "AHHH." Then, before joining it to "Ha Ha Ha!" he choked. He assumed an orc expression of surprise and pain, and his fingers loosened. St. Helens dropped out from the orc's grasp.

There were scales around the orc's middle, and a sword belt. St. Helens grabbed the belt buckle and held on. He swung out and dropped, as from a branch of a tree. He lit, knocking his breath out, hurting his ankles and knees. The drop might have killed him, but he landed on springy grass on his hands and knees, taking up some of the shock.

Something wet hit his face. He looked up to see the orc chieftain dancing wildly, holding his own foot in his hands. Blood was on the foot, and it was green. As St. Helens realized this another drop flew down and hit him in the mouth.

St. Helens saw Mor Crumb reaching down to him. He grabbed the hand and was hoisted up on a big war-horse's broad rump.

"What'd you do, Mor?" St. Helens gasped.

"Stabbed a toe," Mor said. "Hang on. We're retreating!"

At this point St. Helens included to argue. The horse galloped. St. Helens hung on to Mor. Ahead of them their army was running as if their lives depended on it. Behind them—

Their horse shied and St. Helens fell off as the huge boulder zipped past. He landed hard—he was on the verge of developing a dislike for falls!—and he feared that this time he was done for. Almost certainly he had broken his back, the way it felt. Brudalous was coming for him at racehorse speed, not with a sword but a large knobby club. Evidently the orc intended to pound him down into the ground, where he'd stay. Giants in fairy tales, he thought as the mad world whirled around him, always used clubs. They were probably too stupid to know the use of swords.

He tried to rise. He couldn't. He closed his eyes for what had to be the end.

Dragon Horace sniffed. That was Merlain's grandfather about to get his head smashed. The man was not Horace's favorite, because he had a bad attitude about dragons, but blood was tastier than water. Or thicker. Merlain had spoken fondly of the man, and asked Horace not to hurt him. So he ought to help, like it or not.

Having thought of it, Dragon Horace did not ponder the risks and possible consequences. Tail swishing, body wriggling lizard fashion from side to side, he charged.

The man-thing stood taller than three large meer standing atop each other's backs. He smelled more fishy than human. By the time the man-thing saw him, Dragon Horace was there. He avoided the swing of the club as he would a meer's antler, crouching low to let it pass. He smelled blood on the toe, and blood was always tempting no matter its color, but there was a foot and ankle attached. To pull down big game was always the first order; it could not be eaten while it remained afoot. Pull down, disembowel: the rules for hunting were straightforward for Horace.

His teeth found the ankle and bit through scales that went CRUNCH, and thick fishy-tasting skin. He tried to get a good big bite and pull back, tearing. But Dragon Horace was young in dragon terms, barely out of the hatchling stage. The truth was that he had never fought a really hard fight.

The giant's club dropped. The foot lifted, Dragon Horace holding on and coming up with it. Teeth ground against anklebone. A long, loud scream of pain signaled that he was accomplishing something. But the foot did not come off, showing that he was not doing enough.

Dragon Horace sensed the giant's hand grabbing for his tail. That was a growl-growl. A dragon's tail was one of his main weapons, as the orc should have been aware. Anyone who tried to grab it was asking for trouble. Horace smacked the hand with his tail, using all his young-dragon strength. It sounded like a whip crack, which it was in its fashion. The orc roared again, snatching his hand back.

Dragon Horace had had enough of this. The big thing wasn't going to come down, so he was going up. That was another fundamental law of hunting: if you couldn't pull down the prey, open its throat. It was a good adage, and a philosophy that stood the average dragon in good stead. Horace started foot climbing a scaly leg.

The giant whooped and howled and roared with impressive volume, and beat on Horace's back. The dragon was unconcerned. His back was strong, his hide was metallic, and his guts were well encased. His copper heritage protected him. He climbed on and on, his claws hooking under scales and over scales and, wherever it was possible, finding their lodgings unerringly. Up there, somewhere, was a neck with a pulsing vein in it. The blood might be green and thick and taste fishy, but certainly it was going to be pleasant. Even though he was doing this for principle rather than hunger.

There it was at last: the throat. Bordered by two great gills, covered with scales as thick as tree bark. Lovely!

Horace dug in, ripping off scales. He opened his mouth, ready for the big, satisfying, life-taking bite.

Hands pushed him away. A big head came down as the hands held him out at arm's length. A mouth opened, revealing teeth as long and pointed as an adult dragon's.

Horace strained. The orc strained. Something was going to have to give sometime.

* * *

"There's another, Charles!" Kildee exclaimed, pointing wildly at the approaching giant insect. The thing's twin wings beat rhythmically as it veered in flight.

How many did this make? Charles wondered. He had slain so many that he had lost count. The fish were feeding well now, courtesy of his sword. It seemed to be divinely guided. Every time a predator came in for the kill, a kinglet or Glow screamed warning, and he reacted almost automatically, guided by her sight.

Glow?

He lost the thought as it came. He was a hero now in every sense, and with every chop of his sword and every bounce of a downed insect he was wishing that it were not so. The green glop on his face and sword stank and his arms ached and still the idiot insects came on. If only they would leave him alone, he would leave them alone! To fail to strike them down would mean getting stung or eaten, maybe carried off to feed the larvae. He would have liked to stop and shiver, but the constantly coming insects gave him no time.

Charles! There!

He swung hard at the head and thorax of a needle-shaped creature Kildee said was a flydragon. That was, considering its nature, not too silly a name. His sword bit deep. Green ichor spurted, and the weight of the flier and its momentum sent him close to the edge of the pad. The body crashed into the water and fishes boiled around it, tearing it to bits, devouring it while it was struggling. The gossamer wings were the last to go, carried off by an arrow shape that thrashed as it swam like a serpent or dragon.

"More!" Kildom shouted. There were more. Three—no, four of the creatures. If only there were some way of escaping them! Someplace to hide. Someplace, at least, that he could rest his back against.

The giant flower on the next pad! They could take refuge in its bell, and there it would be easy to keep the insects from crawling inside. What a wonderful thought. Wonderful that he, unlike certain royalty, had brains.

No, Charles!

Who was that calling mentally to him? Not Merlain; she had disappeared with the opal. But someone he knew, if only he could see her, if only he could remember. But right now he was too busy saving his hide.

He leaped to the adjoining pad, hearing fish jaws snap as he cleared the water. Those fish weren't his friends either! But they couldn't attack far outside of the water. "Kildee! Kildom! Come!"

"Charles, wait!"

He wouldn't wait. If they didn't want to be attacked by flydragons, they'd stay close to him and his flashing sword. He ran as fast as he could to the flower and climbed its waxy bell. Once inside, he'd challenge any bugs!

"Wait! Wait! Wait!" *Wait!*

What was the matter with them? The flydragons in the sky were still only specks, but coming in. The kinglets had better hurry.

The flower petal moved, like a tongue. Charles slipped. He fell inside the bell and slid downward. Someone screamed in his mind. Great stamens shook above him, bringing down a sticky yellow powder. The inside of the flower was dewy with crystal drops. He tried to turn around, but his feet slipped.

"Here, Charles!" One of the pains was reaching down to him. Gratefully he took the pain's hand.

No!

"KILDEE! HELP!" With a great cry of anguish the pain who was Kildom succumbed to undulating motions of the petals and came down on top of Charles, crushing the wind from his body.

Just as Charles was struggling to recover his breath, the face of Kildee appeared where Kildom had come from. Kildee screamed once, threw up his hands, and somersaulted off the edge, down onto them, then on past into the depths of the flower.

"HELP!" Kildee cried from the lower chamber.

The flower sucked. Charles and Kildom were pulled down to where Kildee lay downward and stuck.

Charles tried to move an arm and then a leg. He was stuck now, really stuck. He should have heeded Glow's warning. If only he could remember who she was, and why he cared about her.

About them, in the dim radiance of the flower bowl, numerous insects were stuck, as they were around the flower's stamen. Some were living, some dead, but it was evident that this hardly mattered; none would escape.

"Well, Charles, that was dumb!" Kildom said, with a certain annoying justice. The kinglet was stuck facedown, and they were almost head to head. "Don't you know an eatin' lily when you see one?"

Charles struggled with a feeling of frustration and hopelessness. He had been successfully fighting off the flying insects. He had gotten himself and the kinglets into this worse mess, by not listening to their warnings.

Finally he said the only thing there was to be said. "I do now," he sadly confessed. He closed his eyes.

Glow appeared, with a fragment of her dream world behind her. "Oh, Charles, I'm so sorry!" she said tearfully.

Now he remembered her. "I should have listened to you."

"But help is coming—maybe," she said, attempting to be positive. "In a while, I think."

"Until then, can we play together?" he asked. At least he was with her again.

"Until then," she agreed, taking his hand.

Merlain wondered, Was this the right frame? It seemed to be, but how could she be sure? The opal had after all taken her to a wrong frame when she left the convention. But then she had thought of her house and yard and her mother and Charles, all together, and that couldn't be done in her home frame. What was the poor opal to do, except take her to where these existed?

This time she had wished for the frame and place she had left. That was important: frame *and* place, and maybe time too. To give the opal accurate instructions. So it should be right. But where were the boys, then? Where?

A flower on a nearby pad took her attention. It was the size of a small house and it was vibrating. The bell of the flower was sooo large, and the way it was shaking—she had never seen a flower do that.

Could there be something living inside the flower? Maybe the boys? But if that was the case, why didn't they come out?

Well, might as well see! She leaped over to the adjoining pad, got her feet wet, and approached the flower carrying the opal. She wouldn't want to drop the opal!

Charles! she thought cautiously, fearing to get too close. After all, it might not be the boys, it might be something really bad. Sometimes there were things that pretended to be friends, but weren't. Like the fake Auntie Jon.

Merlain? He seemed to be waking from a dream; Glow was just leaving and being forgotten. *Don't come close to the flower! It's dangerous.*

So you ARE in there! she thought, relieved. *Come out!*

Can't. Sticky stuff. Kildom says we'll be digested like the big insects.

This was certainly bad news! *You've got your sword?*

Stuck like glue. So is my arm.

What are you doing in there anyhow?

Swarm of insects—big insects. Seemed a safe place. Only it wasn't.

Dumb! she agreed. *Which pain thought of it?*

Neither one. It was my dumb idea. They tried to stop me and fell in too. Don't come any closer.

You want to be digested?

NO! But at least you can escape.

Then I'll get some help. I have the opal, and now I know how to use it. I can go back to the convention, and—

No. Kildee says there's no time. They'll keep you there and question you, and not believe you're not fibbing, and by the time you get someone to listen to you we'll all be eaten.

But—Yet she knew his point was valid. Adults never listened to children when it counted.

Kildom says the opal will teleport you to anywhere you want to go. In this frame, not just out of it.

Was that true? That might make a difference.

Go get someone who knows about these flowers—FAST!

Yes, yes, I will. Charles' thought had been really urgent. But who could she go to? Some adult. Grandfather St. Helens would know. Grandfather St. Helens claimed to know everything. And he was too ornery to do things the sensible adult way. He might actually listen to her.

Merlain stroked the smooth, slippery sides of the opal and thought about how she wanted to be with her ornery grandfather.

Just like that, she was there. But her hope of help was no closer to realization.

Grandfather St. Helens lay on the ground. And there was Uncle Lester's big father on a big horse. And there, just a little way from both of them, so close they might get stepped on, was the orc king, Brudalous. He was holding something out at arm's length that was all wriggles and copper color. Something alive.

Oh, no!

Merlain! it responded, recognizing her thought. At least that was the way she interpreted the signal.

For what Brudalous held was her very dear other brother. Dragon Horace and the orc, both busily snapping their teeth at each other!

St. Helens didn't know whether to believe his eyes. Had he taken a blow to the head when falling? That couldn't be his cute little six-year-old granddaughter who had just appeared here on this battlefield! Yet it certainly looked like her. One moment nothing, and the next heartbeat she was there. Unless he was hallucinating, which did seem to be an excellent prospect, all things considered.

Suddenly Merlain was much nearer the struggling combatants and looking up at them with what her grandfather

knew were weak eyes. She had a nice little personality, but
not the best sight. Maybe the two went together.

"BRUDALOUS, YOU LET HIM GO!" Merlain cried
out in a shrill, childish voice. "HORACE, YOU BEHAVE
YOURSELF!"

The dragon dropped from the orc's grasp, lit on his feet,
and ran to her. Her little arms reached out, as if to a beloved
pet. Copper-scaled, pony-sized dragon, coppery-haired girl
joyfully met, and the child hugged the monster and the
monster's tongue licked the child.

"Merlain! You've got the opal! Give it here!" the orc
king said. He seemed surprised. His recently injured hand
was reaching out, and he was crouched down, waiting. The
opal was, after all, what everything was about.

Merlain was busy wiping greenish and reddish blood from
Horace's dragon face. She was using a piece of filthy but
once purple-colored blouse. She seemed quiet uninterested
in the outstretched hand.

"Merlain," St. Helens said, coming to his senses, sitting
up on the ground and managing, with a remarkable effort,
to find his voice. "Give the opal to your grandpa."

The little girl glanced at him. "Are you hurt, Grandfather
Volcano?"

"No." He stood up, surprised to discover that he really
wasn't. "I'm not hurt, but the opal—"

"I need it," Merlain said. She took hold of Dragon Horace's very small and quite unusable wings and put one che-
rubic but ungirlishly dirty little leg over the coppery
monster's head. She was straddling its neck region. Her face
came down until she rested her small chin directly above
the dragon's brow.

She paused, now glancing at Brudalous. "I know it's your
opal, Your Majesty, and I'm sorry we stole it, and I'll give
it back to you, honest, but right now I just have to have it
to save my brother and friends."

Then she spoke to the dragon, who had been quiet while
she bestrode him. "Stay with me, Horace."

She held the opal in front of her, seeming to caress it.

Suddenly she and the dragon weren't there. The only sign remaining of their presence was one drop of dragon's blood and two of orc's blood on the flattened grass.

Brudalous and St. Helens looked at each other, similarly bemused, for the moment comrades in astonishment.

Merlain and Dragon Horace were on the giant lily pad facing the pad with the huge flower. For her part Merlain was surprised. She wondered whether Horace was. She had not quite believed that it would work: that she could transport him here as well as herself. But she had hoped, and now she was relieved. She had wanted to save Horace, and to help the others, and this might accomplish both. She hoped.

Charles?

Here, Merlain.

Charles, I brought Dragon Horace.

You brought our brother? Why? What good can he do?

I don't know, Charles. But you know how dragons are. Strong. Besides that, Horace is smart.

Don't waste time, Merlain! Our skins are burning and our clothes are crumbling.

I won't. She turned to the dragon. *Horace, Charles and two of our friends are in the flower. They can't get out. Can you help? Please help.*

Dragon Horace walked to the edge of the path. He wriggled into the water and crossed the short jumping distance in a couple more wriggles. A predator fish tried to bite, but Horace simply brought his snoot around and snapped that fish out of the water. He crawled up on the neighboring pad, and two big (and stupid) insects attacked. Horace snapped twice, and both were gone, with only one insect wing fluttering to the pad. After that the insects stayed clear of the region.

Horace crawled up to the big white flower and sniffed it. *Careful, Horace! Don't let it hurt you!*

Horace's thought was a reassuring tongue flick that Merlain knew was his signal for affection or anger or understanding. It was an all-purpose response, meaning whatever was necessary.

Horace wriggled up to the flower and tried a deep, hard

bit on the outside of the bowl. A greenish sap spurted forth, and from the depths of the bowl came a keening that hurt Merlain's ears.

I don't think it likes that, Horace, she thought, satisfied. Then she reconsidered. *But look! The hole you made is closing up!*

Dragon Horace spat out the piece of flower he had taken. Evidently he did not like the taste, so was not inclined to try other bites. Instead he levered himself up to a drooping petal at the top of the bowl. He peered down inside.

WHOOSH!

Dragon Horace was pulled partially inside by a sudden suction. His front claws dug into the flower and he hung there, his head barely visible to her, the rest of his body inside the bowl. Now she understood how the boys could have gotten trapped; that flower had some tricky mechanisms!

A thought come from inside. *Merlain, Dragon Horace's tail is just above my face!*

Well, grab on to it, Charles! Her brother was so dumb, sometimes!

I—can't. It's too sticky in here. I can't move my arm far enough. We're stuck. I think his tail is stuck too.

That flower needs a whipping! Merlain thought. *Dragon Horace, do something!*

Horace said, "Gurlump!" He seemed to try to pull himself up, straining where his claws held the petal. He was strong; he began to come up out of it, dragging the side of the bowl into a wrinkle.

Suddenly the great bell, the entire flower in fact, shook, vibrated, and echoed forth a Whup, Whup, Whup! It was the sound a leather strap might make.

Merlain! He's beating up the inside of the flower! Skin's tearing in here! Insects are shaking loose!

Well, you want out, don't you?

Merlain! I'm loose! The glue isn't holding! Horace's tail is whipping it into froth! Kildom and Kildee are loose!

Good enough! Stop it, Horace! she thought to the dragon. *You have overcome the flower. They want out.*

The beating stopped. The flower quivered and its petals drooped. It had been defeated.

Merlain, I've got hold of his tail now!

Then climb out.

I am. "Kildom, Kildee, don't be afraid of the dragon. He's our brother."

Merlain fidgeted until first her brother and then the royal pains emerged from the bell. They were all well slimed, filthy with pollen, and with insect parts stuck to them. Some of their skin had turned red and was peeling as if from sunburn. Dragon Horace waited until they had dropped to the pad, then pulled his tail free, dropped, bounced, and rebounded. Stuck to his formidable tail were great patches of cream-colored flower skin.

"Oh, the poor flower!" Merlain said. "I didn't want you to hurt it!"

Brother and pains exchanged a glance which was surprisingly similar to the glance grown men exchanged in the presence of idiotic but harmless women. Merlain was sure it was coincidence.

"Of course not," Charles said. "Why should anyone want to hurt a flower, just because it was going to eat your brother!"

"Well, that's its nature. You have your nature. The pains—excuse me, I mean the royals—have theirs. Horace has his. I have mine. All the poor flowers wanted was a meal. Are you boys hurt?"

"We'll recover," one of the pains said, peeling off a strip of browned skin from his flushed right arm. "Eatin' lilies take their time."

"Oh, I'm so glad!" Merlain said. But right now she had to think of getting them cleaned up and presentable. It was always best to make a good reappearance, particularly when out of thin air.

CHAPTER 19

Ultimatum

"You still wish to invade Ophal, Commander Reilly?" the orc demanded.

St. Helens shook his head, glancing at Mor and wishing he was elsewhere. It had been a bewildering series of events. He felt Brudalous was ready to retreat himself; he knew he was. Technically both armies were infringing on Klingland territory, though his army represented the Confederation to which Klingland was a part. With the official rulers gone and King Rufurt of Rud acting as temporary, things got a little sticky in the legality department. His army was more within the law then the orc's army—but what did that matter, in war?

"I'd like to call it quits," St. Helens said, "though I haven't the authority to surrender. All I want are the children."

"We do not have the children, as you now know. They not only invaded Ophal by themselves and destroyed a landmark and a seamark, they did other damage as well."

"I'm certain the Confederation will pay. It's only right."
How he hated being in the wrong!

"And they have stolen Ophal's greatest treasure." The
orc leader put down his big knobby club. He drew his huge
sword from the ground where he had stabbed it, brushed
off its shiny blade with a scaled hand, and resheathed it at
his side. He picked up the club again. The club had a leather
thong that went over a thick shoulder, and the orc leader
did not place an arm through the loop of the thong. "The
girl said she would return the opal, but how can we depend
on the word of a child?"

"It wasn't an official act," St. Helens said. "If we can
settle this matter without fighting—"

"Without your being destroyed," the giant corrected him.

St. Helens swallowed, eyeing the club. It galled him to
back down on anything, and there was the prophecy. Yet
little Merlain had admitted guilt, and still had the orc's opal.
Astonishingly, though not unnaturally, he felt that he had
had enough.

"It's a matter for heads of state," he said. "I'm only a
gen—eh, an officer."

"You may not be for long," Brudalous warned. "I am
the sovereign ruler of Ophal, and I demand a face-to-face
meeting with the rulers of the Confederation who stole our
jewel."

"That can probably be arranged. Boys will be boys, Your
Highness."

The orc lifted the club slightly, positioning it over St.
Helens' helmeted noggin. He showed his shark's teeth in a
grin that was horrible. "Orcs will be orcs, Commander,
especially when crossed. Your Confederation has three days
to make all right. If nothing is done by the end of that time,
I will invade with all the orcs that are necessary. Ophal will
have satisfaction, one way or another."

St. Helens believed him.

King Rufurt raised a hand above the viewing crystal Helbah had left him and listened to the words Brudalous had

spoken. He brought his hand down in a slashing motion, blanking the crystal as effectively as if he had made the proper pass. He stood alone in the silence of his private room in the palace, considering what he had just seen in the polished hunk of crystalline rock. The facets, acting magically now, reflected back his own heavy features with particular emphasis on the nose that would have looked equally well on a comedian or village drunk.

"So, St. Helens," he told his images. "So, round-eared temperamental friend. You'd negotiate if you could, wouldn't you? Even you can see that as warfare goes you have met more than the Confederation's match."

King Rufurt, former king of Rud, now just a mere figurehead, looked out the window onto some flower beds and a bright day. It wouldn't be so pretty here if the orcs conquered. Nothing in his original kingdom would ever again be the same. Orcs were ugly creatures, tall and reputedly brutal. He knew nothing about them except the legends he'd heard as a child. Witches were almost as strange, he thought, though he had been married to one.

Would Helbah and the missing Kildom and Kildee do the right thing for the Confederation? He believed they would, yet there was so much he didn't know about them. Isolationism had totally disappeared since the advent of the prophesied Roundear.

Would Lester Crumb fulfill the mission he had gone on? Would he get to the witches' convention and talk to Helbah? What about the roundear and his magic gauntlets? Truly, potential history—or was it history in process?—was a great uncertainty. He hoped Helbah and the roundear would soon return, and that the two of them could and would clear up the mess and salvage something.

Who would have thought that innocent children could cause such mischief!

"Wasn't the little dragon cute?" Phenoblee massaged his hurt hand, magicking it into wholeness. She had started with his throat, where the nasty beast had ripped off scales.

"Cute! Cute is hardly the word!"

"Oh, but it is! All coppery and bright! And the most remarkable thing is that it's from the same spawning as the tads."

"Wonderful. But if those Confederation creatures don't make things right, we're going to have a war. We have to have our opal back!"

"Not really, not with our superior intelligence."

"That's not enough without the opal! We need it to jump around and behind the enemy forces. Without it, we'll have to move on land only by foot."

"Oh, I forgot about that! I can conjure you and individual troops back here to me, and return you to your army there, but that won't do you much good in a combat situation."

"Yes. Female, are you going to help us fight while we're stuck afoot, or are you going to cry over those pests?"

"You won't ask me to hurt them?"

"No, but we have to defend ourselves. If the humans want a fight, we'll give them a fight. We have before. Even without using the opal."

"With Hermandy. But now it's almost all the rest. Only Throod and Rotternik are not involved, and Throod will probably provide mercenaries."

"I'm certain your magic will be superior to anything they can throw against us, wife." Actually he had his doubts, now that the opal was gone, but she was the best they had remaining.

"Oh, Brudalous!" Her loving arms reached out for him.

Brudalous knew he was in for another long, fatiguing night. The things he had to put up with to gain a proper advantage in battle! As if that pesty little dragon hadn't been nuisance enough!

Merlain saw the big ugly bird first. It had the appearance of the witch who had pretended to be Auntie Jon and had shown her true form finally at the convention. Had that mean witch followed her here?

Not quite sure why she did it, Merlain whipped off her

cloak and threw it over Dragon Horace. As happened with invisibility cloaks, it seemed to stretch to cover him. She looked to the sky and saw the bird coming fast.

"What'd you do that for?" Kildee asked. The boys were sitting cross-legged, studying the books they had. They had been engrossed in the ugly pictures of the spelling book and had not seen the bird.

"Get under there, on Horace's back!" Merlain ordered, her understanding of the situation solidifying. "Stay there until I tell you!" To the dragon she thought: *Stay hidden! Keep them hidden!*

Something in her voice caused the kinglets to obey. Not a word of painish argument escaped their lips. They scrambled under, their faces turning ghastly pale as she pulled the cloak across and drew it taut on their backs and heads.

"Be still!" Merlain warned them again.

A moment later a great ugly swoosh lit in front of her. Immediately it turned into the horrid old witch with her bad breath, ghastly pale complexion, and assorted hairy warts.

"Give me the opal!" Zady ordered the frightened little girl. She held her hand out confidently, too contemptuous of the child to use her magic.

"No, I won't!" Merlain said rebelliously. When the witch had assumed the semblance of good Auntie Jon, the brats had not said no to her, but that had changed now that her identity was known. Well, no matter. The girl backed up on the lily pad as the round-eyed Charles stared at her. At Merlain's words the silly boy drew his undersized sword.

Zady wanted to laugh. This idiot child thought to confront the most powerful malignant witch in any of the frames with a mere sword! A mock sword at that! One whose magic he did not understand, and which wouldn't do him any good anyway. What a farce!

Charles' young forehead crinkled. The child had no barrier and she could read him as clearly as if he were shouting.

Now, Horace! Now!

What was the foolish brat doing? Calling someone mentally? Horace? Which of the benign warlocks had been named Horace? And what could he do, from far across the frames, even if he heard the child's pitiful thought?

"GAWOOF!"

What? That sounded almost like a—

She turned to see a small coppery dragon bearing down on her in a burst of speed. Just then an unwatched foot kicked her ankle, hurting her and causing her to delay her magic. The dragon's tail swooshed, striking her across the chest and face. It stung ferociously! Zady fell off the lily pad. She splashed into the sea, and water caught her and closed over her. Something living grabbed her foot and pulled her down.

"BLUB!" the witch exclaimed angrily. "BLUP, GLUP, SUB!" These were not precisely words of magic. There was too much water in her mouth and nose and then in her stomach and lungs. When she got out of this, she'd teach those brats! She'd teach them proper!

"BLUB!" she said with determination, producing excellent bubbles. "Blub, blub, bluuuuub!"

The tentacles holding her foot pulled her through the water closer and closer to a huge, thick-lipped mouth on a great dark shape.

How humiliating! She, the most accomplished malignant witch in all the existences, reduced to baiting fish!

"Hurry!" Merlain screamed.

The kinglets threw off the cloak of invisibility. They had remained covered, though Dragon Horace hadn't. Now the cloak whipped away from them on a gust of wind and they knew there would be no recovering it. Kildee was sorry he hadn't gotten in a single lick in the fast-concluded fight. A kick to the ankle and a whip of the tail had sent the old witch flying before he could get into the action. He looked out at the dwindling water rings, thankful that she had not reappeared.

"Hurry and do what, Merlain?"

"We've got to get out of here!"

"Why?" Kildee nodded at the water. "She's done."

"We don't know that! You know how strong she is! Witches can survive almost anything!"

"I know that, Merlain. But your dragon brother and I finished her." Deliberately he invented a part for himself and accorded her none. After all, he no longer needed to be polite to her, now that the danger was past.

"Come!"

Reluctantly, staring into the water, he dropped off the dragon's back. Merlain took his place and motioned frantically to the others. In a moment Charles and Kildom were behind her, and she was on the head of the dragon with the opal.

"Well, stupid, you want to stay?" Merlain asked.

Kildee was annoyed by her attitude, but decided that this was not quite the time to set her straight about the prerogatives of kings. She wanted him mounted, so he mounted. He took hold of his brother and held Charles' waist, while Charles held Merlain's waist.

"You certain this will work?" Kildee asked. "All of us, one opal?"

"Shut up," Charles said. "My sister has to concentrate."

"I mean they're sure to take it away from us," Kildee continued. "Even though Kildom and I boss everything, including you. Helbah thinks we're children."

"Brats," Charles said.

"Yes, she thinks we're brats. But—"

"I meant *you!* Shut up! She can't do anything while you're yakking!"

That got Kildee's dander up. "Well, I want to go exploring! I'd like to see that three-headed thing that aided your father and affected your birth."

"The chimaera? You'd faint on sight of it."

"Maybe. But maybe you'd faint yourself."

SPLASH! A very red, very angry witch's face broke the surface right at the edge of the pad. Her mouth opened and started reciting a spell. A hand lifted high out of the water, clawed fingers spread wide and grasping.

Behind her the inert form of a large water monster drifted away. It had made the mistake of annoying a witch. Already the smaller predators were zipping in to bite chunks out of it.

Kildee, belatedly, shut up.

They were surrounded by flowers and bird noises and trees. They were in some sort of garden. Everything smelled green. Back a distance was a castle.

Standing before them, looking down, not at all disturbed by their presence, was a large, coppery-scaled creature whose body resembled that of a scorpiocrab complete with a long, copper sting. One of its heads was that of a warrior. A second head was that of a beautiful coppery-haired woman wearing copper earrings. Between the two human heads was a coppery dragon's head several times as large as Horace's.

The three heads came down on long scaly necks, examining the visitors from three sets of coppery yellow eyes. The eyes of the woman head blinked, and her eyebrows arched.

"Merlain, Charles, Horace," the woman head said in dulcet tones. "Why has it taken you so long to visit your godparent? And who are these inferior mortal creatures? Their minds are as incapable of mind-to-mind communication as your father's."

Merlain swallowed an opal-sized lump. So this was the head she had been named after: Mervania.

"Good, now we get delicate meat!" said the warrior head under its copper helmet. That part was Mertin.

"GRUMMPTH!" growled the dragon head, not quite managing to say its own name.

The twin kinglets were petrified.

Merlain let out her breath. If Mervania didn't allow Mertin and Grumpus their culinary wishes, it was going to be an interesting visit.

Zady pulled herself up on the lily pad. On hands and knees she coughed and choked and vomited up muddy water, a couple of small wiggly things, and the severed tail of one aging fish carcass.

Oh, the ignominy of it! Tricked by brats! Thrown into the water! Pulled down and taken into the mouth of a clamopus! Then, greatest indignity of all, spat out of the creature's shell, a rejected morsel!

Of course she had had to do something about that. Once she focused, a simple gesture had caused the monster to be abruptly deshelled. That had taught it respect, just before it died. But meanwhile, the children had had time to organize, and even as she formed a restraining spell, they had used the opal to escape.

"You brats!" she said aloud. "I'll get you for this! I'll make each of you suffer even worse than I had intended to! I'll—CHOKE!"

She coughed up a slimed minnow, then the picked-clean skeleton of a long-dead minor snake. She contemplated the mess, retched some more, turned her stomach inside out, and emptied every speck. She stood straight again, wobbly but alive.

She was ready now to do some serious destroying! She would get all of Zoanna's old enemies and those born after her! She would end a prophecy by destroying every round-ear this frame had! She would make a mess even Mouvar couldn't manage!

Until now she had been merely malignant, as was her nature. Now she wasn't just malignant anymore. Now she was mad.

A predator insect swooped in, got a good look at her face, and spun out of control. She hadn't even noticed it.

CHAPTER 20
New Boots

"And so, my friends," Helbah told the assembled witches and warlocks from the podium, "that's why we are going to need your help. Lester here"—she placed her hand on the young man's shoulder,—"says that the war with the orcs has already started. We know the folly of that. With the opal the orcs can go anywhere and get any number of reinforcements. Nor are they devoid of magic, though they are a standoffish lot who never attend our conventions. Even if we all pledge our help, the outcome is uncertain." She paused, looked at the most insistently waving hand, and nodded.

A young warlock with a somewhat villainous expression stood. "Helbah, we all admire you for what you did to rid the frames of Zoanna and Rowforth. We'd all like to help. But it seems to me that the trouble in your home frame is chronic. Why should we, with our own frames to think about, risk everything?"

God save us from the practical ignoramuses, Helbah thought, keeping her mind guarded. "If not for the joy of aiding a colleague and preserving her domain, then for the opal.''

"Opal? *The* opal?"

"Yes. That one. When this is all over, we can hold it in common property and use it whenever there's trouble."

Murmurs and whispers and thoughts flashed. The questioner almost sat down, then reconsidered. "That's all very well, Helbah, if we could win, but the probability is that we cannot. The orcs will get all the reinforcements they need from other frames and counter magic with magic, force with force. The result could be a lifeless frame when you're done."

"We can use the opal as the orcs use it, once we have it," Helbah said. "Then no outside force could prevail against us."

"We don't have it, and never will."

"Pessimist." But she looked around the audience and saw that most were of the warlock's opinion. That was bad. If she couldn't raise an arm of magical practitioners, even with the promise of the fabulous opal, there could be no hope. What a disastrous convention this had turned out to be! It was all Zady's fault.

Zady? Just maybe . . .

"Sit down," she advised the warlock. "Now I am going to tell all of you what you haven't considered. The orcs are my Confederation's opponents in war, true, but the orcs are not the real enemy. It's the same situation as when Kelvinia declared war against Klingland and Kance. The enemy then was Zoanna and Rowforth. Then enemy now is Zady. Dare I suggest to you what that means?''

Murmurings went through the audience. Then Helbah struck: "Yes, Zady, the most malignant of the practitioners of malignant magic! Zady, who violates not only my home frame but who came here and violated this very convention. How many of you have had your property taken? How many have felt kicks and pinches, been tripped, and suffered even worse indignities? How many of you have been spied upon, or forced into actions you did not intend? How many of you like one lone Malignant taking over our convention and making it a shambles?''

Now there were outcries. She was getting through to them. What loyalty to the frames had not accomplished, personal annoyance was. No benign witch or warlock wanted to be mistreated with impunity by Malignants. The very fact that this had happened at their convention struck at ancient rivalries.

Now they were on their feet. Now there was shouting. "We're with you, Helbah!" a burly warlock called. "Death to Zady! Death to Zady! Extinction to her evil kind!''

Helbah felt relieved and vindicated in her attempt to persuade the nearly unpersuadable. It was all these indignities that had done it. The pinches, pricks, bites, and gooses. Ultimately it was the brat kings deciding the issue.

"Wait! Wait!" a warlock cried, standing, raising his arms for attention. "Zady's in jail here. You caught her, Helbah.''

Damn, she had almost forgotten that herself.

"I'm afraid not." A uniformed officer strode onto the stage. "I've come here to make an announcement. Zady, it seems, has again done the impossible. She has escaped from confinement and also from this frame.''

There was consternation. Helbah, listening to the uproar, knew that she had won. However narrow, however puny and risky a victory.

Zady, win though she inevitably might, would not win unopposed by the right-thinking benigns.

By noon it had started. Witch after witch, warlock after warlock, was stepping into the busily flashing transporter. The line led back across the station and curled past the baggage area. Other lines at the other transporters were noticeably absent. Every conventioneer, it seemed, whether apprentice or adept, youth or ancient, was going to Helbah's frame to bolster her army.

Lester Crumb watched them proceed with open mouth. The line moved slowly because there was only one utilizable destination transporter, and that one was underwater. Lester imagined the crowd of waterfowl bursting from the river and taking to the air. With beating wings they'd fly the length of the river, past the eerily glowing walls, and above the flights of ancient stairs. They would land past the ruins of the old Rud palace, and Helbah, who had gone on ahead, would be waiting.

He turned to Kelvin, and to his pointed ear and roundear relatives. Jon seemed to be smiling at something; he wasn't certain what, but he hoped it was at the prospect of their being alone together soon. With this great spectacle before them, he couldn't understand why any folk would be chatting among themselves.

"You and your father and Heln have to use the other transporter?" Lester asked.

Kelvin nodded. "You know the warning in the home installation. Helbah wouldn't let any of us risk ignoring it."

"Only roundears can use it," Lester agreed. "I never understood why Jon thinks it's nonsense."

"I don't think it's nonsense," Kelvin said. "I've seen too much magic and science that was anything but bluff! Anyway, why take a chance?"

"Right." He watched the prettiest nude body-stocking witch he'd seen all morning step out of the line, into the transporter, and vanish. He was married, and he was not forgetting that for a moment, but sometimes maybe for just the merest fraction of an instant he might have felt the tiniest flicker of temptation, had he been a less constant man. He could tell by Kelvin's similar pause that he had a similar thought. But of course the wives would be likely to misunderstand. Anyway, those luscious young witches were probably centuries old in reality, and not at all innocent. "You'll wait until we're all gone?"

"Have to. Unless you want someone turning you into a bird."

"No! That I don't want."

"Oh, Lester, it'll be fun," Jon said. "You'll enjoy it."

"No, I won't because I won't do it! I don't want you birding it either!"

"Oh pooh, Lester, I've done it before."

"I still don't like it."

"You take good care of my mother and sister," the Roundear of Prophecy advised. "Father and Heln and I want to be up above the pointed-ear installation in the rowboat. Just in case you really won't change."

"I won't," Lester repeated. But watching the three of them cross the station to a vacant transporter, he was not exactly certain. He remembered how much trouble his oink-headedness had gotten him into before, being separated from Jon, and Jon being impersonated by that old hag Zady. That would never have worked if he had been along; he would have known his wife no matter what! So he realized, deep down, that if shove came to push, he would probably have to yield.

Charlain took his left hand in hers and patted it. Jon took his right hand and held on tight.

Across the floor John Knight was already setting the co-ordinates on their chosen transporter. In a moment John Knight had stepped in and was abruptly gone. Kelvin picked up Heln, not without grunting—she was no longer quite the slender bride she had once been—and as quickly followed him. There was a flash and that particular transporter stood vacant as before.

Kelvin stepped out of the home transporter, put Heln down with relief, and looked around for his father. John Knight had crossed to look out the chamber door. He turned and came back.

"Boat still there?" Kelvin asked. It had better be, he thought, though Helbah would get them rescued if it wasn't.

His father nodded. "All's as before."

"Except for those," Heln said. She was pointing to the stand and its familiar parchment warning that only round-ears were allowed here, and signed by Mouvar. Beside the parchment was another that had not been there before. Beside that one was a pair of boots whose leather sheen exactly matched that of the magical gauntlets.

Kelvin hastened to look, as did his father. The new parchment read simply: **"You will need these, prophesied Roundear. Mouvar."**

Kelvin wondered. "Mouvar? He knew we'd be here?"

"Precog," his father said. "He was here before—must have been. Either that, or someone else sent us to the chimaera."

Kelvin remembered in a flash their inexplicable journey to the chimaera's world, caused by a change of the settings. He had thought it was the doings of the terrible king of the silver world, Rowforth, who had outwardly so resembled their king Rufurt. But possibly, just possibly, it had been Mouvar who reset the transporter. What a notion! It suggested that Mouvar, instead of being long out of things, remained active to some extent.

"Don't look at me," John said. "It's your boot size. You're the Roundear Mouvar prophesied, not me."

"Yes, I'm the hero," Kelvin said. It was a bitter, mocking expression, as always. While his feisty sister Jon might have delighted in being so named, he did not and never had.

"Your boots are a bit worn," John said. "Try these on."

Kelvin knew that there was no help for it. Sitting down on the metal floor beneath the strange lights of the chamber, he drew off his old boots, adjusted his socks, and pulled on the new boots. He expected them to be stiff and uncomfortable and to chafe, because that was the nature of new boots. But these felt very comfortable, as if he had worn them all his life. How could Mouvar have known his size so accurately?

He held his gauntlets beside the boots, and it seemed that both were of the same material. Dragon hide, perhaps, with a scale pattern. Yet Mouvar was said to be from another world and a frame that ran on science, not magic. What would he have had to do with dragons? Or was it that at a certain stage science became workable as magic, and magic became workable as science?

"They look fine," his father said, touching the toes with his fingers. "I wonder if they do anything, or whether this was merely a sartorial favor?"

Kelvin shrugged. "If they protect my feet, it's enough." He set his old boots by the stand and looked in vain for an additional scrap of parchment that might give information about the boots. There was nothing, and even the book that had told them much did not have reference to the boots.

"We'd best be getting out," John said. "Your mother and sister may be taking to the air already. Lester too, I suspect."

Kelvin nodded and thought of the ledge and the boat as he took his first step, leading off with the right boot. He felt no sensation of motion, but his seeing blurred, and things came back into focus only as he finished taking the step. Was he getting dizzy, being overtired?

"Kelvin!" The exclamation was Heln's, but it seemed to come from a distance. He looked around.

To his astonishment, he stood exactly where he had visualized going, right on the ledge above the boat.

His father and wife quickly emerged from the cylindrical chamber with its round door. John was shaking his head, his mouth open with amazement.

Finally John spoke to him. "Now we know what they are, Son. Seven-league boots, as in the storybooks."

"What's that?" Kelvin asked, not remembering that particular story. The amazement of the happening remained; he was bewildered. Nothing had surprised him quite so much since the time Mor Crumb placed a sword in his gauntleted hand and he found that he, or at least the gauntlet, could actually swordfight. Could do it with unparalleled speed, power, and accuracy.

"That's on Earth," his father said. "The story you and Jon learned was about distance-spanning boots. Otherwise it's much the same."

Kelvin thought back to his childhood, and to the more

recent but stranger childhood of his offspring. Spanner boots. It was what his father had said was teleportation, or something: magical transport across great distances, without having to ride a dragon or enter a transporter booth. It did seem like a better way to travel.

"I—" Kelvin said, with his usual eloquence of expression, trying to think of exactly what had happened.

"With those and your gauntlets you should be a match for Brudalous or any orc, I'd think. That must be the Mouvar plan. Maybe we don't need the benign army. Maybe you really are enough of a hero to handle this all by yourself."

Kelvin swallowed. Take on the whole orc army? His father couldn't be serious! He wondered whether the boots would teleport him into adjoining world frames, as the opal was reputed to do. After a moment he asked him about that.

John Knight's forehead furrowed. "That strikes me as a damn good question, son," he said. "Try visualizing yourself back at the hotel desk."

"Kelvin, don't!" Heln protested, grabbing his arm.

That was reassuring; he liked having her fuss over him. "It's all right, Heln. I'm a hero, I think. Mouvar wouldn't leave me anything destructive." He hoped. Mouvar's fantastic tools could be used for good or ill, depending on the competence and nature of the user. The gauntlets had proved that. But he was good, and would try to be careful.

He thought of the polished wooden desk and the hotel manager who had registered them. He nerved himself and took a step. He looked.

He was one step closer to his father.

Maybe the manager wasn't there right now. Maybe he should just think of the floor and the desk. He did so, and stepped again.

He was another step closer to his father.

Maybe he should think just of the transporter booth in the station. His next step, he told himself, would take him just outside that booth. He stepped, and looked up at his father.

"I guess they won't transport me across frames," he said, deflated.

"Try stepping out to the palace ruins," his father suggested, seemingly unperturbed.

He thought of the large rock where John Knight and King Rufurt had once played chess. He took the step, his sight blurring. His sight straightened and there was the rock. Emerging from the hole in the ruins were three swooshes, flying wingtip to wingtip. The swooshes lit by him and changed immediately to his mother, his sister, and Lester Crumb.

"Kelvin!" Lester said. "How'd you get here?"

"New boots," Kelvin explained, and stepped back to his father and Heln on the ledge. He swallowed, shook his head, and motioned at the boat. "I'll row, Father. Might as well put the gauntlets to work." Then, briefly, he explained about the success with the boots. They knew it, of course, having seen him vanish and reappear.

John helped Heln into the bow and eased himself into the stern. Kelvin carefully stepped into the middle, eased himself down on the seat, took the oars in his gauntleted hands, and shoved off.

Rowing, as always with the gauntlets, was restful. The gauntlets moved his arms and shoulders and back without his quite having to think. In this they were like what his father had described as exercise machines. Kelvin had never understood the point of the machines, since it was easy enough to exercise just getting from place to place, or simply doing chores. But Earth was a strange place; he had always known that.

They rounded the curve and passed the great whirlpool that emptied into the Flaw. The Flaw was what made interframe travel possible, though its full nature was beyond the comprehension of ordinary folk. The gauntlets took them by in a wide swing, bucked the river current, and left the phenomenon behind.

He looked into Heln's face and saw the wonder and awe she felt for this region, as he himself had had the first time.

Now they were sweeping toward the slight dimple that marked the location of the transporter for the pointears. Four birds flew up and out, swimming from water into air with the swoosh's specialized wings. Heln waved at some of the birds, though there was no telling who was who until they changed back into people. These seemed to be the last four; no more birds appeared as they rowed on.

They stopped at the rickety moss-covered dock, and here John moored the boat to an old pylon while Heln gazed with him up the rickety stairs. Faces were looking down from the top flight. Were they Lester and Jon? Possibly. Again Kelvin wished that he had stronger eyes.

"It's Jon! And Lester!" Heln cried. She waved excitedly and they waved back. Well, now he knew. John joined them, wiping his hands on his pants.

Kelvin thought of the climb up the stairs and had an idea. "Here, Heln," he said. His gauntlets obeyed him properly by picking her up in his not really very heroic arms. This time she was feather light, and he was relaxed enough to appreciate her other qualities.

He took the one step. Now he was beside an astonished Jon. He set Heln down and waved at his father. These boots were going to save a lot of walking!

"Kelvin, you don't have magic!" Jon said resentfully.

"Funny, I always thought he did," Heln remarked innocently. Then the two hugged.

"I told you—new boots," Kelvin said, and got into explaining as his father trudged up the stairs the old-fashioned way.

"And you think you can really fight the orcs with those and the gauntlets?" Lester asked, impressed.

"I can try if I have to," Kelvin said. It was the answer he had finally settled on when faced by maneuverings of the Prophecy. He didn't like being a hero any more than he ever had, but it seemed that he had no choice.

His father reached the top of the final flight. He took a couple of breaths. "Where's Helbah?"

"Here I am." Helbah stepped out from behind Lester.

"And I see that there are matters all of us are going to have to settle."

Kelvin felt an unheroic plummeting inside. Did this mean that her expectations were like those of his father? That with this new gift from Mouvar he could do all the gory orc fighting? Without magical or military help?

"Oh, stop it, Kelvin!" Helbah said, as if reading his mind. "I know you haven't any liking for war. That's good. None of us have, either. That's why we're Benigns."

"Uh," Kelvin said. She took him by surprise so often! That was the nature of witches, he supposed. His own mother had also seemed at times to know his thoughts. Maybe it had been inevitable that his children would be true mind readers!

But he knew that Helbah couldn't read minds in that fashion. The witch Zady could, but Zady was something else. Indeed she was! That vision of her in her young buxom aspect—phew! But he felt guilty just remembering that. At any rate, he knew that some folk had latent abilities, as Helbah put it. He and his father, he was certain, had exactly none. He wondered about Kian, his half-brother in another frame. Was Kian as devoid of powers as was Kelvin himself? Probably, otherwise Kian would have known right away that his own dear girl, Lonny, really loved him and intended to marry him. Kian had been every bit as slow to catch on as Kelvin would have been.

"Well, Kelvin?" Helbah was looking at him expectantly.

"Well, what?" Obviously no magical powers, latent or otherwise.

"Woolgathering again! Boys! They never listen to anything!"

"You tell him, Helbah," Jon chimed in. "He never listened to me either."

Helbah fixed him with sharp, penetrating eyes reminiscent of a preybird's. "Just what, Mr. Heroic Roundear of Prophecy, are your immediate plans and orders?"

CHAPTER 21

Godparent

"These are our friends, Kildom and Kildee, kings of Klingland and Kance and now rulers of the Confederacy," Merlain said, hoping she remembered her protocol correctly.

Coppery tresses shook on Mervania's head. "Oh, I know that, for pity's sake! I can see into their minds readily enough. Where do you think you got your telepathic abilities, if not from me?"

"Us," Mertin corrected her.

"Groowthm," added Grumpus.

"Yes, from me, meaning this body with three heads." Mervania smiled, satisfied.

Merlain opened and closed her mouth. *Don't! Don't*, she pleaded with her mind. *I want to be my mother and father's. I don't want to be the child of a monster!*

Ungrateful brat! Without my help you three wouldn't exist.

Yes, I know. The magic powder Helbah administered at our birth. But before that—

Before my antidote there was another powder derived from parts of one of my kind. That was administered to your mother, Heln, through the connivance of Zoanna, the witch queen of Rud destroyed by your father with the help of Helbah and her helpers, your grandmother and aunt.

Then we're not even yours? Merlain thought, further discomfited. *We're some other monster's!*

Hush! That's not a nice thing to say. Of course you're not ours, and you're not, as you so meanly put it, some other monster's.

But . . . ?

You're your parents'. Your own parents. Keln and Helvin.

No, that's Heln and Kelvin!

Whatever. Human seed.

But if that's so—

Magic, and not even very complicated magic. I'm surprised you weren't taught.

I was taught! Merlain flared mentally. *I can read a little and write a little and everything!*

You and Dragon Horace. Merlain, you were taught nothing. You've got a very extraordinary mind—for an inferior life-form.

Inferior life-form! Daddy said you called him that!

And your grandfather, and the uncle you've never met. Humans are inferior to my kind, and to a lot of kinds.

"YOU TAKE THAT BACK!" Merlain shouted out loud, and to the bewilderment of the young kings she raised her tiny fists.

The chimaera was amused rather than annoyed. *Facts are facts, kid.*

"Take it easy, Merlain, can't you see she's baiting you?" That was Charles' thought. So he had tuned in!

"OUCH!" Charles cried, slapping himself.

The two young kings looked at each other with completely open mouths. It was as if they had both been rendered mute and idiots.

Merlain had to laugh. It was just too comical. Then she had to put her fists down and look away from the beautiful woman face the to face of the stern, copper-helmeted warrior.

Mertin, she thought. *Does Mervania always tease like that?*

Always, Mertin grumped. *Toys with our food, is what she does. When she meets human men, she hides our body and shows just her face, and tries to make the men think she has breasts and things, and they get all excited and think there's a big romance in the offing, then are really surprised when we eat them. But now, at least since your father's visit, she doesn't let us eat. You would really taste good, Merlain, as a human child should.*

Oh, now, Mertin, Mervania cut in. *You know we won't eat our own godchildren. Not unless they get really disrespectful.*

"Groompth!" said Grumpus.

"Hissss!" said Dragon Horace, not to be outdone.

Merlain wondered. Was it that they wouldn't eat godchildren, whatever they were, or that they wouldn't eat fellow monsters? Were she and Charles and maybe even Dragon Horace going to be like them someday?

Silly child, you certainly did inherit your father's obtuseness. Of course none of you will be like us. All you got from my powder was life and the ability to use your minds. From Zoanna's tampering you have your dragon brother, and just a touch of dormant malicious nature that her aunt Zady preyed upon.

You know about Zady? Merlain thought in surprise.

You didn't block me from your mind. Not that you could, of course.

Merlain wondered how she could have been so dumb. And after having heard her grandfather tell the story over and over and over. The chimaera had not only known their thoughts but all the notions that made up their thoughts. Thus Mervania had teased her father on first meeting by showing just her neck and head, and hinting at a stunning human-woman body, as Mertin had mentioned, and forcing him to remember scary stories from earliest boyhood. Kelvin hadn't remembered well at all, though his father and half-brother certainly had. Yet the chimaera had looked into Kelvin's mind and read it so thoroughly that she remembered for him.

That's right! Mervania thought. *You reason well for such a little girl.*

I have to. I'm smart.

For a you-know-what.

Y-yes. She wouldn't, she absolutely wouldn't, think inferior life-form.

But you just did.

Sigh. *Mean, snoopy old copperhead.*

Mean? I haven't hurt you, have I?

Teasing. Teasing hurts.

But it's oh so amusing to me, godchild.

Yes. Daddy said that it was. Then she remembered something else: that though her father talked of the chimaera's teasing, he also talked as if he had some affection for Mervania's head. It was because she was so very, very beautiful, as Merlain knew she was herself. Men were always stupid about beautiful women, as her father and grandfather had been. Even when they knew that there was no good in those women.

Why, thank you, Merlain, but you needn't try to conceal your thoughts. If you had thought them right at me, I wouldn't have balked. Yes, I am beautiful, by your father's standards. With your coppery-colored hair and eyes you may one day be beautiful as well.

I am now!

No, no, that's your vanity. Vanity can be a tremendous asset to a woman, but it has to be grounded in reality. When you're all grown up, then you'll be beautiful. Now you're merely cute.

Cute!

As a kipy or a pupkin. An amusing little animal that has a lot of growing up to do. If you're permitted to grow up, as I doubt your witch enemy intends.

Merlain shivered. The others were looking at her in wonder. Charles knew what was going on, but poor Kildom and Kildee could only conjecture. True, the kinglings knew about the chimaera and were smart, but there was no way they could talk to each other with just their minds. As far as Kildom and Kildee were concerned, she was just standing here making faces while the beautiful woman's face above her now and then changed expressions.

"Please speak aloud," Merlain said. "So that all of us can hear."

"Oh, very well!" Mervania said tartly. "But it's so slow and tedious. Don't you and Charles ever tire of having to make animal noises for every little word?"

"It's our way," Merlain said defensively, realizing that the chimaera had a point.

"Yes, yes, you are secretive. Your father wasn't, very much, though he tried to be when he was here. You and Charles just mind-talk when it's convenient."

"Yes."

"I know that! You don't have to agree aloud when it's obvious."

"I do at home," Merlain said. How many times had she been forced to reassure some adult that something said was true, regardless of the facts?

"Well, you're not home," Mervania said severely. "Do as I do, here."

"I'll try," Merlain agreed.

"You will. There's no sense in your not doing it. You do after all have the gift bestowed on you through my agency at your birth. Slow thinking shouldn't exist in you. Now about that opal . . . ?"

"Y-yes," Merlain was startled out of her wits.

"I want it."

"You can't have it."

"Why can't I?"

"You're confined. You'd use it to leave here."

"Suppose I say I wouldn't?"

"We wouldn't believe you." *You're a monster, after all. Brat! The word of my kind is never broken.*

That's not what I heard! Merlain thought before she could stop herself. Actually her knowledge of the creature was scanty, formed mainly by her grandfather's stories of what had befallen him and her father and the faraway uncle Kian.

"Well, kid, if you feel that way—" A sudden swoop of the chimaera's feminine arm stopped at Merlain's clenched hands. "Please," the Mervania head said with teasing gentleness.

There was no way of resisting her. Merlain was as powerless to keep possession of the opal as Charles had been to avoid his own slap. She started to place the gem in the waiting hand.

A cracking sound startled her. Mervania drew back her hand with a startled shriek. Horace flipped back his tail, having delivered a really proper whiplash.

Charles thought, *Merlain, get us back!*

Scared, more urgent than she had ever been, Merlain grasped the overgrown pebble and thought home.

They were on their own front lawn alone. She and Charles and Kildom and Kildee, and Dragon Horace. The chimaera was elsewhere, as was appropriate.

Dragon Horace, for the second time since their adventures had begun, had acted quickly without the intervention of human thought, and saved the day.

Mervania gasped, shaking her stinging wrist. *The poor hatchlings! The poor hatchlings! I only wanted to help!*

That's what you get, Mervania. Humans are for eating.

Shut up, Mertin. You have all the sensitivity of Grumpus.

"Groooowomth," Grumpus agreed approvingly.

They are our godchildren, like it or not. I want to help them and their father to save themselves.

Foolish! Mertin thought. *You wanted to keep them here to bother us.*

Yes, Mervania conceded sadly. *If we hadn't used the opal to save their frame, the five of them would still have made nice pets.*

CHAPTER 22
War

"And it was really Merlain?" Kelvin asked his father-in-law incredulously. He could hardly believe the things that had been happening to him, or for that matter to all of them.

St. Helens nodded. Was it Kelvin's imagination, or was his father-in-law getting just a bit more character lines, a few more gray hairs in his shiniest of black beards? His own father had once cracked that St. Helens was starting to look like "Gabby" Hayes, whoever he had been.

"It was my granddaughter! She just appeared with that copper-scaled dragon. Then after she told off Brudalous tree-top-tall as if she was the Princess of the Universe, she and the dragon both vanished."

"It has to be the opal," Helbah said, stroking Katbah on her arm. "Somehow she must have gotten it."

"She has it, for sure," St. Helens agreed. "The orc demanded it, and she said she was going to give it back, but not until she helped her friends. Then she was gone, and we never saw her again."

"That means Zady must have her," Kelvin's mother suggested. With her red hair she looked more the witch than any of the army they had brought; Kelvin had been noticing this more and more.

"Not necessarily," Helbah said, scratching Katbah under the chin. "It's possible that she's free."

"Can't you find out?" Kelvin demanded. Here were the most expert practitioners of benign magic around, and instead of doing things to find the children they were debating their whereabouts.

"Be patient, young gentlemen," Helbah said, thumping him on his forehead with her gnarled hand. "We're about to try."

The crystal was out in a moment. The witches hovered and Helbah activated it. Colors swirled and scenes shifted while Helbah made a countermagic to nullify Zady's privacy spell. Finally there was Zady, looking angrier and more insane than Kelvin remembered.

"Greetings, Zady!" Helbah spoke to the image. "Did you lose something?"

"What's it to you, you benevolent wimp!"

"Why Zady, it's everything. I thought you knew."

"I know those brats will suffer unspeakable pain! And you, and you—" she said, her clawed finger pointing first at Kelvin's mother and then directly at Kelvin. "All of you I will destroy!"

"How are you going to do that, Zady? We're onto you now. We know the tricks you've been playing. Do you think you can handle us all?"

"I'm not alone, Helbah. Look!" The imaged Zady made a magical pass and the scene in the crystal became that of an orc army. Brudalous was leading the troops. They were marching with determined strides across the border where St. Helens had encountered them.

"See," Zady taunted. "Your war with the orcs has started. Brudalous is angry because you haven't responded to his demand. He's not waiting three days. He wants that opal back."

"Without that opal, they are only orc troops," Helbah

scoffed. Katbah looked up at her, seemingly sensing the absurdity in her words.

"Not with my help, dearie. I'm now their ally. I can give them witch's fire and protection."

"Zady, you just want to destroy this frame."

"Yes, all of it."

"We have the numbers."

"I can get more," Zady promised. "Zady is not without her resources. Already we are nullifying all those foolish lesser Benigns you sent out; they will not be able to help you, and it will be as if they never tried. You Benigns have been asking for extinction for a long, long time."

Kelvin shivered. This was no longer between orcs and humans, if it ever had been. It was, because of Zady's maneuverings, between the Malignants and the Benigns. He almost felt sorry for the orcs, caught as they were in the middle of a fight.

"We have more than you can muster," Helbah announced. "We have Kelvin."

He wished she hadn't said that.

Zady's eye turned to bear on him. Her form changed, and there was the beautiful redhead, wearing a cloak that showed just enough around the edges to titillate him. She gave him no time to react as she spoke to the benign witch. "You base your hopes on that boy?"

"You know the Prophecy," Helbah said. "You know Mouvar."

"The Prophecy won't apply once this frame is destroyed," Zady said evenly. Her cloak was slowly turning translucent. Kelvin tore his gaze away just long enough to see that no one else seemed to see anything unusual. This show was for him alone. "One frame in an infinity! What does it matter? As for Mouvar, I think he lied!"

"You *hope* he lied," Helbah said. "This frame is under benign protection now. None of us can see far into the future any more than you Malignants. But must I remind you that Mouvar is of a different order? He's from another world than ours. He sees ahead and prophesies. What he prophesies comes true and always has."

"This time it will be different," Zady promised. Her eye turned again on Kelvin. Her cloak was now almost invisible; her remarkable lush torso was spread out before him.

Unseen imps massaged Kelvin's spine. The old witch sounded so certain! And she wasn't old, now, to his eye. She was as young and ripe a creature as he had ever tried to imagine. Compared with her, the pretty nude witches seemed like children.

"You make a mistake, Zady," Helbah said grimly. "You are up against far more than you realize."

"Oh, yes, I'm just wetting my pants," Zady mocked her. The last of the cloak disappeared, giving Kelvin a clear view of the region of her body to which she was referring. There were no pants there. "It's you and these others who made the mistake. You destroyed my niece Zoanna, and now you and my niece's entire conquered frame will pay."

"She never conquered, Zady. She and her father only tried. Kelvin defeated Zatanas and her in the way for Rud. Then Kelvin defeated the witch Melbah, who was my lookalike. Together Kelvin, his relatives, and I defeated Zoanna for the second time and destroyed her and her latest consort, Rowforth, the look-alike of the proper king."

But while Helbah was reminding the enemy witch of recent history, the beautiful creature was slowly turning her body for Kelvin's view. It was superb in every part, front, side, and rear. Kelvin knew he was crazy to respond to it, but he wanted that body with increasing intensity.

"History," Zady said to Helbah. "Nothing but history. The present war is the war that the Malignants will win."

"Are you prophesying, Zady?"

"Yes! I prophesy our winning and your destruction. Only a few of you will I keep alive to entertain me for a time." Once more her eye touched Kelvin, and he felt its smoky power.

Helbah pulled herself up to her full stature. It wasn't much, but it seemed impressive the way she stood. Her mouth firmed, she stuck out a long claw similar to Zady's before she became the redhead, and her voice cracked.

"Know then, Zady, that you are wrong. Know that I, Helbah, benign witch, prophesy the opposite of what you prophesy. Know that we will win this war and destroy you."

Zady only smiled, and Kelvin's knees turned weak. If it had been possible for him to step through the crystal to be with the enemy witch, he would have done it.

Helbah waved a hand and the crystal blanked. Then, to the astonished others, she said: "She's right, you know. For every Benign we have, she has a Malignant. The two cancel out. As near as I can see the future, the war with the orcs is as much as lost. That's why I did everything possible to see that it never began. Kelvin, I don't want to be the pessimist, but the Confederacy has less chance of defeating Ophal than Kelvinia had of winning against Klingland and Kance. We're depending on you this time as never before."

They were depending on him—and he knew that if he ever came face-to-face with Zady in the flesh, he would be completely unable to attack her! He knew she was a terrible enemy, and that she was an ugly old crone. But that lovely redhead—

They were surely lost.

Brudalous screwed up his handsome green face, so much like that of a widemouthed trass, even to the gills, and considered that he had just led his troops past the border. Now they had left Ophal and were in the southern region of Hermandy, a former bad neighbor that was now part of the Confederacy. He hated having to trudge the whole distance afoot, but until they recovered the opal there was no choice. He had had to walk back to fetch the main part of his army and guide it here, after Phenoblee conjured him back here; only now could they proceed to the main engagement.

Abruptly, as if the land knew its boundaries, the trees became armpit height. He and his troops, equipped with the best of throwing and slicing weapons and clubs, walked down a road wide enough for war-horses or orcs. Ordinary humans such as St. Helens or the legendary Roundear would have found it more than sufficiently wide. But orcs were giants by human standards, and that meant that on both sides his scaly elbows now and then scraped the top of a tree.

"Commander?" Mosday, the officer who had witnessed the destruction of Helmport, the orc official showpiece, repository of the opal, touched him on the shoulder. Not given to the trapping and make-believes of human armies, Brudalous' soldiers practiced little in the way of ceremony.

"Yes, General Mosday?"

"This is where the child and the dragon appeared." He pointed at the scruffed ground where they had so ignominiously fought, or tried to fight, the child's strange companion.

"I know that, General. What's your point?"

"She had the opal."

"That's why we're at war."

"Not entirely. They declared war before the child got the opal. I don't think they knew she would get it."

"But if she gives it to them, Commander, how can we—"

"We must first of all get it back, or force them to give it back. The child did say she would return it; if we keep the pressure on, she may even do it."

"Yes, Commander, but—"

"We are superior fighters. We can win even if they should surround us with warriors from other frames who are their look-alikes. Even without the opal. Remember how we fought Hermandy in the past?"

"Yes, Commander. It was fun. Hardly even a challenge."

"And Hermandy was the most warlike of all the human kingdoms. Their warriors were always reputed to be the best."

"Yes, Commander."

"We needed no magic then. Our opal resided in its proper place in Helmport. We hardly needed our weapons."

"No, sir. The humans were weak."

"As are all humans, compared to orcs. What matter if they have magic? We have Wizard Krassnose, and Phenoblee, our proper witch queen. Either alone is as powerful as any humans who dare call themselves either Malignants or Benigns." That, of course, was obvious. But it was fun repeating it.

"Yes, Commander. Krassnose can throw the fire or protect us from it. He is a good wizard, and orc rather than human. Orcs are always better in everything than humans."

"Right, Officer Mosday, for we are a superior people. Other races left the water far behind, but our people are closer to our beginning. We breathe water when we want, while all the humans do is drown."

"Unless they have magic."

"Yes, as when the ability was given to those children."

"Commander, why didn't Krassnose save our castle? He could have vanquished the giant."

"Krassnose is too kind. Too much of a Benign to be a warrior. To have dissolved the giant would have meant destroying a child." He was putting the blame on the wizard, but actually it was Phenoblee who had given him the word: no harm to children, no matter what. "Moreover, the child is a king, and not an ordinary king."

"I know. The young kings who age slowly."

"And therefore may live long enough to learn."

"They live such short lives, don't they, Commander?"

"Yes, because we refrain from destroying them. Otherwise they would live no lives at all."

"We could destroy all human races in the frame, couldn't we, Commander?"

"Of course. And I doubt if we would even need the opal to accomplish it."

They marched on, under the steaming sun, satisfied with their familiar and reassuring dialogue. Perhaps the main reason they had suffered the humans to survive so far was that not only were the humans normally no trouble, they served as such an excellent example of inferiority. What was the point in being superior if there was no standard of comparison?

At noon they reached a village deserted by the humans in the face of the advance. For want of something destructive to do, Brudalous kicked down a heavy brick wall and walked through what had been an army garrison. It was stupid, he thought, and when he saw the horse jumping and neighing in fear, he bent down, picked it up, and put it down gently where it could run in the forest. He thought of gentle Phenoblee.

Good King Rufurt shook his head at the size of the witches' army Kelvin had brought him. "You really think these will make a difference, Kelvin? All these scrawny women and effete men? With orcs?"

"They'd better," Kelvin said.

He hoped they would, but since every time Helbah opened her mouth, it was to say that they faced certain defeat, he was not certain. He was beginning to learn that magic had its limitations. Warfare with swords and spears he understood; he didn't like it but he understood it. Magical warfare was another matter. Orcs, being magical creatures like dragons, lived forever unless something unexpected happened to destroy them. In the many centuries in which they had lived, orcs had had ample opportunity to master magic, be it called malign or benign. Orc magic, according to legend, was powerful. The only reason orcs hadn't conquered all was that they cared nothing for conquest. Indeed, his father-in-law had been brave to the point of insanity in challenging Brudalous. The dragon, his and Heln's own flesh, he had to remember, had no concept of bravery or cowardice; in this Horace was like all dragons. So only St. Helens had been brave, though the dragon had been more effective, it seemed.

"What do you think about it, Kelvin?" the king asked. "Why don't some of your high-powered magicians and witches get the gem?"

Kelvin sighed. "Helbah?"

"We tried," she said. "None of us can even locate the children."

"So you think Brudalous has them?"

"That would be a guess if not for his army. He would not be invading the Confederation if he already had what he wanted. Zady may or may not have them; she interferes with all our attempts to find out. No matter what spells we use, she fuzzes the crystal. But I suspect that means she doesn't have them, because if she did, she wouldn't conceal them, she would use them as hostages, and would be gloating."

"You think she knows where they are? Even if she doesn't have them yet?"

"If she does, she's not telling. Probably she knows. There's no one interfering in her searches. Our Benigns are here, while her Malignants are free for magical duty."

"It amazes me that she's so powerful." How well he was coming to know an aspect of her power! Even when he couldn't see her, that voluptuous redhead now haunted him. "Can't you hit her with fire?"

"She's keeping hid. She's good at that. Besides, she'd counter it."

"Kelvin, how are we going to stop the orcs?" The king motioned at the crystal showing the orc army laying waste to an inoffensive and unoccupied village. If there was one thing Hermandy's peasants knew, it was to make themselves scarce once orcs appeared.

Kelvin studied the image. Brudalous looked like a monster, but so far the orc leader hadn't killed anyone that Kelvin knew about. Yet if armed men went against him, there was certain to be bloodshed. St. Helens had been exceedingly lucky. At that moment, it was evident, the orc king was merely making a demonstration of power. If he got his opal back, he would probably quit the war. Zady said she was helping the orcs, but it didn't look as if the orcs cared about her one way or the other.

They should return the opal! That was the only way to end this bad business. But how could they, when they didn't know where it was? If Zady got it, she would keep it away from the orcs so as to keep them rampaging; that might be what the witch meant by helping them. The orcs and humans really had no quarrel with each other; it was Zady's interference that had started this mess!

"How long before the orcs reach Hermandy's capital?" he asked.

"A day," Helbah said. "If we do nothing to stop them."

Stop them, Kelvin thought. He just wished there was some certain way to slow them down. In the meantime what did he really care about? It was his children who were his real concern. Were they prisoners? Were they being tortured? Were they, and he shivered at the thought, already dead? He realized that whatever private fascination Zady had worked on him would be meaningless if she had harmed his children; the very thought of harm to them made him want to throttle her, even if she assumed the lush-redhead form.

"What's the matter, Kelvin?" Heln asked, seeing his face.

How could he tell his wonderful wife all of what was going on in his mind? He knew he loved Heln, and that he hated the evil witch. Yet that beautiful image remained to haunt him. "Worry," he said. "Worry about what to plan."

"Spoken," St. Helens said with disgust, "like a true tactician."

"We'd better make a stand," his father suggested.

"Yes, I guess we had better do that."

Next day the orcs came marching down the highway with their drawn and so-far unbloodied swords. The Confederation's army was massed and ready to meet them. Kelvin knew that the time of no bloodshed was almost over; the orcs might have been making a demonstration, but they would quickly make the war real if the humans tried to make it so. That, unfortunately, was what the humans were about to do.

The catapults whuffed, and agile and quick orcs either caught the missiles on their shields or easily ducked or bobbed away from them. Several of the orcs, more enterprising than the rest, sheathed their swords and caught the missiles in their hands. Great muscles bunched and the missiles came whizzing back to them, killing and injuring men, smashing catapults and equipment. It had started.

"Damn," said St. Helens. "If this were magic, you could counter it with the Mouvar weapon. But all they use is muscle."

Kelvin nodded. He was adjusting the levitation belt. He had set the butt of the chimaera's copper sting firmly in the ground and was preparing to hurl some lightning. Since the bolts were not magically generated but were drawn from the earth, it was not so readily countered.

He set off a burst. The lightning flared and cracked and the orc who had just wrecked a catapult was hit on his well-scarred chest. The orc was flung back, burning and smoking.

How he hated doing that, Kelvin thought. His hands, freed of the magical gauntlets for the time being, rubbed the sting's coppery surface. He extended his hand nearly to the flexible tip, concentrated, and focused on drawing forth and hurling the lightning bolts.

Flash, flash, flash, CRACK! Orcs fell, toppled, burned, and then one of their number—could it be Brudalous himself?—raised a shiny shield and intercepted the lightning. The bolt struck and was deflected. Shield edge joined shield edge as the orcs united their defense. It was what John Knight called a phalanx, and it was proof against the bolts.

Slowly the orcs advanced behind their protective barrier. Lightning struck before them, behind them, and to either side. The orcs seemed impervious to all but direct strikes; they advanced, as through a fiery rain.

"You're not getting them," St. Helens observed.

That was obvious. "Something seems to be interfering. The bolts don't go where I want."

"Either their magic or Zady's," Helbah conjectured.

"Well, we've got a few protective spells working for us, too, and it looks as if we need them."

As the witch spoke, long swords were flashing. The orc vanguard had closed on the human front and waded in. Men's bodies, armored or not, went flying in halves. They were almost like harvesters, those orcs, and the human warriors were almost as helpless as stalks of grain.

Kelvin could stand it no longer. He took a step with a magical boot and was out where he wanted to go, facing Brudalous. It was suicidal and brave and stupidly heroic: exactly what was expected of him.

Brudalous smiled. "Ah, the boy with the boots and gauntlets!" He was evidently pleased.

Kelvin's gauntlets acted with a precision strike with the sword at the orc leader's vitals. Only the lowest ones were in reach. It was such a fast move, so precisely timed, that nothing could have countered it. Nothing but magic.

The sword bounced back, having met an invisible barrier before the barrier of scales. Its tip glowed red and smoked. A witch's cackle filled the air, and Kelvin realized that Zady, somehow, invisibly, was there.

"Your Benigns are no match for me and neither is Mouvar's science!" It was the evil witch's voice, coming from the empty air.

Science? Kelvin had believed that Mouvar's devices were magic. But some had said that magic and science were so close to each other that they sometimes merged, and each acted in the fashion of the other.

"What do you want?" he gasped, addressing Zady, knowing as he spoke that he was being foolish, playing her foul game.

"Want? Why your worthless young body, of course." The words were harsh, but now the voice was that of the lovely young redhead, and that gave them a rather different meaning.

Kelvin knew he should fight her in whatever way he could. He should strike at the spot her voice seemed to be, and curse her. But he didn't. He just stood there. He saw the orc king standing similarly, not trying to strike, though he had an opening. Brudalous was leaving Kelvin to Zady.

"I don't see what you see in that old hag," the orc murmured. "There is no accounting for human tastes."

Paralyzed, frozen as he had once been by a giant serpent's stare, Kelvin found himself whirling upward. He was being sucked up as if by a whirlwind. The ground spun dizzily beneath his feet, and he hadn't even activated his levitation belt. Science or magic, he was ignominiously caught!

Perhaps his belt could save him. He touched the controls—and his fingers, even through the gauntlets, felt as if they had plunged into fire. He was up so high now that he was finding it difficult to breathe. She was throwing him from the world, she—

Then he leveled off and began to descend. Far, far below was a mountaintop. He gasped, choked, trying to draw in air.

He was falling now with a velocity that made everything blur. He was tumbling heels over head, the sky and the mountain changing position. He was falling to a mountaintop, and on it was a little speck he knew was Zady.

He wanted to move his fingers on the belt control. Having felt the flame once, he couldn't regain the will to force his fingers to obey. Yet if he didn't—

His gauntlets moved his fingers for him.

CHAPTER 23

Kid Stuff

Merlain and the others watched the battle from the forest where Dragon Horace had taken them. She felt quite winded and whirly from their jumping across frames. But now they were back home and there was nothing more interesting than this little battle between orcs and not-orcs.

They watched as the catapults sang and the orcs dodged or reached up and caught missiles and hurled them back. A great rock fell on a beautiful black war-horse, crushing it like a fly. The horse's feet stuck out from beneath the huge rock. One of the warriors screamed; another shook his fist at the still-distant orcs.

"I don't like that," Merlain said. She felt tickly and sick in her tummy. She knew her eyesight wasn't good, but it was good enough to see the red stain.

"Well, what can we do about it?" Charles asked in an unreasonably normal tone. "If we had more of the Alice Water, one of us could teach those orcs a lesson. But Kildee had to ruin that."

"I didn't!" the young king snapped.

"You did," his brother supplied, "but it was accidental. You didn't mean to."

"That's right," Kildee said.

Dragon Horace yawned. Since he'd eaten the better part of a meer carcass earlier in the day, this battle wasn't interesting. Besides, one skirmish with an orc had taught him a hard lesson: though he was a dragon, he wasn't all grown up and invincible.

"Oh, look!" Merlain cried. "Daddy's doing something. He—"

She blinked at the thunder and the lightning flash. An orc fell over, clutching its singed chest. Now another lightning bolt followed, and other orcs fell, some of them smoking where the jagged bolts had struck. Orcs cried out and shields were lifted, catching the bolts, rerouting them to where they exploded in the woods, setting fires.

"Oh, I don't like that!" Merlain said. "The flowers and the little animals will burn!" Her eyes widened until they hurt as the small clouds formed and rained on the fire. Magical doings, she knew, and she hoped it was Helbah working the magic to put out the fires.

Now the orcs were advancing with shields raised. More bolts of lightning, but they seemed to have lost strength. The orcs' big swords swung and cleft men and horses. Merlain hid her face.

"Oh, look, Merlain, Daddy's doing something else!"

She opened her eyes and saw that Charles was right. Kelvin, their father, was out there meeting the orc leader. Now Brudalous would learn! Now Daddy, their daddy, would put everything right!

Daddy's sword flashed and seemed to rebound before striking Brudalous' belly. Then Daddy stood there, and the orc stood there, without anything else happening. Then Kelvin shouted and waved and flew upward, his arms and legs jerking. He flew up, up, up into the sky, not at all as she would have imagined he might fly. He did not seem to be using his levitation belt. It was as if something was hauling him through the sky. He got so high that he was a blur to her eyes, and then a speck, and then she couldn't see him at all.

"DADDDDDY!" Merlain cried, realizing that he was in real trouble.

"We've got to help him!" Charles said, grabbing her arm. "It's the witch who has him!"

She knew that he was right. He meant the evil witch, of course, the one who wanted the opal.

She climbed onto Horace's neck, motioning to the others to follow. They scrambled on, the kings looking scared and unsure of themselves, which meant they probably would not be too much trouble.

"Where are we going, Merlain?"

"Shut up, Charles," she explained in her usual sisterly way. She thought they should follow Daddy and help him. But—and it astonished her that she hadn't thought of this before—Daddy was a hero. Mightn't he be mad if they interfered? Besides, follow to where? By now she couldn't see anything but empty sky.

"Merlain, you must not procrastinate!" a voice said from the apparent sky.

"What? What?" That had sounded like—it had to be!—the chimaera's woman head, Mervania!

"Yes, yes, I'm here, but only in astral form. I took a dragon berry so that I could follow you. Only I must say I'm surprised where you are!"

"Daddy—" Merlain began.

"Yes, yes, but with that opal, which I can't touch in astral form, you can go where I tell you. I can follow him and then come back here and tell you. Wait!"

Merlain blinked. She felt no breeze and saw no other indication, but she knew the chimaera's persona had gone. Would she see Daddy again? she wondered. Should she trust the part of the creature she was named after, even a little bit?

The two kings had round mouths. They, like Charles, had heard her conversation and not understood. There was much she had to explain. She just hoped that Mervania would come back to them as she had as much as promised.

Kelvin's gauntlet pressed the red button on the belt. It slowed his fall, but still he was being pulled down. Down, down, down to the ugly old witch on the mountain. The gauntlets remembered how to move the control and did, though to him it felt like touching live coals. His body swung around, his feet touched ground, and he was down.

"Greetings, Kelvin," the ugly old witch said. She squinched up her eyes, studying him where he stood.

Kelvin waited. He did not think a return greeting was expected.

"From here you'll get a better view of the slaughter," the evil creature explained. "But don't worry, I'll bring your brats here and fill out the show with a little added torment. They and their ugly lizard brother first, before your weak and tearing eyes."

Kelvin had it in mind that he couldn't see as far as the forest from up here; also that Zady had no reason to comment on another's ugliness.

He should have known. Instantly her expression was one of rage, showing that she gleaned his thoughts.

"You'll pay for that, Kelvin Smartmind! And I'll fix that goody-goody wife of yours too! I think I'll give her to a horny orc. And your red-haired mom, she thinks she's a witch, so she should be part of a witch's ceremony! First a little session with all the malignant warlocks with big parts—that should last a day or two, depending on her stamina—and then starting the real fun—"

Kelvin thought to leap at her and try to break her neck. But Zady made a gesture, and he knew as she finished it that he was in trouble again. She had become the luscious young redhead in her translucent cloak. He knew it was still the evil old witch, as terrible as ever, but somehow he just couldn't attack that beautiful creature.

She smiled and stepped toward him. She took his flaccid hand and brought it up to touch her cloak at chest height.

He felt the material, and he felt the full firm breast beneath it. *This body was real!* It wasn't illusion!

"No, not illusion," she murmured in a low, thrilling tone. "Just as my power is real, not illusion. I can assume this form when I choose; it is magic and requires effort, so I normally don't bother, but if you behave, I will maintain it for a while." She leaned forward and kissed him on the mouth, and her lips were as firm and warm as her breast.

It was impossible even to think of opposing her now. He knew it was more than just a form change; she had enchanted his mind too. But he was powerless. Where magic was concerned, he was, to say the least, among the disadvantaged.

"Exactly, Kelvin," she said. "But there is that prophecy, and there is something about you, so I seek to salvage you rather than destroy you. If you cooperate."

He knew he shouldn't cooperate. He should wrench free of this and do something heroic. But he couldn't.

She reached around him, but it wasn't an embrace; she was removing his levitation belt so that he could not fly away from this precarious mountaintop perch. Then she stepped away from him. She flung it over the edge and it disappeared. "As I was saying, Kelvin," the witch resumed with a pleased and terrible though beautiful smirk, "you can watch everything from this mountaintop. All it takes is a little bit of this."

Zady threw down a bluish powder and there was a *poof* of purple smoke, which resolved into a miniature scene of a battle between men and orcs. Battle was hardly the word. It was, as she had said, a slaughter of brave men by stolid orcs.

"Stop it, Zady! Stop it!"

She glanced back at him over her shoulder. "You must phrase that request correctly, Kelvin. Say 'Please, gracious lady, I beg you to stop this, and in return I will do anything you ask.' Will you do that?"

He could not attack her, but he found that he was not compelled to lie. She wanted to coerce him into joining her, or at least into not opposing her at such time as she let go of his will. It must take effort for her to hold him like this. At least he could avoid giving her the satisfaction of his capitulation. "No."

"Then why should I stop it? It's fun!" She turned back to the scene. "Now, as for those pitiful excuses for practitioners of the art—"

She gestured, and the scene changed to that of his family and friends and the witches and warlocks from the convention. All were looking on at the battle, helplessly, as if held by a powerful spell. Helbah, attempting to do a spell of her own, moved with exquisite slowness, reciting words and making gestures that would be finished only after the slaughter was complete. It was a magical spell such as Helbah herself had employed to slow invaders, but here it was used to keep her and her allies helpless.

"Yes," Zady said, "mine is the more powerful magic! As for your brats, including the scaly one—" She gestured.

The scene was now in the forest. Trees were on every side, and the four children and the dragon bunched together, the children clinging to the dragon in apparent fear. Scorched and burning grass was almost to their feet; the deflected lightning bolts had started many fires. Between tree trunks a young warrior grimaced and bled and died in full view of the children; his entrails trailed back, back from the way he had come.

"Zady, stop it!" Kelvin cried. "Stop it, please!"

"Well, did you say 'please' that time; that's an improvement." The forest scene vanished. Zady laughed a witch's cackle. She seemed far more formidable to him now than she had when he had wrestled her at the convention. But just as beautiful. This was no merely evil person; this was something from a nightmare. A dream that cursed him with the guilt of illicit desire even as he viewed its horrors.

"Daddy!"

Right beside the witch Dragon Horace appeared out of empty air. Astride his coppery back were Kelvin's twins and the missing kings who theoretically governed the Confederation. Merlain, her red-copper hair and green eyes making her very witchlike, held a large ball of scintillating colors in her two cupped hands.

Kelvin realized with another shock that the witch's luscious redhead form was much like the child's appearance—as it would be when she became adult. No wonder he couldn't hurt it! But now he understood something he had not, and it gave him power he had lacked before.

"Give me that!" Zady said to Merlain. She snatched at the opal.

Horace, not at all cowed by the witch's presence, snapped as quickly at her hand. Zady drew back just in time, her hand beaded with Horace's saliva.

"Give me that immediately, you brat!" In her distraction, the witch had let go of her form change, and reverted to her natural appearance.

"No!" There was a stubborn set to Merlain's chin. Kelvin knew that look; he had seen it on her mother.

"Then I'll just have to hurt your daddy. Let's see, I can turn him into something. A fish."

Zady made a gesture, and Kelvin heard "POOF!" He gasped for air. He could move, but it didn't do him much good. His tail and his fins vibrated frantically, but he could not leap out and kill the witch.

In his panic and distress he called out. "Screeek!" That was all that came from his mouth, forced out by his painfully squeezed swim bladder.

"Turn him back! Turn him back!" Merlain cried, horrified.

Twisting his body to move his head, Kelvin worked his gills. He wanted to tell his daughter to never mind, to be gone, to get out of the witch's clutches and take the opal with her. Otherwise they would all be lost. The witch would only kill them all, once she had what she wanted. But he couldn't say anything, and in spite of himself he wanted air.

"Why certainly, dearie," Zady said. "But first—"

Another gesture produced a puff of smoke that obscured everything. As the smoke cleared before his lidless eyes, a great flopping came from overhead. An eagawk with extended talons froze in midair. A predator bird with a taste for fish.

Kelvin flipped and flopped for all he was worth, even while he was suffocating, but there was no getting out from under that apparition. If it *was* an illusion.

"Don't! Don't! Here, take your old opal!" Beside herself with fear for her father's life, Merlain threw the oversized gem at Zady's head.

Zady gestured and caught the opal in open hands. "Why thank you, dearie." The predator bird disappeared. It had indeed been an illusion.

"Gasp, gasp, gasp," Kelvin gasped. It was the last thing he would say, he was sure. How ironic, dying as a fish!

"Now turn him back!" Merlain screamed.

"Why certainly." A quick gesture, and Kelvin was choking and gasping in his natural form, drawing in great shuddering breaths.

As soon as he could speak, he said, "Zady, you've gotten what you wanted. Now you'll let us go."

The luscious form reappeared. "Will I, Kelvin? Not while I have use for you."

But that form no longer fascinated him. He had come to understand its derivation.

"Oh, so it's like that," Zady said, reverting to natural again. Once more he had been so foolish as to let his thoughts flow freely, and once again had given away any advantage he might have had.

She gestured, and he was frozen in place, unable to move a finger. Why hadn't he simply jumped her when he had the chance!

Zady stroked the opal, but did not vanish. It was only a gesture, he knew. She pointed a finger at him as if it were a weapon. Then, with a nasty smile, she moved the finger to point at Merlain.

The little girl slid down from the dragon's head. She walked stiffly and with unseeing eyes between Kelvin and the witch. The twin kinglets and the little dragon seemed to be frozen by the same spell.

"Should I let her live, Kelvin? Should I make her a witch like myself? The child does have talent."

Kelvin thought of what he had learned and guessed, and now knew to be a fact about malignant witches. They were bad, very bad. He could not wish his daughter to become one, even to save her life.

"Oh, Kelvin, your thoughts are so predictable! And not even an elementary mind screen."

What, he thought with determination, *are you going to do?* It wasn't as if he even wanted to know, because he knew it would be worse than whatever he imagined.

"Well, Kelvin, there is this little war. . . ."

You can have the Confederation. You can have this entire frame. You can have everything and anything you want.

"Of course I can, Kelvin. And so wisely put."

Kelvin's brain was spinning. He wanted so badly to destroy her. But Zady, unlike her extinguished niece, unlike even Melbah, Helbah's extinguished look-alike, was a very accomplished witch. She seemed to have no weaknesses. Now, with the opal, she was certainly the strongest witch in all the frames.

"Thank you, Kelvin," She rewarded him with the return of the lovely form. *Are you ready to join me, and be loyal only to me? To have your daughter become a malignant witch?*

"No!" For he realized that as powerful as she was, she still feared Mouvar's Prophecy. She wanted to neutralize it by neutralizing him, and apparently it was safer to convert him to her side than it was to kill him.

Zady made smoke appear. Merlain, propelled by the witch's commanding finger, walked to the very edge of the cliff. Below the cliff, Kelvin remembered, was a very long drop. Zady looked at him from beautiful eyes, but her intent was ugly. She had used him as a lever against his daughter; now she was using his daughter as a lever against him.

Are you sure, Kelvin?

How could he betray not only his friends, family, and frame, but the Prophecy itself?

Zady gestured with her finger. Merlain stepped to the verge of the cliff and teetered there. "Oh, Daddy, Daddy, I'm so high up! Don't let me fall! Daddy, Daddy!"

Kelvin felt his heart being torn out.

"Shut up, brat!" Zady snapped. *Kelvin, do you reconsider?*

You know I can't. Besides, I know you never keep your word. All you're doing is tormenting me. You'd never turn Merlain into a powerful witch. As a witch with power she might oppose you.

Not if you supported me. You two are a package.

That did seem to make sense. If she had them both, she would always be able to play one off against the other, exactly as she was doing now. How could he go along with that?

If Zady was disappointed by his continued resistance, she gave no direct sign. She moved her finger.

Merlain stepped off from the cliff.

"DADDDDDDDDIEEEEEEE!"

He could visualize her falling. Even as he did, his foot moved swiftly of its own magical accord. The almost-forgotten boots propelled and carried him. His equally forgotten gauntlets drew his sword. His sword blade swung, cutting through Zady's upraised right hand and slicing on through her neck. Her head jumped free of her body. It turned in the air, the eyes focusing on him for a moment. The expression on the ugly face was surprise. She had finally made a mistake and let him act. It was as if that bothered her more than the loss of her head. The irony was that it had been his Mouvar gifts that had done it, not him.

With sight that was suddenly under his control, he saw the opal fall from the witch's slackening hand and bounce on the ground. He saw the young dragon's snout snap forward, the jaws opening. The opal dropped inside. The dragon had swallowed the opal!

But Kelvin was still moving, propelled by the boots. He

charged past the dragon, to the edge of the cliff. His hands clapped together and his ankles touched. Boots and gauntlets together pulled his body down and outward.

Below, Merlain was already a fast-disappearing speck.

Knowing nothing at all but appalling terror, Kelvin dived after her.

Move, Charles! Mervania's thought came. *This is not yet over. Neither your sister nor the witch are doomed yet.*

Charles blinked. He had been able to move, but afraid, and hadn't known what to do anyway. Now the witch's body lay only a few steps away. Her severed head and hand lay separate from the rest of her. His father's bloody sword lay where he had dropped it on his way off the cliff. Of father and sister there was no sign. Not from here.

"Kildom, Kildee, I can move. The spell's broken."

"We'll have to get down from this mountain," Kildee said.

"We have to make certain the witch is dead," his brother corrected him.

Dragon Horace gave a snort. Previously he had given a choking sound.

"Oh, he swallowed the opal," Charles said. "Do you think he'll cough it back up?"

Kildee shrugged. "Helbah may have a potion."

"The puke maker," his brother explained. Evidently they had had experience with it. He scrambled off the dragon and went to look over the edge of the cliff. "They're still falling," he reported. "It's a long way down."

"Maybe they'll land in water," Kildee said.

Charles carefully slid one leg off the scaled neck of his brother. He didn't want to go too near the witch or the ledge. But the pain was right: they had to make sure the evil creature was dead. Since his father had done the deed, he felt that there could be little chance of her recovery. But poor Daddy. Poor Merlain. He hoped the chimaera was right about them. He could not accept the notion that they were doomed; he hoped Kelvin would be able to use the levitation belt to save Merlain. But now he remembered that his father hadn't been wearing it, which was odd; because—

"Charles, look!" Kildee cried, pointing at the witch's hand. It had raised itself on its fingertips. As he watched, it walked, like a scorpiocrab, around the head and to the arm stump in a pool of blood. It turned, backed, flopped, and somehow reattached itself.

"Stop that, Charles! Before she's whole!"

"How, Kildee?"

"The sword! The sword!"

Charles didn't ask. Kings were, after all, kings. Besides, it was he, not they, who was descended from a hero.

As he took a step toward the body it got up on hands and knees. The just-reattached hand looked a little weak, but was bearing its share of weight and functioning properly. It was obvious that the head would also work, once replaced.

The eyes in the head clicked open and glared malevolently at him. "Stand back, brat!" the head ordered.

Charles could see that the head intended to reattach itself. It wanted him to stand back. Therefore he shouldn't.

"CHARLES!" a royal pain shouted. "Snap out of it! You're not under her spell now."

"But you will be if you delay," the other kinglet chimed in. "Once she can make gestures, we're done. She's destroyed your father and sister, maybe; don't let her destroy your kings!"

Charles thought that his priorities were slightly different. But the pains did have a point. If the witch recovered, it wouldn't matter whether his father saved his sister; every one of them would be doomed.

Apparently Zady couldn't make magical gestures until she had her head on so she could see what she was doing. Once she could gesture, she would freeze them in place again, or turn them into fish. So he had to stop her from pulling herself back together.

Maybe he should have Dragon Horace handle it. But no, if the young dragon ate her, the withered old meat might make him terribly sick. Witches were not very good eating, by most accounts.

"Hurry, Charles!"

"One step nearer and you die!" the head warned. The body, crawling through spilled blood and over bare rock, had reached the spot. Blood dripped from the neck onto the stub below. In a moment the body would lower, the hands would grab the head, the severed neck halves would be pressed together, and she would be reunited. He didn't have a lot of time.

Charles, another Mervania thought came to him. *What do you think your father would do if he were here and free?*

Instantly Charles acted. One step, one hard kick, and the head of Zady the Malignant went flying off the cliff. As it rose into the air it wailed, and as it plummeted the wailing came back at a lower and lower pitch. His grandfather John Knight called that doppler magic; evidently the witch had not lost all of her powers.

Something stung Charles' right calf. He looked down to see Zady's gnarled fingers grappling, their dirty nails already biting into his flesh. Blood squirted black and foul-smelling from the neck and onto his foot and leg.

"The sword!" a royal pain shouted.

Yes, Charles, the sword! came Mervania's thought. *Quickly, before the body heaves you off the cliff!*

Charles needed no further urging. As the hands of the headless body pulled loathsomely at him, he reached down and snatched the handle of his father's sword. He lifted it, struggling with its weight, and positioned the point above the witch's heart region.

Not that one! Mervania thought. *Use your magic sword!*

But Charles knew his sword was only a toy, and he doubted it was really magic. Ignoring the spouting body that was soaking him with gore, he drove the blade down until he could drive it down no further. He pushed down on it, giving it all his weight.

The body struggled like a pinned bug. Blood and air rushed up at him, fountaining in a noisome mess.

He was pressing down on his father's sword. Its blade was moving through a deflated costume and skin, occupied now only by bone and gore.

Zady had to be fully and truly dead. At last.

Kelvin found that he could move a little as he plummeted, but his boots and gauntlets directed him. He saw sheer rock walls to one side, a green and brown landscape to the other, and within it the ribbon of a distant river. Ahead, way down, he spied a gradually enlarging speck.

Merlain was tumbling over and over in the air. She was growing bigger as his faster-moving body caught up with her. She was inadvertently presenting a high proportion of surface to the passing air, so it was slowing her, while he was making himself as streamlined as possible. He saw a smear of dirt across her face, and—

"DADDY!" she cried, spying him.

Purple skirt, once-white panties, then again her face. It was changing from terror to hope. Somehow she had known he would rescue her.

His arms, propelled by him and the gauntlets, reached out and snatched. He caught her, pulled her close, and held her tightly to his chest. Green trees rushed upward.

"Daddy! Oh, Daddy!"

He clutched her close. Soon they would be dashed against the ground. His flesh and hers would splatter. But she would die without fear, believing all was well.

"Daddy, Daddy, I didn't know how well you could fly!"

If only this tiny girl were right in her estimate of what was happening. She thought he had the levitation belt. But Kelvin knew better. Zady had deprived him of it. She hadn't been concerned about the gauntlets or boots, just the belt. She should have taken them all from him, but perhaps she had been distracted, and really thought he would soon be joining her side. That had cost her. Nevertheless, he and his daughter were falling to their deaths, wrapped in each other's arms.

Now his boots were kicking out. He was going over, backward, somersaulting at the boots' command.

Was it possible that Merlain could be saved? No, he knew better. They were falling too fast. Sky and ground had finished changing places. His boots were extending down.

"Daddy, we're slowing!"

They were! Just as rock-strewn ground appeared, his right leg moved. Tree branches and a brook underneath, and the foot coming down. Gently, gently, to a completed step.

They had not died. The boots had brought them to a soft landing. The boots had known when they propelled him off the cliff.

"Daddy! Daddy! Did you see it? The eagawk had Zady's head!"

What an imagination his daughter had! He lowered her to the ground. His knees bent. His vision blurred. The green, green grass came up ticklingly to his face.

Exhausted, he was collapsing, having taken but a single step.

CHAPTER 24
War's End

Helbah blinked as the battle before her suddenly began to move. She hadn't been aware that it had slowed down, or that she had slowed too, but now she was. The orcs were winning. She had started a spell to help her side, but without realizing it, she had slowed to ineffectiveness. Zady had been the cause, and Zady would pay, but first there were the orcs. Just what, if anything, could she do about them?

"Surrender, Helbah, unconditionally," a voice from midair said.

"Mervania?" She had wondered when, if ever again, she would hear the chimaera female's voice. The last time had been six years ago, when Kelvin's twins were born and Kelvin and Jon and Charlain had aided her against a common enemy. How long that was in human terms, how short a time for such as she was.

"Speaking," the insufferable astral traveler said. "Save your friends, Helbah. Surrender."

"That would be wise," Helbah conceded. "But Zady—"

"I'll tell you later. Things to do. You get busy on that surrender while you still can."

Helbah grabbed her crystal from the table she had set up. She held it in front of her eyes, concentrating.

Brudalous.

There was a flash in the depths of crystal geometry. The unhuman face she'd summoned floated there, his eyes narrowed by the squeezed-down scales on his forehead. The orc leader was aware of her.

"We surrender unconditionally," Helbah said. Those were difficult words, but necessary under the circumstances.

"You have the authority?" The orc tested her.

"My charges do. Our Confederation can't win, even with magic. Ophal has won. Call off your warriors."

"Hoist your surrender flag."

"Don't!" Helbah called to St. Helens. That worthy, reluctantly but not too reluctantly to all appearances, hoisted the white square. It flopped, ghostly, on its pole.

"The opal, Helbah. That's what all this is about, you know."

"First things first. There's Zady to be attended to."

"That Malignant has the opal?"

Does she, Mervania? Helbah thought at her rescuer.

It's on Overlook Mountain with the hatchlings. The returned thought was a rescue in itself.

"I've just learned that the opal and the children are together," Helbah told the orc. "You won't hurt the children?"

Brudalous looked as startled as his fish face could manage. "Hurt the tadwogs? You think we are monsters?"

Helbah decided upon expediency and did not answer. There were people who thought witches were monsters too, when it came to that.

"I know your word is your mooring rope," Helbah said, using an orc expression. "The opal is the orcs', and always has been. Zady is not your friend; she tricked the children into stealing the opal for her. When Zady is vanquished from this frame or, better still, destroyed, when the children are safe, and we have the opa—''

"You have until tomorrow morning," Brudalous said without lightness. "If the opal has not been returned by then, beware of the consequences."

"I may need more time," Helbah said, but she said it to an empty crystal.

Charles looked up at the bird circling their mountain peak. It was a swoosh, and swooshes did not belong up above mountaintops. But this was a magical place anyhow, with fresh green grass and breathable air where science would have had thin air, ice, and snow.

The swoosh landed between him and Horace and the pains. There was a familiar *poof* of pinkish smoke and good witch Helbah stood where the bird had been. Except for location it was similar to what had been commonplace at the convention.

"Well, young man," Helbah said in a stern tone of voice. "What have you to say for yourself?"

Charles swallowed a lump he hadn't been aware had formed. He didn't know a nice way of saying it, so he said it just as it was. "I killed her, Helbah."

"Killed who? Your sister? Not your sister!"

"N-no. But she's dead too, maybe. I mean, I hope not, but since she—I've tried to mind-talk to her, but there's nothing, so—"

"I will verify that in a moment. Whom did you kill, Charles?"

"Her," he said, pointing to the deflated skin with the sword stuck through it and the black cloth.

"That's . . . Zady?" Helbah seemed to be struggling for the right thought, but didn't sound displeased. "You did this to her?"

"Yes, Helbah." It was going to be a relief to tell it. "She turned our daddy into a fish, and then—"

Helbah listened without interrupting, as adults were capable of doing when they put their minds to it. When he had finished, she shook her head. "You won't mind if I see for myself?"

"No, Helbah." But he didn't know what she meant.

Helbah produced some powder from under her cloak and dashed it to the grass, making some sounds in her throat. A pinkish cloud formed above the grass and spread out and stayed. In the cloud were Zady and Horace and the royal pains. All were there in image, exactly as they had been when recent events had occurred. It was one of those picture recalls that Charles had heard about. Interested, he watched as Merlain went over the cliff, and their daddy dived after her—without his levitation belt. Then Charles killed the witch again, and—

"Wasn't Charles brave, Helbah?" the one twin asked.

"And weren't we smart to tell him what to do?" his brother added.

Helbah casually delivered a double cuff to the now-crownless heads. Charles' maternal grandfather often answered foolish questions in the same logical way.

"She may not be completely dead," Helbah explained. "Her body is, but her head wasn't."

"What can a head do?" one of the twins scoffed. Charles knew the scoff was foolish: a severed reptile's head, after all, was alive and would bite an unwary person until after sundown.

Helbah said, "The crystal. Brudalous must have—"

Dragon Horace vanished. Yet Helbah had made no magical pass in his direction. It took Charles a moment to realize what had happened.

"The opal still works," the twin he thought was Kildee said. "Even in his gizzard."

The probable Kildom nodded. "You'd have thought Helbah would have thought of it. He doesn't want to cough up anything. He wants back in the forest."

Helbah raised a hand as if to administer more discipline. Kildom covered his pointed right ear and held his face back. At that moment Kelvin stepped onto the ledge, from the spot where he had left it. His left foot came down in its shiny new boot completing a stride.

Charles had to consider whether this was more of Helbah's magic. His father did not have his sister, so he knew she was gone forever. The fear and grief he had been suppressing welled up.

"Your sister's safe, young Charles," Mervania's voice said from the air. "Your father just saved her. Foolish boy, to think he'd let her drop!"

Charles collapsed with relief. So he had not been able to mind-reach his sister because she had been out of range!

Kelvin said, "Thanks, Mervania. Thanks for telling him. Thanks for bringing Helbah."

"I brought myself," Helbah said, her witch's feathers ruffled by any suggestion that she needed help. "You left the girl alone?"

"With her brother. Dragon Horace popped out of the air and ran to her. I don't know how he did it. Did you send him with a spell?"

"The opal," Helbah said, seeming a bit bemused. "It seems he swallowed the stone."

"Oh. And she wanted him, and they're telepathic. She called to him with her mind."

Charles took note of that. Apparently Horace could hear her mind from farther away than he could! They had never had occasion to test it before.

"Right," Helbah said. "For a dumb hero you sometimes show a flash of near intelligence."

"Thanks, I think," Kelvin said with a wan smile. "I never asked for the job."

"None of us ever do!" Helbah snapped. "Now about Zady—"

Kelvin eyed the shadow pinned with the sword. "You did this to her?"

"Your son did, because you had not quite finished her. He's a good boy."

"Y-yes. Where's her head?"

"He kicked it. It fell after you left."

"Oh, that must be what Merlain meant. She said an eagawk was carrying Zady's head."

Helbah groaned. "You dummy, you should have gone after her! The crystal won't focus on just a head! And there are so many eagawks in these mountains! I doubt if we can locate it!"

"The head will die, won't it? She can't come back."

"She can! After twenty years to grow another body, she can! And all her old evil will be stored in that old head, however new her body is."

Kelvin seemed daunted. "A new young body? She has that much energy in reserve?"

"A witch with adept powers always does! We can be hurt but never completely destroyed without the application of fire to the vital part."

"Oh. Now you tell me."

"You should have known, dummy hero! Your experience should have told you something! Twenty years from now you just may have to complete the job. And she may have a far more attractive body than before."

"I know what that will look like," Kelvin said, evidently daunted.

"I will kill her!" Charles said, finding a new bravery on seeing his father's seeming cowardice. "I'll complete the job!"

"Yes, Charles," Helbah said, patting him on the head as if he were her cat. The royal pains looked on with expressions of disgust, but she seemed unaware of it. "Yes, I think that you just may."

CHAPTER 25

Glow's Return

As the Roundear dived off the cliff, he struck off the head and hand of the witch. The opal went flying, and the small copper-scaled dragon caught and swallowed it in a gulp.

"There! You see there!" Brudalous was quite beside himself. He poked at the magically created replay scene and so far forgot himself as to hug his wife. "Phenoblee, you've done it! You've found our opal!"

"What did you expect, husband?" She leaned into his hug, her body striving to remind him that spawning time was very near. "Helbah was right: Zady wanted the opal for herself, and tricked the children into stealing it. Zady was never our friend. We should not have been fighting the humans. That's why I did not interfere to help Zady."

"Now all you have to do is kill that creature! Turn it inside out, magic the opal back here, and—"

He didn't like her face. It was wearing that expression. "NO!"

"No?" He was and was not surprised. "But—"

"Watch!"

She gestured again with the conjuring weed. Under her gestures the mountain scene changed. Now they were following the little female tad as she fell. She tumbled over and over, crying out. Her father appeared, plunging head down and cleaving air as a diver cleaves water. The father caught his spawnling. An eagawk flew by unobserved by him, carrying the malignant witch's head in its talons. They fell together, adult and tad. They turned up and over, and then the father's foot shot out, down, and gently onto solid ground. The humans had reached the base of the mountain unharmed.

"They *do* have magic!" Brudalous admitted as he admired. "I don't think I could have survived a fall like that! Even a great orc athlete with a bit of lightness magic would have splattered. Of course I began to suspect they had magic when those pollypoles kept breaking out of our—"

"Watch, I said!"

In the scene before him the father left his female tad and stepped back to the top of the cliff. It was all in one stride, a long, long step that was not actual flying.

"I admit that *is* impressive!" Brudalous exclaimed. With such powers at their disposal humans might be more competitive than expected. In fact possibly, just possibly, they might battle Ophal to an eventual draw. The carnage, for orcs as well as humans, could be far greater than expected.

The scene was now of the little tad female all alone. She put out her little arms and instantly the small, coppery dragon was there. She hugged it, kissed it, rejoiced in its presence. The dragon tasted her face with his forked tongue, and explored with tickles the insides and outsides of her unusually round, visibly dirty ears.

"Why not now, Phenoblee? Now while it is separated from the adult humans? Yank it inside out! Slap the opal from its gizzard!"

"Monster!" Phenoblee exclaimed. She drew away from him, as if she did not actually want his fry anymore. You see what those two mean to each other, and you want it destroyed? You're almost human in your sensibilities!"

"But—" Now he'd done it! He'd have to mollify her as he had never mollified her before. This time a simple compliment on her magical abilities would not be adequate.

"I don't want to harm the dragon or the tad," he said carefully. "But dearest, our precious opal—"

"Is safe. The stone still works its magic, and the humans have surrendered. Let the dragon retain it and guard it until it's needed."

"But—"

"The tads will grow and the dragon will grow. Always the stone will remain, for the opal is indestructible. It enables us to cross frames no matter where it is, as long as we know its location and can orient precisely on it. Obviously it wasn't safe where we kept it before! With proper precautions, there can be no safer place than inside that dragon. Dragons don't excrete stones; they keep them in their stomachs to help grind up their unchewed food. The dragon is protected by the human Roundear of Prophecy; no one will molest it if we don't. The human girl tad has done what she said she would: she has returned it to us. I will send her a message to inform her of that."

"But—"

"The Confederation serves us now. It surrendered to us, remember? Those tads and that dragon tad are now part of our domain. The opal in the dragon is in our power."

"But we don't want the Confederation! We don't care about the land at all!"

"So we'll ignore it. Except for the dragon."

Brudalous tried to argue. But gradually, convincingly, as always, Phenoblee persuaded him to do it her way. The worst of it was that she was making sense.

"What is that you're wearing?"

Helbah's sudden question took Charles by surprise. Equally attention getting was the sting of her fingernails as she gripped his shoulders.

Charles took one more look over the side of the cliff, wishing again that he had better eyesight. He had thought that with his sister safe and his father back that it would be turning-into-bird time. Helbah's actions said there was more.

"This," Helbah said, tapping the sword at his waist. "Tell me, and don't you lie."

"I never lie," Charles lied. Then he remembered how much and how frequently he had lied or tried to lie under Zady's tutelage. It didn't matter that he had thought she was good Auntie Jon. It hurt that she had succeeded so well.

"Zady gave you this, didn't she?"

Charles shook his head. "I stole it at the con. She wanted me to."

"Kildee and I got books," Kildom said. "Merlain and Charles are less literate, so they got toys."

Helbah cuffed a royal head. She was looking at Charles, not the pain. On her shoulder Katbah stared fixedly at the sword. "Go on, please." The last word had the ring of "or else!"

"I found it in a room at the hotel, and—" He launched into his tale, telling just what he remembered as happening.

"That isn't all," Helbah said when he stopped.

Charles looked at her, baffled. "Yes, it is! All I remember—except one more thing I remember now. Zady said the sword is magic, but she didn't seem to worry about it, and it never seemed magic. But it did work very well when I fought those big insects, as if it were guiding itself some. Then when I killed the malignant witch, Mervania the chimaera told me to use my sword, but I knew it wouldn't be enough, so I used Father's sword. And that's all."

"It is only the beginning," Helbah said. "Look at me, Charles."

He met her gaze. Her eyes seemed to become as big as dinner plates, and he was falling into them. "Remember the rest," she said.

Suddenly Charles remembered his dreams. The sword had been in his dreams too—and then there had been Glow.

He found himself talking, telling all about the little girl he had met only in the dreams. Beside him Merlain was nodding; she had picked up some of it too.

"And I love her, I think," he concluded. "But I always forgot her, until the next dream. She's just a dream girl."

"Perhaps." Now Helbah held out her hand and waited.

Reluctantly Charles unbuckled his belt and slipped off the scabbard. Giving up the sword hurt as bad as anything he had ever done. Now he realized that it was the sword that had given him his dreams of Glow; they were sword dreams, with it assuming the girl form so it could talk with him. By giving it up, he was giving up those dreams; he knew that. It was as painful as saying good-bye to his sister or the pains would have been.

Grimacing, holding back unmanly tears, he handed the sword to Helbah. He had stolen it; he could not keep it. He understood that.

Helbah drew the blade from the scabbard. It glinted, glowed, and flashed. She slid it back. She examined the shining face on the scabbard. Finally she handed it back to Charles, to his astonishment.

"It is not for you to keep, Charles," she said gently. "You did not actually steal this sword. It belongs to no one but itself. It was in storage, part of an exhibit. It called to you, bringing you to itself, because it was lonely."

"So was I, I guess," Charles said. Certainly he would be lonely after he lost it!

"We must abate the enchantment on it."

"Yes, I guess," he agreed unwillingly.

"You do want to do the right thing, Charles."

"Yes. I just wish the right thing was for me to keep it. So I could be with Glow again, in my dreams."

"I want you to do exactly what I say, Charles. You are to draw the sword all the way from its scabbard. You are to bend down with it and wet the tip in Zady's blood. As you do this you must say 'With this blood, I free thy soul.' Say it, Charles."

Charles repeated the words. He was afraid the old witch had lost her mind. Even if Zady had a soul, she couldn't possibly want it released. He wished he could say the wrong words.

Helbah was waiting. Katbah eyed Charles as if daring him. His father seemed to be studying him with awe.

He drew the sword. ''With this blood,'' he said as he wet its tip in the remaining gore, ''I free thy soul.'' There; he had done this preposterous thing.

POOF, as of exploding gas. There was blackness and stench all around him, getting on him. He could not see and he could not breathe. It was the soul of the evil witch, he knew, freed from the gore.

In his hand, the handle of the sword transformed into soft flesh, as it had in the dreams.

The blackness cleared. The air became sweet. Standing beside him, holding his hand, was Glow. He swallowed. She was real! Solid flesh and bone. Glow's bluest of blue eyes widened. Her hand tightened in his. Her little bow mouth opened in an expression that he knew mirrored his own. She spoke, and her words were as real as her hand.

''You're—*real!*''

''Of course,'' he said, surprised. How strange that she, his dream playmate, should say that!

''I thought you were a dream. I thought everything was a dream.''

''It's all right,'' Helbah said, touching her. ''You're real now. Fully real, in your natural form, as is your right.''

''But—'' Glow looked prettily flustered.

''Oh, I suppose I have to explain. When she was young, Zady slew Dawn, the sunwitch, out of envy for her beauty and goodness. You, Dawn's lovely daughter, were changed by Zady's art into an enchanted sword. It was an additional torment to your mother, before she died. As a sword you would kill and inflict injury, as often on the side of evil as Zady could arrange.''

Helbah paused, wiped an eye, and resumed speaking. ''Only the blood of the evil witch who enchanted you could free you. That was why Mervania wanted you to use that sword on Zady. Fortunately I was able to fathom this spell

in time, before Zady's blood was lost. Charles and I together have unlocked the ancient spell."

Then Glow was crying, great tears rolling down her
chubby cheeks. She let loose of Charles' hand and hugged
him. Then she turned to Helbah and embraced her. "I remember you, Aunt Helbah, but you were younger."

"It was some time ago," Helbah said, and Charles realized that that could mean centuries. No wonder Glow had
gotten lonely!

"But what will become of her?" Merlain asked. "With
no family—"

"I will raise you as my daughter," Helbah said, stroking
the lush softness of Glow's blond tresses. "I always wanted
a daughter, but Zady's spell left me barren. The sunwitch
was my friend. You will have these two"—she indicated
Kildom and Kildee, who were standing with opened
faces—"as brothers, and Charles and his sister as friends."

"Oh, Helbah, oh, Helbah," the beautiful child sobbed.
"That will make me so happy!"

"You are, like some witches, able to mind-speak," Helbah continued. "You will be able to read your brothers'
thoughts and warn me of any mischief they contemplate."

Kildom and Kildee looked at each other with raised eyebrows. Even the joy of having this beautiful girl as a companion and sister had an accompanying curse. With Katbah
and Glow watching them, they would have little chance to
trick Helbah. In time the kings would be forced to learn
things Helbah wanted them to, repugnant as that notion
might be to them. They would begin to be the kings their
destinies demanded.

Charles, his hand temporarily bereft of Glow's, sought
his father's hand. He remembered Kelvin's story of meeting
Heln and somehow knowing that there was much more
ahead than behind.

Kelvin, an expression of confused happiness on his face,
simply reached down and stroked the back of his son's
equally happy, not fully comprehending head.

EPILOGUE

Charles and Merlain crouched in the brush where they could watch the clearing. Their mother and father emerged from the trees, following the path. In a moment their mother had placed with almost reverent care the large blue bowl of chopped meat before Horace.

Dragon Horace, having been advised by Merlain's quick thought, nuzzled up again to their mother and rubbed some smell on her. Ignoring his actions, Hela fed him a tidbit with her fingers.

Charles wrinkled his nose at Merlain. *Dragon Horace doesn't like that! He's just eating to please you and Mom. He'd rather eat what he catches.*

Yes, Charles. But isn't he polite! Is it any wonder that Mama loves him? She didn't used to admit he existed.

Fine! But privately he was thinking that she was making him a sissy. Horace could catch anything he wanted now, thanks to the opal he kept. What the dragon would prefer to eat was not the cooked meat his mother brought, but raw flesh that quivered or old flesh that stank.

You understand that business they did the other day? That orc business?

Why certainly, dummy brother. The Confederation is now governed by the Alliance. The Alliance is ruled only by orcs. Kildee and Kildom have the say over human-dominated kingdoms. Those, dear brother, are Rud, Aratex, Klingland, Kance, and Hermandy.

Six kingdoms. The five you named and Ophal. And people say there will be seven to fulfill the Prophecy.

Six kingdoms united with our daddy's help. But according to the Prophecy, there are a total of seven. Throod and Rotternik, of course, make eight.

The prophecy's crazy! I, Charles the First, proclaim that Grandpa Knight is right!

I, Merlain the Only, proclaim that it is you and not Grandpa who is crazy!

Merlain the Only, explain if you will about Horace.

Figurehead. Absolute monarch. All six kingdoms in the Alliance acknowledge him as overking, and he keeps the opal for us. Only, of course, he decides things even less than Kildee and Kildom do. He just is. Should the opal be needed by the Alliance, you or I will tell him and he will help us as we ask.

Merlain chewed on a stem of bluish-green grass. Her smile showed that she was increasingly content with the way the world was going.

Charles' smile showed that he had established mind contact with Glow. Merlain and Horace could communicate farther between themselves than with others; Charles and Glow were similar. There were wonderful mental pictures being formed for playing in.

It was a great, fine time in Rud, Kelvinia, the Confederation, and the newly formed Alliance.